The Divorce Sonnets

The Divorce Sonnets

A Novel by

Harry H. Taylor

LOUISIANA STATE UNIVERSITY PRESS
Baton Rouge and London   1984

Design: Albert Crochet
Typeface: Linotron Aster
Typesetter: Moran Colorgraphic Incorporated
Printer and binder: Vail-Ballou Press

ACKNOWLEDGMENTS

The first chapter of this novel appeared in *Cimarron Review* in April 1983, under the title "The Rub of Love." The author gratefully acknowledges permission from Dragon's Teeth Press to quote from the poem "Paula," © 1975 by Paul Baker Newman, as well as a National Endowment for the Arts grant, funded in 1976, when this book was little more than an idea. Appreciation and gratitude are likewise extended to Daryl B. Adrian, English Department Chairman, Ball State University, whose kind and patient understanding over the years allowed the author additional time to write.

Grateful acknowledgment is also offered for permission from Miles Laboratories, Inc., to quote the registered trademark PLOP, PLOP, FIZZ, FIZZ, OH WHAT A RELIEF IT IS.

For Barbara
For my mother and for Armand Serent

It is certainly American
to go too far.

P. B. Newman, "Paula"

The Divorce Sonnets

ONE   Calvin Hart had an extremely high IQ, and his innocence, if anything, merely accented it. He was twenty-one, but he did not look his age. There was something downy and unblemished about the face, and despite a short hitch in the service, the peacetime forces, his body had that same bland, smooth, padded cast.

After the crowds, the cramped barracks, the regimentation, the world suddenly seemed magnified, expansive. He was eager to get on with Life. He was cleaning his room and packing for college, heading down after the holidays to find a job and an apartment before school started in the fall.

He found his grandfather's alligator bag. The old man had shot the brute in Florida, back when Florida had been wide open, and then brought it home in this condition, including clasp, lock, and handle. When tanked, Calvin had led it out on the end of a rope, then got down on the floor and grappled with it. The bag always won, landing on top. He half considered giving up this pleasure now, and with his foot he pushed it back in the closet.

Calvin's grandmother was leaving, too. Sarah Elizabeth was selling the house where he had been raised, a big square three-story brick across from the park, and she was putting the furniture up on the auction block. She was going back to the Cape. She was one of those large, broad-shouldered, big-boned Scudder girls from Eastham. She had short, coarse white hair and clear blue eyes. She chain-smoked and was not all that careful where the ash went. She had a clipped, abrupt air, and when people spoke, she would pierce them with a sharp, cutting look, as if she were seeing through their lies, evasions, and half-truths.

She did not have a high opinion of humanity in general

1

and would say so in a minute. She divided people into those who had horse sense and those who did not. If someone did not have horse sense, she often said he wasn't worth the powder it would take to blow him up. You could tell, just in her tone, that she wasn't going to pay for the powder, either. Calvin's father had fallen into this class.

Calvin wasn't particularly crazy about her selling the house, but he kept his objections to himself because arguing with her was like arguing with a stone wall. You couldn't get through, and if you were wise, you saved your breath. He was going away, too, but just because he was, just because he had his whole future ahead of him (as she was so fond of saying), he wanted to think of the place as still there, in Bridgeport, Connecticut, intact.

In the meantime, he had trouble even holding onto his own stuff. He couldn't find several cartons, and he had his machette in one. He told her that if she was planning to contribute his weapon to the friendly little neighborhood auction coming up, just because she was after every last red cent, she could forget it. He needed that knife.

She considered this speech through the cigarette smoke. She managed to sprinkle ash on her chest, then tried to brush it off, but she just smudged it further into her blouse. "I couldn't *get* a red cent for that knife," she said.

He had never asked her about her differences with his grandfather. He was not about to start now, but, given these, she still should have some feelings about all those years spent in this house, shouldn't she? He decided not. "Sarah Elizabeth," he said, "you don't have a sentimental bone in your body, do you?"

She actually looked surprised for a second. "Why, no," she said, "I do not."

He gave her a look without saying anything else. What was the use? She had several rentals that she was keeping for income—places his grandfather had kindly taken off the bank's hands during the Depression. When she went on one of her many cleaning fits, she would stash cartons in various webby basements in these buildings. When he thought about it, he realized that he could be spread fairly thin around town.

He picked up the keys and went out to his grandfather's car, a big Hudson that still had a Willkie button on the visor and a gas-rationing stamp on the windshield. He backed down the drive and cut through the park, heading over to a likely spot. When he found his stuff, he would carry it back into the house and then clump up into his room without saying a word.

The cartons were wedged in together, difficult to get at, pulpy from the damp, close to falling apart. He rescued a planter's suit and pith helmet, a World War I airplane pilot's jacket, an overcoat of many colors, and a black cape lined with red silk, a magician's cape, which he had picked up in a secondhand novelty shop. He believed he looked fairly dramatic in it, but he chiefly wore the item because it irritated Sarah Elizabeth.

The wind was picking up, the light growing ashy, and the rundown upper sections of Main no longer kept themselves lit. Businesses were moving out in patches here and there. He found an old landmark, a vacant theater, once a legitimate theater, then a burlesque house during the war. An agency now rented it out for charity performances, gouging various organizations until it could be sold, torn down, and turned into a parking lot.

He braked across from the building and pulled behind his grandmother's second treasure: a bicycle shop, a barber's, and a cigar store on the first floor. The second floor had once been a public dance hall, briefly an Arthur Murray studio, now a girls' ballet school. He forced the first-floor door open against the wind and climbed the disinfectant-smelling stairs.

The place was awake, although he had not noticed a light below. He felt confused for a moment, as if the room were filled with more light than there was. The mirrors reflected the room, reflecting the figures, which sparkled with repercussions; the girls spun in scattered clusters, fluttery and

3

wobbly, their skinny chests heaving, their skins moist. The instructor was in and out of the pack, a seventeen- or eighteen-year-old. Her dark hair, severely bound in back, accented the broad forehead, the sharp cheekbones, the face's generally clean, sculptured look. The black leotard clung, stretched across the small, swelling crests, the brief curves, and hard little hips.

He crossed the floor to the storage room in back, where he ran into several boxes on a closet shelf. He found the photograph albums with ivory covers, metal clasps. Wearing swerving gowns with mutton sleeves, their hair in coils, the hatchet-faced women in the wedding groups looked directly into the camera, their chins raised as if in defiance. In the studio photographs of the period, done in sepia, the trailing muslin dresses trimmed with lace at the cuffs and at the hem, the babies all looked regal and pompous, as if about to take over some backward nation at any minute. The fat round faces looked polished, and the bald heads, huge and shining, could have come from some hard, metallic mold. He had originally run into these treasures while he had been digging through several dusty boxes outside an antique shop, and now he was rescuing the families for the second time.

He packed and sorted. When he reached the main room again, the place was dim, the space diminished, the apparitions gone. He nudged the door open with his cartons, then came around to where he had parked the Hudson. He had to back through the narrow, unlit alley without touching the trash on both sides. He cleared these dangers, but he just missed a car that was pulling away from the curb. They both slammed on their brakes, and his cartons hit the floor.

He jumped out and came around. She was trying to get the stalled car started when he opened the driver's door. She was in street clothes now (pea jacket, plaid skirt, flats), but her dark hair was still up, partly loosened in back.

"If you aren't careful, you'll flood it."

She did not look up. She was intense and frustrated. "Oh, brother! That's news!"

He was stamping his feet in the cold. "Move over. I'll try."

4

She shoved over and put her purse in her lap. "This old thing does this all the time. Now I think you've finished it off."

"We have to sit here a minute and be patient."

"I don't *feel* patient."

He lit a cigarette and put his hand on the wheel. A car passed, illuminating the theater across the street. "Do you know much about that place? It has a long history. My mother took me to see *The Cherry Orchard* there when I was around fourteen. Everybody mumbled, and I didn't catch a word. I remember the trees starting to go down at the end, though, just before the curtain, the only sound that was at all clear. They did not show you the trees, of course, but the props started to shake."

She sat hunched over beside him, her hands between her knees, trying to keep warm. "Would you try it again, please?"

"The cardboard wall trembled," he said, pumping the accelerator a bit. He could smell gas. "Real trees could have been going down back there for all I knew. They could do a lot with that, along those lines, don't you think? What if the cardboard house comes down, then the theater itself starts to shake. It could fall across the audience, bit by bit, just before the curtain."

"Try it again. Do you know how *cold* it is here?"

"Wait a minute," he said, getting out of the car. He went back to the Hudson and returned with his cape. He draped it over her shoulders. "That's better, isn't it? It's a good thing I came along when I did!"

"What is this cape I'm wearing, in this dream?"

"It's a cape."

"That figures. Are you an actor, or what?"

He was just a talker, like his people on both sides. "Good Lord, no! What made you ask that? My great-aunt, my father's aunt, drifted into the theater, though. I just vaguely remember the woman. She was very courtly, very majestic. They don't make women like that these days. We took her into the country once. She had never been in the country before, and, as far as I could tell, she had never seen a cow or

5

a horse. She found a cow to be a marvelous mechanism when she finally located one."

She was looking at him for the first time. Huddled under his cape, she sat studying his face. "Do you make these things up as you go along?"

"She also acted as if she had never seen a tree. She wanted to pick an apple. Not apples, either, which is another activity. Just an apple. Isolated. She was always on stage, and when she found the place she wanted, we had to stop. She either charmed or frightened the farmer into submission. In any case, we had to troop out into the orchard. She went ahead in the full-sleeved dress, her light hair half-bundled around her head. She made an art of it. Reaching up into the branches and pulling her own apple down. She convinced us that she had a miracle in the palm of her hand. I suppose she did. I can see her now, turning it around and around in the late afternoon light. 'Just look at this,' she kept saying. 'Just look at what I have! I have an apple in my hand!'"

She was still watching him. "Well?" she asked, when his silence finally registered. "Was I supposed to say something? I was just listening to the sound of your voice. It's hypnotic, like an actor's."

He wasn't flattered because he didn't hear what she said. He seldom heard praise. "This meeting's very curious, isn't it?"

"Oh, yes."

He was starting a fresh story when the engine finally kicked in. The car shuddered and shook.

Kasey Thatcher lived in a small three-story brick apartment house out on Fairfield Avenue. The buses running from Bridgeport to Fairfield rumbled by on the hour, and a truck route passed on its way to Black Rock, then down the coast, past Westport.

She was a high school senior who shared the place with her adoptive mother, a widow who was a kitchenware buyer in a local department store.

Kasey had several times pointed out that she had been

adopted, a fact which appeared to give her more leeway than most when it came to explaining herself. She had tinkered with her Christian name through the years, first changing it from the original, Kristine, to Kriss, to Carol on to Caroline to Casey. She later changed the spelling, ending up with Kasey, a far cry from Kristine. She did not often use her last name because she said that Thatcher wasn't her real name, anyway, was it? Her real name could be just about anything, probably far more mysterious, like Gonzalez. She assumed that she had come from a tragic, certainly illicit relationship.

She wanted her own apartment, but since she couldn't afford it, she had gradually worked out a compromise; she had divided Kay's down the middle, and as long as the woman stayed in her half, Kasey felt fairly independent. Kasey had the main bedroom because she needed the big closet; she also had the living room beside it. Kay had the kitchen, which was big and airy. She kept a chintz-covered rocker and her heavy oak dining room set back there, products which had come from grander times. She had the small bedroom behind the kitchen.

She had to pass through Kasey's half whenever she entered or left the apartment, which dispelled the illusion some. "Well," she said once, when Calvin was there, "the world isn't perfect and probably wasn't meant to be."

Kasey had just raised her brows, intent on bearing up as best she could. "She doesn't know everything. She doesn't even know what a french kiss is yet," she told Calvin, as if that pegged her about as well as she could be pegged.

She stood leaning against the doorframe, a tall, heavyset woman whose feet generally hurt long before the day was out. "Miss High and Mighty over there. She gets more notions from the movies."

Kasey just shrugged. She leaned toward Calvin in the dimness, her sharp little breasts tilted forward against the black wool sweater. She kept her eyes on his. "I don't see many movies," she said, as if she meant more.

Kay often spilled the beans without thinking about what

she was saying. "Kasey's a lonely child. I'm not saying that she isn't, because, in many ways, she is. The trouble is, she wants too much, sets her sights too high. Whatever happened to that basketball player? He took you to New York, didn't he?"

Kasey was still looking at Calvin. "Oh, swell! The Roseland Dance Hall. Mirrors. Stars. I suppose you think that's class."

"You had a good time, as I recall."

"He wasn't terribly mature."

Calvin romanticized the cramped apartment just because he was used to space. The cubiclelike living room seemed shut off, dim, secretive, and pleasant, in part because it was in the back. Its single window looked down on more brick. The couch and the two chairs were covered with the same grayish, nubby stuff. A portable phonograph and records were spread out across a battered blond wood coffee table; murky pastels of dancers hung on the walls, and a canary swung in a cage over the couch.

Kasey had kissed him up there when Kay was still at work, in the middle of the silent afternoon, the bird scratching above their heads, complaining, ruffling its feathers, dropping seed. She had taken him by surprise, her soft mouth against his for a moment, then gone, but their first kiss, cutting him off in midsentence, half-opened his eyes. Well, then, now what? Did she want him? Seriously? All the way? She was *just* seventeen.

He was up and down with her. He was in and out of the house at all hours, and he wasn't sleeping. When he wasn't with her, he was just marking time. When he wasn't with her, he felt as if he were trying to push through some kind of blunt, dead texture that buried both color and dimension. When he was alone, he showered, chose colognes, played records, pulled books out of cartons looking for needed poems. He was no longer seriously packing.

Sarah Elizabeth was just about through packing, but she wasn't taking much. She could get what she was taking in a small truck; the rest was ready for the auction block: the rugs, the hard sofas with their tapestried backs, the oak bookcases with leaded-glass doors, the sepia prints, the gilt clock encased in its glass dome, the gateleg tables, the lacquer jars, the plants and their stands.

He found the rugs rolled on auction day, the chairs up on tables, as if moved from flood level. The space looked alien and upended, too light.

She came through with a box of china and set it down on the floor. "Calvin," she said, turning, "are you still planning to go to college?"

"Yes. Of course. Why not?"

"I have kept my thoughts to myself as long as I could, but I have decided to speak my piece."

He had never argued with his mother because Grace had needed all the reassurance she could find. He did not argue with his grandmother because he couldn't get anywhere doing it. She just drove through all resistance like an army tank. He knew where she was driving now, but he wasn't going to help her get there. "Oh? And which piece is that?"

"Your grandfather could not easily praise people, but he admired you. He admired your studying and your fine school grades. He had his high hopes. That is why he put by the trust. He wanted you to make something of yourself."

Able Thomas had also chained several snarling bankers around the fund, ready to go for Calvin's throat if he touched it before he finished college. He was actually supposed to *make* something of himself before he started counting the money. "I know. I get the cash in my old age. I don't have to worry about funeral expenses."

She lit a cigarette, coughed and spit into a handkerchief. "You *have* brains. You just don't have much horse sense. You're short on that, so be careful before you get in too deep with that girl. Don't do anything rash. Don't commit yourself. Don't saddle yourself with a family before you finish your schooling. You've got your whole life ahead of you yet. You've got a lot of things you'll want to do," she said.

He knew that she was thinking about his parents' impulsive high school marriage. He couldn't think about it himself without seeing her point. Unlike his father, he was going to do something with his life. He couldn't commit himself now. He couldn't alter the course he had mapped out for himself, a career somewhere between business and the liberal arts.

However, he was probably safe. He loved Kasey just because she was elusive, finally unobtainable. He was sure that he did not have a chance. "She can't be tied down, anyway. She wants to dance," he said, just to rile Sarah Elizabeth. He knew what she thought about the stage.

"Well, I've had my say. I'll just have to let it go at that."

He parked behind the school buses that were already lined up in the crescent-shaped drive, their motors running, their exhausts smearing the snow along the curb. Cars were coming and going, their chains crunching over the smooth packed places, then suddenly hitting the cleared street. The sun fell through the sliced cloud formations, glinting weakly on the car hoods.

He saw her working her way through the crowds, separating herself from the groups that fanned down the steps onto the walk. She was carrying her books against her breast, her dark hair rolled under at the ends, just brushing her shoulders, swept across the forehead.

Then she was climbing in beside him, bringing the street's freezing, fresh breath, arranging her books on her lap, tucking in the pleated skirt. Her firm bare legs looked slightly bluish, her flats darkened, dampened at the edges.

He did not think of himself as vulnerable because he believed he was so closed, so careful, but she suddenly touched the emptiness inside him. The touch was so total, so comprehensive, he felt shaken, exposed.

She never greeted him in any conventional fashion. She was just suddenly beside him with some new plan or plot. "Could we take a long drive?" she asked, watching his face. "I've got something to tell you."

"We could go up to the apartment."

10

"*Then* we wouldn't talk." She was a teaser. She teased a lot, then watched his face. "Well? Would we?"

He started the Hudson, edging it out, around the buses, then stopping before entering the street. He pulled into the traffic. He shifted gears, keeping his hand on the knob, turning after the light. He passed an empty coal truck, its shovels banging in back. The sun was going in, the sky turning grayer.

"Sarah Elizabeth had her auction today. I left before the looting started, people pawing over her linen, her china, and her best corsets. Fighting could have broken out by now, and she will have had to call the police. I can see those cops now with their pleasantly impervious faces, steadily clubbing down the elderly and the infirm. The people who survive will be trying to get the chairs, tables, and couches down into the waiting trucks. We'll be staying in a shell. We'll be camping out. We can roast something freshly killed in the fireplace."

"It doesn't matter, does it? You'll be leaving for college any day now," she said, teasing, perhaps testing.

He refused to rise to the bait. "You sound like Sarah Elizabeth."

"Oh? Why?"

"Just because you do," he said.

He had been driving through premature dusk without realizing it, and he put on his lights. An army convoy passed, going in the opposite direction, disappearing one-by-one under a railway trestle. Buses lumbered by, stopping at corners, and when their doors opened, activating the light, he could see the faces inside briefly outlined. The wind came from the harbor behind him. He could dimly see the cranes and shadowy rigging etched in space. The sky was curdled and swollen, the horizon faintly reddish in the factory districts. The crowds crossed against the traffic, stepping around the hardened slush. He went through semilighted sections and then dark. Christmas trees lay bundled in side lots.

The car was overwarm. The heater was blowing up little puffs of dust around their feet. She unbuttoned her jacket,

11

then unwound the scarf. She once told him that she used to be heavy. He couldn't believe it. She was always hinting at a past more mysterious than the present, a past filled with sickness, fevers, extra fat.

"That's my life," she said—having been so quiet for such a long space, "somebody coming into it and going. I often wonder why it isn't the other way around. Do you think that all parting's like a little death? I sometimes do. It's as if two people take their last breaths. Then they begin again. Or try to. But it's just not the same. Because the numbness comes. *I* still feel as if I came from such a parting, a parting like that. It could have been very beautiful," she said.

He headed out of town, passing railroad tracks, water towers and old billboards which were still advertising war bonds. The traffic gradually thinned, then ceased. The street had a desolate, ashy look. The emptiness was gritty, tangible. The stoplights, going off and on, shone palely in the few store windows. The dusk deepened, changing texture, and it started to snow. They passed two-story frame houses with deep front porches. Then a brick school and a massive Catholic church with no particular design or shape.

"My father drank. He was on the stage, some, when he could crawl up to it. He was a comic. He had many disguises. He did impressions. He did numerous accents. He was all talk. He could also throw his voice. He built his own dummy, a tiny, gnarled, ugly figure, like an elf. It wore an elf's hat. He loved that elf, and when he wasn't speaking to anyone else, he would talk to that. They told each other their troubles. They always had many."

He had blundered down a side road in the dark. They passed a small cemetery on a hill, its fence half-fallen, its broken, grayish stones leaning in different directions. Then a dump. He crossed railroad tracks and over a bridge. The snow was coming down harder now, tufting the trees. He suddenly stopped the car.

"My mother never fought with him or anyone else. She seldom raised her voice. She was very quiet, very gentle, very remote. She said little. She endured mostly, but he walked out anyway. We moved into my grandfather's house."

"Oh, Calvin. You must have been an awfully lonely child, like me."

"I kept busy," he said, abruptly.

"You aren't like other men," she suddenly observed, meaning the jostling, hardy high school crowds.

He felt defensive. He was shy about his differences, not proud. He shrugged, looking out at the snow, his hands still on the wheel. "Oh, I guess. I'm a charmer, I am. Aren't I?" he said bitterly.

His self-preoccupation and apparent diffidence both worked on her like a stimulant, and she took him by surprise for the second time. She leaned over toward him, before he realized what was coming, and, without warning, she kissed him on the mouth.

He turned toward her, trying to get his arms around her, but her mouth, once so squarely planted on his, did not stay on his.

She leaned back to study him. She ran her fingers across his face, across the cheekbones, down to his mouth, where she lingered, as if she were trying to memorize the structure.

The falling snow was still mantling bushes, half draping fence rails. The moment had a numinous power of its own, transforming what it touched.

"I love snow," she said. "I love watching it fall."

"I love you."

She put her fingers across his lips again. She shook her head. "This is too intense, too perfect."

"What were you going to tell me?"

"We aren't going to do this again."

He felt numb, instantly drained. He sat up. "*What? Why?*"

"Because you're going away to college, and if I get any more involved, I'll be hurt more."

"But why can't we take advantage of what we *have?*"

"I just told you why."

13

How could he lose her now, when he had just found her? How was he going to survive without this feeling of fullness? How was he going to live outside this nimbus? "Oh, Jesus, Kasey, you can't do that! Listen! Will you? Kasey?" He was on the verge, the very edge, ready to get in too deep, ready to propose marriage. Ready to skewer two futures on the spot. Then he took another breath. The moment passed. "Can I at least *see* you again?" She was already combing her hair. "Alone, like this? It isn't wise, is it?"

He met her after school again the next day. "Unlike the rest of us, my grandfather wasn't a talker," he said, as if picking up the conversation where he had left it. "In fact, he seldom spoke, as if the art of conversation were something he had not cared to master, and what interested him besides his business would be hard to gather. When he smiled, which was seldom, something about the mouth slightly altered, as if some evil or some great wrong briefly amused him."

She was in heels, stockings, and her hair was up. "Before you get started, I've got something to tell you."

"I know. We aren't going to see each other anymore."

"I've got to work this afternoon."

"So that's why your hair is up, a bad sign. I might have known."

He hurried down Fairfield, over to Main, then north to the dance school. He drove recklessly, passing cars impatiently, hardly pausing at stop signs. He parked in front of the building and sat tapping his hand on the wheel.

"Goodness, you're a moody person! You look like Tyrone Power, a bit. Has anyone ever told you that?"

"How long will all this take?"

"Could you pick me up at six?"

He drove farther north to kill time. More collections of little businesses. Cigars and newspapers. Hats blocked. A butcher, a shoe repair. The hospital, and then the florists and fruit stores, grouped around the mother building like chickens. He pushed farther up Ox Hill, straight into the country.

14

When he got back, she was waiting in the doorway, carrying two grocery sacks filled with dance costumes. He threw them in the back and came around. "He was tall and fleshless. He held himself very erect, as if he had a plate in his spine. He wore those stiff detachable collars with studs until the day he died. They had to be sent out to be 'done,' but, by the forties, he had difficulty finding places that would take them."

She was sitting sideways, her legs pulled up under her, the dress hitched slightly above the knees. He was fumbling with the dash lighter while he kept his eyes on the traffic, and she took the lighter out of his hand, held it up for him.

"He wore a suit at every meal, and when he removed his coat after dinner, he put on a black, scratchy wool sweater. He did not smoke or drink, but when Chiclets first appeared, he took up that vice. He carefully unwrapped the cellophane and bit the gum in half, to save half, you see, and his cardigan pockets were always filled with half-bitten Chiclets, curled cellophane Chiclet wrappings."

"And he's the one who left everybody rolling in money."

"*I'm* not rolling in it. I'll be living on the GI Bill."

She romanticized his house, his people. She wouldn't visit his place or meet his grandmother; she wanted to keep their lives separate, apart. She saw his as much grander than it was or ever could be. "When are you leaving for college, exactly?"

"My grandparents fought constantly, and, as far as I can tell, that could have been their single pleasure in life. When her mother left her the house on the Cape, they bickered about it when they didn't have anything better to bicker about. He wanted to sell it. She wanted to keep it."

It was snowing again. Streets darkened. Lights in shops. Christmas music. Tacky, damp decorations and then the snow.

He parked. Came around and took her arm, still preoccupied. Going into the cramped soda parlor together. Dark oak, high glass cases, grayish marble counter, oval tables, chairs with curved wire backs. He kept his voice down because the place was empty. A boy was mopping up behind the case, his head and shoulders visible. They could hear the mop crossing the tile, clinking against the pail. He finally came around, wrung the mop out in the grayish, sudsy water. He stood there without a pad, waiting to take their order. Calvin ordered two hot chocolates, then sat across from her, picking at the charm bracelet on her wrist.

"She wanted to keep the place in repair, but, except for a single trip up there after she died, he wouldn't have anything to do with it. He had a heart attack when I was in the service, and when I came home, I found her packing. She had faced all her responsibilities through the years, you see, including me, and now she was going home."

They both moved back when the hot chocolate came, and he released her arm. She did not eat what a bird ate and did not like anything sweet. She sat spooning the cream off into the saucer. "You'll be going there in the summers, won't you?"

He knew she was thinking of some estate, probably on the water with its own dock. "It's a small three-quarter Cape. The winters are hard on houses up there, and by now it will need work. She'll get up on the roof with a hammer herself if she has to."

"We've got to be going."

"We've *always* got to be going."

"Oh, yes."

"Sarah Elizabeth is the spitting image of those people, the Scudder bunch, prosperous farmers. They first depleted Plymouth, then drifted down onto Nauset to deplete that. They spread from Namskaket to the herring brook at Billingsgate. From Slut's Bush to Jeremiah's Gutter. In gales, high winds and howling snows. Harrowing Quakers, drying salt, boiling tar."

It was snowing harder out. He opened her door. "Why're we always riding around in circles in the snow?"

"I love snow. It's so peaceful."

He turned off Main toward the darker, looming stretches

around the park, and then stopped. "What if I just took you along to college with me?"

"We weren't going to talk about the future. Remember?"

"*You* said we weren't going to talk about the future. I don't remember any bargain having been struck."

"You have such a *rich* voice. You could sell anybody anything. Do you know that?"

"I'm not getting very far with you."

"You have your whole life ahead of you, Calvin."

"We both have," he said, sounding bitter, as if its vastness merely irritated him at the moment.

They left the car and crossed through the park. They climbed up onto the seawall. The Sound was building below, throwing itself against the rocks, gradually thinning out, then dragging the loosened stones down. They couldn't talk in the roar, and it was too cold to stay.

They climbed back into the car, and he decided that he was going to propose. "Let's go back to your apartment, where we can talk."

Flakes glistened on her coat collar, melting in her hair. "Why? We've been talking, haven't we?" she asked, which was more teasing. She didn't suggest an alternative.

He spun out of the park in a huge, sloppy U-turn. He crossed onto Fairfield, then swung left, past a no-left-turn sign. He parked on a side street, then pulled her packages from the back. She held the downstairs door for him, and then went on up ahead. She had the door open when he reached the landing.

He put the bundles down just inside the door in the pleasantly stuffy, steam-heated air. "Well, everything's the same," he said, getting out of his coat. "Very peaceful, too. Your mother's canary is still up, though."

She took his coat. "It isn't hers. It's mine."

"Oh?" he said, rubbing his hands. "Whatever possessed you to want a canary?"

She hung their coats in the closet, stretching up to pull the hangers down, half in the closet's light. "It's a long story."

17

He was trying to decide what was actually different about the place, and then it dawned. Her mother wasn't in. Kay was usually back shortly after six. Pushing pans around in the kitchen and complaining about her feet. "Well, then? Tell the story."

"I once went with a basketball player from Black Rock. He was skinny and blond, and I told him once that he looked like a canary. It was a joke. He didn't. But when we broke up he gave me a canary. I was supposed to remember him. Always."

They were sitting on the couch. He was playing with her charm bracelet again, picking at it, turning it this way and that. He could smell her damp hair, snowy fresh, the dress's damp, salty, wool odor. "And have you?"

"Oh, yes. Some."

"I'll never feel the same about that bird."

"Oh, it isn't the same. That bird died."

He dropped her wrist. "And you went out and bought *an-other* canary?"

"Yes."

"I don't know much about you, do I? Why is that, do you suppose?"

He kissed her, and this time—to his surprise, she settled in against his mouth, gradually opening hers. She moved, barely, getting closer, giving up—a slip's soft sound, and his hand, crossing her dress, crossed a garter belt. He started to fumble with a zipper when he heard someone in the hall, and he stopped. He tensed.

She still kept her eyes on his, a dark, opaque color. She was still elusive, quiet, watching, waiting to see what he would do next. A little puzzle. "Mother's away overnight."

He was listening to the bird scratching in the cage overhead. Then everything registered. The works. The swelling wonder. The many meanings. They were going to have an affair after all! No strings. No rash promises. No long-term contracts. They were both free human beings. They still had their futures ahead.

He got up and took her hand. He assumed they were using

18

her bedroom, like normal adults, but she shook her head; she wanted to stay where they were; the bedroom was too personal, too frank.

She had her reservations, but he never knew where they were going to strike next because, a few seconds later, while they were still standing up, she had her hand between his legs.

He could later remember a certain amount of fumbling, trying to get around the coffee table, back to the couch, where she stuffed her underthings behind the pillows. She wouldn't remove her dress, but he was suddenly nuzzling her breasts through the scratchy material, those trembling circles, such small, plump cups.

He fell between her parting thighs, and she squirmed against his weight, her eyes shut, her arms around his neck. She had a sharp, hard little mound. He had difficulty entering, and he came quickly. At the same moment all his urgency broke. "Oh, marry me, Kasey!" he cried out, another, more tearing explosion. "Marry me, marry me, marry me!"

TWO Kasey talked about the possibility through that winter and into late spring. She told him that she would not marry while she was still in school. She was just skimming through with a low C average, but she wanted to hold onto it because when she stepped up onto the stage to get her diploma in June, she did not want to be one of those people who just squeeze through on a safe D. She had more pride.

She also told him that she would not marry him while she was still in school because if she married him before graduation, everybody would think she was pregnant. "That's the only reason girls get married while they're still in high school, isn't it?" she said. "Just because they're pregnant. Just because they're dying to settle down, go domestic. They act as if they're proud of their little achievement. A girl pregnant thinks she's the only one pregnant."

When she developed that line of thought, she would start to waver in general because she told him that although she wanted to get out of Kay's place, out into the real world, she wasn't very domestic. She was going to go on taking dance lessons, and, when June rolled around, she was going to work at the studio full time.

He agreed with all this. "You can be completely independent with me," he said.

She hesitated. "Do you mean it? Or are you just saying all this now? You could be ready to promise anything right now, and then go back on it. Men change when they have the woman where they want her," she said.

He told her that he meant it. He said that marriage usually stayed fresher when the two have their own lives, anyway. "Because everybody," he added, "stays more mysterious."

20

Kay Thatcher considered them both to be babes in the woods on the subject. She did not always try to hide her amusement, either.

She considered Kasey to be a very special child just because she was adopted. She had spent her life trying to justify her adoption, as if she had somehow intruded on the infant's own choices. "And so how lucky I was when I turned out to be right," she told Calvin, gradually leading up to the subject on her mind. "Kasey is very special. She's talented. She's moody, and she needs special handling. She needs a lot of understanding and patience. If you don't push too much, she'll always come around."

When she was annoyed with her, she could play it the other way, of course. She could claim that the girl had her sights set too high, but she had actually set them there. She had worked harder at it after Mr. Thatcher's death, a railroad man who had fallen from a water tower shortly after Kasey's arrival. She had started her career early: first tap, then twirling, then classical ballet, where she belonged.

Calvin had other problems. He couldn't get Kasey interested in sex without a great deal of steady urging, and he was still urging when Kay showed up at six.

"Excuse me," Kay would say, coming through, trying to mind her own business. She would go back into her own territory, change, and put her feet up for a minute before she started the evening meal.

Kay was a trusting, mild-mannered woman in many ways. She said that she had faith that Kasey would never do what she was not supposed to do.

"Which is?" Kasey would ask, teasing, wanting to keep her on the hook.

Then Kay look miffed for a minute. "You're no dope," she said, using the vernacular for emphasis. "You know what I'm talking about."

However, when Kasey missed a period, Kay pulled herself together. "Well, that's that," she said. "We all know what we're going to do now."

She barged into the living room as soon as Calvin showed

up the next day—Kasey's part of the house, and she was making plans before he could get his coat off. She was a partly lapsed Methodist, but she was willing to talk to her old minister. An Anglican, Calvin wasn't impressed with these flighty, recent sects. He wanted to be married in a more substantial atmosphere, but, as she said, they couldn't wait that long—not for priestly talks, published banns.

When Calvin called his grandmother to break the news, she said nothing for at least thirty seconds. "Well, beggars can't be choosers," she said, and because she was so short with him, he kept the rest of his thoughts to himself.

She showed up for the short ceremony. She sat on a folding chair in a boiling, baggy cloth coat, holding the wedding present on her lap. She had it bundled up in old newspapers, tied loosely with kitchen string, a battered pewter pitcher which had been in her family for years. He was touched because she had kept it away from the auction, her first and only sign of affection that day.

They had a weekend in New York. Calvin was on his own at last, and with a girl. He felt strong when they reached Grand Central. The air was hot and baking, that distinctly exciting summer city smell. The crowds and tall buildings were exciting, certainly stimulating. However, when they reached the hotel with its huge, crowded lobby, its long, noisy, disorienting corridors, he felt less elated. He never entirely recovered down there.

He took her to a foreign restaurant that was in the same district, but he felt small when he saw its size and heard the waiter's accent. He overtipped. They both fell silent for long stretches. He purchased tickets for a play, but the house was half-empty, its furnishings shabby, and they had trouble following the plot. She asked him questions about it that he could not answer. When they came out, he had trouble getting a cab. While he was standing there, half in the street, his hand up, an empty cab refused to stop. He flushed, and, for a moment, he couldn't look at her on the curb.

She was distant and quiet. She was continually watching

him, as if she were discovering things about him she hadn't noticed before. She wanted to know about his former affairs because she had once taken them for granted. He couldn't count his army experiences, hardly "affairs," and he switched the subject.

He asked Kasey about hers. She wanted to put the past behind her: Kay's preaching, Kay's cramped apartment, her own backwater high school existence. (Kay considered high school activities like cheerleading to be tacky; she supposed Kasey to be too mature for much else.) Kasey wanted to forget her old sense of separateness, her general unpopularity. She certainly wanted to bury her single previous affair, her part in its awkwardness, its corny vows and secrets. She just smiled her inner smile. "I asked you first," she said, staying mysterious.

While they were packing, getting ready to take the train back, she suddenly rushed to the bathroom. She locked the door, and he could hear the shower running. He knocked. He asked her if she was all right, but she didn't answer. She stayed in there for the better part of an hour, and when she finally appeared, she looked very pale. "My period's just started," she said.

They did not discuss its implications, but on the way home, her eyes grew misty. She still looked pale, certainly close to crying.

He did not try to talk, for once. He just picked up her hand and held it, a cold little hand without movement or strength, while the train swerved, swayed and slowed, stopping at local stations. Then gathering speed, rocking around the curves, finally hitting the straight stretches.

They camped out in Sarah Elizabeth's vacant house until they could find their own place. They lived in his bedroom, a cluttered oasis in that resounding shell: his clothes and hers, piled up everywhere; his books and papers; the novelty items and old costumes; several cameras, his barbells; a fencing set and a chessboard; some prints and pots. He had also rescued eight plants from the auction block, a way of

23

decorating when they found their place. He did not know their names. He called every plant a coleus.

He couldn't keep away from the latest gadgets out, either. He bought his first hi-fi during this period, but he also kept his old phonograph. Everybody was trying to dump his old 78's on the market, and because he could pick them up in bushel baskets, he also bought up 78's. He kept his modern jazz collection beside her records, beside "Sleeping Beauty," "Swan Lake," and the Andrews sisters.

Kasey lived as if nothing had changed. She transferred her routines from Kay's apartment to his grandmother's house. She worked out as soon as she rose and worked out again just before she went to bed, partly a dancer's duty, partly just hers because she was always in search of extra flesh, ready to pounce on fat. She padded around in those sloppy warm-up stockings complaining about the cold in July because she didn't *have* any meat to spare.

When he first stirred, he rose talking, walking down the hall to the bathroom, ready for the day. He was anxious to get going, to find a job and a place, to put down roots. He was trying to find both at the same time. While he shaved, he filled the tub. After the numerous army shower stalls, he fancied a smoking soak. He would lower himself into the high, old-fashioned piece with rolled sides, clawed feet. Then half pass out in sheer bliss.

He came back into the room, searching for his clothes in the clutter. "The veteran home from the tropics, his life ahead, just beginning his marriage. Having fought in the swamps, the warm slush. Heaving and swearing, swinging a cutlass."

She was sitting on the bed peeling off her warm-up clothes. "I thought you said you missed the war. I certainly can't see you fighting in it."

"When we reached Manila, we came in through a blowing drizzle. The city, gradually appearing, looked as if it had just fallen: broad avenues ripped up, statues toppled, buildings rubble, bridges down. The sight looked permanent, dura-

ble, and ancient: Athens, Persia, Rome, just beneath the skin."

"Well, *I'm* going to shower. We better hurry if we're going to get going."

While he was there, the city gradually changed, of course, taking shape around the new constructions, the heavy flow of dump trucks. The whores came back; the bars spread; the lights grew brighter, the gangsters more evident. Just before he left, the whores were beginning to appear inside the army compound itself, clinging to the sides of jeeps and pulling up their dresses in the laundry tents.

He chose a fresh white shirt, tied the dark, narrow tie, a sincere tie, a badge; breeding, right? He was going to find a job and an apartment with that tie. "No landlady will find any hell-raiser here," he said, talking to himself. "Coming in at all hours drunk. Falling up the stairs." He looked down at his shoes, then up at some imagined landlady, a harridan. "Madame. I have always had trouble with these feet. Since I was a pup. Now, if you could just give me a hand here."

He came down into the kitchen to start the coffee. He was getting the donuts out when she appeared: Kasey in a striped skirt, clinging rayon blouse and heels. Hair pulled back behind the ears, and then from them dangling brass bits. She looked older than he at the moment. She was still a little mystery.

She drank coffee, but she wouldn't eat. She pulled over the donuts, as if she just might try one, but she seldom did.

He would fret. She was working full time now—clerking in front when she wasn't instructing in back, and he wanted to send her off with at least a donut in her stomach. He packed her a lunch because if he didn't bother, she certainly wouldn't. She was far too immaterial to remember anything as mundane as noon.

He brought the Hudson around. The day was already baking, and they rolled the windows down. He pulled over some books, which fell, then crammed them into the back, be-

25

tween his cartons. He had a photographic memory, and he moved them in and out of his life quickly, like highly perishable merchandise.

"My grandfather wasn't great on going anywhere," he said, starting the car, feeling a story coming on. "When he took a few days off in the summer, he would get out this car, this very car, and take the family for an afternoon spin. He would leave early after lunch. He always planned to be back in time for dinner, too, because he did not like to drop any money along the way."

He cut through the park to get the coolness. There wasn't much. The Sound hardly stirred.

"He always took us to the same place, too. He would drive up into the country and then park on a hill, where we were supposed to admire the view, a little valley below. The hill was called Chicken Hill, although I do not remember the chickens. Was it shaped like a chicken? Perhaps."

He swung back into the traffic, toward the day's business, their life ahead.

"When he parked he always said the same thing. He would show us the valley, as if it were one of the Seven Wonders, and then he would say that there was no prettier spot in the whole world, as if he had circled the whole world many times himself. Then he would turn around to look in the back of the car, just to be sure that I didn't have my head in some book."

She sat quietly looking out. She unscrewed the earrings and dropped them in her lap.

"Sarah Elizabeth wasn't all that crazy about Chicken Hill. She wasn't all that keen on Connecticut in general. She was fond of saying that Connecticut didn't have any real weather, and, when it came to that, Connecticut didn't have any real people, either."

He pulled in front of the dance studio, unconsciously cutting in front of a car. He did not hear the horn. "That view appeared to last him all year because he only went once a year. When he came home, tired, wanting his supper, he

would prowl around wearing a self-satisfied look. He felt as if he had given the family a real treat and did not owe it anything else."

Calvin found a job toward the end of that week. He was going to be working in a factory's accounting section, a new wing that looked down on warehouses, marshes and recently constructed parking lots. He had lunch and then started the search for an apartment.

Places were scarce, and because the rent ceiling had not yet been lifted, every property owner had something to sell, a little item that explained the difference between the rent and what he actually needed. These people did not really care whether he was interested in the deal or not because if he wasn't, somebody else would soon be.

He was still searching on the weekend when Sarah Elizabeth's agent finally sold her house, a new pressure now. Besides, he was supposed to start work on Monday, which would crowd his time up further, pushing him to look through the evenings. Or else.

The day was still stewing, but suddenly gusty. A warm breeze suddenly lifted parts of shop awnings, turning their scalloped edges up.

He skirted a broken-down bureau that sat in the middle of the otherwise empty room, like bait. Feeling defensive, as if imposing, he silently examined the stained, dripping tub, the ancient gas range, the cracked, buckled linoleum. He finally came back to the bureau. "I like that fine, very rare old piece. It could be fixed up. What do you think?"

The woman continued to stare into space.

"How about fifty dollars? Would that do?"

She looked completely put out. "Why, I couldn't let that go for fifty dollars," she said.

He left.

His second try was more depressing. The place was dark because buried in the back. The single window looked down on a metalwork shop.

27

The landlady was sweeping and did not stop. He had to step around the dust pile. He opened the cabinet door over the sink. The paper had not been changed. A cockroach scuttled back, out of sight. He shut the door quickly, less his noticing offend.

The woman continued to sweep. She had a sharp, narrow face and faintly penciled-in eyebrows. She evidently had no furniture to sell. However, a cat strolled just ahead of him, wandering from kitchenette to bath, as if it were showing the place off. A clue?

He leaned down to pet the scuffy animal. It hissed, tentatively, as if about to be offended. "I like that cat. Is it Persian?"

The woman studied the creature with mild surprise. "No, not so I ever noticed."

"Well, there's Persian in it, I'm sure."

"I wouldn't know about that."

"Would you take fifty dollars for it?"

She looked put out, too. "Well, now, you know, I'm pretty attached. I live alone, and, without that cat, I don't get much company."

Where was the wonder?

"You want more for it, right?"

She didn't answer.

He left. He loosened his tie outside and threw his coat in the back of the car.

He passed railway crossings and trestles, pockets and bottoms in the factory districts, warehouses and workers' parking, fields of scrap iron, then several rows of two-story buildings, children playing on the steps in the cindery air. They watched as he slowed, checking numbers, then speeded past. He couldn't get himself to go in.

He saved the Black Rock address until last because the rent was steeper than the others. He drove out Fairfield and parked on a side street with big trees. The small brownstone apartment building had no lobby, certainly no elevator. The one-bedroom apartment was on the third floor on top, but in front. Despite the open window, the place was simmering.

Calvin looked around briefly, carrying his coat. He leaned out the window, looking at the trees. "It seems to be peaceful here."

The janitor was showing it. He did not comment. He was as grandly noncommital as the others, but he just worked for an office downtown, and, as far as Calvin could tell, he did not have his thumb on the scale.

"I'll take it."

The janitor just nodded. He took him downstairs to his place in the rear. He evidently ran his empire from a dining room table in his cramped apartment. A radio was going, and a woman was arguing with a child in the kitchen.

Calvin got out his checkbook to give him a month's rent in advance. He had just about exhausted his savings, the few bonds, the mustering-out pay, and the small veteran's bonus. "I love those old trees," he said.

The janitor put his cigar down on the edge of a dish. He looked hesitant, and then, when he cleared his throat, Calvin knew there was going to be a last-minute catch. What if he had to buy a few of the trees? "I'll also have to take a damage deposit from you, son," the janitor said.

(Money. You know how these things work.)

Calvin could hardly believe his luck.

He threw his coat on the seat and picked up some beer on his way back to the house.

They painted first, covering the standard grayish pink with a flat white just to get an extra sense of space. He would open a beer after breakfast, push their things into the center, and put down newspapers. Those summer weekend mornings were already like noon shortly after the sun rose, and he stayed in his shorts. She painted without shoes or skirt. She wore one of his old shirts, the tail trailing below her bottom. She would start with her hair tied back, but as it gradually loosened, she would push it away with the side of her hand,

29

steadily smearing her face and her dark hair. She got bored before he did, and she stopped shortly before lunch. She would shower and then hang out the window, trying to get some air. "You know what you're doing better than I do, anyway," she said.

They bought their basic kitchen needs and their few linens in the dime stores and the bargain basements. They picked up a few pieces of furniture in the secondhand shops. They purchased an expensive, name-brand mattress and frame to put in the living room under the two windows, a bed that could double as a couch. He was going to set up his desk and his bookcases in the small bedroom. He hung up his prints and set the sick-looking coleuses on the sills, where they could recover.

They ate out on Saturday nights and came back late, when the traffic was just beginning to thin. They threaded their way around the neighbors' children who were still out because of the heat, going past on orange crates, the rollerskate wheels beneath a part of the din. They made love on the new mattress in the haze, when the place was still burning like a low oven, a street light spotting the dusty, motionless foliage outside, the children still up, shouting to each other as they passed on the orange crates.

He started a long, narrative poem about his army experiences, but when he got halfway through, he realized that his language was lumbering, his thought prosaic, and he gave it up. He half suspected that he was too verbal to write. He knew that he talked too much, but he did not want to consider the problem at any length. When he tried, he ended up talking about it. He took night courses in accounting, business law, and the modern British novel.

Kasey said that she couldn't read because she couldn't stay put in one place that long. "When I try to sit still for any length of time, my skin starts to crawl," she said. "Don't you ever have that feeling?"

She would sometimes dutifully glance at a page over his

shoulder, as if she felt she should be interested. She would try to engage him in conversation, asking him what it was about and why he was reading it. Did he need to know that for anything? He would finally show his impatience by marking his place with his finger and looking up, prepared to endure.

She appeared to have no interests of her own other than dance. She danced because she craved both the moment's attention and its brief, steadily perishing aftermath. She needed the fleeting, bittersweet, shadowy sense of loss that followed every performance. She didn't follow the dance world as such. She knew little about what was going on in the field in general because she did not read the literature or attend anyone else's recitals.

She was raised to feel special, but she often felt handicapped in some obscure way; and when he moved into any area, she soon abandoned it. When he gradually took over the cooking and the cleaning, she just fell back, filled with a cloudy, floating sense of ennui. She would drift into the kitchenette and watch him work, half wanting company.

He felt jumpy and unprotected when she was in these moods, as if she wanted something specific from him that he could not understand, or, once understanding, even give. Half-guilty, he tried to tempt her with food instead. He threw her the margarine bag to give her something to do, and while he went on talking, telling her stories, going over the past, she would just sit there in silence, squeezing the colored tab through the pale, lardlike stuff.

He rolled up his sleeves, leaned his cigarette against the sill and put the mixing bowls in to soak. "Kasey? Do you know what I just realized the other day? Do you know what interesting fact about you I've uncovered?"

She finally preferred his talking about himself because his probing often threatened her ability to select, to forget, to gloss over the unpleasant. She waited, wondering what weakness he had uncovered.

"You left that canary at your mother's. Why? Because it

31

doesn't mean much now, or just because it still does?"

She felt on firmer ground for a moment. "What do you think?"

He took a beer out of the box. "Probably because it doesn't."

"Oh, really? *That's* interesting."

"But then I still don't know much about you, do I?"

"No," she said, "you don't."

"Not yet."

She overestimated his perceptions, his ability to pry. She stiffened. "The past is my business," she said, wanting the subject closed.

When she was angry, he was instantly concerned. He could not stand harshness, anger, any general rejection. He fussed, rubbing the back of her neck, wanting the status quo back. "You're tense," he said. "You're so tense! Why is that?"

She stood. "Don't touch me right now!" she snapped. "Don't hover!"

He grew tense, too, but backed up. "Wait until you try this meal I fixed," he said.

She was always starting fresh: tearing up old diaries and pictures, burning notes, getting rid of last year's clothes, changing makeup, cleaning out her record collection. What she put behind her could disappear overnight. He could never tell just what was going to go next.

He couldn't always sleep, and once, while he was lying on his back, his hands behind his head, staring at the ceiling, he started to mull over their wedding trip. He cleared his throat. "Kasey?" he called, softly, He rolled over, touched her shoulder. "Are you asleep?"

She stirred, moved her arm across the pillow.

"Did you just marry me because you thought you were pregnant?"

She didn't answer for a moment. He thought she was still asleep. "I don't know what you're talking about," she finally said. "I never thought I was pregnant."

32

The heat finally lifted. They could breathe in the place, now, and when it was chilly toward dawn, he climbed over the mattress to shut the two windows. They added a blanket. The radiators finally came on, knocking back and forth at first, hissing, the one in the living room answering the one in the den.

Kasey was working on a big show, the school's winter publicity drive, put on to bring in more business. She was out for long stretches. She came in later and later. She couldn't sleep when she reached the bed, but she was too strained, too tense to want sex. She turned gaunt and hollow-eyed. She caught a cold which she couldn't shake. She kept a fever, and her throat got worse. He finally took her to a doctor.

He kept soups and broths brimming on the back of the stove, but she wouldn't touch more than a taste at a time. She lived on aspirin, sulfur gum, and warm Cokes. She shook the cold a week before the recital, but she still looked fairly grim.

He drove her over in the Hudson on those frantic opening nights. Staying close, he carried her changes backstage, gingerly moving around among all those startling made-up pubescents and prepubescents. Enclosed in all that wonderfully creepy, self-centered, self-conscious intensity. Cooped up in themselves and highly strung. Dancers watching sideways to see if he is watching them. Sitting or warming up. Squatting with legs spread, feet pointing out in their stiff, glittering little skirts, waiting to go on. Low undertones. Chitchat and backbiting. Once on, they all sail off into sheer moonshine.

The mothers filled up the first three rows, clutching beaded evening bags, the house behind them empty. He watched Kasey from the third row. She was still what he had first wanted, the goddess Artemis. Dewy-eyed, fresh, virginal, and partly mysterious. He realized that he would never be able to penetrate the last, slight touch of strangeness; there and then gone, demure and elusive—but just *be-*

cause all this was true, he did not feel anymore complete than he ever had. He did not feel closer to her. He could not share; he could not take. She rose from sex as if untouched. He did not feel married. He did not feel settled down.

When the recital was over, it was worse backstage: mothers barging past in trailing gowns, the general crowds, the shoving and noise, the ripe odors, the doors back there constantly opening and closing on brief, semihysterical scenes: a girl heaving and weeping, a group jumping up and down, hugging, in happy tears; most still flying through in costumes.

He couldn't hurry Kasey out of hers. Get her to climb out of it and come down. She poked in the half-lit dressing room. Back and forth past the mirrors. Kasey after Kasey: the heavy brows and thick lashes, the huge eyes, the hollow cheeks, the breasts just pale points. The backs bent like bows while these figures were unlacing. The ridges shifted; the planes changed.

"I was different. Wasn't I? Wound up and really going, all alone. Floating. I was really floating. There wasn't any stage. There wasn't any floor. I've been better, technically, but I've never felt so free. So myself, too, but not me."

He paced, chain-smoking. "Yes, you were different. Come on. Let's get something to eat. I'm starved."

"Oh, I could go on and on."

He finally took her arm and firmly steered her toward the car. "You had a good house," he said, trying to sound involved.

She paused outside. She broke away from him, wallowing in the night air. She was determined to stay overcome. The moon would help but there was no moon.

"Come on, Kasey. Before you start running a fever again."

He turned out of the parking lot, the last car left back there and entered the street—passing closed shops, package stores, neighborhood bars, a corner building with its false façade, dentists' offices and law firms on top, once a piece of his grandfather's real estate.

Kasey removed her shoes and tucked her legs up under her.

34

"I looked down, tonight, and I saw this strange-looking woman in the front row. Dark, beautiful, foreign, perhaps Greek, and for a moment, just a moment? I wondered who she was. I wondered if I would run into my own mother some day like that. Sitting in the front row in a silver mink. She would come out of curiosity, just to see me, without telling me she was there, or disturbing my life. She turned out to be nobody, though. She didn't even look so foreign when the lights came on."

"My grandfather was a foreigner. He was born in England," he began, starting a fresh story, something to cheer her up, get her mind off the stardust. "He came over when he was still a boy, but he worried about England just as soon as Hitler started to kick up a fuss on the continent. He would sit glued to the news: H. V. Kaltenborn, Elmer Davis, Raymond Gram Swing, Edward R. Murrow.

"He went through some alteration. He grew restless, as if he had awakened one morning to discover that perhaps his own life was not what he had meant it to be. He decided that he ought to see a few things himself while he still could, and while the King was visiting the White House, eating hotdogs and drinking Ruppert Beer, my grandfather decided that we were all going to see the World's Fair."

She was combing her hair, putting the pins in her lap, concentrating on what she was doing, slowly coming down to earth, where, with luck, he could join her.

"Now going from Chicken Hill to Flushing Meadow is quite a jump, but he appeared to realize it himself. He first brought up the idea sheepishly, as if he knew he was revealing himself. Sarah Elizabeth just looked at him as if he had taken complete leave of his senses. 'That,' she said, 'would be the *last* thought in my head.'"

He looked at Kasey sideways. "When he got an idea, he held onto it. He would brood over it in silence and cunning. He would sometimes drop the subject, as if he had forgotten it, but he was soon back on the track."

"That woman turned out to be under the weather. While she was walking around afterwards, I saw her. She was staggering some and she was loud. When I run into my real mother, will it end up like that? A disappointment? Couldn't I for once have something that turned out right?"

He was now deep into Bridgeport. He turned left, across the tracks, into the eastside wilderness. Then over the bridge into rundown neighborhoods, shady districts.

Kasey put her comb back and closed her purse. "Where are we, anyway? I thought we were going out to eat."

He missed the place and had to back up. "Somebody told me about this. We're going to do something different tonight. We're having an adventure, which will help you get your feet on the ground. You'll need your shoes. So put them back on."

The windows were cloudy, the floor covered with linoleum, the air filled with a spicy, tomato smell. Onions, oregano, and what else? They sat in a booth against the wall.

"He kept at her about it. 'It has a robot down there that talks and smokes cigarettes,'" Calvin quoted, getting his grandfather's gravel voice down more or less right. "'It would be very educational for the boy.'"

A big, dark woman finally came around the counter, drying her hands on her apron. Broad shoulders, compact fat, and then the grave, strong face.

He ordered and turned back to Kasey. "'Educational?' Sarah Elizabeth just said. 'Educational, my foot! When you get fired up on something, when you dig in like that, wild horses couldn't drag you off the subject, could they? Do you want to know what really burns me to a crisp?'"

Calvin looked around the room without seeing it, gradually getting into stride, carried away. People looked up. Kasey put her hand on his wrist. "'Everything burns *you* to a crisp,' he told her, shouting now."

"Calvin? Please! You don't have to shout too, do you?"

He just wanted to finish this part of the story. "'You'll go down there to some swamp, you'll let a lot of strangers take your money, but you won't spend a red cent on anything you don't want. You won't put a lick of work into Mercy's roof.'"

Kasey looked around her, up at the ceiling, and back. She shifted in the booth.

"Then that would start him off. He would groan loudly, because they were back on what he considered to be an old subject. 'Oh, murder Christopher Columbus!' he would shout. He never swore; that was the strongest he ever got. 'OH, MURDER CHRISTOPHER COLUMBUS!'" Calvin quoted again, shouting. He was playing with the silver, pulling over his cigarettes, partly standing behind the table. He did not notice the woman back with the order until Kasey squeezed his hand. He finally sat down, leaned back, out of the way.

She was staring down at the huge, bubbling dish. "What *is* it?"

"It's a sort of tomato pie. Try it."

"Who invented it? Is it Jewish?"

"No, it isn't Jewish. Why should it be Jewish? It's Italian. Try it! You eat with your fingers. Look! Here. Like this."

"It's sticky."

"Of *course* it's sticky! It's supposed to be," he said, chewing, going crazy over this. He was thinking about ordering another. "Doesn't this bring us all down to where we belong? Won't this stuff stick to your bones? It's good, isn't it?"

She shook her head while she was drinking her Coke. She put the glass down suddenly. "You're different from what I first thought."

He waited. Well? How?

"You aren't as mature as I first thought. You aren't as secure."

"I never went around telling you I was *so secure!*" he said.

Calvin endured a second recital, an arthritis benefit. When they were both half organized again, he decided that they were going to recapture the old days, his metaphor for some old-fashioned sex.

He cleaned and cooked. He even talked her into a drink. She tried the mild daiquiri, then put it aside while she watched him at the sink.

She was getting herself up differently these days. She sported padded bra cups, spongy bits. She wore very little makeup, and she pulled her hair back severely.

She was wearing an old, bulky cablestitch sweater at the moment, and the wool, stretching in spots, showed the slip beneath, which worked him up. However, he had to get this show on the road first. He salted the roast.

"I've decided to take a stage name. What about Stacey Rainbolt?"

Kristine Thatcher; Kriss Thatcher; Carol or Caroline Thatcher; Casey Thatcher; Kasey Thatcher; or (perhaps) Kasey Gonzales. Then Kasey Hart, the last one less real than all the rest.

He picked up a beer. He rescued her daiquiri on their way into the living room and set it down in front of her. He knew that he was going to be abrasive just because he was desperate—wanting everything to be perfect just this once, but he couldn't stop himself. "Who are you *now*? It sounds so Indian."

"Well? I *could* be Indian."

She was too hairy to be Indian. She was too hairy to be Stacey Rainbolt. The springy, curling stuff appeared to crop up over night, and if she did not shave regularly, it soon curved around the leotard's crotch. When she left the tub, he would have to rinse down the soapy remains that still bubbled around the drain, peppered with these bits.

"I have these cheekbones, of course."

"All right. I'll give you the cheekbones."

"You didn't. But somebody did," she said, still in her own world.

She had a lonely existence, he decided, because solipsism could not support two, and if she was going to reshape her world every other minute, then she had to retreat. She had to burrow in, until the space around her seemed once more divided down the middle.

He still could not stop himself. "Why not Stacey Thunderbolt?"

"That sounds *too* unconventional."

Her florid imagination could flare up in spots, but, at the same time, her limiting intelligence cramped its scope. He suddenly realized that, in many ways, she *was* conventional.

38

"You will eventually leave me for some dancer, a bleached blond with a cold, cut-glass face and a fancy jockstrap. Both of you will go straight to the top. Berlin. Rome. Moscow. Paris. I will take care of you both. Keep the books. You'll need someone who has his feet on the earth."

She was still leaning against the bookcase, where he had placed her drink. "*You* want to be taken care of. You're always *waiting* to be taken care of, aren't you?" she asked, finally looking at him. She didn't sound short. She could still be on his side, waiting for him to share the joke.

He could be abrasive, but he could not confront her directly. He spotted his stovepipe hat sitting up on some books, and he put it on. He lifted his hand and straightened the brim. "I've never claimed to be a terribly independent person. It isn't one of my great strengths."

"Oh, yes. You want to be taken care of," she continued, as if he had been arguing with her. "Mostly, really, and I just wasn't cut out for that. We both just married the wrong people."

"Oh, Kasey! Be reasonable! You don't mean that! You're just down!"

"Oh, I loved you once, when you weren't around, when I could just think about you. I loved you when I first thought you were going away," she said, looking as if she would love him again if he would just *go*.

His heart bulged against his chest. What did all this mean? Where was it leading? Weren't they going to have sex tonight? "What do you want me to *do*? What do you want me to *say*? How can we get back to where we were, then?"

"Will you wait awhile? Will you be patient? Will you just leave me *alone*? Will you stop *hovering*?"

He felt as if he had once been touched on the shoulder, and, in that moment, chosen. Now the spreading radiance was gone. He had stepped back into a gray, dimensionless hum.

He was suddenly hopping around her, thrusting his face into hers. "I was going to New York. I was going to school. I had a future. Before I had to settle down in a third-rate college so you could dance in a fourth-rate troop. If you *really* believed you could dance, you'd want to be in the city, too, where things are going on. You know that, don't you?"

Her controlled anger took him by surprise. She was suddenly in the closet, pulling down coats, trying to find hers. "You *wanted* to settle down. That's all you ever talked about. I had more freedom with Kay. I'm going back there."

Was it over, just like that? Were they through?

Kasey picked up her clothes while he was at work—leaving the closets empty, but the apartment, filled with his possessions, did not look that much changed. He lit a cigarette, prowled around, and then climbed into the Hudson.

Kay opened the door, and he crowded past her. Kasey was just coming out of her bedroom in a bathrobe, drying her hair. He tried to hover without actually hovering. He was going to change. "Listen, Kasey, all this has been good. A small fight, and we've cleared the air. What do you think?"

She just shook her head. "I don't believe what I'm hearing," she said.

Kay suggested a cooling-off period. Calvin was willing, Kasey indifferent. "All right," she said, turning her back, "but I won't see him."

Notice what he won, a curious status quo; they weren't seeing each other anymore. That was the best deal he could get.

He moved his clothes and costumes into the closets. He slept spread out across the big mattress, trying to fill up space.

He wrote several letters and then tore them up. He was drinking more. He prowled around in his coat of many colors, peering out windows, talking to himself, his glass in his hand.

Fuzzy with rum, he drove out to the studio in a late afternoon downpour, and when someone at the desk said she was busy, he broke into the practice session. Wearing the soggy coat of many colors, waving his hands, he scattered those shimmering pubescents in several directions. "All right," he said, "I'm ready to back up all the way. You're a very talented dancer. You outshine them all, and just because you do, we'll stay in Bridgeport, where you can put a little life in things here." She escaped into a back bathroom and locked the door. "Oh, come home! Come home, Kasey!" he called, pounding on the door. "Where you can put a little life in that place, too!"

Kay called that evening. She sounded nervous. "You need to talk to somebody," she said. "You need to get a little calmed down. I was wondering if you wanted to talk to our minister."

"Hoppit's very prissy, isn't he?"

"His name is Habbit, and he isn't prissy. You can tell him anything, Calvin. He'll listen."

Habbit. Hoppit. Who cared? What difference did it make? He was *her* prissy minister, not his.

"I know you're defensive. That's natural. You've been hurt, and so you need someone to lean on. You're *both* very high-powered people who don't know how to communicate."

She sounded like Hoppit herself, and that was just a sample. In any case, he was a very private person. He wasn't crazy about any such confrontation. "Is *she* going, too?"

"I can't make her do what she won't do. I've finally learned that through the years."

So he was right from the beginning. *He* was considered to be the unsound party in all this. *He* was supposed to unburden *his* soul. She got off scot-free, a balanced little adult.

"Kasey's bound and determined to do what she wants to do. She's talking about divorce," Kay said, finally unburdening *herself*. "She's talking about seeing a lawyer, but if she does that, she's going to have to handle it alone. She's going to have to start standing on her own two feet."

He decided that he had also better see a lawyer. He had never told her about the trust, but why take chances? He was just a veteran, and you couldn't wring blood out of a veteran on the GI Bill.

THREE   Calvin drove down to New York in midsummer, shortly after his divorce. He was beginning again, a year behind his first schedule. He was striking out, his life once more open-ended, but why, then, wasn't he excited? Why couldn't he enjoy the challenge? Why was he just going with his emptiness, his ragtag depressions and anxieties, a few steps ahead of panic?

The Hudson bulged with his possessions. He hadn't tried to open the old car up on a highway before, and he had difficulties from the start. The fanbelt broke on the Merritt and a back tire blew on the Hutchinson River Parkway. He started to lose oil close to New Rochelle, and while he prowled around the car in his third service station, his shirt sticking to his chest in the searing heat, he argued with the attendant about the work involved. What if he blew a rod? If he blew a rod, he blew a rod, then. He carried extra oil instead. He reached Riverside Drive in the five o'clock rush and finally turned into the city, looking for the midtown YMCA. He wandered deeper into the maze through the frantic criss-crossing traffic. Several streets were being torn up, the jack-hammers were tying into main lines, and he made poor time. Cabs cut in front of the Hudson, swerved around the excavations, the garbage trucks and the backed-up vans, the drivers leaning on their horns and slamming on their brakes at the last minute.

The hotel lobby was filled with milling people. He finally got his key at the desk and walked back outside to find something to eat. He wandered through the crowds, stopping to read the menus tacked up on restaurant windows along Broadway, but he decided he wasn't up to a full meal. He bought two Italian sausages from a street vendor and ate them as he headed north, the warm buns slightly damp from the steaming shredded onions.

He stopped in a bar for a beer. The place was crowded and noisy. A waiter passed in the dimness, weaving his way around the customers, carrying a tray over his head, heading for a back room. Calvin crossed to the bar.

A neat little man with a fleshy face, a fancy dresser, was talking to the bartender. "We're just protoplasm," he was saying. "We're not solid matter. We're just protoplasm. We're liquid. Protoplasm is just liquid. Flesh is just liquid, but arranged in suspension in cells of dead substances. We're mostly water, and you can break water down into two components: hydrogen and oxygen."

The bartender picked up the empty glass in front of Calvin and wiped off the counter. Calvin ordered a beer. The bartender was still listening to the man without looking at him or Calvin. "I don't like to think about things like that," he said.

The little man was still talking. He turned to Calvin, as if he were going to include him in the conversation, but he changed his mind. He turned back to the bartender. "For instance, why do you suppose the Arabs wear those robes?"

The bartender didn't answer. He drew a beer, put it in front of Calvin and picked up his dollar.

"They wear those robes because they would dehydrate without them. They have to conserve their own sweat, and the robes act as insulation. If their sweat dried they would dehydrate. Have you ever seen a dehydrated man?"

The bartender brought Calvin's change back. "I just don't like to think about those things," he said.

When he got back to the hotel, he pulled his suitcase out of the car and went upstairs. He took a leisurely shower in the huge shower rooms, which reminded him of the service. A few people came and went, usually sticking their heads in to look for someone else; but it was early, and he had the shower to himself.

He climbed into bed naked because the cell-like room was so humid. He stripped back the top sheet and bunched up the small, clean-smelling pillow under his head. He expected to pass out instantly, but he didn't. The sudden privacy was slightly paralyzing. He lay on his side, staring at the long, narrow window where the streetlight still slid past the edges of the drawn shade. He lay listening to the half-muffled traffic sounds, a distant, steady hum that gradually diminished after dark.

He thought about Kasey, trying to remember specific details. He could not see her clearly, but he could catch certain angles, like the side of her face and the set of her shoulders. He could just see her shape on the mattress in the shadowy Black Rock apartment, the children below still out in the street, shouting to each other as they passed on the orange crates.

He woke in the middle of the night, still tasting the greasy sausage, and his stomach turned over, throwing him off balance. His thoughts, scattered, eerie, undirected, played over him in wave after wave. He got out of bed, hurried down the hall, threw up in the public sink, and felt better. He fell asleep and did not wake until noon.

He camped in the YMCA while he looked for a place—out each morning with the classified section and a street map. He ate breakfast in the same drugstore, scanning the papers while he sat at the counter. An orange drink rose and splashed against a globe behind the help. The clerks, rushing orders back and forth, squeezing past in the narrow space, just touched, without noticing, the damp spots already spreading under their arms. The customers milled around behind him, reflected in the mirrors, trying to get waited on, coming and going—women in white linen, soft cotton, and backless, clinging rayon.

He kept close to the West Side while he hunted, from 73rd Street through the high 90s, between Broadway and Riverside. He walked through the small parks, the dusty edges of green that dotted Broadway, and then down to the Drive, where he couldn't afford what he wanted. However, he couldn't stay in the YMCA. His coat over his arm, his tie loosened, his shirt sticking to his back, he explored side streets lined with brownstones, their shades pulled in the middle of the day.

He finally chose a cramped, barely furnished efficiency, a boiling fourth-floor walk-up where he could store his cartons until he found something better. He shared the bath, cooked on a hot plate, and slept in a high, shapeless bed that sat in the middle of the small cell. He finally took the bed apart, cleaned the frame, put it back together, and dragged it over under the single window, where he could get a little air after dark.

He wrote Kasey several times, trying to rescue old feelings, certain auras, certain scenes: the falling snow, the leafless park, the Sound curling below, and then Kay's overheated apartment; but he finally tore these letters up. He wrote letters to Sarah Elizabeth—talking about the past, recalling that trip to Flushing Meadow on a chartered bus, for instance, "dredging it all up," as she would have called it, and he also tore these across the middle.

He could still remember the journey to the fair—the cold morning gray and then the drizzle. It had drizzled all the way down. The Connecticut industrial towns passed the bus windows through the smudge and the changing, splotchy water shapes. The drizzle finally stopped without altering the air. The day stayed muggy and close.

They trudged around, covering acre after acre, covering as much as they could. His grandfather bought a china bulldog in the British pavilion, a Union Jack painted across its back, but the Germans did not have a pavilion.

"There's a war coming," Able Thomas said, carrying his bulldog in a brown paper sack. He looked delighted.

Calvin's mother was appalled because she always tried to look on the bright side. She could find a bright side when nobody else could. "Why!" she said, having planned to stay cheerful through their vacation, "*what* a thing to say!"

They trudged through the Heinz exhibit, where they

picked up pins shaped like tiny pickles. Sarah Elizabeth threw hers in the trash on the way out. She wasn't carrying around free advertising for anybody.

They gazed respectfully on Elsie, the Borden prize cow. They studied ancient Christian manuscripts under glass. They saw the Futurama.

"Your father would have loved this," his mother said— leaning over close so that the others could not hear. She sounded as if he had died a graceful, meaningful death, instead of having just disappeared. She was in fact still married.

His mother and his grandmother moved at a faster clip through the less respectable amusement sections. They passed fan dancers, and then a girl in a bathing suit who lay inside a huge block of ice. How did she do that? The barker extolled her talents as they passed. The show was just starting, and Able Thomas disappeared. He caught up with them later, looking partly sheepish and partly renewed. Nobody spoke. His mother took his hand.

The sky darkened early, and a breeze sprang up. The flags snapped crisply, and over the reflecting pool the colored lights came on. Standing in the crowds, close to his people, he could feel the distant fountain spray and see the changing colors. Then Kate Smith sang "God Bless A-MER-i-ka!" and he got gooseflesh. The war was coming on, and everybody knew it.

He had dreamed about that woman in the block of ice several times through the years. She had her arms against her sides, her knees together, her chin lifted, looking out at him, the eyes wide open. She suddenly smiled. Now her stillness had not bothered him, in itself, but, considering the stillness, considering the general rigidity, the little knowing smile always terrified him, shining up through the ice. He always woke at that point, bathed in sweat.

He was gradually learning the subway system and the crosstown bus routes. He took the IRT up to Columbia University, walking through the main gate under the fragile, sooty foliage, cutting across the campus under the low, massive stone buildings, past the library where Minerva sat halfway up the stairs, granite-faced and square-figured, her arms extended like a Roman emperor's, the Broadway traffic a distant hum in the summer heat. He prowled through the bookstores while his heart raced, wanting book after book on the spot. He couldn't wait for fall. He finally registered for two summer courses before he found a job.

He was finally typing letters of credit on Wall Street from four P.M. until midnight, hours which kept his days free. The typists threaded the forms into the big, humming IBM's, lit cigarettes, or opened packages of gum, and started the production rolling shortly after four. They kept a radio on, and while they typed, calling to each other across the room, they listened to the weather reports, the news, and the latest popular songs.

Calvin was already a crack typist, the fastest on the foreign department floor. When he started work with the others, shortly after the hour, he would light an Old Gold, open his bottom desk drawer, stick his foot inside, as a brace, and begin. He could talk through the heaviest work load without glancing down at the machine.

He talked about Mercy Scudder—Sarah Elizabeth's mother, his great-grandmother, the famous New England ghost. "She always wore a man's worn mackinaw and a man's old felt hat, its brim pulled down around the ears. She was an independent, stubborn old woman right up until the end, a troublemaker from the word go, and if anyone could come back from the dead, she could come back from the dead," he explained, pausing to light another cigarette, littering the papers beside him.

"She could talk a blue streak, and if she decided that she was going to talk to you, the effect was generally numbing. She spoke in long, rambling, involved, transitionless sentences, without having to pause for breath or consider her audience. She liked to believe that she understood the world better than most did, and she would say she could call a spade a spade. 'Like the truth or lump it' was a favorite expression. She would get up and argue everybody down in town meetings, and if she did not like the way the vote went, she threatened to pull her ancestors out of the local cemetery and move them down to the next town, where they could be properly appreciated.

"She died in 1944, shortly after France fell. She wasn't cold when she first appeared. We were on the road, still on our way to the funeral. Mrs. Fox tells the story. *She* was in, trying to straighten up the three-quarter Cape. Mercy tried to help with the cleaning. She would not cease her doing," Calvin said, trying to approximate Mrs. Fox's language. "She put an old chest where Mrs. Fox did not want it put, and when Mrs. Fox tried to move it back where it belonged, Mercy dragged it back where she wanted it. 'I gave up,' Mrs. Fox said, 'because arguing with ghosts is like arguing with children, and what's the point?' She slammed doors. She set a spinning wheel going. She tried to get an old musket down. She talked a blue streak, as usual. She complained about her high taxes, the low Anglicans, and the new lax zoning laws. She finally floated back into the buttery, where she disappeared," Calvin said, embroidering on the buttery, competing with the radio: the weather, the late news, and the popular singers, Eddie Fisher, Perry Como, and Patti Page.

Calvin ran into an interesting Staten Island rental in the fall.

NYU Students! Huge Space!
Privacy! View! Desperate!
Quiet!

He drove over the following Saturday, crossing on the ferry, still carrying extra oil. He cut through the half-deserted streets and climbed the steep hill. While his future roommates waited, he poked around the big, dusty, half-furnished flat that overlooked several warehouses. Given the warehouses, the neighborhood was empty after five. A clock face shone through the trees like a big, blank autumn moon.

Charley Klick was a veteran who had been in the army of

occupation, like Calvin just missing the war himself. He still had his army crewcut, like Calvin, but he was a blond. He was so blond he looked blanched, bleached out. He sported a small, light, almost invisible moustache. He wore baggy pants and loud, loose sport shirts. He was short, but, in compensation, he worked out, and at that point of his development, he had a thick, compact, jointless look. He was a business major.

He was just a freshman, but NYU did not awe him much, and he already knew shortcuts. He had been on a high school swimming team, but he was taking a beginner's swimming class to pick up some quick, easy requirements. He told the instructor that he was in the class to help overcome his fear of the water, and halfway through, he was already standing in the pool up to his chest, splashing his shoulders and getting his face wet. He told the man that he could not have made such progress with anyone else. He shook his head while he was telling the story. "I made that skinny little bastard's day," he said.

He had originally come from southern Ohio, but he had gotten himself mustered out of the service in New York, and he had not gone back home. "Skip that shit," he said, without explaining. He stayed fairly evasive about his background, Ohio coal-mining stock. "My old man believes the earth is flat," he said once, a remark that appeared to have no particular context at the time. "That dumb shit. When I said it wasn't, he said that any fool could plainly see it was. Then he slammed me up against the side of the head. That didn't make the earth flat, but I saw a few stars. I hate *dumb* shits like that. They're going to *stay* dumb all their lives. They're proud of it, too, as if being that dumb is quite an accomplishment."

Charley was going with three girls at the moment; they served separate functions. He loved to dance, and he had a girl who was supposed to be a great dancer. She was best on her feet. He screwed a second, who was best on her back. He just ate the third. He saved her up until he felt like eating, and then he gave her a call. "She's wonderful," he explained, "like a big, warm, friendly, freshly baked pie."

Floyd Deeds did not believe half these stories, and he said he took the other half with a grain of salt. Floyd Deeds was different, a prelaw student who believed in logic above anything else. He was older, and he had seen some of the war. He had been a second lieutenant in the Pacific, and he still carried his bars around in his wallet. He was trim and spare, and he kept his military bearing. He was quiet, faintly priggish, and if he was not openly patronizing, he appeared to suggest that he knew the world in a way that the others could not; but, at the same time, he wasn't going to hold it against them if they did not push. He came from well-to-do Westport people; and because Charley was a climber, Calvin associated Charley with Gatsby's mysterious friend, who had "gonnegtions." Calvin thought of Floyd as Charley's Westport "gonnegtion."

Floyd had two chief worries. He worried about the Red Chinese. He knew that the U.S. was going to have to take the Red Chinese on sooner or later, and, as far as he was concerned, the sooner the better. He was far less worried about the Red Russians than the Red Chinese, who weren't white. "I'll tell you what the problem is," he explained, "because it's short and simple. The Chinese don't make any sharp distinctions between life and death, and when you're dealing with that kind of mentality, you're dealing with trouble."

Charley Klick teased Floyd Deeds some. He called him Good Deeds. He would go through Calvin's boxes until he found his Viking helmet. "Hey—Good Deeds?" he would call, placing the helmet on his head. "You better get ready! You better arm yourself! The Chinese are coming! The Chinese are coming!"

Floyd seldom rose to such bait. He knew what he knew, and that was that. You could say what you like.

Floyd also worried about his sister. Fern was smart, but she could not or would not consider her future. She was not interested in college, as such, but if a class caught her eye, a music appreciation or an art appreciation course, she took it without credit. She sampled here and there without worrying about a degree. She worked in the Barnard library bindery, and, as far as Floyd could see, she was willing to stay there for the rest of her life. She did not appear to be worried about ending up an old maid, either.

She was twenty-six and still unmarried. She was getting on in years, but she did not know much about men and acted as if she did not care to. She just wandered around the city's art museums and took in the concerts by herself because she was such a loner. She said that men were too much trouble. They were always concerned with themselves, with the impressions they made, and they could not sit still long enough to listen to a serious piece of music. She liked the opera. She particularly liked Russian opera; but how could she concentrate on a long Russian opera if someone was fidgeting around in the seat beside her? What was the point of going with someone if you couldn't hear the music? She reminded Calvin of his grandmother, and, at times, he could understand Floyd's position. "She's just got her priorities all wrong," Floyd would say, shaking his head, a logical, efficient person in an illogical, inefficient universe.

Floyd ran into Fern in the Village shortly after the first of the year. Calvin and Charley waited while he talked to his sister—the shambling student herds and the uptown tourists milling past their shoulders in the crowded, narrow street.

Fern was not attractive in the conventional sense, but, when a general impression emerged, she could strike some people as interesting looking. She had a broad, open, intelligent face.

Fern was in a hurry, down there to hear a folksinger, and when Calvin suggested that they all go, she hesitated for a moment. He decided that he was being rebuffed. "Are you sure you all *want* to go?" she asked, finally looking pleased. She had short, crisp, auburn hair, her best feature. "Because you don't *have* to, you know."

She was far less aggressive than Floyd had led him to believe. In fact, she soon struck him as modest, quiet, and self-effacing. She wasn't flirtatious or intimate, or, for that matter, guarded. She was a very direct person, the way some shy, lonely people can be direct, as if they know they have nothing to lose.

While they were coming out of the café that night, heading across the street to find a drink, Calvin started talking about his former marriage: Kasey Thunderbolt and the cloud-capped towers, the Cokes, the sulfa gum, the post-recital inwardness, the apartment filled with his dying coleuses.

Fern couldn't make head or tail of it. She could not understand the girl's pretentiousness, and because pretentiousness bothered her so much, she did not comment on that. "You must have been very confused during that period," she said, unable to find anything amusing about his previously smitten state.

Her directness appeared to be both intelligent and at the same time dimensionless, without subtlety, edges, or shadows. Her intelligence touched him, as intelligence always did.

The group was born that night. Like most loosely knit groups whose members have separate lives, diverse interests, and tight schedules, they could let weeks pass without seeing each other, but then, just when they appeared to be drifting apart, someone was getting something up again. They prowled around together for various separate reasons, from January through May, but that period, that whole period, had about it in retrospect a kind of fresh, innocent shimmer.

They spent long, gray Sunday afternoons in the Museum of Modern Art or the Metropolitan. They shot down Fifth against the head-on wind, chins lowered, hands in their pockets, nobody talking, just enduring. They hurried onto the partly sheltering side street, 53rd with its elegant brownstones, the museum's welcoming flag. When they came in through the revolving door, getting out of their heavy overcoats, these excess burdens, their skins stung in the brief transition. They picked a floor and spread out—Fern taking longer than anyone, alone with a picture without talking, taking notes, or posing. The three usually ended up waiting for her in the hall. They were up and down stairs, under the floating Calder, then out into the brown, chilly garden.

Floyd once ran into some of his Westport connections out there: bland, mild, well-bred people, and if Calvin wanted to patronize them, he couldn't without feeling as if he were slightly betraying parts of himself. They tried to keep up. Everything you did pleased them. Everything you did was either super or fabulous, and the attention they lavished on small items could be unnerving. They had been heading in a different direction, but when they discovered where the group was going, they changed their plans. They decided to tag along.

Fern combed the *Times*—making lists, plotting the weekend, underscoring the rare events, the special shows. They walked beside the park, its leafless trees etched against the rolling, mottled sky. They passed the Paris, the Plaza, the fountain, and the carriage horses. The horses had their noses buried in their feed bags, and when they raised their tails, they dropped steaming clumps behind them.

"That's art," Charley said, ahead of his time. "That's art. Let's take it along."

They reached Fifth and then turned north, four spread out across the walk.

Charley raced through Calvin's books. He read as if books were virgins, to be trapped, taken, and discarded. He was reading Joyce at the moment. "Horseshit has clarity, wholeness and harmony," he insisted, unable to leave a joke alone.

Calvin threw his cigarette away in the wind. "Horseshit."

Fern was heading up the steps first. She wore comfortable flats, and she had a long, determined mannish stride.

Charley poked Calvin. "I've insulted her," he said, impressed.

Calvin shook his head. "You've bored her, which is worse."

They caught Ruth St. Denis, a living legend, sowing grain in the Metropolitan Museum basement, where the mummy cases had been stored. They sat on hard, collapsible chairs while the old dancer posed with veils, striking interesting positions.

Charley complained on the way out.

Calvin stopped to light a cigarette. "The miracle is she's still breathing. Can't you just enjoy the breathing?"

Charley missed little, there because he wanted to know what he should know, in case he should need it. Since he had the usual vulnerabilities of the opportunist, he saw this period as an achievement rather than a process. The single-mindedness was less willed than naturally implicit, and, like his selfishness, his drive grew from an incompletion that slightly resembled innocence.

They hung from straps in the swaying IRT—rocking up-town to catch an Eisenstein festival, slowing at local stops, then picking up speed for brief periods. Calvin watched a paper cup rolling back and forth under a seat across from him, wondering why the group stayed together, such odds and ends.

"*That's* no problem," Fern said, standing beside him. "We do *because* we're such odds and ends."

Calvin felt checked. He thought of *her* as a little strange, but why him? He was just an average child in the dying upper middle classes, respectable, respectful, guilt-ridden, and unnerving.

They climbed up out of the subway and into the ashy light. Heading for the Thalia, they passed shoe repair shops, corner groceries and Chinese restaurants.

Floyd was arguing with Charley about the girl he was half going with at the moment.

Buffy Trulock came from the Westport set, one of Floyd's "gonnegtions," a small, slightly heavy blond with brown eyes. She surprised Calvin. She was less bland, less literal-minded than that crowd. She sailed; she supported the right charities; but she had survived polio when much younger, and although she had no visible signs of the affliction other than a slightly twisted left arm, she seemed to have been made permanently deeper by it. She could even strike people at odd moments as backward, as if she had sat out some earlier, crucial social development. She was thoughtful where the rest of her crowd was merely earnest.

"I just don't like the way you treat her, that's all," Floyd was saying. "She's a very serious person. She's a Catholic girl, and you shouldn't be taking her so lightly. If you want to see her, see her, then. Go with her, but just don't call her up when you think you can't find anybody better around."

"She's a nice girl," Charley said, missing the point. "She has several big brothers in bonds."

Fern took them up to the Cloisters in late April. Floyd and Charley fanned out inside as usual.

Calvin needed the group, the sense of the whole, but, at the same time, he was gradually growing closer to Fern. He stayed by her side. He was talking about his last trip to the Cape, the journey up to Mercy's funeral service.

He suddenly stopped in midsentence, realizing that he was going on again. He said so. "I talk too much, I know," he said, wanting reassurance.

Fern could only tell the truth. She respected it so much. "You have many other sterling qualities," she said.

They walked out into the garden together where the twiggy stuff was just starting to come alive. They stared down at the broad, gunmetal-gray river, the bridge like an abstract painting.

"I *do* make you slightly nervous, then, don't I?"

"That isn't your fault, Calvin. Attractive people always do. I feel as if they're not quite real."

Calvin felt checked again. "*I* am? I bother you that way?"

"Oh, my heavens, yes, you are! Like a movie star, for what that's worth," she said.

Fern loved foreign restaurants. She knew the best, least expensive spots. These places were seldom crowded, but the service was still slow, sometimes close to nonexistent. They had gypsy music, roving fortune-tellers, Turkish dancers. Fern particularly liked the Russian stops.

Charley instantly took to caviar. "Red food," he said, spooning it down directly. "What would Westport say if it

55

knew you were eating Red food, Floyd? Could you get back into the yacht club?"

"The Russians know how to eat," Floyd said, giving them that.

Charley wasn't seeing Buffy these days. He was currently half-going with a psychology major, a thin, freckled girl with outrageously large breasts.

"The Russians are civilized," Fern said. She always wore the same clothes: a plain blouse, usually white, a navy blue skirt, and those comfortable flats.

Calvin decided that her auburn hair was particularly attractive that night. He said so. "You ought to wear it long," he said.

She shied away from the attention as usual. She started to put her hand up to her head and then dropped it. "I'm not the type," she said, wanting the subject closed.

"Why? What type is that?"

She didn't answer him directly. "It would be pretentious of me. I don't like appearing to be what I'm not."

"What are you, then? You're a mystery, that's certain."

She shook her head, partly annoyed. "No, I'm not. Don't make me into what I'm not. I'm just a quiet, fairly dull person."

He tried to object.

"No," she insisted, interrupting him. "I am what I am, and that's it. I'm dull, and I don't mind. Can't dull people live, too?"

Striped curtains hung from brass rings at the windows, where a heavy May storm was thrashing against the glass. When Calvin looked back on that period, he remembered the cold winds and the blowing squalls; but the weather merely added to the comfort within.

The Korean conflict broke out in June. Calvin and Charley couldn't settle down. They skipped work and canceled summer school plans. They hung out in bars, watching the news. They saw their first UN session, interrupted by commercials and performing children's puppets. The Russians stayed away, and the U.S. resolution carried. Congress gave it a standing ovation. Even Governor Dewey supported the intervention. Truman called up the reserve units first.

Floyd was resigned, as if college had merely been a pleasant if inconsequential interlude between the wars. He gave up the flat and handed over his keys. He was going back to Westport to see his family before he climbed into uniform. Fern was going with him. Like her brother, she was composed, and if she was worried, she showed nothing. Everybody shook hands all around, and then they left.

Charley turned on Calvin. "We'll be next, right after they grab up all the reserves they can get, and just when I was starting out."

"But we're veterans."

"Oh, shit! That helped poor old dumb Good Deeds a lot, didn't it? They sure as hell got him! Hell, we may be veterans, but there isn't any justice. We're young, we're single. We don't have a chance. A lot of old bastards in Congress will be calling for our blood. We could end up in a body bag yet."

Charley took a daily paper for the first time in his life and he bought a war map. The 24th and the 25th divisions came in from Japan, but they got separated, then sliced up. The Pusan perimeter started to shrink. The 24th was thrown out of Taejon.

The city was going through a heat wave. They wore their shorts around the flat, drank beer, and constantly took showers.

Charley was on the phone off and on through that period. He would drag it into the kitchen, where he could talk to Buffy behind the door. When Calvin came through, he would find him sitting on the floor, his beer, and a filled ashtray beside him. He finally got up and came out one day looking more pleased than not. "Well, that's it," he said, off to pack, "I'm going to be a married man."

Calvin was alone again. He couldn't read, he couldn't concentrate. He started talking to himself, and his drinking picked up. He prowled around the empty, simmering flat worried about the war and wondering about his future. He couldn't be positive that the country wouldn't have to end up grabbing off the younger veterans. "I'm going to go crazy if I don't get a change," he thought. "I've got to get myself out of this state."

He decided that he was going to visit the Cape in August just to escape the city heat for two weeks. He wrote Sarah Elizabeth a fairly long letter. He caught her up on the news and hinted about a brief stay.

While he waited for an answer, he kept remembering his last trip up there, heading for Mercy Scudder's funeral. His grandfather had bought himself a new suit for the event, a gray pinstripe with a soft felt hat. They left early because he had business in Springfield first. The rest of the family toured Springfield while his grandfather conducted his business; and when he returned, they had lunch in the car. He was in a good mood. He looked faintly festive while he sat behind the steering wheel in his new suit, eating a hardboiled egg. He was happy because he was killing two birds with one stone. He was burying Mercy, and he was conducting a little business.

Coming over from Brockton, dropping south toward Plymouth, they had driven through places that still had that snug, enclosed inland look. The foliage was still dense, the vegetation fresh. However, the trees gradually shrank, the soil got more sandy, and the scrubby stuff started to show up. Then the humidity changed. Sitting in the back of the car beside his mother, he could not smell the wet, rank air yet, but he knew that it was coming. He soon spotted the first small inlet, and then the sky completely opened. "Oh, just *smell* it!" his mother kept saying, taking a needed holiday herself. "Oh, just *smell* the change!"

Sarah Elizabeth's letter arrived just before he was leaving for work, and he read it going over on the ferry.

"Fog, being blown in from the shoals, has stayed for the better part of a week," she began. "From time to time it appeared as if it would lift, but it did not. As a consequence, I have been confined more than I would choose to be, and, having a moment, I will get some matters off my chest.

58

"I have your letter in front of me as I write, and I do not agree with most parts. Your mother never raised her voice or argued with anyone, as you say, but that is because she never heard the other side in the first place. Grace had a bland, dead center inside her, and when outside pressures or pleasures reached that center, they just blurred themselves against it and perished.

"Your mother and your father were not suited, as you say, but I do not know who *would* suit them. They had an unhappy marriage, as you also say. The words, they tell me, that bind. That is a very curious notion because words of course cannot. Some will tell you that only the human heart does that. However, I have never put too much stock in the human heart, either. I am not usually given to confessions, as you know, but I will reveal myself here. I was not happy with your grandfather, but marriage is generally not a happy state, and I learned to cope. Always cope. I am relieved to hear that you are now in school full time, as your grandfather desired, but I have different opinions about your divorce. Divorces finally don't change a thing, do they? They don't change a thing!" she insisted, writing the last sentence larger than the rest.

She never wrote without a specific purpose in mind, a purpose that usually appeared toward the end of the letter.

"Do you remember the Westwoods from around Birchley? There is of course no earthly reason why you should. They are distant cousins on your grandfather's side. They have certain British connections, but they are more British than the British, and that says a lot. They were left a little property over there last year, and before the body was cold, they were on a plane. They poked around the ruins and consulted the courts, but what the Germans had not destroyed, the British taxes took. Well, they returned fit to be tied. I'm afraid I wasn't properly sympathetic because I wasn't surprised.

"They recently turned up on my doorstep here. Dorothy looks dreadful. She ought to be in a home but isn't. They pretend instead that everything is all right. I was busy at the tine, and while they prowled around as if they had something on their minds, I finally had to offer them some tea. They said that they had come all the way out to the Cape just to see me. Now why in the world would anybody want to do a thing like that?"

Calvin's problems increased. The toilet on the floor above him wasn't working right, and some dampness started to spread across his bathroom ceiling. It gradually got worse. He called the landlord several times, a firm in the city, but he didn't get any satisfaction. He wrote a letter, threatening to sue if the upstairs toilet came down, but he didn't get anywhere with the letter, either.

He finally decided he was going to move. He was going to look for something up and around Columbia, and he started to pack.

He was half-packed when Fern called, back from Westport, and he told her about his plans.

She paused. "I'm not trying to be coy about this," she said, "but if you want to sleep on the floor, you can stay here until you find a place."

He finished packing. Holding his chin high, above his cartons, having difficulty seeing, he edged through the door, into the hall, took the sharp turn, then descended the narrow, dark stairs into the piercing heat of the street, where he wedged everything into the car. He carried his last beer with him and opened it on the boat as lower Manhattan came toward him through the haze.

Fern lived in a brownstone facing the Hudson River. When he first entered the small efficiency, he saw the view before he noticed the apartment. The sky was flushed; a narrow streak of red was fading over the New Jersey cliffs. A freighter passed, heading north, trailing wide, glistening patches of oil that rolled and swelled on the water's barely wrinkled surface.

Fern did not have much furniture; she slept on a pullout couch, but every available foot in the place was filled with books, records, and prints. He fell in love with everything on the spot.

She fixed a Russian dinner that night, starting with cold bits of fish. Cold borscht next in plain white bowls. They added their own sour cream. The stuff floated around, gradually breaking up among grated, fresh new beets, bits of shredded onion.

"Oh, this is wonderful, wonderful!" he kept saying. Thinking about his old bathroom ceiling, he felt under a slight strain. The contrast, given these wonders, made the event appear far more formal, more still, than she could have meant it to be.

"Oh, *Fern*, this is wonderful!"

She nodded. "Isn't it," she said. She assumed the food was being praised, not the cook. "I love these colors. So basic."

They finished, and she took the bowls away.

He was anticipating stroganoff or shashlik, but she returned with a boiled flounder under fresh mushrooms, soup greens, small shrimp and more sour cream. He could taste vinegar, bay leaves, peppercorns.

She put on a string quartet. While she was away, working on the dessert, he stretched. He was stuffed. He was stuffed.

They moved to the couch where they could see the view. They sipped strong black coffee and nibbled on small rye honey cakes.

The evening sky changed, deepened. A barge passed without ruffling the water, its pinprick lights winking from bow to stern.

She brought him an ashtray. "It's always busy out there."

"It's better than television."

"Oh, heavens! Much. Yes."

"Oh, it's wonderful."

"You may not think so tonight when you have to sleep on the floor."

"Oh, I'll love the floor."

"You certainly sound smitten."

"Why didn't you ever tell us about your retreat here?"

"I didn't know it was *that* important."

"And now the group's gone."

"Such as it was," she said, a woman without illusions.

He loved her auburn hair, her grayish green eyes, her

61

broad, open, intelligent face. At the same time, this intelligence protected them both from a closer involvement. He could just talk.

Pusan held in late August. The stalemate wore on without the World War II draftees. He gradually realized that he was probably safe. Life was continuing, the future open. He didn't have to hold his breath anymore.

He bought the wines, the vodka, and the beer. She made cold cabbage soup, spinach soup, lentil soup. She cooked sweet and sour pot roast, Russian meat patties, stuffed cabbage, kidney stew. She fixed cherry dumplings, cottage cheese tarts, and snowballs in rich custard sauce.

He paced with his untouched snowballs. He was talking about that last trip to the Cape, when they first rounded the bend. Mercy Scudder's three-quarter Cape sat back off the main drag; the dirt road wound through the shade, the sudden, brief patches of light. Ramblers clung to the low stone walls, and you could smell that damp, woody coolness.

Her place sat alone on a rise: a single window on one side of the door, two on the other, a chimney showing through the bowed roof. She had a small, square parlor on the right, a small downstairs bedroom on the left. The huge kitchen, once called the keeping room, was in back. It still had its huge fireplace and wide plank flooring. A spinning wheel's pedal had worn the wood smooth around the hearth. The old buttery was still there, the borning room now a downstairs bath. He stopped abruptly.

She was pulling out the couch at the time, and when she straightened she was slightly flushed. She knew everything. She knew that he was trying to set the scene for some trauma to come. "Go on, if you need to. It can't be that bad."

He suddenly realized that she was letting her hair grow. Its crisp auburn ends now fell unevenly around her soft neck, just touching the bathrobe's collar.

She was still not going to overdo much, though, and when he kissed her for the first time, she considered her reactions very carefully. "My! That was very interesting," she finally observed.

62

He laughed with delight. He kissed her again—for a longer period, until she finally patterned her lips' movements after his. Her mouth, gradually adjusting, suddenly softened. He drew away. She was watching. She was still lucid. "What do you want me to do? Should I be doing something now?"

He took both her hands and guided her over to the open bed. He was worried about any moment's awkwardness just because it was her first time. He didn't want to frighten her, but he apparently did not. She was pliant, interested, direct, and uncomplex. She was surprisingly unmodest. Her narrow freckled back and her thick, reddish bush just about broke him up. Oh, she was a wonderful woman! She wasn't just intelligent.

He turned the lights out afterwards and then came back to the rumpled bed, an act so domestic, so immediately natural that he felt soothed to his fingertips. He wasn't on the floor any longer. He kissed her neck, her shoulders, her back. When he started to grow again, she turned in surprise. *"Can* you, again?" she asked. "In the same night? Is that normal? Could anybody?"

He was completely charmed. He asked her to marry him.

"Oh, *Calvin!*" she exclaimed, half amused, half deeply touched, *"you* don't have to do *that!"*

FOUR The curtain was rising on that whole period: housing developments and shopping centers; 3-D movies, Davey Crockett and Miltown; the Sixty-Four Thousand Dollar Question and the American Bandstand; chlorophyll toothpaste and dog food; the Weavers and Gordon Jenkins; Bill Haley and the Comets; pop-it necklaces and the skull-hugging poodle cut; charcoal suits with pink shirts, pink hatbands. The war, togetherness, and the boom.

When Calvin first met Fern's parents, her people had another couple in for dinner. The four supposedly shared mutual interests because they came from the same generation; but these people were already settled and hence a part of their times; they had two children and a mortgage. The conversation generally circled around these items.

During the course of things, Calvin mentioned Sartre. The wife's reaction was remarkable and immediate. "Oh, I admire you people so," she said. "You're so serious! Honey?" she asked, turning to the husband, "aren't they? They're *thinking*. Don't you just envy them?"

What had he done? He had just dropped the atheist's name in passing, but, years later, the reaction still struck him as fixing the period: a jittery, polite balance between being on edge and staying cheerful.

A building contractor, Fern's father wasn't sitting still, either. George swung them around through the changes the next day. His development hadn't been completed yet. There were open lots between the houses where the trees were still being torn out. Open two-story structures sat dripping and sopped in the slanting gust, their flooring exposed. A few finished places had started lawns; a few more had straw

64

covering, but on most plots, the rain was turning the loose sod into mud. Big, mud-splattered cars sat in the drives; rubbers and boots lay on their sides near the doors.

George's own place was a bigger copy of those same Colonials. A rough stone fireplace covered the far wall in the family room, but it had no screen or andirons, and the fuel sat up on cinderblocks. There were two huge couches and a console TV set, but, other than these, the room was bare. The dining room was bare, and they ate back in the big kitchen. The house, in general, was no more than half-furnished—a solid-looking piece here and there among the empty stretches, as if the family were just starting out.

George was a big man with a lot of drive. He had a dark history of fierce drinking behind him, separated from his current success by several hospitals, two bankruptcies. When he had finally climbed on the wagon for good, he had assembled the whole family to witness the moment. A good Catholic father, he thought in terms of the whole. "All right," he had said, at that point, patting heads and squeezing shoulders all around, "I'm off the sauce. I'm giving up the squirrel juice. I'm not touching another drop. But I need everybody's support. Can I count on it? Let's see a show of hands." He had ceased drinking years ago, but he did not kid himself about his illness. He still needed constant attention and praise. The children hopped to.

The mother wouldn't. A small woman with huge brown eyes, Helen treated everybody the same. She stayed detached. She had a delicate, cynical, half-teasing air. If she had once worried about Fern ever finding a man, she didn't show it. The relationship appeared to amuse her more than anything else. "Why, he's so young!" she said, in front of the engaged couple, without having to stress the age difference further.

She could stand back, removed, as if in control, not needing anything, not needing anyone, because other people had the problems. She was chilly, slightly cold, always amused, half-teasing, ready to help; and what was happening? She was calling priests who might know other useful priests. She talked about Calvin's taking instructions. A Catholic marriage was taken for granted.

Fern had once been fervent about the church. She had centered her early adolescence around it, in love with various nuns and the notion of the religious life. She loved the ritual, the language, and the music. She loved the art, the architecture, and the vestments. She had later connected that same life with numerous hardships: cold baths, stale bread, frigid winter morning masses, complex, seriously sustained penances. She had thrived in both periods, a dedicated, interesting, if one-sided child.

She hit a curious malaise in late adolescence. While praying at the altar rail, she put phalli on the figures hanging from the crosses. They were sometimes blurred, often quite specific, more or less accurately remembered from the art museums. With effort, she could wipe them out of her mind for a moment; but, if she relaxed, if she started to pray again, for instance, the cocks came back. Although the period was brief, she never completely recovered. When she started college, she stopped going to church altogether.

If Fern cast a cold eye on the world in general, she treated her people as if they were more fragile than most. She didn't tell them that she was no longer going to church. When she came home she went. She put on her heels and her garter belt and borrowed a hat. She genuflected when she passed a church up there like everyone else, and if this uncharacteristic blandness ever bothered her, she did not show it. She did not talk about her parents much. She took it for granted that Calvin would see what he wanted to see, and she let it go at that.

She hadn't prepared him for her mother's stand on a Catholic marriage. She waited until he got it from the horse's mouth, as if preparing him couldn't have helped much. She did not express an opinion while she was up there, either. She held fire until she was back on the train.

"We'll marry in the church if you can bear up under a few instructions, but I'm not a sentimental person, and I don't want a big wedding. I don't want any fuss. I am what I am, and that's that," she explained, returning to her usual decisiveness.

They wanted to get married over the Christmas school break, and he shopped around for the right man. He was intrigued about the instructions part because he had done a certain amount of reading in modern theology at least. He planned to sit down across from some well-educated priest and talk his head off. There was no sense letting him assume he was dealing with an idiot.

Father Ash was a big heavyset priest who moved quickly and gracefully, like a harried old actor. He came to the point before Calvin could sit down. "We'll have to give you some instructions first," he warned, as if Calvin hadn't known that, "because you'll want to know how your wife thinks. Catholic girls are different from Protestant girls, and when a Protestant boy runs into that difference without warning, there can be trouble ahead. We'll get some appointments set up, and if we're still talking to each other, I'll marry you here, in the study. I can't marry you in church in front of the altar."

Calvin had been raised in the Anglican church, which was certainly close to the Roman one. He still attended off and on, unlike Fern (which could be pointed out), and he wasn't happy about being treated like a complete outsider. He glanced at the crucifix over the priest's desk. What would Father Ash do with that when they were married in here? Drape it so it wouldn't be offended?

Father Ash went through the Ten Commandments on their first official appointment day. He asked him various questions along the way, and then, while he was fishing in his pocket for his cigarettes, he asked him if he honored his parents.

Calvin himself never knew when he was going to be guarded and when he wasn't. "When I was growing up, we seldom mentioned money, but a great deal was indirectly implied about our class. When I appeared in a tie, Mother would say, 'Oh, don't *you look nice!*' When I came down in a suitcoat, she would say the same thing. 'Oh, don't *you look nice!*' When I didn't look nice, I knew it because the subject wasn't mentioned. My appearance just wasn't brought up; and my mother, in her need not to offend, always said less than what she meant. In any event, I once got downstairs and through the living room in a fresh shirt without being observed. So far, so good, I thought, but, just as I was going into the kitchen, my mother caught me. 'Oh,' she said, 'don't *you look nice!*' Now my grandfather had been doing some work around the house. His toolbox was still out on the kitchen table, and his big, heavy claw hammer caught my attention. I wanted to hit her over the head with that hammer; the thought was so clear, so sharp, so electric, that sheer happiness accompanied it for a moment, and then the thought passed. I did not hit her with the hammer, of course. I smiled. She smiled, and I kept going, on my way out the back door."

When Calvin showed up for his next appointment, he found somebody else on the other side of the desk. Father Martin did not try to explain the change. He had a cold, and this slight incapacity appeared to anger him. He blew his nose loudly and stuffed his handkerchief in his back pocket. He leaned forward while he was putting his handkerchief away. "Father Ash tells me that you're quite a talker," he said.

Calvin did not disagree.

"Well, I know you want to get married as soon as possible, don't you? Everybody's in a hurry these days. Nobody can wait. That's all right, too. I'm here to help," he said, not sounding like it. "So I wonder if I can just run through some main points without fear of interruption."

Trouble did not break out until the third appointment. Thinking about Kierkegaard, Calvin said he believed precisely because it was absurd to do so.

The priest turned sallow. "Absurd? Absurd? Absurd? What? What? What? Why?"

"Because you can cut the ground out from under the enemy in one stroke. You can let the rationalists go their own way. You can just stand there waving when their boat pulls out, and you can wish them luck. Who has to get hot under the collar in that case?"

"*What* enemy? *What* boat? What *is* all this stuff? Church doctrine is rational. I've been trained in logic! I believe in reason!"

Calvin stayed controlled while he continued to bait the priest. "Look, you can't prove that God exists, because, whatever you proved, by definition, wouldn't *be* God. You're forgetting that the spirit blows where it wills."

"Logic! Logic! Logic! That's the trouble these days. Nobody's logical. Aristotle! Aristotle! Aristotle! Whatever happened to Aristotle?"

"I'm talking about Kierkegaard."

"*Who? Who? Who?* How do you spell that?"

The third try was with a much younger man. "Please spare me Kierkegaard," he said, as soon as Calvin walked in, "that much, much misunderstood, highly overrated man. Please spare me Bultman, too, while you're at it. Bultman me no Bultmans."

Calvin switched tacks. He had some interesting theories on the Immaculate Conception. Father O'Day half-listened while he tapped his pencil against his knuckles. "Let's get to the point, please," he said several times, before he finally interrupted him in midsentence. "What are you, the boy in the temple? How would you feel about dispensing with some of the bull? I have a hunch that something is bothering you besides Mary's birth. Do you want to talk about that? Do you really want to *talk* for once?"

Calvin decided to listen instead.

"All right," the priest said, searching for his glasses, "all right, all right, all right . . . We're not talking theology. I'm not talking theology to you. First of all, Christianity offers a certain perspective. It's a fairly simple, fairly obvious one, but who else offers it? It says that somebody else may count at least as much as you, and although you may not be able to live up to that, you'll have it there to consider. It just may give you some relief. You could have a way of coming to grips with certain otherwise overwhelming obsessions."

Calvin finally hit the last obstacle in the final appointment. He supported birth control. He had been using rubbers all his life, and he wasn't going to stop using rubbers now. He wasn't ready to populate the world. He wasn't adding to India's problems. He was talking about Malthus when the priest finally cut him off.

He sighed. "Just sign the papers," he said wearily, a practical man with a lot on his mind. "Just sign on the dotted line and keep your sex life to yourself."

"I can't do that. I can't lie."

"Well, I can't do anything for you if you won't sign the papers, son."

Fern was there on the last shot. She had not imposed her opinions on him before, and she did not impose them on him now. She just looked serious and pale, ready to respect his stand.

"I'm sorry."

"That's all right. That's perfectly all right with me. We just won't tell the Holy Father that you stopped by."

Fern was still sitting there perfectly still. She finally cleared her throat and moved her hand.

The priest looked at her and shrugged. "I went as far as I possibly could. This hasn't exactly been easy."

She nodded. "Well, if he can't sign, he can't sign. I'll cope alone. I've coped alone before."

She broke the spell just because she sounded both so straightforward and so dogged. At that moment, close to crying, he picked up the pen just to reassure her.

"Calvin? Are you *positive*?"

"Sure I'm positive. Look at me signing," he said to the priest. "Look at me signing while I'm telling lies."

"Don't tell me what they are," the priest said, picking up the paper. "I don't want to know what they are."

They had become so domestic that the marriage rite itself was a slight imposition, a break in the household pattern. They were sorting laundry when they realized that it was time to dress for the afternoon appointment. Calvin shaved while Fern bathed. He was letting his standard crewcut grow out, and he was working on a moustache. He looked like a boy actor who has been trying to put on a few years for an older part.

Fern had purchased a serviceable gray dress for the event. It fit too snugly across her square hips but fell more or less evenly at midcalf. She was not sure about it now. She hated to shop. She grew half-paralyzed as soon as she saw a dress rack, and she tended to grab the first thing in sight.

While he was still in his shorts, he kidded around some. He brought out his second-hand tuxedo and a red silk cravat.

"Come on," she said, half-resigned to the dress. "If we're doing this, we're doing this. So quit posturing and get decently covered. *Not in that.*"

Considering the occasion, he hailed a cab. The driver skimmed through one caution light after another, block after block, and when he finally hit a red light, he took that.

Calvin's face felt stiff and his heart raced. He was surprised to realize that he was nervous. He glanced at her dress sideways, wondering if he would grow used to it. "I think I like what you chose," he said.

"The less attention paid to it the better. That's my guess."

Father O'Day had come out to watch the street being torn up, and he was waiting in the vestry entry. When he saw them, he knocked his pipe out in his palm and scattered the dead ash on the walk. He shook both their hands, just touching the tips of their fingers. They followed him into the vestry, where he picked up two clerks as witnesses. The clerks followed the three up the stairs.

While the priest mounted, he talked. "Well, here are my customers, the philosophers," he insisted, soutane flapping above his white socks. "Kierkegaard, correct? *Fear and Trembling*, right? He's much, much misunderstood. He's also highly overrated."

He turned the bend into his study where he had Fern's parish records spread out across his cluttered desk. He asked for the marriage license while he was still talking about Kierkegaard. He had had to work them into a busy schedule, and he glanced at his watch. "What is it, the leap?" he continued, not able to leave his point alone. "Well, this is the leap. You're making the leap now," he insisted.

They walked out of the Catholic dimness and back into the afternoon rush fifteen minutes later. The traffic was heavy, and the passing trucks threw up grayish, half-melting, mid-March slush.

"I liked that last one. I liked Father O'Day. I liked the name. The others did not have priests' names. Ash, Elm, Oak. What are they, anyway, druids? Is that why their theology was vaguely blurry?"

"There was an Ash," she said, trying to sound patient, "but there was no Elm, no Oak."

"You'll also notice that he didn't blindfold the crucifix. A nice touch. Very tasteful, too. Very welcoming. Jesus wasn't weeping, either. Did that strike you as important?"

"I don't always notice these crucial things."

"I'm glad we married in the Church, *the* Church," he said, then stopped because he finally realized that he was irritating her. "Well, I've obviously stepped past some line. You're offended."

"No. I'm not 'offended,' as you call it."

Why was she so angry then? Was she still a Catholic? She was still a stranger. He did not know very much about her after all. He dropped the subject.

They ate lunch in the Russian Tea Room, and they saw a Griffith film. Fern seemed tense and jumpy, far less her neutral self than usual, and they turned up in the stuffy, laundry-strewn efficiency just as the evening crowds were beginning to fill the streets. Calvin felt slightly let down and sealed off.

Fern was starting a period early. Strapped and bandaged, she pulled on three sets of cotton panties before she climbed into her pajamas. She sensed his disappointment. "Well, if I can't perform, I can't perform, can I?" she said. "I can't do what I can't, and that's just about that."

Their marriage, taking shape, growing more concrete, dependent upon its daily routine, fell into a steady, unvaried regime.

Calvin woke when the world was still blurred. He spent the night addressing vast, faceless audiences, a performance that more closely resembled a natural force than human speech; and when he first woke he could still hear the wordless, rippling, half-muffled tidal swish in the back of his brain.

Scratching, stretching, anxious, depressed, still partly erect, he discovered the toilet seat while he was in that waking state, a webby, soft dislocation. While shaving, while in the shower, while out around the place, putting the coffee on, pulling his books out, he lost the last of that heavenly chorus, the night swell. He did not look up from his books until the city returned: jackhammers, car horns, the rattle of garbage cans, and the clanging, heavy metal doors that swung open on the backs of delivery trucks.

Fern stirred when the room was getting its corners back, prints and pots appearing last. She slipped into the bathroom where she liked to soak, half-hidden in the lather, her private moment before her full day started. She didn't spend much time in there once she left the bath. She wore her hair short again—being right about that; the stuff was too fine, too curly, to lie down right when long; it jumped up and frizzed. She appeared in her sensible blouse and flats around him in the kitchenette area, getting the coffee while he grudgingly moved some of his books. "Good morning," she said, on her way to the door to get the paper, to find out what was doing in Korea. "You could say that."

Floyd wrote infrequently, usually to Westport, less often to his sister. His letters were bland and impersonal; his people could seldom do more than guess where he was or what he might be up to, and because he was so guarded, his letters were never censored. If his family merely judged from what he talked about (the weather, his health) they felt closer to the war through the newspapers.

Events rose and crested. The armies settled down opposite each other across the 38th Parallel. Truman fired MacArthur. Ridgeway first sat down with the enemy that summer, arguing about an agenda, and then the country stopped reading about the conflict.

"Boys are still dying over there, but people have lost all interest. They don't care," George said, a big MacArthur supporter. He had been an FDR Democrat from the beginning, but he had turned against Truman. "They don't even call this a war. If it isn't, what is it? Some Boy Scouts on a hike? Doing a little bird watching? When you're dead you're pretty dead."

George alone voiced his fears. Helen just raised her brows at these exaggerations, knowing what she knew. Which was what? Who could be sure? Fern wasn't much better. In that world, the women distrusted the feelings. They kept their own council, and, as far as Calvin could tell, they played their cards close to their chests. Helen at least seemed half-amused at human folly. Fern just wanted the subject changed.

Calvin took the trash out just before they left, his first connection with the outside. He couldn't really do much in an efficiency with this curiously satisfying ritual. He wanted to go from room to room collecting, but he made the brief chore last. He bent down to get at it under the sink, then emptied ashtrays, balled up papers, old class notes and drafts. He carried the trash down the silent, dimly lit, carpet-smelling hall to the third floor chute. He sometimes ran into someone in the hall, out to walk a dog. He was beginning to recognize the building's dogs in the street. He could tell them apart from the sounds of their tags, clinking against their collars.

They left together, heading toward an eight o'clock class, the job in the library bindery. He could walk to school now, and this convenience, like the aura around his domestic routine, often gave him a placid sense of belonging and well being. At that hour, on upper Broadway, now light, if grayish and overcast through the long winters, hanging bulbs still burned in the backs of package stores, dry cleaners, and secondhand bookshops. The newspaper stands were open, and, on the corner, across from the subway entrance, filled with its cold-warm smells, a clerk was out with a metal pole, unfurling the awning in front of the drugstore, where students already milled or sat clustered over coffee.

There was always time for a story, if he hurried—getting it in between the damp-smelling Drive, the steep trip up the side street and then through the main gate, his last shot. He once told her about Kasey's parrot. She turned, puzzled, overly interested in accuracy. "I thought you said it was a canary."

"No. A parrot."

They stepped into the street while he was talking, getting a firm grip on her arm, switching the story some, working it out now at his expense. His eyes felt gritty in the blowy cross.

"Oh," she said, on the other side, "you think love solves everything, or, if not love, then sex."

The huge parrot sat in its cage against a cream-colored wall, ruffling its oily, greenish feathers, cleaning its beak, eyeing them suspiciously, refusing to speak.

"Calvin? Did you try to save your last marriage at all? Did you give it half a chance?"

"I was ready to do what I could. When it started to go, I was supposed to talk to a Methodist minister, but you know what happens if you hang around Methodists. They soon have you rolling on the floor, speaking in tongues, and handling serpents."

She just raised her brows like her mother. "I won't," she said, "attempt to pursue that."

She kept such an anxious, exact hold on the real. She constantly separated the unauthentic from the authentic, the pretentious from the unpretentious, but, aside from her family—her "poor people"—who could pass her rigid test?

She was close to her brother, closer to him than her parents—close in some dim, obscure way he could not understand or follow. She certainly did not approve of Floyd's wild militarism or support his otherwise overly conventional view of the world; but she overlooked these misguided enthusiasms in order to keep her concern intact. "Poor Floyd," she would say, like many liberals who knew him, people who could not share his many anxieties; but she appeared to use the phrase in some deeper, more basic sense.

Calvin was taking a business degree and wandering around the edges of the liberal arts, a process that kept him hopping through the full year. He did not take the summers off. Floyd was overseas, where Calvin could not see any future. She was right about her brother, but he did not mention it. Floyd was an embarrassment.

Calvin was on campus through the mornings—alone, surrounded, secure in his various slots, a jumble of sounds and odors, ideas and facts, the sides of faces, the steam-heated stupor; and then the sharp cold, the purposeful, unseeing coming and going, across to the next class, where the settling in began again: coughing, nose-blowing, chairs moving, scraped back, coats piled up, and the room, thinking about arranging itself, fell into a ragged, loosely attentive whole.

He was now working part time afternoons with Choice and Corners, investment counselors. He called them Choice Cuts, an ancient family business with a good deal of style and little future. He ran errands and helped on reports.

The old man, the grandfather, put out to pasture, still showed up every morning anyway, driven in from some prospering, remote, weedy spot. He still carried his lunch in a brown paper sack, and when he called Calvin in, he pulled it out of his desk. He wanted company when he ate. He had the only visionary head around. He pushed a single point: If you want to follow the power flow, then you have to look across the country as a whole, ignoring the centers for a moment, catching it in one glance, because it was going to be flattened out, a vast grid where everything was soon going to connect to everything else. "A vast community," he would say, while he was opening his thermos, "without people, or people, you see, as parts." Then his ancient eyes would twinkle with pure enjoyment. "You'll be there, boy," he would say, as if Calvin's future were related to the joke.

Calvin listened. Certain people could always slow his talking down, sometimes stop it: other heavy talkers, non-stop artists, for instance, then father figures, awesome older males.

When he left Choice Cuts, he had to run while the financial section was slowing down, the few shops closing or shut. The guards were already locking the main gates in front of the banks and the big brokerage houses. He slipped into his bank through a side door, then crossed the marble lobby into the elevator, its grillwork decorated with ancient Egyptian fertility symbols. He was now a floor supervisor, and, as soon as he stepped from the elevator, into this huge, unpartitioned, neon-lit area, with its confusions, its ringing phones, its many people, he ran into night-shift problems, which kept him going until he finally checked out.

He caught the IRT back, feeling half glazed, still half stimulated. He was tired and hot. His mind still turned. He always carried a book. He was working his way through *Finnegans Wake*, and while he sat in the swaying car, while the passing patches of light alternated with the streaking dark, he kept close tabs on H. C. Earwicker's universal adventures.

Here Comes Everybody home—letting himself in, feeling around for the vestibule light. Circling the pulled-out couch where Eve slept in the dimness, her arms around an extra pillow, her knees bunched up. Home, he opened a beer. Home, he cut into the ham sideways, picked it up with his fingers—chewing, pacing, to and away from the small refrigerator, trying this and that. He sliced a tomato in half.

He could still go on. He was horny, for instance, but Fern did not wait up for him before Friday night. When he once complained about his continually horny state, she blamed him. "Well, it's your fault," she said. "It's those tight jockies you wear to bed. You insist on wearing them, and then they work you up."

He opened a fresh beer on his way into the bathroom. He put the bottle down on the floor while he masturbated, and when he felt normal again, at least less needy, he took a long shower. He dried off, then climbed into his tight jockies before bed.

The Korean issue lingered through his senior year. The bargaining that broke out from time to time just raised false hopes.

Floyd's letters grew less frequent. Fern wasn't comfortable in New York or Westport. When she was in New York she thought she ought to be home; when she was in Westport, she was at loose ends because she didn't feel as if she had any real function there. She just followed her mother around. If Helen needed the company, she didn't say; but if Fern tried to leave early, the air changed.

Poor George, poor Helen. When the father was still saddled with his drinking problem—getting into the sauce and passing out in the garage, back before World War II, the mother had walked out on him for weeks at a time, leaving the children home to cope because they had school. Floyd and Fern had held down the fort through those periods. They could never tell where they were going to find George next—passed out in the garage, or lying flat in the front yard. Helen couldn't divorce him. She was Catholic.

The Chinese launched a major drive in June. Calvin bought his commencement gown early and wore it around the place just to get used to its feel and flow. He liked the way it flapped around his heels. He was getting the gown out when Fern called into the bathroom. "Well, that's that. Mother just phoned. Floyd's missing in action."

Fern stayed composed. She was so consistent. Everything followed from everything else. It made her very difficult to track. She decided she had to go home for a few days, and she started to pack. "I can't *do* anything," she said, "but hang around. I guess I'd better hang around them through this bad period."

"Don't you want me to come? Don't you want me with you?"

"What for? You've got your graduation coming up. You

78

stay here and put on your ceremonial splendors. We could both use the change," she said, sounding like Helen: that delicate, removed teasing.

"We don't know he's dead, Fern. He could still show up."

"Missing in action is as close to dead as you can get, so don't embroider on it now, please. It won't help."

"I wish I *could* help."

"Well, false comfort certainly won't."

He carried his commencement gown over in the boiling sun and put it on at the last minute. The rows of folding chairs were packed so close together that he could not move his legs or cross his knees. Under the layers of clothes, costume after costume, he could feel the sweat running down his chest. While he sat there half listening to the speakers, he could dimly sense his own nakedness: his various moles and marks, his fatty places and soft spots.

The commencement pomp abruptly toppled toward the close; the marching lines coming out did not hold; the families moved in, separate cells that surrounded the graduates here and there—open spaces yawning between, growing larger, and the last marchers, alone, giving up, broke ranks. The few strays avoided each other. Calvin felt pierced with an immateriality that left his hands heavy.

He changed in the apartment but he couldn't settle down in the emptiness. He was soon out again—over on upper Broadway, walking south toward the increasing activity. He walked with his hands in his pockets, his head down, sensing his surroundings without seeing them; but small details increased in size and focus: curbs, traffic signals, subway gratings. He saw himself weaving through crowds like this for the rest of his life, going to keep going, as if the movement itself counted, as if it could eventually add up to something besides more movement. He felt intact and cumbersome.

He lost all track of time, and when he looked up, the light was thinning. He was standing in front of a small seafood bar and grill where the curtains were half pulled across the plate glass windows. He saw a waitress preparing for the dinner hour inside, putting silver on the tables, smoothing out the cloths, and lighting the candles in the blurred, softened air. The tiny individual candle flames shone without moving in their pear-shaped jars. When the girl hovered over them, her face briefly glowed, then the shadows returned. She was small, dark, faintly curved, and she was wearing a silvei chain on her left wrist.

He was suddenly parked in the Hudson with Kasey, watching the large, ragged flakes wheeling across the windshield. The snow-mantled bushes, draped fence rails. He was not in love with her now. But he had not been in love that way since, either, and he could not shake the screening, blurred feelings, the painful sense of loss and yearning that the crowded city streets merely increased.

He woke that night with these same feelings. He heard some people across the hall—a small group at the opposite door, talking, laughing, carrying on; they got the door opened, and the hall was quiet again. He climbed out of bed and stood at the window. The moonlight glittered across the Hudson; and while he looked at the few stars, the shadowy trees, he realized that he was going through some crucial inner change.

Fern's absence brought her close. Her being gone made her more desirable than she had ever been. He needed her so now. He pulled out her clothes and buried his face in her blouses, trying to reconstruct her nakedness, her narrow, freckled back and long, graceful arms. "Fern," he called, "Fern, Fern . . ." The name, spoken aloud, gathering softness, vaguely hypnotic, cast a sustained spell over the room.

Fern turned up in a new slack suit, boxy and padded across the shoulders, too roomy behind. The outfit gave her a hefty, broad look. It was not flattering in general, but because she looked so unfamiliar in it, somebody else for a moment, the total effect vaguely moved him. She had also had her hair trimmed. She started to apologize as soon as she got inside the door. "Mother bought this, and so I wore it back on the train."

80

When Fern was home, Helen tried to get her in shape. She hauled her around to off-season sales. She always paid cash, pulling bills from her purse as if she were scraping around to find her last cent. Like Fern, Helen had little interest in clothes as such, but she could express her disapproval through them. Whatever Fern was wearing was not right. When Helen picked out something else, she always ended feeling as if she had not redressed the balance, either. "I'm a lost cause, though," Fern said now, ready to blame herself before she blamed the clothes.

"You look very fashionable, as if you were beyond reach. I'll fix us a drink."

"I want a bath first. I just want to get composed before we fly too far away from the truth."

He had cleaned the apartment in her absence—moving back some of the clutter, rearranging the pots and prints, stacking and sorting through a lot of loose books; but she did not notice what he had done, or care.

She closed the bathroom door shortly after she returned, and when he heard the tub running full force, he knew that she was going to be in there for a good stay. She was preoccupied; she had more on her mind than her marriage. He knew that he was going to have to be patient and giving at all costs. It was going to be a long night.

He fixed himself a drink and put the glass down on the counter while he started the meal—another welcoming gesture because he had shopped all morning. He washed the lettuce and put that aside while he worked on the rest of the salad: goat cheese, black olives, hot peppers.

"The thing is," he said, trying to shout over the running water, "that delicatessen that was such a treasure is closed. I had to walk down to 83rd Street before I could find any first-class goat cheese. Everybody else evidently had sold his goddamn goats."

She couldn't hear, or didn't answer. He had talked to himself for five days. He was still talking to himself now.

He finished his drink and fixed another. He put on the Goldberg Variations and sat down—trying to get composed, too. A stubborn streak of red hung over the broad, unmoving river. As it faded, and the dusk gradually assembled, like the next movement in a piece of music, or the changing mood in a play, an excursion boat passed, its lights reflected in the water.

She finally appeared in pajamas and her big, bulky robe. He jumped up to fix her drink. "You're missing your early evening view. You've already missed it for five days. I'll have to catch you up on what's been happening. When do you want me to put the steaks on?"

"Suit yourself. I'm not hungry, so don't fuss—please."

He finished the salad and put the steaks on. She hardly touched her drink. She wasn't against drinking, like some children from drinking backgrounds. She drank some, at times, but at others she couldn't be less interested. She was also growing less interested in food in general. She was not interested in special meals anymore, and if he didn't fuss, she didn't.

He turned the steaks and carried her drink over with her plate. "I forgot wine. I was so busy trying to run down the goat cheese."

She glanced at the meal with some interest, trying to look attentive, because he was obviously doing what he could. "This is all fine," she said.

He felt a depression coming on, the kind that could wipe him out for weeks at a time. "Floyd could still be alive, Fern. He's pretty resourceful."

"You said that several days ago. If he's dead, which is more likely, it would be easier on them just to know."

And on you, too, he thought, but he did not say it. He could not draw her out. He knew that he had trouble dealing with other people's problems; when he tried, he soon felt engulfed, curiously violated; and if they did not want their privacy invaded, he certainly wasn't going to invade it.

While they ate, he could hear people at the door across from theirs. Every few minutes there were new arrivals, and when the door opened, he could hear the loud, popular music inside; then the door shut, and the hall was quiet.

"We're missing an orgy."

She agreed. "Evidently," she said. She could not care less.

They finished the meal in silence. He jumped up to put the dishes in to soak—moving them around in the boiling suds with a fork, clattering plates. He cleaned. He fussed.

Fern got up to pull out the couch. "I'm turning in early. You don't have to."

"I've got some brandy. I've also got something else."

"Why? What?"

He poured the brandy while she was still tucking in the sheets. He went into the bathroom to put his pajamas on, and while he was still in there, he picked up the package he had hidden behind the towels.

"Oh, good! A gift!" She sounded uncertain, edgy because she couldn't escape the moment's attention.

"Well, open it, and don't save the ribbon."

"It's so elegant."

"Isn't it?"

She pulled out the surprise—turned it around, this way and that, concentrating on the silky, peach-colored night-gown, avoiding his eyes.

When he had bought it, he'd had a softer, dimmer presence in the back of his mind. The color was garish against her hair, her ruddy skin. "Well, what do you think? You don't have a gown, do you?"

"No. Because they usually just hitch up on me through the night."

The brandy spread, filling his brain, gradually reaching the sides of his face. "You're very curious, very closed," he said. "You don't talk, like me. And so you don't have much release."

"I don't know if I have all that much interesting *to* release. I wouldn't want to turn anything into what it is not." But the brandy appeared to loosen her, too. "I don't know why everybody has to have an unhappy childhood in order to be interesting," she said, certainly talking more than usual. "Is that a requirement? If you did, you did—if you say so. On the other hand, we were fairly closely knit. I'm not ignoring certain problems, but we were all on our own a lot, and that, you see, made us closer than some families." She paused, as if she were wondering just how much she was going to reveal.

His family wasn't always unknit, either. In their own way, given their differences, they could be close. He wasn't *always* trying to romanticize the past by making it more tragic than it had been.

He was suddenly talking about that last trip to the Cape, on their way to Mercy Scudder's funeral, when everybody's spirits were high. "We reached the house late," he said, getting up to freshen his drink, "but Sarah Elizabeth hauled me out of bed before dawn, or just as the grayness was breaking. She gave me a start. She was wearing Mercy's threadbare man's mackinaw and that old felt hat, pulled down around the ears, and, for a moment, I thought it was Mercy herself—my great-grandmother, who later became a famous ghost."

He turned off the light over the sink and came back to the couch with the brandy bottle. "She picked up a rake and a bucket, and while we headed down the road to go clamming, she got more personal than she had ever done before or since. She told me about her childhood there, back in the days when there hadn't been any other houses around. She fussed about the few houses now, scattered back there in the woods, and when we reached the bay, it was furiously changed. That's what she said, 'furiously changed.' *She* was furious. 'That place is new, and that awful place is,' she said, ignoring the no-clamming signs and the keep-out notices. She did not have any truck with these newcomers, and they didn't give her any trouble, either. She climbed over fences and scuttled through backyards. A dog appeared. She just turned around and pierced it with her look. 'Go away!' she shouted, stamping her cigarette out with her foot. 'Go away, before I use this rake!'"

He heard more people across the hall, a small crowd at the door, talking, carrying on; the door opened and the silence returned.

84

"I saw the bay just as the sun was flaring up," he said, off to the bathroom. He lifted up the toilet seat and raised his voice. "The tide was out, the wild rank salt smell was strong, and in that growing light I could see the clean, slightly ridged sandbars that stretched ahead, row upon row, recently created."

He came back carrying his pillow and slipped in beside her. "'Now this is more like it,' she said. 'This is the life. This makes some sense.' The gulls skimmed overhead, briefly landing in packs. As we approached, they scattered," he said, close to her back, his arm across her hip. "They landed again several yards off, pecking hurriedly, ready to take flight. 'Isn't it?' she repeated, as if she were determined to fix the idea squarely in my head. 'Isn't this the life?'"

Fern tried to move free. "I don't want sex tonight."

He could smell her hair, the soapy odors around the back of her neck. "I was just going to hold you. You've had such a hard week."

"Well, I don't want holding at the moment."

He moved away and turned on his back, his hands behind his head. "We haven't had sex in a long time."

"I know that."

"You didn't like the gown."

"Calvin, I can not be what I am not."

"Which is not what?"

"Why does everybody have to love sex so?" she asked, in that low, neutral, inquiring tone. "Does *everybody* have to love sex so? Is that some kind of basic requirement? Can't there be differences? Can't I live, too?"

He lay awake for a long time. He finally dozed lightly, just under the surfaces of consciousness. When he woke shortly before seven, he felt as if he had just left the previous conversation.

Fern was already stirring. He watched her dressing—in his alert, unfresh state—putting on her hose, stretching the stockings up around her thighs, pulling down the garter belt straps.

He half sat up, fumbling for his cigarettes. "What's going on now? Where are you headed?"

"I'm going to church."

"*Why*?"

"Why? Why is that so surprising? I'm going to church because there is nothing else I *can* do at the moment."

"You could have asked me."

"Why? You aren't Catholic."

"I'm Anglican. That's close."

"You can't take Communion, and I don't know why you'd want to go. You certainly haven't ever done anything except take pot shots at my church."

"Fern? Listen. I'm lonely."

Her wintry, bleak intelligence could cut through his passions in a minute. She considered loneliness to be a given condition of existence, a cliché that was not worth bringing up. "Oh, *Calvin*," she said, with such emphasis, with some forebearance, "*I* know *that!*" She certainly couldn't do anything about it, could she? So why couldn't he be resigned like her?

Calvin still admired Fern. The colder she was, the more intelligent she seemed. He accepted her values without question and formed his interests after hers. He had no better examples around. Other women seemed shallow in comparison, given their short-shorts, pop-it beads and poodle cuts, and he was in the middle of a nervously optimistic, shallow time which depended upon adjustment, togetherness, and getting along.

The Korean armistice lay behind, opening a bullish market and a period of feverish productivity based on the installment plan. The suburbs bulged; the radio carried a jingle that ended "Buy, buy something that you need today." In contrast, there was something healing about the apartment over the Hudson—with its prints, pottery, and books; the civilizing thread ran through her choice of music, from the Gregorian chants to Mahler's choral pieces.

When he had first moved into Fern's small, already overcrowded efficiency, he had stored most of his possessions in her basement—out of reach like the crippled Hudson with its oil problems; the car stayed up above Grant's Tomb, the World War II gas rationing stamp still on the windshield, fading in all weathers.

But now, as time passed, his things began to appear upstairs, taking up the last of the space: more books, records and prints, maps and jugs, a few favorite costumes like his planter's suit and pith helmet, finally his grandfather's alligator bag and the antique photograph albums with their hard ivory covers, metal clasps.

From time to time, he talked about finding a larger place. "When I move at night, when I try to shift positions, my arm threatens those jugs. Whole civilizations going over," he suggested, "and who would ever find us in the rubble?" However, he did not seriously look for another place because they did not want to give up their view.

He was now working full time for the counseling investment firm until something better came along, the bank's foreign department job behind him like the last war. He was out of town a lot; he was constantly going, and he discovered that the separation helped the marriage, making them both less tense, making him less focused on her. She called their random, infrequent couplings "more adult" just because she was so duty-oriented, and he wasn't surprised to find his sexual interests in her less demanding. Resignation could be a lot like quicksand: once you sank into it, you kept going, and if this was acceptance, it had its compensations. He had more freedom. In theory, at least, he could look elsewhere.

He was not a woman chaser in the usual sense of that term. He was cautious where other men were bold; his needs humiliated him and put him on the offensive, made him desperate, and, in his desperation, he could be cutting and cold. He talked too much. He could talk nonstop, as if he were fending off a confession, some great self-revelation. His irony frightened women in that generally bland, cheerful period, and his straitlaced manners kept them at a distance. His puritanism was in many ways like Fern's. They weren't entirely unsuited.

Still, at the same time, he was looking again: a girl in the typing pool around the corner from his office, an elevator operator in the same building, a clerk in a drugstore, a waitress where he ate lunch, the new neighbor across the hall, a young model who lived with a photographer. He ached with a kind of total, muted, guilty, self-absorbing desire that left him feeling glazed and cut off, separated from the creation. He couldn't have confessed to Fern even if she hadn't been his wife because she would have considered such desire shallow—a part of a false, frenetic, shallow age. He supposed she would have been right, too.

He could slip out of town without notice. He slipped up to Bridgeport in the company car to check on his grandfather's trust: previous farmland that now edged shopping malls, woody regions close to housing projects, utilities in small towns that had since become growing cities.

This intricate structure had been put together with an enormous amount of care, and if he did not exactly feel unworthy, he felt considerably awed. He wanted some shares in a highway construction equipment business and in a newly emerging motel chain which was heading west, but he was going to leave most of the trust untouched for the time being.

He left the bank just before closing and cruised around his old stamping grounds—his mind still on the same thing, a possible affair like the first. Even after all these years, Kasey's not being in sight seemed strange. The radiance was gone, too. The streets looked normal.

He stopped to eat in a hotel dining room where he had once taken his first wife, an expensive evening out in those days, meant to be special, but the furnishing now looked shabby, the carpets worn. He ordered a martini, but drinking alone merely increased his growing sense of emptiness. His good fortune now seemed to accent this loneliness, an obscene compensation which left him feeling unadorned and raw.

He drove past Sarah Elizabeth's old place just before he

left town. The snowball bushes had been cut back all along the porch, showing the dirt and the worn patches below where the sun had not reached. A child sat on a strange swing set in the side yard, looking down at his feet, dragging his shoes under the seat in the dust. He glanced up as Calvin passed. Calvin increased his speed, heading back to the city.

When he got back, he felt unhinged and unsettled. He was soon talking. He was telling Fern about his last trip to the Cape—everybody together for Mercy Scudder's funeral. He still remembered the beach walk with Sarah Elizabeth with such pleasure; he loved gulls; he loved the songs they sing, the racket they make—the best part of the day because when they returned, he was back in the normal world. His grandparents were at it again.

"Tooth and nail," he said. "He wanted to sell Mercy's house as soon as possible. She didn't. She knew what she was doing. She was saving it for her old age. She used to tell him so many times. 'Things won't always stay the same,' she would say. 'We won't always both be here. One of these days one of us is going to be missing, one of us is going to die,' she reminded him, 'and when *that* day comes, I'm going back to the Cape. I'm going back to the Cape where there's some real people and some real weather.'"

He was pacing around the bed in his World War I pilot's jacket, the goggles raised, nestled into his dark, unruly-looking hair. He had a cigarette and a beer, a new expensive brand that struck him as too mild. "*That* remark always raised his blood pressure, as it was intended to."

Fern was half asleep. She turned and placed her hand over her eyes. "Do you still need that light? Do you think you could get through your revelations without it?"

He opened a fresh beer, and on his way back he turned off the light. He was quiet for a moment. "*Tell* it, then," she said. "Tell what you think you have to."

"They were still at it when we went to the funeral. They argued about the house in undertones during the service, and they snapped at each other later over the open grave. When

89

we got back to the house, my mother was terribly upset. She was white and trembling. 'Oh, *stop* it!' she cried, 'just *stop* it, now, *both* of you!' Nobody had ever heard her raise her voice before, much less like that, and, in the silence that followed, Able Thomas changed the subject. She was off balance that whole day, though."

"Why do your costumes help, Calvin? What touch do they add? What do they do?"

"She *stayed* off balance, too, and when my father finally turned up—out of nowhere, after all those years—she could not have been expected to take the appearance in stride. He couldn't have been less than a bolt from the blue. He had come for the funeral—although he was late, as usual, missing that as he had missed everything else. 'I always admired Mercy,' he told her, 'the one in-law with some flair.'"

"You always tell these stories as if you were just passing through, observing the scene," she observed, half sitting up. "You never talk about your own reactions."

"I *was* just a passing observer," he said, feeling unconnected, still safe.

He wrote to Sarah Elizabeth the following week, his third attempt to communicate since his second marriage.

"Well, Dorothy finally died, which was a blessing, considering how long she lingered, and if she has gone to her Maker, as they say, she might just ask Him why He kept her waiting," she began. "I am as devoted a Christian as some, I should imagine, but that does not mean I do not have a few questions myself. When something just doesn't make much sense, I have to say so.

"I have just returned from the funeral, but the less said about the whole trip the better. There is no point in going anywhere these days. The world has filled with servicemen, although the war has been over for some time, and they are all entirely too talky. I know that they are away from their homes, I know that, of course, but this doesn't excuse certain liberties taken, does it, and while I wish these boys well, I don't believe that the brief contacts people form on trains, planes, and buses can ever amount to much. I don't believe they can amount to a row of beans. Generally speaking, they are a complete waste of time because they unduly raise false hopes. I am wandering, I know, but I am not used to being exposed to so many people. The crowds confuse me and I tire around people these days.

"I do not, as you know, generally moon over nature, but when I got back I could not have felt more comfortable in the solitude. There was to begin with a smart shift in the weather. It blowed, the wet lifted, and, wanting to clear my head, I went for a walk. I tramped through the dwarfish woods behind my little place for the better part of the afternoon, going around those little low salt ponds. I came around, toward the sand, which was rounded in hills and hollows, barren and darkening, toward the supper hour. I passed beach plums and wild roses overgrown with woodbine, then tramped back to the house through the poverty grass. That Mrs. Fox was waiting and probably had been for some time. She is poor or so she claims and does for people around here. She is too interested in others' business. Anyway, she could not do for me, and I sent her packing. She was heading for Provincetown, although what she sees there I can't say, being nothing but dunes and always filled with outsiders. I am sorry I can not have you up here this August as requested, but I will be painting then, the house will be torn apart, and I will have no spot to put you.

"I have your last letters in front of me as I write, starting with the announcement of your second marriage, and I am herewith enclosing a check for five dollars. I do not know what you need or what your preferences are, besides there is nothing here *to* buy, which is as it should be, but I expect that you can get what suits you with the money. I also understand that you have finished with your schooling, which must be a relief after all those books. Now you will want to prove yourself, as they say, and I expect that you will be successful at it. You have many of your grandfather's better qualities. You have it in you to be.

"You ask about your father. I certainly do not, cannot,

blame myself for what happened during that dreadful afternoon. I have put both your parents' deaths behind me, and I strongly urge you to do the same."

Calvin ran into his new neighbors from time to time in the elevator—the model who was living with the photographer. She looked younger than Calvin; the photographer looked older. Clara actually looked younger than she probably was, though. She was small and faintly curved. She was usually in black leotards and scruffy ballet slippers—back from posing in a life class at the Arts Students League downtown. She had long, fine, thin, very pale blonde hair. Her mouth was unpainted, her eyes elaborately shadowed, a strange contrast, and because she looked so out of place in a public elevator before sundown, she seemed to fill up the space despite her size. The theatrical effect, slightly cloying, asking for attention, struck Calvin as vulnerable and human after his years with his less pretentious wife.

The photographer was a big man in work clothes: boots, flannel shirts—a big, imposing, fairly silent presence beside her. He seemed to be filled with some sort of compressed tension. He was always patting his crewcut, stroking his big, shaggy beard or shuffling his feet. Calvin could often hear fighting going on across the hall when the door opened—a lot of crazy screaming back and forth, his voice almost as shrill as hers, but when they weren't fighting, when they were standing together in the elevator, for instance, he could sense the half-muted pull that existed between them. Even when Clara was talking to Calvin, he could tell that her mind was half on the photographer, the Paul Bunyon figure who stood beside her.

They were both fairly blunt, open, unguarded people, given the average New Yorker, and they were soon talking about getting together for a drink. They did not set a date at first, and then, when the photographer did, they couldn't work it out because Calvin was going to be on the road that weekend. The photographer shuffled his feet and looked down at his shoes. "Well, keep punching," he said, getting off the elevator first. Calvin waited for Clara. She looked around. "Goodness," she said, "me next?" Randy was already halfway down the hall.

In any case, they eventually mentioned the rental open over their heads—a one-bedroom apartment with the same view. Calvin got the key from the janitor and poked around up there alone the following day: a good-sized living area, slightly larger than his own, a small bedroom, both with a view. The empty apartment badly needed paint. The place was generally unclean; the trash had not been taken out. He found lipstick stubs in the medicine chest, a sex manual in the linen closet, and a pair of torn black lace panties still hanging over the shower rod: secret lives gone, but their remains still humming, like the haze around a reactor's core. He rented it the same day.

He decided that he was going to clean and paint before he moved in, and he held onto the apartment below for an extra month. He asked for a week off from the firm—his first since he had joined it, and because he looked forward to throwing himself into operations like this, he did not hurry the process.

He spent several days just walking around the shell first, from the living room to the bedroom, from the bath to the kitchenette, savoring the task ahead, deciding where everything was going, measuring and taking notes. He finally purchased everything he needed at once: the cleaning materials, the paints, the thinners, and the brushes.

Fern did not have her days free, but she turned up after work at first. She stripped the greasy range and soaked its parts. She scrubbed down the bathroom because she did not trust him with the basics, but she did not try to go further. "I won't intrude anymore unless wanted," she said, at the door one night, tired, ready for bed, "which doesn't look very likely, does it? You're evidently in your element."

He kept the door open while he worked—putting down the flat white first, covering the standard dingy green, less dark where pictures had once been hung.

Clara did not like staying alone, and when the photographer was gone, she climbed the stairs, knocked on the side of the open door, and came in, without waiting for his reply, stepping around the paint cans, the paint thinner, and the paint-splattered newspapers in her scruffy ballet slippers or sometimes in bare feet.

It drizzled through that spring and turned dark early, and he would finish under a naked ceiling bulb. He would finally put down his brush and light a cigarette—while Clara stretched like a little animal at the window, breathing in the fresh damp chill that rose from the Drive. The wet shone on the pavements under the streetlights. "I love spring," she said, leaning on the sill, looking out—while he studied the soft pink neck, the small shoulders, the narrow curve of the back, "drizzle or not. I hibernate like a bear all winter; I don't want to leave my bed, but, when spring comes, here I am, out. I just want to shed my skin."

He imagined the sense of something wanting to start, to come together, to grow, an intimacy created through the magic of the outer world, through the weather, the spring smells, the dusk, the shadows cast across the ceiling, the two presences in the empty room, cut off from the rest of the building. However, when he considered her sharply and critically, when he realized that there was nothing personal in her eyes or in her voice, when he realized she couldn't stay alone because she wanted to be watched, seen, noticed, admired, without being involved, or imposed upon, when he considered these things, and remembered the photographer, he knew that he was trying to construct something from the air, from his own needs and hungers. Wisely, he never touched her. Wisely, he stayed removed. Wisely, he played her game—admiring her while they both pretended that nothing more serious or dangerous was actually happening.

He ran into Fern's mother in the lobby waiting for the elevator one afternoon. He had gone out to get a cleaner; he was wearing his tropical suit and pith helmet, and Helen didn't recognize him at first; he was on his way back to his apartment upstairs, above theirs; but now he had to get off at his old stop. He felt for a moment as if he were living two lives. Helen was in shopping. Unknown to him, Fern was having her in for lunch. "We're moving," Fern told Helen, when she saw the boxes around, brought up from the basement, "I think—if he's sharing his new lair."

That delicate, teasing irony was less common these days. Fern appeared to be growing more and more indifferent to him and to the people around her. When the couple next door invited them over to a party the following weekend, she was just civil. She stayed noncommittal through the week, but when the weekend came, she refused. "You go. They're your friends," she said dully, not judging, but not interested, either, "and you could use the change."

New York still glittered with every possibility, in planes and angles, in shafts and spires, gray and golden, mysterious and overcast. He followed Fern to museums and concerts, to plays and readings, to films and recitals, to mimes and fairs, but when they returned to their isolated, fourth-floor apartment, back to their window, their marvelous view, he realized what was wrong: She just wanted to look.

Calvin was going to a party. He was going to be part of the flow again, back in circulation, not merely sitting in the middle row in some half-dark house waiting for the curtain to go up on someone else's troubles. He showered, shaved, and chose his best cologne, his heart beating like a boy's on his first date.

He finally told himself to slow down. He shouldn't go over there anticipating the moon—sound advice, too, because when Clara opened the door, he was staring into an empty, disheveled room: photographs pulled down, leaning against the walls, chairs and ashtrays overturned. The TV news was on, without sound, the Army-McCarthy hearings; the Senator was looking directly into the camera, glaring into the room with its forlorn air, its look of past violence, and then a commercial came on. A girl in a short skirt was hugging a giant cupcake.

Clara was distraught. "Randy's gone!" she said, squeezing his arm. "Randy's gone! We started fighting last night, over nothing, just nothing! We fought all day, and then, this afternoon, at the last minute, he just walked out! He took half his pictures with him. Oh, Cal!" she exclaimed, actually wringing her hands, a wonderful little moment of pure melodrama. "What am I going to do? Who can I turn to? I'm alone!"

He tried to calm her. He tried to soothe her while he talked. He tried to ask questions, but she didn't want calming. She didn't want to talk. "Oh, hold me!" she said, wanting more than holding. She was soon searching for his mouth with hers and trying to undo his belt at the same time.

He was still overstimulated the next morning, and he woke talking. "You were right, as usual. You wouldn't have enjoyed the evening," he said, working his way around the cartons to the bathroom.

Fern was bent over the *Times*, taking notes, planning the weekend, plotting out their course of action: films, museums; a traveling pottery show was in town.

"I'll condense," he said, coming back from the bathroom and picking up an empty carton on the way. He started to strip the bookshelves. "I'll just sketch in the guest list: two lady librarians who came together and who were obviously living together, not far off, but sensitive, secretive about where; why? Their secretiveness was constant, general, persuasive, delicate, polite, unpushy. An interesting problem, and if they did not want to share what was going on, they wanted to share their secretiveness."

How was he going to get back to Clara? *When* was he going to get back to Clara? Clara needed him. Fern didn't. Fern didn't need anyone, but, just because he felt clogged with guilt, he would have to do his share here. He would spend the weekend doing extra duty, following her around from place to place.

He picked up a box of books and put it on the table. He poured his coffee. "Another couple, a broad-shouldered, broad-backed team, newly married, I think, both chess lovers, math lovers, geology lovers—interested in agriculture, in Africa. He's getting some kind of grant, and while they're waiting to go, they read widely in the subject. He was slightly more stiff than she, more military, more ready to be affronted, and because his softness was so close to the surface, she spent the evening constantly running interference."

Fern folded the paper and picked up her notes. "I've got to shower. You can save those lovebirds for another time, when I'm not so pressed."

He followed her into the bathroom to finish the last part at least. "Then a tall, graceful, pale, hollow-cheeked girl who appeared with a recorder. She was good. She was mellow and sweet. She played the standards, like 'Greensleeves,' and, in the polite silence that followed every number, the guests just smiled, looked at each other, shook their heads. Oh, they envied the talent!"

He was still thinking about Clara—her strength, her softness, her childlike eagerness, her outlandish affections, and brazen giving. He felt half off-balance, crazily unfocused.

The phone rang. "I'll be right back."

Helen was off on a cruise, planning to sail the Caribbean with some friends from church, the altar guild's outing under the Southern Cross. Elderly Catholic ladies in backless summer dresses bobbing across the blue latitudes. Oh, blue latitudes, oh, moonward swell, you're part of the package deal.

He was appropriately impressed. He showed up again in the dripping cloudiness just as she was stepping out of the shower, her neck arched and high as she patted under it. "That was your mother."

"Just the facts, please."

"She's going on a cruise." He followed her out while she was belting her robe. "Then there was the prize, a big, beefy, shy inarticulate soul with sloping shoulders, bushy moustache, a facial twitch, a genius, I believe, who is translating Japanese verse."

He was back stacking books while she dressed. "'Here,' he said, when the music faded, the last note gone, 'let me see that.' He turned the recorder over in his big, lumpy hands, as if he were trying to find out just where the music came from; did this little thing do that? Nothing in his universe gets by him. He has to study it out. Did he ever say anything else? I don't think so. Huddled over in a bulky sweater, looking hot, his hands dropping between his knees, he looked as if he were trying to memorize the pattern in the carpet. All those little intelligences humming, and I hardly spoke more than a sentence or two myself."

"*That's* hardly likely, is it?"

He shifted some books from the table's edge. Getting ready to move upstairs, he had stacked books around the room, and he had to watch his step in the clutter. He needed boundaries, limits, walls, order—a place to settle, a way to contain an intangible weight within, a weight that otherwise threatened to fly off in all directions, and while he was between the two apartments, unsettled in either, he felt hollowed out, impersonalized, too light. "Fern," he asked, picking up a carton, still thinking about her last remark, "why did you marry me in the first place? You didn't *have* to. You weren't pregnant, and I didn't exactly *beg*."

She was out in the hall, edging around the cartons stacked there, reaching up on the top closet shelf, and if she heard she didn't answer. She finally came back with her suitcase and opened it up on the unmade bed. "Because I was alone, and I wrongly thought I shouldn't be. I must have let more popular opinions get to me."

"Meaning your brother's?" She didn't answer. "Right?" he said, after a minute. "And you also told yourself you liked sex."

"I told myself that for awhile, yes."

He was tying cord around a carton. "Getting the truth out of you isn't exactly like pulling teeth, is it?" he said, without looking up.

"No. That isn't one of my many sins."

"Good Lord, woman," he said, looking at her at last, "don't you ever allow anybody any illusions? Isn't that *in* you *at all*?"

98

"I don't understand why anybody would want them."

He watched her packing, still feeling removed, partly disconnected. He suddenly realized that she was in her heels and her one good dress. "So? What's up now? Why are you in your Sunday best?"

"That wouldn't be too difficult to figure out if you ever noticed what was going on around you. She's leaving home because he's drinking again. I've got to look in on things."

He picked up his cape and his stovepipe hat. Where was his overcoat of many lurid hues? "Which may not be that bad."

"My brother's disappearance has taken its toll. I knew it would."

"Since he hasn't been reported dead, I still say there's hope."

"You can go on looking through your rose-colored glasses if you insist," she said, shutting the suitcase.

What about moving, though? What about the apartment? What about this *wreck*? What about her pottery show, too? He couldn't have told her that she *couldn't* go because he couldn't get close to the subject. He couldn't deal with her family relationships because they were too personal. He felt secure with her precisely because she didn't invade, didn't make any demands, either; her parents were her parents, her troubles her troubles—in contrast to his own constant chatter about his degrading childhood. Second, he remembered Clara; he could now see Clara today. At the same time, though, he felt ill-used, deserted. "Taking care of your father always comes before taking care of your marriage," he suggested, because he saw how wrong she was, too. "Because *that's* in bad shape!"

"Oh, *Calvin*!" she said, ready to go, but sitting down on the bed instead. "*I* know it's in bad shape! But just what do you envision my doing about it? Do you want to talk? Is that it? Do you want to talk *seriously*, for once? Do you want to try to work out some ground rules with me, before we go any further?"

He felt threatened, unsafe. "I want a divorce," he said, sounding calm enough, but he had difficulty breathing because he had so much air in his chest. However . . . it was out. At last.

She stood. "Well, then, suit yourself. You'll have to get it."

He picked up her suitcase. She bent down at the same time, but he grabbed it. They were awkwardly close for a moment, close to bumping into each other, knocking foreheads, in each other's way. She thought that he was trying to stop her from going now, but he was just carrying it. "Why? Because you're a *Catholic* again? Because you're now back among the *saints?*" Still in his robe, he lifted her suitcase high above the junk piled in the hall and opened the door. "Is *that* it?" She didn't answer. She clung to her resignation. What came came. *She* never got out of line!

Although it was now May, and sweet-smelling out at that hour, the Drive misting, the trees with their foliage taking shape, the small, square, bleak hall, with its four closed apartment doors, still had its wintry, sterile odors. He rang for the elevator. While she was finally talking just behind his left shoulder, a long speech which he did not take in all at once. "I'm generally not an alarmist, *but,*" she began, an interesting thesis sentence. "I'm trying to stay in control, but I've missed a period. I can just endure this relationship as it is—*just*, mind you, such as it is, but I *can't* imagine what would happen if we actually had children. Because I can't see *you* having them. I don't know what would be worse, a son or a daughter. I *certainly* wouldn't want *you* around either!"

Calvin's irony usually kept him reined in—his irony, his exaggerations, his metaphors, his stories, his compulsive chatter in general. Oh, when talking, he told nothing! Indeed, he could keep up this balancing act for a long time without slipping, without falling across the thin edge between his ravaged needs and his worse hatreds, but sooner or later the adrenalin gusted through him like a flame chasing a fuse.

Fury, pushing, plucking, shoving, lifted him up, outside

100

himself. He was now dancing around the elevator hurling his invectives. "Witch! Witch! Witch!" he kept shouting. "Blackhearted, sour-smelling witch! *I'll* get the divorce! *I'll* get the divorce, all right! I'll get it! I'll get it!"

He leaned on the elevator button again, although the car was on its way up, and when the door opened, he kicked her suitcase through, just missing Clara's husband's legs. The big, wild-eyed photographer was coming back home, loaded down with his photographs. He had some in his arms, more stacked against the walls of the elevator. "Holy shit!" he exclaimed, in fright, his eyes growing bigger.

And there Calvin was, his first genuine attempt to strike another, his fists raised, in front of Fern's retreating back: Calvin Hart, the nut, the maniac, the basket case.

FIVE Charley Klick turned up while Calvin was packing, getting ready to leave both apartments. Charley paced, following him around, and downstairs, full of advice.

"I've been meaning to get over, buddy. I've been keeping tabs on you. I always knew what was going on. . . . Buffy runs into the family every so often. She used to date Floyd. . . . You've got them all up in arms. Why do you have to act like a madman? Why don't you run up there and see if you can't quiet things down?"

Klick had aged. He was heavier, and his pale blond hair was just beginning to thin in front. On the other hand, he had that weathered, healthy-looking sheen which comes from a lot of time spent on a golf course.

"I know it's a strange family. . . . In some ways those two women can be as hard as nails, but if you'll scratch under the surface a little, you'll find a lot of heartache.

"If you went up there, I think you could deal. When a marriage breaks down, it takes two people. You aren't still claiming you're entirely innocent, are you?"

Charley was fairly diversified these days. He was playing around with commodities, but he was also selling bonds in his father-in-law's firm. He was doing well. Calvin suspected that a slump was around the corner, but the moment was still bullish.

"Christ, buddy, look around you! Consider what you're doing! Look at all these books, these records, this art! You both have the same tastes. You're both intellectuals, and, in the long run, you both had a good life set up here. Look at this river view! Why would you want to give up a view like this! You're both a lot alike, too. You're both interested in the cultural life. You're both intelligent. You're both remote and old-fashioned. You're both pretty cool cucumbers!"

Charley finally changed his tone when he realized that he wasn't getting anywhere. "Well, I tried to get through to you, didn't I? I did what I could. I carried the word. . . . It's your life, buddy. It's your life, strange as it is. . . . You're going to have to live it. *I* certainly wouldn't want to."

Wearing his rumpled planter's suit because he claimed that it insulated him from the sticky heat, Calvin was carrying the last of his cartons up from the basement at the time. He realized that he was getting low on string and brown wrapping paper.

Organize, organize, organize; only organize!

"You can tell them you pulled out the stops, Charley. They'll understand. They can't blame you."

"You *look* young, certainly younger than your twenty-seven, twenty-eight. But you're actually old before your time. You never played the field, did you? Next time don't be so anxious to settle down. . . .

"You're certainly old-fashioned," he continued. "You should have lived back in the Dark Ages, when everybody was still pure. You ought to let yourself off the hook more. Two mistakes, and by now I imagine you imagine you've seen the world. Well, I've got news for you. You can still have a little fun without cutting your own throat."

Calvin thought about bringing the Hudson down from the Grant's Tomb area while there was still some innocence in the morning air. That May was treacherous, gusty, and damp, overcast by noon, laden with bulging skies, sudden squalls.

"The trouble with you is you're too straitlaced, Calvin. You talk like a book. You're a nice guy, too, in certain ways, but you're also extremely boring. You don't know when to back off."

Calvin picked up his car keys and pith helmet. He held the door. "I'll walk you down. I've got to pick up the Hudson. I've got a pretty busy day. I want to get out of here before dark."

"Why? What are you going to do now? Where are you

headed? Are you going to run off half-cocked again? Escape? Is that it? And in that beat-up old clunker? You're *different*, buddy! You really are!"

Calvin patiently waited beside the elevator with his ex-roommate—keeping his eyes away from Clara's door. As far as he knew, the photographer had not emerged since he had come back. Making up, they probably did not leave the sack except to eat.

Charley stepped into the elevator ahead of him. "You haven't told me where you're going."

"I've got to pull myself together. I just want to get out of here before she comes back. I'm tired of fighting, Charley. I'm tired of scenes. I'm tired of her refusal to *have* scenes. I'm tired of her cold airs."

He couldn't shake Charley in the street, either. He stuck close on the walk up to the car. "You didn't answer me before. You never played the field, did you? Too bad. Two bad marriages, and now you think every woman is a sour apple. Maybe you can only get the sour apples, though, the ones as desperate as you are."

"I may turn them into sour apples somewhere along the way."

"That's a thought, too, of course."

The morning was crushing, humid, heavily overcast. The sun was enclosed in a grayish, cement-colored gauze. Except for a few mothers with young children, the park was empty.

"I'm not you, though, Charley. I don't treat them like objects, either."

"When I get a moment, when I get back from the coast, I'll have you up to Westport for a solid, home-cooked meal. Steak, baked potatoes, apple pie. We've got twins. The boys wear those goddamned coonskin caps around the house all the time. You put those hats on them, and they both think they're kings. In fact, they'll probably never know what scrambling for a buck is all about."

"Well, you've done it. You've settled down. I'm not sure, though, there's all that much change."

"I'm too busy to chase tail these days, if that's what you mean. I've got too many responsibilities. I've got to put a lot of good solid food on the table, and I'm saddled with a pretty heavy mortgage. I've got two cars. I've also got a lot of conservative Catholic in-laws. I've learned to listen to their troubles. They think they have troubles, anyway, and I listen."

"I was willing to listen to mine up to a point. I know Fern has her problems, too. I understand that. But she finally had to choose between her parents and her marriage, and she picked her parents, particularly her father."

"Yes, but that generally changes when they get children of their own. We had ours fast."

"She thinks the rest of the world can make it on its own, and, if it can't, she couldn't be less concerned. She doesn't think too much of the world in general, which includes me. I'm left looking bad because I couldn't personally share all their various interlocking griefs. I wasn't terribly close to her brother. Who *could* be close to Floyd?"

"Listen. I don't think that Good Deeds is dead. I don't think he's even missing in action. He wrote to Buffy once, just before nobody heard from him again. He wasn't in the infantry anymore. He was transferred."

Calvin removed his pith helmet and wiped the back of his neck. "To what?"

"I don't know. I'm not positive. I had to read between the lines, but I think he was shifted to Intelligence. I think he was planning to blend in with the landscape. I'm just riding on a hunch. I told Buffy not to mention it. I didn't want her to get anybody's hopes up."

"Well, you wouldn't. Fern's a born fatalist. Whatever's bad could get worse. She's probably right, too."

"The world's growing pretty sinister. There's a lot more going on than we realize. I like Ike, but he doesn't really know the score. World War II was just a ball game. We *need* a good Fascist on our side now. We need old Good Deeds out there to keep an eye on things."

"I'm not sure I'm too crazy about that notion."

"He's only stupid in certain ways. He *told* us the Chinese were coming, didn't he? We were pretty innocent at the time."

Calvin suddenly remembered the empty flat with the leaking toilet above him in the summer heat. He had been closer to panic then than he had realized—in part because he could have been back in uniform, his student days cut short, in larger part because he had felt left alone again, alone enough to marry Fern. When was he going to learn to draw back, to rely on some core within?

"Hell," Charley was saying, still admiring his former innocence, "we didn't know which end was up."

But, Calvin thought, *you took care of yourself, Charley. You got out. You married Buffy; you married into her family's money, then got her pregnant, because you thought by then that the Chinese could be after you, too.*

Oh, he knew! A survivor from the word go. A survivor from southern Ohio coal-mining country, from ignorance and dirt. So probably who was to judge? Charley was both infuriating and amusing. "Floyd also partly asked for his troubles. He was very disapproving. He was a lot more like Fern than not. It *is* a strange family."

"The brother and sister were pretty close, weren't they, when you think about it?"

"They once had to take care of each other. The mother walked out of the house when the father was drinking. She couldn't divorce him because she was Catholic, but she left them to deal. In some ways, they grew up pretty fast. In others, they don't know anything. They haven't faced their bitterness."

"Well, my in-laws are pretty strange, too. That's New England. A lot of moneyed Connecticut oddballs. You never know what they're going to do. Everything's class. Done just so, with linen napkins, napkin rings, and then my mother-in-law feeds the dogs at the table. She'll let them eat right out of her dish. Hell, at home we didn't let the dogs in the house."

They reached the car. Calvin unlocked the door and pulled

out a can of oil. He walked around in front and lifted the hood. "Connecticut isn't New England, Charley. It's just an expensive New York City suburb. You have to go farther north than that to hit New England, so if you think you've married into the real thing, you haven't. You're lucky."

Charley stood on the walk staring at the Hudson. "Oh, Christ! I don't believe it! Does it still run? How come it hasn't been towed away yet?"

Calvin slammed the hood and threw the empty oil can in the back. "It runs. It just has some oil troubles. If I decide to get on the road again, I'm going to have to put some money into it."

"*Oil* troubles? Are you kidding? Why don't you just put the thing out of its misery? Why do you have so much trouble spending a cent?"

The engine took a few minutes before it caught. The motor was scratchy, sluggish, but it finally started. He kept his hand on the moving gear shift, waiting to try first as soon as the shaking stopped.

Charley lit a cigarette beside him. "Are you still with that old-fashioned firm? That family place where the great-grandfather shows up every day with his lunch box?"

The cold, enclosed air inside was musty, slightly engine-smelling, and he rolled down the window. "Oh, yes. He turns up at Choice Cuts the first thing in the morning, but he's long since retired. He can't stay home."

"Choice and Corners? They're all embalmed there."

The light was thinning, the air growing more dampish. He wondered if he could get packed before the rain hit. "He doesn't trust this bullish period. He says there's a slump on the way, and if he says it, I listen. He's the only one with a head in the place. He doesn't have anything to do all day except keep his ear to the ground."

"Well, he must have rocks in his head. I don't see any slump ahead."

Calvin shifted, easing into the street. Aside from the fresh oil smell, he could also detect a faint electrical odor. What was that? "I forgot. You like Ike."

He was going to have to pick up string and wrapping paper before he could finish packing. He climbed the steep side street and slipped onto upper Broadway while the car still shook some, leaking oil, surprised at its own life, but steadily gaining confidence. A pre–World War II Hudson heading into the future, ready to try if he insisted. He insisted. The will was a marvelous mechanism. He couldn't be completely crazy if he stayed so concentrated.

"What are you doing, trying to advise people about their investments, anyway?" Charley said. "You don't inspire much confidence, do you? Don't you put people off a little? You have that old-fashioned, half-romantic, half-remote air about you that couldn't help. I don't say you have to do a lot of backslapping, but you don't come off like somebody in a Rotary Club, either. Your looks are also against you, and your voice is too rich-sounding. You look like a movie star, and you have too much presence. You need to be imbibed from a distance. You also ought to be showing a few years; you ought to be getting a little thin on top, as if you were a securely planted family man with responsibilities out in New Rochelle somewhere. Look at you! You don't even know where you're going to sleep tonight, do you? You're going to turn into a regular drifter."

He could still interest investors without half trying because the firm had its old connections, its family clients, and since the place wasn't all that interested in new business, he was secure enough there.

He wasn't all that content, though. He didn't want to sit around there forever. He was looking over the field, but he was having trouble locating somewhere else. Potential employers were searching for bland, adaptable company men; and whether it was his college transcripts, peppered with liberal arts courses, or his personality, they apparently did not see him as cut from the right cloth.

"I've been thinking about a change."

"Well, you've got to change your image first. You need to be more like everybody else."

"I'd probably stick out."

"I could put you onto something. It's out of town, though. In fact, it's out of the state. It's in Indianapolis."

"Now that I'm free I wouldn't mind leaving the city, these stale centers of power," he intoned, thinking about the old man's eye for the future: America flattened out like a grid.

"Well, they're interviewing here right now. I can put you up where I stay when I'm in town. I've got to get back tonight."

Calvin pulled over to the curb in front of a hardware store. "I've got to pick up some string."

"*String?*"

"I've got all that packing to do."

"You're two people. Do you know that? You're several people. You're very disconcerting, buddy. Listen," Charley said, climbing out, too. "I've got to get back downtown. I can catch a cab."

While he was camping out in Charley Klick's cramped, transientlike, semifurnished midtown efficiency, the neighborhood was being demolished around him, another going up. The girders swung overhead like matchsticks; the cement trucks wove in and out of the clogged traffic in the hot, sticky air, the on-again–off-again screens of warm, bitter rain.

While he was waiting to meet Charley's Indianapolis contacts, he could hear sweet, clear recorder music coming from the door across the hall, starting around ten P.M. and going on with few interruptions slightly past twelve.

Recorders were everywhere at the moment. He saw them on subways and crosstown buses; they rose and fell on elevators; they showed up at Nedicks; they were carried through the Village streets, appearing in San Remoes and Minnetta's, there among the Beat Populations (beards, crewcuts, khaki pants, sandals, the girls in leotards, black ballet slippers); and if he had created a girl with a recorder at Clara's nonexistent party, the coincidence was not all that curious.

Still, when he lay in bed on the pullout couch, unable to

sleep, he could not hear the ghostly recorder music without recalling his earlier invention and wondering if he hadn't summoned her into being now: tall, pale, thin, almost breastless, lighthaired, shy, silent, seemingly ineffectual, a lost soul until she picked up the recorder, when she was so obviously in command.

Was she any the less invented than Clara herself had been, a girl he had not seen since he had spent those few hours at her side? His brief period with her had already faded: sensations cannot be recalled, and her cries and tears, so clear at the time, could not have any substance now. And if he had not invented her desperation, assuming desperation could be so short-lived, he had misconstrued her general need for a particular person; she could have chosen any other male in the building who happened to show up at the time.

In fact, was she any the less made-up than Fern herself, who had chiefly lived in the mind's eye—a softer, more pliant, more understanding presence than she had actually been? Was she any the less made up than Kasey, who, despite her own confusions, self-deceptions, roles, and names, was probably, in reality, as flesh and blood, a lot less mysterious than he had wanted her to be? How many real people had he failed because he had invented substitutes?

Why couldn't he just deal? Why was there so much discrete unhealth in him?

He felt isolated and tender, vulnerable and thin-skinned, too self-indulgent, too self-centered, too self-serving, too absorbed in dark, soft inwardness, piercing, private, joyful. Self-love: the fear of the void. I have to notice myself while I'm still around. Nobody says I'm living forever.

He could probably be homosexual if he didn't work himself up so over women's flesh: their breasts, bottoms, curves, and secrets; sex stood in the way, sundering him from any likely experiments.

He could not face his refusal to confront a woman like another human, though he had to admit he did not cherish any confrontations. He was afraid of anger, as if anger should be beneath him, as if only getting on was healthy and exact. So

110

he converted his aggressions into passivity, his dislikes into temporary admiration. Show him a woman with killer instincts, with death wishes, and he could call this maturity, a realistic view of what is, at least for awhile, as long as he could hang on.

Eventually, though, his bitterness surfaced and got the better of him. He boiled and boiled and boiled and finally boiled over. The murderer in love, who claims he has his rights! All his softness, his vulnerability, his charm, his stories, his self-sacrifices, his cooking and cleaning, and then, finally, the assassin's rages. He sheds his apron and goes for the knife. He yelled for divorce as if it were the last cleansing, creative act on earth. He felt like one of the world's great confusions.

As high school valedictorian, he had once quoted the Great Thinker: "Man is timid and apologetic; he is no longer upright; he dares not say 'I think, I am,' but quotes some saint or sage. He is ashamed before the blade of grass or the blowing rose. These roses under my window make no reference to former roses or to better ones; they are what they are; they exist with God today. There is no time to them. There is simply the rose; it is perfect in every moment of its existence."

But these very valedictorians, quoting Emerson, ranking first in scholarship, having worked hard, always with their noses in books, could not have lived like roses. He certainly didn't, given his anxieties and depressions, his fierce, jumpy nerves and hungers. His misery was himself. He didn't know how to give up.

His mother, large, solid, sweet, hazy, absent-minded, an Emersonian, diluting a diluted doctrine, had not believed in original sin. In fact, she had admitted to no inconveniences, no flaws or problems. The worse her troubles became, the more set her mouth, fixed in a little distant, frozen, otherworldly smile.

She looked through people, generally, not at them, as if there were something far more interesting just behind them; but when her troubles grew, she particularly seemed miles away, sheltered in a better world. Her strongest expression of disapproval was limited to *"What* a thing to say!" as if nothing could *be* wrong until it was put into words. And so she had feared language because of its possible releases.

She had kept her life on an even keel, a well-bred visitor who politely overlooks the antics in a madhouse, his father's routines: studying himself in the mirror, practicing his ventriloquist's exercises, checking for lip movement, holding his nose at the same time because when he was correctly making the sounds he could feel his nose vibrate; his father in retreat during one of his "depressions," talking to the dummy on his knee when he wasn't speaking to anyone else, the two of them chuckling together in the corner, telling stories, reading the comics ("Gasoline Alley," "Orphan Annie," "Bringing Up Father"), playing word games, testing each other on allusions, Sophocles, Chaucer, Shakespeare, shaking their heads, bent over, collapsed in laughter, then straightening, dead serious again, off on another tack, a fresh direction.

Because she believed she had a sunny disposition, because she claimed that she could discover the good in anyone, and always looked on the bright side, his mother had been a master of endurance. She was a survivor. In her way, she lived with her troubles. She would never have left his father; he left her, twice. She did not believe in divorce anymore than her mother did. Two contrasts, Grace and Sarah Elizabeth shared the same opinions on that subject: divorce wasn't possible. When you married, that was it; you cut your own pattern. You are that fate which befalls you.

And here he was now, the son and grandson, the heir, the end of the line, walking out on his second marriage, heading for his second divorce. He was worrying about keeping the settlement reasonable because if she *was* pregnant, she could try for the moon: from romance to business, a modern rut.

Oh, why was divorce so American anyway? What stresses and pressures do we put on relationships that make them terminate so conclusively and so haphazardly? What demands do we make on fixity itself, as if we were apparently the most rooted people in the world, which finally cause us

112

to end up in court, sitting beside an attorney in our best clothes?

And here he was now, the son and grandson, the heir, the last of the Puritans, listening to ghostly recorder music after midnight, dwelling on it, music that could just be in his head, like the girl he created to go with it. He drank beer after beer, keeping it close to the bed. He was growing a heavier moustache. He was putting on weight because he was living on beer and grabbing drugstore milkshakes. He kept his Viking helmet within reach, but slept nude. He bought skin magazines and practiced self-abuse, trying to take off some of the edge. He talked to himself and talked back to the TV: Ed Sullivan, "The Sixty-Four Thousand Dollar Question," "Talent Scouts," "You Bet Your Life," "What's My Line?"

He worked on TV show ideas when he couldn't sleep. He had something going called "Every Friday." Every Friday a master of ceremonies, a sleek head honcho, drags out four or five hooded contestants who vie with one another on a coast-to-coast hookup. Faces covered, just the eyes and mouths showing, they unburden themselves before millions, confessing, going through some agony, some half-buried guilt they've carried around with them for years. The audience applauds its favorite, the one who has gone through the most suffering. He gets to take home the jackpot, the TV console, the Miami vacation, the Lincoln Continental. . . .

He particularly liked "This is Your Funeral." Every week someone designs his own, picks his mourners, his music, his orators, and setting; stars are flown in from Hollywood; great musicians appear for fantastic sums: opera singers, concert organists (or Bill Haley and the Comets); famous actors like Paul Robeson or Orson Welles read from Norman Vincent Peale. . . .

And where was Charley Klick, the draft-dodger, the cunt-chaser, the con artist, the steady talker, the coal miner's son? Where was the heel of our time? Settled in Connecticut (New England to him), a home in Westport, among the dogwood, the apple blossom, the iris, the maples, and the elms, the charming stone walls, the old churches, and cider presses, the spinning wheels and cut glass, the golf courses, and summer theaters. Among the bond salesmen and bankers, the advertising executives and brokers, moneyed commuters and bookish book club members. (*The Robe* was big at the moment.) He was probably playing canasta these days or cooking in his backyard, wearing a funny apron and chef's hat, drinking Cutty Sark, feeding his dogs Pard, chlorophyllin added, sweeting their breaths. . . .

He could see him ordering Buffy around, that plumpish, small blonde with the strange soft brown eyes, the slightly withered left arm. ("Christ, Buffy, where's the steak sauce! How am I supposed to eat steak without steak sauce?") And twins, too, with Davey Crockett hats! He'll always have the latest. "While I have my remoteness, my amusing inadequacies and Old-World repressions."

He put down his beer and rose unsteadily. The talker talking to himself again. All those little intelligences humming, and he needed the outlet. He felt a depression coming on, the kind of depression that could wipe him out for days, for weeks at a time. He wove toward the bathroom. Leaning, looking around, locating Charley's lightswitch. Weaving, he raised the toilet-seat lid.

"Writhe right there a moment, will you?" he requested, looking behind him at the rumpled couch, the filled ashtrays, the week's worth of newspapers. "I have a lot to tell. I'll get another beer. We'll have a little parley." Standing. Swaying. Smiling, Leaning, Pissing, Lonely. (So watch it!) Zipping up. Swaying face in the mirror: strange, dark, aggressive, unsafe. He had his father's mouth.

In the whirling quiet. Riverrun. . . . Oh, out past Thumperton Landing, Herring Brook, Dead Woman's Pond, First Encounter Beach, from curve of sure to brake of day. . . .

Great-Grandmother Mercy buried. The pilgrim's pilgrim gone to her fourfeathers, and when we turned home, mine appeared: a ghost from the past with trick coins in his pockets.

Beware! Oh, I'll be kingdom-comed!

Oh, organize, organize, organize; only organize!

114

Floyd surfaced with the French in Dienbienphu, and he flew home. He found Calvin through Charley. If he was still in the service, doing whatever he was doing; he wasn't in uniform. He looked thinner and grimmer, but he was otherwise pretty much the same.

Floyd was laboring under a delusion which Calvin never got straightened out during that strange, brief visit. He believed that Calvin had been keeping a second apartment—probably for women on the side, and when Fern discovered it, he walked out.

On the whole, he avoided personal matters. He had come to deliver a message. "Fern's definitely pregnant," he said, refusing to sit down. "She's a Catholic, and this puts her on the spot."

"I know. She can't divorce me. I can divorce her, though."

"She agrees to stay married for the sake of the child, but she won't live with you."

"What kind of deal is that? I'll see the child anyway. I'm going to ask for visiting rights."

"Nothing doing. She doesn't want you anywhere near her child."

"She can't stop me. The court will give me visiting rights."

"She won't let you see it."

"She'll have to, if she wants a settlement."

"She doesn't want anything else from you," he said, still standing near the door.

That was that, too.

Penny-pinching, string-saving, hoarding, grasping, staying close to his things, loaded down with his possessions—books, records, loose papers, check stubs, accounting sheets, some original poems, bric-a-brac, fencing swords, ancient alligator suitcase, jugs, pots, costumes, art, old photograph albums, he crossed town in the early morning traffic on the first leg of his trip west, off to Indianapolis, heading out for the territory.

First, the hissing, the sharp, crackling sounds, and then the smoke curling up from the hood. In control, as if he were not surprised, certainly refusing to panic, he edged toward the curb. By now the smoke was fleeing up from the floor, circling his possessions, his compact little civilization. A passing trucker jumped out with a fire extinguisher, but Calvin couldn't save a thing.

He bought a Mercedes that afternoon—writing out a check in full without batting an eyelash because he could pass a car like that on to his heirs. Because, beginning again, he was interested in a little style this time, the kind of flair he wanted to grow used to. Given some status, he could pass as normal, a young man with a future coming up.

He rose early again the next morning and crossed into New Jersey while the choppy sky was still ashen. The curling chemical fumes stayed close to the ground, yellowish in spots, tannish or rust-colored in others. It was raining when he hit the Turnpike. The wipers worked frantically in the sulphurous gloom. The trucks curved past, throwing up wet. They changed gears on the steep inclines, then opened up as they barreled down. He twice pulled off to pause overnight in roadside motels. He half slept while the trucks were still pounding past, a dull unceasing roar that touched the surface of his sleeping state.

The weather finally broke. The rain lifted. When he crossed the Indiana state line, he drove through a warmish, eerie dusk. The open fields looked sopped and spoiled. In the distance, seen from the straight, unchanging highway, the few trees appeared to be faintly menacing; the woods grew slightly yellowish for a moment, just before the dark hardened.

He blundered into and then out of small towns. He passed a filling station, a closed country store, two Pentecostal churches, a low, semimodernized red brick school complex, and a clearing where wrecked cars had been dumped. A closed drive-in movie came up on his left, deserted in the weeds and high grass. On the other side, toward town, there was a motel, a truckers' stop, the separate wooden units already lit with pale, greenish neon tubing. After the motel, the small eating places began: The Corner Cupboard, Jeter's Chicken Shack, Welcome Inn, Harriet's Home Cooking, Country Corners Café, Chicken Haven, The Oaken Bucket, Snack-A-While, and Betsey's Hum-Dinger-Drive-In.

There was something so forcefully alien and unreal about all this that for a moment or two he felt too light, detached, dangerously not himself. If he wasn't himself; there was the outside possibility that this new being might be better. But who could tell? Who could be so sure?

SIX Vance, Zimmer, and Harsh had its offices in a nine-teenth-century three-floor brownstone out on West Washington, set back off the tree-lined street among the rows of other steadily converting mansions. The depleted elegance was slightly dispiriting, considering the closed-off marble fireplaces, the empty third-floor ballroom, the abandoned, overgrown rose garden in back. The drafty bathrooms still had their huge tubs with clawed feet, a world of porcelain fixtures, mother-of-pearl toilet seats and leaky taps. The heavy leaded windows stuck in the other seasons. Calvin had an office in a huge second-floor bedroom with a balcony that faced the street. He felt like Maud in the moated grange.

The firm counseled small businesses, advising them on their various bankruptcies and growing pains. He was doing a lot of hack work at first. He was using a library, checking out taxes and tangled government regulations. He ran errands between Indianapolis and Washington. He covered other people's mistakes; but the firm was young, and because the management was unsure of itself, it was open to change. It took chances and created new positions overnight. Its atmosphere was hectic, innovative, and overly-concerned with public relations.

He was moved into a special slot a little over a year later. He was in charge of a TV talk show called "What's New in Indy?" The adaptable, uncertain format concentrated on new businesses and new business opportunities in the area. Calvin did the legwork. He handled the research and the little writing necessary. He compiled the questions, found the guests, and handled the TV shuffle in general; but when the TV host suddenly left, he took over his job as well.

The firm developed financial problems during the 1957–

1958 slump, and when it took the show's increasingly high costs into consideration, it decided to cut back. It phased out "What's New in Indy?" and it phased him out at the same time. He was back in the streets in a strange town, knocking on doors. He was also going through his divorce at that period, but if it was a particularly low point in his life, it didn't last long.

He talked some sponsors into another local show. He was producing and hosting a half-hour program that handled local cultural matters: museums, music, theater, movies, exhibits, special events, visiting celebrities. He was successful and popular. Both the sound of his voice and his engaging good looks gradually brought him a larger audience than such a show could usually anticipate. He carried it far more often than he interviewed, and because talking put him up so high, as if he were riding a creative current, he felt more complete than he had ever felt in his life.

He was still camping out in a furnished single-bedroom apartment, his third move since he had first reached town, and he decided that he was ready to invest in some space. He started looking for a house—heading south, out of the city. When the corner groceries, the Dr. Pepper signs, the concrete-block churches, the dingy bars, and the rundown neighborhoods gradually thinned out, he passed the lumberyards, the auto body shops, the paint stores, and the plumbing suppliers. He finally hit the country: small wooden churches, scattered farms, a golf course, and a newly emerging housing development.

He wandered around a big four-bedroom brick split-level in the development. So far, only a few streets had been cut through. The land around was partly wooded, partly farm. From the upstairs he could see willows, cow pastures, ponds. The backyard gradually dropped down to some tall nut trees that separated it from a vacant lot.

The agent followed him around, poking at this and that, a big, square-shouldered woman in a slack suit, who was also seeing the place for the first time. Opening closets and kitchen cabinets. Enjoying smelling the new smells. "A lot

119

of space here, and you'll have city gas. You won't have to mess around with oil."

"Who owns the vacant lot in back? Has that been bought up yet?"

"I'll have to check, but you can probably have it. When will the family be moving in?"

"I think I'll look around a little more first."

"Suit yourself," she said. "But you said you wanted some space, you wanted some trees, and I pushed the magic button. Why don't you let your wife see what she thinks?"

He looked around, but he took the house and the extra lot a week later. He furnished the house slowly, starting with the basics. He slept in the master bedroom, used a second as a den. He closed off the other two. He wandered around this space with a drink, talking to himself, peering out at his trees.

He bought a lot of clothes soon after he started the second talk show, and he was half going with a script girl. He liked expensive, conservative clothes: charcoal pin stripes, flannels, midnight blue, narrow knit ties, button-down collars, linen shirts with french cuffs, no pockets. He kept all buttons buttoned. His dark hair, not long, was nevertheless no longer used to the army crewcut. Its bristle was gone. He had shaved his moustache for the time being, during that long period before he later decided to grow a beard. He was tall, fairly filled out, yet far less padded-looking than he had been in his early twenties. He still lost and gained easily, putting it on in the stomach, just under the chest. He kept his thighs and his strong-looking legs, both inherited, not earned. Between his talk show, his own business investments, and a little writing, he was too busy to exercise. He was constantly going. A quick-moving, tense, restless man.

Marcie Griffith typed and ran scripts around the studio, a tall, twenty-two-year-old with a broad, freckled face and a tempting, slightly underdeveloped figure. She lived an up-to-the-minute existence. She loved peasant blouses with low bodices, puffed sleeves, full taffeta skirts at midcalf, crinoline beneath, a happy product of a popular culture. When he first met her, she was carrying *Marjorie Morningstar* around. In looks, in energy, in health, in fussing, she was ideal. Her cologne smelled like spring violets in those bleak, windy Indianapolis weathers. Her short dark hair was thick and naturally curly; her shoulders were sturdy, her breasts still like a fifteen-year-old's, her mouth soft and full, her teeth unusually white against her tongue. She had a little habit with her tongue that drove him crazy; she touched the sides of her mouth with her tongue, wetting the edges. Her eyes shone, her skin glistened in the cold while she was waiting for him to open a door or help her out of the car. (She always waited for help through doors or into her coat. He loved her spicy, old-fashioned ways. When she first met people, she looked as if she might curtsy at any moment; she just came short of it.)

She nestled against him in the Mercedes. She would look at him without speaking, with those deep brown eyes, as if she had been going with him forever. When she was seated beside him, she instantly laced her fingers through his, as if she needed the contact badly, and he got used to driving with one hand. What was this miracle, this wonderfully average girl, after he had reached such an empty period in his life? When he was with her, this flesh-and-blood being, the past's final radiance faded: Kasey was insubstantial now, long since preserved in some lost, golden period.

He realized that he was willing to commit himself too soon. He told himself that he was going to have to go carefully; but her bland, cheerful surface protected them both. She ignored his depressions and tensions. She disregarded his various hungers. She had a sensitive neck and ears. She enjoyed steady necking, some petting. He could change her breathing in minutes. He could kiss the tops of her breasts until her eyes grew lusterless, but she always came to at the last minute.

She wasn't going to sleep with him. She could not be appealed to or reached through some deep-down weakness or problem, either his or hers; and this absence of vulnerabil-

121

ity, this lack of generosity and depth, finally wore him down and cheapened her in his eyes.

He took her south to see his split-level in the middle of a silent, listless, hot Sunday afternoon—past Pleasant View, across the Brandyview River, into the Blossomville–Boonepoint area, just north of Shelbyville.

As soon as he stopped, she got out of the car, unaided for once. He couldn't get around to her side quickly enough. She hurried around the house, down the gradually sloping ground toward the backyard. Crunching the first few fallen leaves, peering up through the trees. The fall was dusty and still. Squirrels gorged overhead, dropping shells. He stepped on others, the fuzzy, hard buckeyes that threatened his lawnmower. Tall shaggy grasses covered his extra lot, untouched, just there to look at for the time being. He could smell manure in the distance.

A city girl, she was having trouble with her heels. She wanted to know if he was planning to rake all the leaves himself. She was impressed, but reserved, her eyes half asking a lot of unasked questions. Why, for instance, would anybody want to live so far out? And why would a single man want such a big place? She started to sneeze, and he realized the trip had been a mistake.

He crossed the patio and unlocked the backdoor, but she stayed where she was—planted in the middle of the backyard in her city girl's peasant blouse and full skirt, still looking up into the trees.

"Marcie?" he called, waiting, "don't you want to see the house?"

She started across the yard, gingerly watching her step, as if she were parting brambles. She stayed just inside the kitchen door, admiring the built-in range.

"Come on. I'll show you the whole house."

She hesitated. She was trying to decide if she could trust him. "Oh, I don't know. I know you," she said.

What did she know now? (He knew.)

"You know," she said uneasily, avoiding language—only unclaustrophobic in parked cars.

122

Staying in the hall, she peered into room after room—dining, living, family area. She never got upstairs. When she reached the panel, she was back on the patio again. He was amused, annoyed, finally irritated. He drove her home without commenting on the situation, but he knew that he was through with the struggle. He wasn't going to bother. He wasn't going to see her again.

The sky never lifted that winter. The snow fell from time to time without seriously accumulating, and the ground remained hard. The day's thinness collapsed around four o'clock. The soundless nights dropped quickly. The wind was not constant, but the chill was. He could never get warm enough, and when he was alone, his drinking picked up. He kept the heat high and the lights blazing against the silence outside.

Well, and what next? Was his loneliness, that unmentionable burden, the rule of his existence, the fixed law, his marriages just the brief exceptions? Was this clownish oddity, this unsocial role, to be alone, his logical fate?

Calvin was prowling around the TV station when he first met Sheila Foss. She was in a quiz show with a semi-intellectual format. That day high school teachers were competing from around the state. Her students, the best half-dozen or so, mostly males, sat in the front row, rooting for her, and when she answered correctly, they clapped. She would duck her head slightly at those moments and briefly put her hand to her throat. She seemed shy and introverted, but highly competitive at the same time. She tried to look detached, as if all this were just part of the day's work.

There was a party in the station afterward. Sheila walked back and forth to the punch bowl carrying her paper cup. Her closely trimmed reddish hair appeared to have a slight rinse but was otherwise natural. She was wearing harlequin glasses, heavy eye makeup and a certain amount of fashionable, expensive-looking costume jewelry. She was short, but well endowed.

She chain-smoked while she circled the punch bowl. She would grip someone at the elbow for a minute with two fingers, and then she was gone, off to talk to someone else. Her color was high, her face animated. She used her hands a lot, and he noticed her long, brightly painted nails. She waved her hands while she talked, her fingers spread, her wrists loose.

She recognized him and came over, offering her hand without fuss. Unlike most redheads, she had clear, unblemished skin, certainly no freckles, but her eyes were pale, somewhat greenish, more often light gray. "I'm a fan of yours," she said, "slightly, but I suppose you're used to hearing that. I suppose you're used to being told you look more like a movie star than some of those pokey, small town, so-called stars you interview."

He was just off work. As usually happened just after a show, he felt no need to talk. He felt tired, happily spent. At these moments, periods of shyness rose in him, a shyness that had its roots in distant childhood, a part of some ancient, half-buried existence. This was another person, and although the shyness never lasted, he welcomed the feeling. He sometimes cherished not knowing what to say. "Well, we all do our best," he finally said.

"I suppose they do. They're still just taking up space. I like the literatures. Do you read a lot? You seem to have. You didn't go to college around here, did you?"

"Columbia University. I have a business degree."

"*Business?*" she said, with such emphasis he raised his brows.

"Oh, yes. I wandered blindly into the arts."

"*That* was fortunate."

She lived south of the city, if not as far out as he did, and she asked for a ride back. She stopped at the punch bowl on the way out. She was still sipping from the paper cup when she reached the car. She was talking about TV in general. She talked about it as a medium with a serious future in education. She said that, as a literature major, she believed in the word; but she also had an art major, and from that point of view, she could understand television's power. The image was ancient, and so why wouldn't it have a lot of basic appeal?

It was snowing. A wind soon sprang up, bowling swirls of snow across the highway in front of him, making the going uncertain. Fresh wet sludge clung to the wipers, slowing down the blades.

"Whatever possessed you to want a business major, anyway? That seems like a strange pursuit."

"I have some money to take care of."

She sat beside him still holding the paper cup, empty now except for the melting ice. She shook it, rattling the last of the ice, and drained it to the dregs. "That must be a pleasant responsibility."

He said nothing. He was concentrating on the driving.

She wasn't worried about the weather, and when he mentioned it, she stayed unimpressed. "Oh, piffle. I've seen worse."

"I have too, but I haven't driven in it. I could use snow tires."

"Snow tires are overrated. You don't need them when you're driving a big, expensive tank like this."

She discussed tires and cars. She discussed which years you could trust and which not and why.

She talked about the small town where she was teaching, just south of Indianapolis. "It's a spot in the road," she remarked dryly, not unkindly, "but it's historical, in a sense, and so I try to bear with it. I try to breathe a little life into those sticks."

"What do you do in the summers?"

"This and that. I do a little painting and I try to get a little writing in. I certainly can't get much of my own stuff covered during the regular school year. I have to spend too much time then just knocking heads together."

"You handled yourself well on that show back there."

"I can't say the competition was much."

The wind continued to organize small, careful drifts out in the fields where the emptiness began. It kept the highway bare in spots and heaped it in others. It brushed flat plains of snow across the front wheels. The big warm body of the car was sometimes fluttery and undependable. It once fishtailed slightly, as if demonstrating what it could do if it chose. A semi passed a small Chevy up ahead, throwing up snow. Calvin swore in sympathy, complaining about the carelessness.

She said that truckers knew what they were doing. They could drive better than anyone else. With snow, a little speed helped, so why poke. Why would anyone just want to poke? She said that if more people drove like truckers, the world would be a safer place.

She looked out at the fields while she lit a cigarette. She said that the empty spaces reminded her of *The Heart of Darkness*. She said it impersonally, though, as a fact. She didn't appear to mind too much.

She stayed cheerful and accommodating. She asked him if he wanted her to drive.

He shook his head. "I'm managing," he said.

"Oh, you're managing. You aren't exactly a speed king, though, are you?" she asked.

Her cocky certainties amused him, whether they were authentic or not. If not, it came to the same thing in the long run. Since she did not have to consider how he was taking her, she seemed courageous because doggedly exposed: here she was, as she was.

He finally turned off the highway into her town, passing little businesses, all closed: an insurance agency, a loan company, a watch repair, a shoe repair, a dry cleaners and a hat-blocking shop. There was a feed store, a Singers, and a Sears.

"You take a left at that light."

"Where, though, are the historical sites?"

"I don't suppose you're up to a guided tour tonight."

She lived in a three-story frame with a Gothic turret and a wraparound porch. "Come on," she said, getting out, "before you drop, after that ordeal of yours. You could use a stiff drink."

126

She had a second-floor flat. Books, papers, and school art projects littered the narrow parlor: turtles made from clamshells, masks from milk cartons, totem poles from TV-dinner plates. "All this junk," she said, lighting lights on her way back to the kitchen, "so just pick a place."

He moved some books and dropped onto a corner couch. Feeling dazed and stiff, he rubbed the back of his neck. He could hear her in the kitchen getting the ice cubes loose. She turned on the faucet.

"For heaven sakes," she said, appearing with two glasses, "why are you still wearing that silly coat and tie when it's steaming in here? Don't you believe in ever getting comfortable, or what?"

If she took charge, he did not worry about his role. If she was the aggressor, he did not feel demeaned. In fact, the aggressiveness touched him just because he was its object, hence evidently sought, which was a wonder. "I'm from New England," he said, loosening his tie before he took his glass.

"Oh, Lord, yes! I gathered that."

"I didn't know the West was such a wild place."

She missed his irony or ignored it. "Oh, for heaven sakes! Indiana isn't 'West.' I don't really feel 'west' much east of Denver."

"Are you from Denver?"

"I'm from here, but not particularly confined to it."

"I'm enjoying the leisurely change of pace around here," he said—another irony, which meant he must be feeling less disoriented.

"Then you haven't seen the right parts."

"I haven't seen anything yet."

"No, you haven't."

He got drunk quickly because he was both hungry and tired. They hugged unseriously through his haze. They stumbled around, watching their footing among the high school art projects, maps constructed from regional products: corn, peanuts, oats, soybeans. Two kittens dropped down from a windowsill and began to circle their ankles, as if joining the fun.

He later couldn't recall the transition from the parlor to the bedroom. He couldn't even remember undressing. When she was on her back, her breasts did not completely flatten. They rode in front, massive, loose, partly flopped over the upper parts of her arms, where they slightly creased against their own weight, pointing in different directions. A conical shadow etched the space between the cleft. Except for the small, sharp chin, her face was completely in shadow. She moved her chin just as she raised her knees. "Come here!"

He wanted to be held between her knees. He wanted to be clasped, cradled, rocked.

She knew, she knew, and when she raised her knees, she opened her arms at the same time. "Come here," she repeated. "Come here. Oh, unwind! Relax!"

His orgasm was sudden, painful, and tearing. He finally rolled over on his side as if he were rolling away from himself.

She was up on all fours trying to reach his glass. "You need repairs."

Because she had not come, he felt unsettled, incomplete. "I'm all right. I still have some."

She took it out of his hand. "Oh, piffle-dew! Stuff and nonsense. You aren't even completely relaxed yet," she said, heading back to the kitchen, the cats following.

He lay there in the huge, scruffy, unmade bed, imbibing the stale sheet smells, the stuffy warmth, the sense of shelter, while the snow continued to fall, hitting the windows, muffling the town. He felt gingerly balanced between this comfort and his basic unease: he felt too waited on, too valued.

Sheila was not exactly a relaxed person herself, but she was better at giving advice than taking it. She would have been more self-centered if she had not possessed such a gift. She could spot other people's problems in a minute. She had a sixth sense for what was wrong and why and what it would take to get somebody straightened out. She kept many irons in the fire: she read; she wrote; she painted; but, at the same time, she was not above trying to make people over when she felt the project was worth it.

She had grown up in a small southern Indiana town, which had gradually emerged around a cement plant, and just about everyone there worked for the cement company. Everything in the town was the same gray stucco: the library, the school, the community center, and the seven churches. There was a park with a duck pond, a gray stucco gazebo and a playground filled with heavy gray stucco picnic tables, benches, and sheds. A fine, gritty lime dust always hung in the air, whatever the season. It powdered the snow in winter. It covered the leaves and the grass in spring and summer. When it rained, the showers briefly settled the dust, but when it cleared, the leaves never glittered, the day never really smelled fresh. The schoolchildren could breathe the dust whether the windows were open or closed, and on Sundays the people in the seven churches breathed the dust while they bent over their devotions.

Sheila's father worked in the plant, but he didn't collect guns or hunt like the other men. He was a morose, private person, and when he wasn't on the job, or under his truck in the front yard, he sat around the house drinking beer. He did not approve of the town, but he did not approve of much. He kept his eyes on his wife and his two daughters, Sheila and Lu Ann, without saying a great deal, but his disapproval was as tangible as the cement dust they breathed everyday. When he finally got fed up, he could make his point with a few words or often with no words at all.

When he had once come home to an empty house and a bare table, he searched through the fields down the street until he found several large patches of dry cowflop. He brought the cowflop back, got the plates down, and put the cowflop on the plates. He even put paper napkins beside each plate. When Sheila's mother returned, back with the groceries, she screamed and screamed. She got migraines easily, and when she had unloaded the car, she went straight to bed, pulling the shades down along her route. Darlene told her daughters that T. C. was the cross she had to bear. T. C.

would even look pleased at the remark for a moment, as if he had at last found some function in his life. A small smile would cross his face just before he opened a fresh beer. Unlike T. C., Darlene had finished high school. She considered herself above the cement plant, and she tried to instill the need for education in her two daughters, Sheila, her first, who turned out to be bookish, and Lu Ann, her second, who did not. Sheila brought home straight A's. But if she had been studious, she had to compensate for the four-point average, and she had hardly been reclusive. She dated early, and she was soon hanging around fast crowds. She circled the drive-ins, visited the lime pits, and parked along the river. She also claimed that she could do what any boy could do. She played poker. She drove around town, helping to put out streetlights with a twenty-two. Darlene knew about some of this, but she could not handle Sheila after she was fifteen. She could scream a lot; she often did, but that did not phase Sheila anymore. Sheila was steadily developing her own temper, and since T. C. did not want to deal with her, or couldn't himself, she usually ended up doing what she wanted.

Lu Ann was shallower and certainly more easy going. She was prettier and more popular. She was a cheerleader from junior high on, and she was prom queen in her senior year. When she finished high school, she competed in a state beauty contest. She didn't win, but while she was in Indianapolis, she met a young junior executive in a luggage company. Arthur was on his way up, and if Lu Ann wasn't an intellectual, she was not entirely stupid. She saw her chance and she took it. She married Arthur, moved to Denver, and promptly had three children.

Sheila went to work for the telephone company when she graduated. She was planning to save for college, but the routine was beneath her, and too many people around with less sense ruled the roost. She couldn't understand how some of her superiors had brains enough to get up in the morning. She would come back complaining, frustrated, and bored. She was also spending too much. She liked clothes, and when she realized she wasn't putting anything away, she got discouraged.

She dated a sailor during the Korean War, and, in a weak moment, she agreed to marry him. ("He was cute," she told Calvin later. "He had such a wonderful little bottom and I wasn't unhappy with his legs.") She followed him out to San Diego where he was stationed and spent the war years cooped up in a trailer outside the naval base. When he was off duty, Scott flew model planes in the brush. He would get up before dawn and not return until dark. The humidity was terrible, and the damp got into her books, ruining the imitation leather covers on her Shakespeare set.

He resented her books, and when she read, he paced, complaining about the way the trailer looked. Once when she had just gotten through mopping, he took the mop away from her, ran fresh water, worked up the suds, and started over. "I'll show you how it's done," he said, "and if you watch carefully, for once, you just might learn something that don't come from a book." She could not get him involved in any of her interests, and when she once corrected his English, he hit her across the mouth. He was not usually violent. He was evidently ashamed of what he had done, and he immediately walked out, staying away all night. ("Why," she asked Calvin later, "did I put up with all that? It's a mystery to me, but I was still young. I was still wet behind the ears. I didn't have anymore gumption then than Lu Ann.")

She felt dependent and determined, without an education or a job, out there alone in the desert, in the humidity and the heat, where you could not hear anything but other couples fighting, the endless, identical bluegrass music, and his model airplane engines that sounded like wounded gnats. When he was discharged, they moved in with her parents until they could get settled, but he wouldn't seriously look for work. He was only interested in flying model planes and hanging out with his old friends. He was finally less interested in his planes than in just drifting, and when he met some Beats who were passing through in a van—heading west again, where you could get some serious thinking done in the wide open spaces, he decided to join them. He went without packing or taking his planes.

She divorced him and went back to work in the telephone company because she could not see any other options open, but when T. C. died less than a year later, having a stroke while he was working under his truck, she decided that if she was going to college, she was going to have to act now if she was ever going to act. She borrowed T. C.'s insurance money from Darlene and she started in at Indiana University, working toward a teacher's certificate in two areas because she felt talented in both. She didn't go anywhere during those early years. She didn't date and she certainly didn't have sex. ("I just studied like a house on fire," she said. "Of course, Darlene was worried about her money. *She* kept her eye on me every minute, just waiting for one false step.") She wasn't making any false step.

A freeze set in, glazing and hardening the snow, sealing in that winter underworld which completely darkened shortly after four o'clock. Worried about the pipes, Calvin kept his faucets dripping all night. If he had city gas, he did not have city water, and he also worried about the pump. It was on a separate fuse box, and the fuse kept blowing. He had called twice, but couldn't get anybody out. Sheila looked around his fuse box with a flashlight—admitting for once that she did not know what she was doing, but willing to be interested in the problem. She was not exactly living with him, but she was in and out a lot. "Just to be sure you're still alive," she explained, "in this elegant, overpriced tomb of yours."

They spent most of their time in bed in the master bedroom at the back of the house. They kept the drapes pulled and a table lamp lit. They did not leave the bed unless somebody was interested in a fresh drink or a light snack.

Calvin usually drank gin. Sheila would drink a martini if he fixed it, but she leaned toward bourbon. She drank it on the rocks. She did not like any mixes. She said that mixes always made her feel slightly sickish, and what was the point of diluting a good drink, anyway?

She did not eat much, but she liked steak. When he once fixed her a steak sandwich, she refused the bread. She lifted the lid and pulled out the meat. She said that sandwiches were a waste of time, when she just wanted to get at the basics. When you thought about it, who actually needed that much wheat?

He once told her that a good shot of bourbon was her staff of life, but she was not amused because she was not so sure about the implications behind that. "I can handle it," she said, her face turned reddish, her small jaw set.

She could surprise him in many ways. Although she could talk a steady streak, she wasn't above listening. When they had finished their lovemaking, when she had a fresh drink, she would pound several pillows into shape above her head, light a cigarette, lie back and let him ramble.

He circled the Cape trip several times. "In any case, my grandparents argued about Mercy's house over her grave," he said, picking up where he had left off after his jaunt downstairs to freshen their drinks. "He wanted to sell it. She wanted to keep it. My mother spoke up, probably for the first time in her life. 'Oh, *stop* it!' she cried, 'Just *stop* it, *both* of you!' Nobody had ever heard her so angry before, and they stopped it. My grandfather changed the subject. She convinced them that their arguing over the old lady's grave was pretty tacky, and, for once in her life, she held down the fort. She put down her foot. Her color was high, and, for a moment, she even frightened me."

Sheila stretched across him to reach her cigarettes. "Sarah Elizabeth, though, is the colorful one in that bunch. I don't imagine she misses much."

"When we got back to the house, my father was waiting for us. He had shown up out of nowhere, after all those years. He had come for the funeral, but he had missed it. He was just beginning to get on his feet. He had a business project in mind—a business project! He wanted to borrow some money from my grandfather."

"He wasn't a subtle type."

"He patted me on the head, a stranger. He had wanted a girl in the first place. He did not know how to handle boys.

Any male at all was competition, just because another male. He wanted to be unique. He wanted to be alone in the world with himself."

His straw hat, his striped coat, out of fashion even then. His long arms, wide hands, and strong cologne. "He considered lifting me up, but he thought better of it. 'Well, son,' he said, watching my mother go up into the house alone, trying to escape him, 'here we all are, a united family again.'"

"Oh, bull roar!"

"I never knew what he believed himself and didn't. I never knew what *I* believed and didn't."

"Well, you can always take that kind with a grain of salt."

"My mother was slightly off balance that whole day, and when *he* showed up for the funeral—late, out of nowhere, a bolt from the blue after all those years, she was further thrown off balance. I was fourteen then. I tried to comfort her. 'Oh,' she said, still upset, 'and just *what* do you suppose you *can* do?'"

"Well, what could you?"

"She didn't fall apart when he walked out the first time. She still thought she loved him, or claimed so, or at least *needed* him. She needed her self-respect. His walking out could have been seen as a reflection on her. Sarah Elizabeth had no time for him at all, but *she* saw it that way. Women then were supposed to endure.

"In any case, she didn't fall apart the first time. She coped. She brought me up to Connecticut, into her people's house, and she went back to school. She finished getting her music degree and she taught. She made her own way. She came to terms with her own life as best she could. She was reasonably happy. And then, out of nowhere, he returned. What was she supposed to do? Take him back? She was still married to him, and, given the time, given her straitlaced family at least, I guess that's what she thought she was supposed to do."

"She should have stood up to Sarah Elizabeth."

"And what could *I* do? Did I think I was going to get rid

of him myself? Did I even really want to? Fern once said I carry around more mixed feelings about him than I realize."

"Oh, *fuss*! What would *she* know? You certainly married a lot of not very bright people."

He did not reply. He was still off. He was still wondering about Fern's remark.

"Come here," she said.

He looked up.

She took the cigarette out of his hands. She kneeled in front of him on the bed, gripped him from behind the knees and tried to part his legs. Now nobody had ever gone down on him before, but he still knew what she had in mind. He started to sit up further, but she pushed him back with her free hand at the same time, her fingers spread across his bare chest. He shook his head. "I feel too separated from myself right now," he said.

"Oh, piffle! Don't be so picky! Seize the day. Grab the opportunity while you can. Just let go. Just relax, will you?" she ordered, just before her head disappeared between his knees.

So, all right, he thought, let go. Always the same question, though: *If* he let go, just where was he going?

SEVEN

Calvin started planting soon after his third marriage. He turned up with redbud and dogwood, willow, pin oak, and Chinese elm. He turned up loaded down with flats. Getting the nurseryman's advice, soon forgetting the flowers' names, he started with hardy, basic stuff, the beginner's sure bets: pansies and petunias, waxy begonias and gaudy snapdragons, moss roses in many colors because they spread quickly and continued to bloom through the sticky months. Planning to blend in the backyard with the extra yard behind it, less "yard" now than vacant space, spongy and brown, he spread his purchases out across the two lots, worrying about the final effect. Fussing, he arranged and rearranged. What if he had overbought? What if it just ended up looking like a public park?

Sheila directed from the patio away from the wind, gesturing with a cigarette and a drink in the same hand. She was in halter and shorts with cute cuffs. Very stylish, and she was proud of her good legs. She crossed her knees.

She looked pleased, watching him watch his little empire take shape, his kingdom, but she did not admit it because you could spoil him. She slapped at something flying around her head. "I hope you know what you're doing. Spread out the moss roses more, for one thing. You're putting them too close together."

Sheila's mother was visiting. Darlene Foss was short and small, slightly taller-looking than she was, given the bouffant hair stiffly sprayed, the rigid shoulders; but thin, prim mouth, sharp, prim chin, the alert jawline long and narrow. She was sitting sideways on the picnic bench, claiming to be more comfortable there than in the patio chairs that dipped, clung, encased. She wanted back support. When out of her element, when out of her own house, in fact, she was wary, rigid, too exact, too polite, too willing to please strangers. (In compensation, she was strident when she addressed her daughter.) This edgy quality affected her breathing. She got all her air from the upper parts of her chest. She was less endowed than her daughter. She had a trim figure, and she stayed in shape. She had her hands at her throat, playing with her costume pearls. "Let him alone, *goodness*! He must know what he's doing. Why are you always ordering him around?"

Darlene was sleeping in the newly furnished guest room, its decor Sheila's choice: cream-colored French provincial, fat little night chests trimmed with gold on each side of the big bed. She had also turned the fourth bedroom into her den. She had left her public school job and started graduate school because she wanted to end up teaching in college. She was always reading or working on some paper. When Calvin came home, he could hear the typewriter going in her den, the paints and canvases pushed back, the floor littered with paper. She would appear for a drink while he fixed the meal, her look distant, her mind elsewhere, and when she finished dinner, she got back at it upstairs. When she started a paper, she liked to stick with it.

She was also a graduate assistant, where she was making contacts. She took him to parties where he met a loose collection of settled young couples who were trying to struggle through on graduate assistantships or slim instructors' salaries. He ran into several unmarried drifters, in and out of this university and that, trying to teach while they finished their degree. Both groups were fairly conventional. They threw bottle parties and kept an extra gallon of Gallo on ice in the kitchen sink. Most guests brought beer. Sheila came with an unopened bottle of bourbon from her stock, and while someone was trying to help her with her coat, she was already looking for a glass. She drank fairly hard at these events because she said she had it coming. "I can crank out the work in white heat," she said, "but I feel fairly done in afterwards. I feel like an old draft horse."

She wanted too much, everything; through sheer spunk and drive she was going to maintain opposite worlds, mix and match: the scholar-artist's and the solid middle-class life. She was not a Beat; she courted permanence and respectability; she needed the house as a setting for her free spirit; he could bury her in trees and flowers, keeping them both happy. Things should be expensive and tasteful, assuming they showed. She loved cashmere sweaters, skirts, coats, but when she went to bed, she cast off a battered, grungy bra, an old pair of his briefs, and slept in a T-shirt. (Why spend money on what couldn't be seen?) She cleaned the same way. In certain specifics, she *was* middle class, too. In fact, uninterested in politics, in foreign affairs, she was a natural Republican. Like her mother, she trusted power.

She got up to freshen her drink. On the way back from the kitchen, she let out the half-grown kittens. She did not let them out unless she was around. They scampered around her ankles now. She had to work her way around them back to the patio chair. "I still say you could separate the moss roses more. But . . . do what you want to," she said, sitting down. "He will, too. You watch."

As usual, Calvin only heard what he wanted to hear. Like her, he was locked into his own notions. Besides, even "suggestions" turned into orders in his own mind. In khaki shorts and T-shirt, but good imported pumps, dark blue silk socks, he brought the hose around without thinning the moss roses out.

"He's going to ruin those shoes, but he won't wear the sandals that I got. He won't take off his socks, in either case. He's getting a good tan, though. Very sexy, too, and at night I like the white parts."

"*Please*, Sheila!" Darlene said, more angry than shocked. "I *don't* want to know about your private life!"

"Oh, come *off* it! You've heard about sex before, at one time or another, and you know it!"

"Well, you can *spare* me the details!"

"I'm taking him out of himself."

138

"Well, he spoils you. He spoils you rotten!"

"Oh, fiddle-faddle! *He's* spoiled, too. He's having the time of his life. He's just half-starting to relax."

He was getting used to being spoiled, if just. The florid, hothouse honeymoon period did not let up. It was a wonder. Her need for him—perhaps doubly obvious because his former wives had not appeared to need him or had not shown it, was grandly operatic and constant. After his years of so-called neglect, of women going their own way, anticipating his going his, he wasn't sure he didn't enjoy possessiveness.

At the same time, he had difficulty getting his work done. When he wasn't on the air, he was involved in a lot of leg-work, running people down, handling the sponsors and the format, putting the show together. When he wasn't actually on the air, though, where she could see him, she couldn't understand why he wasn't home, there—with her. They had had some early arguments over the problem. ("Oh, piffle! Piffle-dew! You could get somebody *else* to do the legwork, couldn't you? You *love* running all over the town, impressing people, and you know it!")

"Anyway," she was saying, "I have to tell him what needs doing next. He's cute, but he doesn't have the sense he was born with. He wouldn't *have* a pair of sandals if I hadn't bought them. I also got him a pair of pedal pushers, which he won't wear, either. He lives in his own world. He isn't always tied to this one," she pointed out, proudly—pleased with her find, this ornament she could afford. She shook her head, as if he were a real trial. He was a step or two up from her father, and she did not care if her mother noted the fact. "He's just a baby! But you know men! He neglects his responsibilities. He hasn't seen his own grandmother for years, his closest surviving relative."

What she couldn't run, she kept harping about. He was now only half amused. He looked up with the hose in his hands. "You don't know her, Sheila. She doesn't need me. She likes her privacy and her independence. She'll go out of her way to get both."

Sheila looked at Darlene for a moment. She raised her brows. She shook her head. "Well, there you are! See what I mean?"

Darlene put her half-touched drink down beside her on the picnic bench. "Well, he must *know*. How would *you* know?"

"Oh, piffle! Pish-tosh! *I* know what old ladies like and don't like even if you two don't. She just needs a little attention. Someone to fuss over her a bit. Someone to bring her out of herself. He's neglected her for years, and he knows it. When we can both get some time off, we'll visit. I'll take her out to dinner and buy her a new hat."

"Oh, yes!" he said, stopping to light a cigarette, cupping the flame inside his hands, "here we are. Here I am, with my third wife. Out of the blue. We'll see what Sarah Elizabeth thinks. If she doesn't approve, I can always take her back. She won't. Why should she?"

"Oh, fiddle-faddle! Fiddlesticks! In the *first* place, those pokey women you married before don't count. You didn't have *real* marriages then, and you know it. She must know it. In the *second*, you just *think* you can't stand up to her. Well, if you can't, I can!" she said. "Mother? What about your drink? You've hardly touched it."

Darlene put her hand over her glass. "No. I don't want any more before dinner."

Sheila got up. "Hint, hint. All right, all right! You can help me set the table."

"Well, look at the *time*. When do *you eat*? You both need to *eat*, don't you? It's *after* six!"

"I ran a tight ship, but I was wasting my talents in high school," Sheila said over dinner, on the edge of explaining herself to her mother. "It was beneath me. It was using up too many of my energies, and for what? I was baby-sitting, essentially, and with my brain. I was just keeping them off the streets. It doesn't *take* half a mind to do that. It just takes someone with a club."

Darlene put her water glass down. She put her hand up to her neck. "And *what* are you going to do with your time, just *waste* your education?"

140

"Oh, *Mother*! *Come off* it! Stop worrying about what it *cost* you! I told you, anyway. If you ever *listened*. If you ever *heard* anything! I'm back *in* school. I'm getting a graduate degree. I'm going to teach in college, where people care. Where I can use what I have, where I'm appreciated!"

He did not say much at the table. He was still smarting over her invasion of his privacy in the backyard: organizing, taking his past for granted.

She took a fresh drink with her to bed. She put it down on the night chest while she was still talking about graduate school. She had to get a paper done by Monday. "That so-called professor is a first-class bonehead, though," she said. "He's a cinch. *I* know where *my* A's come from! My high IQ and pure sweat. But he'll also hand out top grades to just about *anybody* coming down the pike. When I start thinking about it, I *just* boil."

She stretched across him to reach her diaphragm, her bra still on, bunching up her big breasts. "*You're* very quiet. Are you *sore* about something, or what?"

"You can't handle everything, Sheila. You can't handle Sarah Elizabeth."

She jellied her diaphragm and rolled over on her back. Knees up, legs spread, she worked in the rubber cup. "Oh, hush. Just hush! We'll cross that bridge when we come to it. You're *really* worried about my going back to school, and you know it. Well, have you been neglected? Have you had any less sex? I can handle both. I won't cut you out. I'll always be right here! Offering you everything you never had!"

He raked the leaves in the fall under the tall, shaggy nut trees, pulling them from around the sides of the house toward the front. He kept them in long even rows until he reached the edges of the grass, where he separated them into several piles, then burned them in the street. The smoke slumbered in among the curled, acrid, dusty stuff, then gradually drifted up into the moist, windless air.

He did not have as much time to work around the house as he wanted. He was getting ready to take on a second show, a **PBS** project that was left fairly open. He could choose his own topic from an array of possible interests: art, travel, politics, books, economics, people, antiques. He had discovered Indiana auctions that summer. Ideal excursions: the day off, the weather warm, the girls in backless dresses or worn, tight, cut-down denims, the cars nosed in, the crowds milling through the streets in those tiny, sleepy, sun-drenched towns. He had picked up two empty steamer trunks for practically nothing.

Sheila stayed busy. She had started last spring taking courses unrelated to her degree just because various subjects took her fancy. She had stayed up half the night working on ancient Greek, and while she was involved, still enthusiastic, she pulled down one A after another in the vocabulary work. She passed the other students in the class the way she drove on the highway; she would pass one car after another, taking this one, then that, pushing down on the accelerator, curving around the last car until she had a clear, open stretch ahead.

She finally came home grumbling about the professor, another bonehead. A language teacher, he knew his Greek, perhaps, but he had no real feel for the literature as such. Any serious idea was obviously beyond him. He did not understand Greek tragedy, and he certainly did not understand Greek myth. She also said that she was growing less interested in teaching college, anyway. What was the point, if she was just stuck around here? What was the incentive if she couldn't teach in a first-class eastern school?

She dropped graduate school because she decided that she was going back to painting, her first love, her chief talent, and why not settle down, try to get somewhere with it? She worked around the clock up in her den on her hands and knees, circling the huge abstraction on the floor (sharp lines, jagged points, dark colors, a single ray of light), her brushes stuck in Ball jars, crumpled tubes, wadded cloths, paint thinners, and old newspapers in every corner. Talking to herself, she dragged on a cigarette and then abandoned it, letting it burn down on the edges of a dish that was crowded

142

with half-finished cigarettes. She would pick up a beer and then forget that.

She appeared now to tell him he was wanted on the phone. She stood in the side garage door in a dressing gown with puffed sleeves, his present. He called, wanting her to admire his work—this precision, order. She stayed in the doorway, gingerly admiring, without moving. Her pale eyes watered. "I can't come any farther with this drip I have," she said, a damp tissue balled up in her fist. "I'm happy for you, though. You've been out here all day, just tearing up the pea patch."

Charley was in Chicago on a business trip, and he was flying down for a visit. He wanted to see the house. "Besides," he said, "I have to keep tabs on your various marriages."

Calvin picked him up at the Indianapolis airport. Charley discussed Floyd on the way back. He had disappeared again shortly after Dienbienphu. Then he surfaced shortly after the Lebanon crisis. He was briefly home, looking in on his family. He checked up on Fern and his new nephew, then he was off. "Someone finally had a letter. He was in Bien Hoa, and he turned up in Guatamala. Where is Bien Hoa? What was he doing in Guatamala? He's a very sinister person, a part of an invisible pattern in the world."

"I tried getting visiting rights when I sued for divorce from here. Nobody could do much or wanted to do much. I'm not sure which. But I gathered I have to fight for visiting rights where the child resides. That means going into their territory, and that won't be easy. I'd have to face their judge."

"He's almost four."

"I *know* he's almost four. Which is also why I'll have trouble getting visiting rights anywhere, right now anyway. I'll have to wait until he's older."

"Floyd doesn't look the same these days. He used to like a little soft living, even him. Do you remember how he used to tie into that foreign food? He's given up drinking, and he doesn't eat meat. Fern went back to school full time to get a degree. She's got a good job in a library up there."

143

Sheila dressed for the event. She was in a pale green cashmere sweater, a big uplift bar, big cartwheel earrings, chains, and checkered pants. She sent Calvin up to change into his pedal pushers and polo shirt. "He wouldn't, if I didn't order," she said.

She kept referring to Calvin as "the new man," her creation. She said that he was already a lot less frozen than he had been, before she had come into the picture. There were still changes to make, but he was coming along. Didn't Charley think he was coming along?

Charley was admiring the house, and he had his back to her. "What would a place like this run him, out here in the west, anyway?"

"You'd have to ask him. He bought it before I showed up, and he never discusses such things with me."

She told Charley several times that he would be much more comfortable if he took off his hot-looking suitcoat. Charley didn't. He watched her closely, as if he were trying to put a lot together, but he kept his own counsel.

Calvin appeared in the same clothes. He set the table, cooked the dinner, and brought the wine in. Sheila seemed more guest than not. She came to the table with a fresh drink. She put the glass down, next to the wine, with great care, but, still unsatisfied, she moved the wine glass farther back.

Charley took all this in. He wasn't much taller than Sheila. Calvin decided that they resembled each other for some reason. Charley caught his eye on him. "Well, buddy, what do you think of the country out here?"

"I love Indiana place names. Pauses in the road, crossings, and spots: Homer and Horace, Acton and Arcadia, Palestine and Noah, Gnaw Bone, Sunny Bend, Bean Blossom and Mount Comfort."

Sheila pushed back the salad as if it were an unpleasant object. She picked at the steak for a minute but returned to her drink. "How can he remember all those names and then call every flower a coleus? How can he get the commonest things mixed up, *in this world,* and still claim to have a business head?"

"He has a business head," Charley said, looking at Calvin. "He's just several people."

"Oh, he's instructive. He's a mixed metaphor, but cute."

"He's from New England."

"Oh, New England. That is as it may be," she observed, sounding detached, crisp, and exact, as if she had meant much more than she had actually said. She was always extra precise, extra exact in the early stages of drinking, as if she were determined to watch herself. However, she could soon pass over into loosened, slurred speech.

(He loved her. Indiana natives will sometimes still use *doctor* as a verb. They'll say, "Who do you do your doctoring with?" Sheila said, "With whom do you do your doctoring?")

He was soon talking about Josh Scudder, the last miller in the family tree, an important man. Millers had once served such a crucial function that they were not taxed, were not pressed into military service, and were not expected to hold public office. Josh was a drinker, a reader, a steady talker, who would debate any point when he was in his cups. "He claimed, for instance, that he did not believe in original sin. He stressed the human will instead. Change, he claimed, was possible, and, if he tried, a man could do better. He was often fined for such foolishness, but the town needed its miller, and he was never severely punished. He was never warned out."

Sheila shook her head and pressed her lips together with mild amusement. "Here comes one of his many stories. I listen to them all, very faithfully, as I should, and when he's done, I divide by half."

"In any case, he fished a half-drowned fifteen-year-old from a salt pond in the middle of a Cape winter. He carried her over his shoulder through the howling winds and stood her up in front of his fire. That was the Hand of God, or so the town said. Take their pious married life. It appeared to

145

set him up. His drinking slowed and his strange ideas partly ceased. He would sit in a corner, his head down, staring at his huge hands, while she talked a mile a minute, pointing out his many remaining faults. However, he still believed that change was possible, and a man, if he tried, could do better. She finally perished under mysterious circumstances in that same pond during another rough winter."

Sheila hadn't been listening. She was still thinking about the Cape. "I always thought those people were all sea captains," she said, speaking too soon, blurring the story's point. "I always thought they caught whales, or whatever."

He watched her closely, noted the small, floating, disconnected movements with the wrists, the hands. She held her empty glass toward him. "Freshen this for me, will you?"

He did not move. She did not need another. "I'm talking about the seventeenth century. You're in the eighteenth. Besides, the Scudders didn't go to sea. Everybody didn't."

"You just *might* check your guests, too, *if* you're of a mind. If you can interrupt your history lesson that long."

Charley looked at his glass and shook his head.

She got up to fill her own. "*They* didn't go to sea because they were so busy buying up all the land in sight," she said, coming back. "No fools, they."

Now she was talking about his Connecticut grandfather. He did not correct her. What was the use?

She tested her fresh drink and got it back down beside her plate without spilling much. "None of *his* people ever let their hair down. He didn't, either, until he met me, and he knows it . . . I *still* feel sorry for Sarah Elizabeth, though. He ignores her, even though she's about all he has left. His various wives kept them apart."

"It had nothing to do with my wives. She's independent."

"Oh, independent my foot! We've been down that road before. You're her only grandson, aren't you? He's a stick in the mud, like her," she said, turning to Charley. "When he isn't working, when he isn't on TV, or tearing around town, impressing people, you couldn't get him out of his own backyard. He sits around communicating with his many trees, like an old Druid. You can't expect her to leave you any money if you won't *visit* her, can you?"

She switched the subject. She knew that Charley was a convert, having married a Catholic. She talked about theology for awhile, leaning across the table with her drink. She wanted to know what he thought about the Pope's stand on birth control, but when Charley looked uncomfortable, she did not push it. She was always ready to oblige. She said that she was interested in Paul Tillich. She was reading all of Tillich she could get her hands on because if there was the slightest hope for modern religion, he was it.

Charley hadn't heard of him. "Calvin tells me you're back in college," he said.

"He may have *told* you that. I'm not now. I wasn't getting anywhere in that extension which *claims* to have university status. That wasn't particularly academic, and I'm well out of it. I paint and read a lot instead. Why should I stagnate? Does anybody here know any good reason why I should stagnate?"

She carried out a few dishes after the meal but soon forgot about them. While she was in the kitchen she freshened her drink. Charley was standing in the doorway while Calvin was at the sink. He was talking to him about some stocks. Sheila put her fingers under Charley's elbow for a minute, her long, red nails glittering against his suitcoat. "Oh, what's so important about business? Boys and business! You two really don't have a lick of sense now, do you, and you know it!"

Calvin took Charley out into the backyard. They paused on the patio in the close, mild, humid evening air. They heard the two cats under their feet, but, as they went down the steps, the cats scurried ahead. The men walked through the recently raked yard, and when they reached the second lot, Charley leaned against a tree trunk.

They talked about world affairs: Nixon's Moscow visit, his candidacy, and the stock market. Calvin was buying into electronics. He was also thinking about purchasing some land south of Indianapolis. The whole strip was eventually going to open up between Indianapolis and Bloomington.

The patio door panel slid back. Sheila was standing there looking around, outlined against the family room light behind her. She looked uncertain, mildly surprised to discover that she had lost her focus. She reached for the top rail, and, for a moment, she looked as if she were going to come down the steps. "Calvin? Are you out there?"

He didn't answer.

"Calvin?" She sounded fretful, and she hesitated. "*Cal?*" she called, louder. Then she suddenly went back into the house.

Charley looked up into the tall nut trees that were scattered through the extra lot behind the house. He admired the new plantings. "This is a great place. Very pleasant. And great trees. They always help the resale value, trees like that."

Calvin could hear the cats ahead in the bushes. He could hear the small paws trying their footing.

"Would I be out of order if I asked you what you paid for this?"

Calvin told him.

Charley whistled and shook his head. "Christ! Do you *know* what this would run you in Connecticut?"

When Sheila opened the panel the second time, she was very drunk. She stood there swaying openly, holding her glass against her chest with both hands. She called again. She tried to manage the three steps while holding onto the rail. The men could hear the ice cubes rattling against the sides of her glass as she came down the steps. In the shadows now, she finally sat down heavily on the bottom step. Because she was briefly quiet, the men knew she was having a drink.

She finally stood again. Swaying, she held onto the rail. She was trying to peer out. "Calvin! Calvin! Are you there? I know you're out there! I know you're out there because I can hear the cats. They're with you, aren't they? They're with you, out there in the poison ivy, and if you don't get it, they will. If you don't get it, they will, and I'll have to deal with poison ivy in here for days. Their eyes swell up. I don't suppose you know that, do you? I don't suppose you know that cats can catch poison ivy, too, and when they do, their eyes swell up."

Calvin said nothing. Charley cleared his throat. They could hear the two cats in the neighbor's yard now, stepping in some brambles which he had pulled out earlier in the week. They could also hear the ice cubes rattling against the sides of her glass.

When she spoke again, her voice had changed. "Calvin," she said, as if really asking, really interested, "what's so important about business? What's so important about that?"

She was quiet for another moment. "Calvin," she finally said, louder. "I know your problems. I know you have problems, but I'm prepared to deal with them. I'm prepared to cope because I know what's wrong. Do you know that? Do you know I know what's wrong?"

She paused again, as if giving her question a chance to sink in. "You haven't accepted yourself yet, have you?" she asked, her voice rising. "Calvin? I'm going to tell you something."

She was quiet for a few more seconds. "YOU ARE ACCEPTED! YOU ARE A PERSON!"

Calvin finally stirred. "I've got to go in before she wakes the neighbors," he said.

Calvin bought fireplace wood. The fuel, hickory, ash, oak, coming down from the country in a pickup, was backed into the wide, two-car drive. The farmer stacked it in the garage, arranged against the right wall, done with such precision that the compact rick looked permanently arranged, set. The farmer—cleaning out the truck, leaving everything because paid for—would also leave the litter. Calvin swept up the small branches, broken twigs, wood dust, and pungent chips.

He carried in several big pieces before dinner and built on his knees, tenderly working with the splinters and the paper. While the kindling cracked, sputtered, and briefly caught, the flames often quieted, going down, partly out. He rebuilt from scratch. By dinnertime, the good-sized flames finally licked through the heavy stuff. Shadows crossed the ceiling. He separated the glowing embers and pulled the screens across the hearth before they went up to bed in the changed air, the faint, ashy chill.

He stopped to pick up the brandy in the kitchen, where the accumulating dishes sat in the sink, soaking in cold, grayish water. Garbage in brown, spotted paper bags leaned against the wall. He took out the garbage and then veered off toward the utility room to wash his hands. The laundry, brought down from various parts of the house, sat unsorted, spread out across the utility room floor. To get in, he had to shove the door against it. The cats sat nesting on the clothes inside the open dryer, looking out. While he washed his hands, they stared at him without moving, interested in the process. He picked them up and closed the dryer. Coming through the house with the brandy bottle and the glasses, he turned off the lights and locked the doors on his trip. Since she did not empty the cat box often enough, the cats sometimes used the rugs, and the living room rug now had blanched, unfresh, touched-up smudges. There were claw marks in the curtains and on the sides of the chairs.

He passed her empty den upstairs. She was working on a philosophical novel in there—the huge, unfinished abstraction propped against a wall, face in, the paint, brushes and pallet knives stacked in a fishing tackle box, the various thinners and paint rags still on the floor. He worried about a fire when he wandered around in there, among the papers and books in disarray, pulled down from the shelves, the filled ashtrays and discarded cigarette cartons. She wouldn't clean because she said she knew where everything was, just as it was, and she might want to go back to painting at any minute. The clutter, because not his, an invasion, threw him slightly off balance. The anger, half-repressed, irrational, increased his vertigo.

"And you talk," she had said, standing in his den, where he had brought the two steamer trunks, now filled with Indiana lore, but neatly stacked: odds and ends picked up from auctions—old albums, journals, postcards, letters. He had a rolltop desk, a Tiffany lamp, two Morris chairs and several huge ebony picture frames leaning against one wall. The upright 1930 Philco no longer worked. "I don't see how you can get anything done in here." He didn't. He worked in his office on Meridian, a functional cell with a modern desk, a couch, several file cabinets, and a hanging coleus. His escape route. When she brought it up, he changed the subject. "All innocence, aren't you? I can imagine what you'd like to be up to down there." She couldn't. He worked. He wasn't a woman-chaser, as such. She knew, too. She finally felt safe.

Elegant in public, in cashmere sweaters, soft wool skirts, she slept in his castoff, unfresh T-shirts, torn at the shoulders, stained around the neck. She slept in her eyeshadow, eyelash paint. While she got ready, she kept a cigarette burning in the filled ashtray on the bedside chest, somewhere within reach among the sticky, empty glasses, the books, the journals, the cigarettes, the girdle with attached stockings and big, soiled, battered-looking bra cups. She was sitting up now holding her bourbon and a cigarette in the same hand.

"I didn't know you had a drink. I brought the brandy."

"Set it down there, then. I can eventually use it."

"I have to get up early."

She liked to talk until two or three. She raised her brows but did not comment on his plans. She watched him while he undressed. "I've been working hard. I've got two chapters completed, just by pushing it. I'm not *positive* about it. I don't know whether I should show you what I'm about, or not. What do you think?"

Her uncharacteristic uncertainty caught him off guard. Well, and what? He did not bother her with what he was doing on Meridian. . . . When difficulties came, demands made, he feared depletion, diminishment. "If I'm going to see it, if I'm going to judge, then perhaps I ought to have the whole thing first."

"Oh, yes. I suppose. Still, you know, I'm not sure I *want* you to 'judge,' as you so precisely put it. I may just want to share it."

Still in his briefs and socks, he shaved in the master bathroom—in all that white and gold trim, matching carriage lamps beside the oval mirror. His reflection struck him as strange: dark, aggressive, closed, unsafe. He saw his father's jawline, his father's chin.

He was soon in the middle of a long story—back on his father's sudden appearance after Mercy's funeral and the trip home. He returned with them, taking it for granted that he was going, was wanted. He was at least trying to brazen it out in the continuing, unspoken tensions, the high, clear silence, in the face of their refusal to accept or reject him yet. Everybody was evidently waiting for someone else to act: to say *you have definitely interrupted our routine, the established if sterile order of our lives.* ("So, crazy man, go away!")

He returned with them: father, mother and son sitting in the back of the Hudson, unnatural to have him there, unnatural to have him that close, unnatural to have him in the back, not driving, but in the rear where the women and the children usually sat. And while they passed through the patches of sun and shade, leaving the Cape in the middle of the week, in the June heat, Calvin (I; he; the other; the buried child) seemed keyed up with this unnaturalness, pro and con. He felt dizzy and rattled, sitting beside the hitchhiker who rested with his head on the back of the seat, his eyes closed, his long arms across his lap, his wide hands loosely clasped. If he could talk a blue streak, he was in their hands now, and briefly mute. He slept. There are people who appear to stay unperturbed all their lives—whatever they do, whatever outrages they commit. Then there are the others, the innocents, who squint, cough, squirm, flush, blow their noses, clear their throats. How uneasy they are, how guilty they seem, just trying to fill the gaps, the vacuum that some great injustice has left!

He was back in the bedroom wandering around, looking for his pajamas. "I can still see the light hair on the backs of his hands, those pale, wide hands, more stuff at the wrists, below his coat's short sleeves. Where did he think we were heading? Why didn't someone take charge?"

152

He was still trying to find his pajamas. He opened a second drawer, fishing in around the unmatched socks, two stray ties, several rumpled sport shirts covered with fine cat hairs.

"I don't know what you'd do if you couldn't talk about all this, sweetie. And I'm here to listen. As those others couldn't."

He was suddenly very tired, and in his new, sudden effort to stay calm, to ignore the chaotic bureau drawers, he certainly did not want to continue his senseless, self-indulgent recollections.

She was going to pursue her point, too. "Because they couldn't, could they?" She put her empty glass down and picked up the brandy bottle. From bourbon to brandy, and once half-warmed, she would stay on that subject all night. "I'm not muddleheaded, library-oriented, dimly withdrawn, like the last sheep-faced, flat-chested ex-nun you managed to get mixed up with, back when you were blind, when you were frozen yourself, half dead. Before you found out about *real* life! When you didn't have a lick of sense, as cute as you must have been, and you know it. Well, I saved you from that!"

She was suddenly up, weaving across the room, a lot more drunk now than he had realized, off into the connecting bathroom. Still talking through the open door, she lowered the toilet seat and sat down. "And you call her innocent! Innocent, my foot! She was about as innocent as a ticking time bomb!"

He slammed the bureau drawer shut as she came through. "I can't make any *sense* out of these drawers! Why do we have to *live* like this! Why is *every* room in the place in this shape! Why can't we have a little order!"

Bleary-eyed and slack-jawed, she stood wavering in the middle of the room for a minute. Then her whole face changed. She grew rigid. Her eyes narrowed. "Oh, I *knew that* was coming! Sooner or later! I could smell *that* in the wind! I knew I was going to be *gotten* there! Well, I'm not your servant! If you want a servant, go get a servant!"

He picked up his brandy glass. "Oh, God! I just want a *wife*, Sheila!"

"There are matters more important than housecleaning, then!" She was hissing, spitting, furious. Blood left her face, then flushed back through it. She was having trouble breathing. "There's *sharing*, for one! And you don't *share*, do you? I share! I listen! I listen, but you *don't*! You couldn't care less! You don't know anything about me, and you don't want to! As COLD as you are!"

"Oh, pull yourself together! Cut down on your drinking!"

"OH, GET OFF IT! GET OFF ME! WHOEVER TOLD YOU *YOU* DIDN'T DRINK! WHAT MAKES YOU SO SUPERIOR!"

He suddenly realized how much he hated her. He didn't need her. He wanted to be free of her—free of all these bombasts, these outbursts, and, at the same time, he withdrew. His sense of removal gathered in his chest, branched out through his head, behind the eyes. The blood-pounding fury was gone. He just felt cold.

She could go on and on, far into the night, more powerful than he when these rages came, but she didn't.

She passed out instead. She was soon snoring on her back, her mouth open, her cigarette burning in a dish.

He put out her cigarette and finished the brandy. The drink gradually diminished his sense of removal, and without that wall, his needs and insecurities returned.

He rolled her over, pushed up the T-shirt and battered her from behind while she was still out. He did not have much difficulty entering because, as drunk as she was, she was completely loose, relaxed. He finally freed himself.

She woke him in the middle of the night. She half sat up, worried and distraught because she thought they had gone to bed without making love. "What's wrong, Calvin? What's wrong?" she kept asking, still half asleep. "Don't you want sex? Don't you want me tonight?"

She attacked the house the next day. She swept and scrubbed. She brought the last of the laundry down and started the washing. She wheeled the vacuum cleaner out. She changed the cat box. She ran fresh water over the dishes. If she worked with such concentration and single-mindedness, she was less angry with him than intent on getting the job done. She was facing it, plowing in, then planning to move on. She worked as if a house *could* be "done," those tasks ever finished, put behind her once and for all.

She straightened her den: the A papers going back to high school, the early college years, aimed toward the teaching certificate, her teaching notes, aids, slides, student tests, her graduate work, projects started and never completed, her painting, the abandoned novel. (Soaked in sex, generally hazy about specifics, he didn't know when she had given up the book. When he finally noticed, she did not want to talk about it. She was short with him on the subject. He didn't take offense. He was patient. He didn't push. He respected her privacy.)

When she finished the house, she shopped. She came back with a crisp, new waistless sheath, patent purse, matching patent pumps with slender heels, pointed toes, then a small veiled, fussy pillbox hat. She had her hair done, trimmed expensively below the ears, carefully curled, and frosted.

Then she wanted to do something, go somewhere. She called Denver, hinting about coming out for a visit, and when that didn't take, she invited Lu Ann back to Indiana for Christmas. "What a cluck!" she said as soon as she got off the bedroom phone. "She's in one of her many states and won't admit it. I can tell, and bored. I may be able to do something about it. She needs taking out of herself."

He left the shower and reached for a towel. Various flavors, smells, Sheila's strawberry soap. Steam rising, clouding the mirror, the bathroom fixtures. He picked up her gown, in among the tangled, cast-off clothes, a pair of his old cotton gym shorts, which she slept in, then stained. A half-filled glass of beer, now flat, sat on the imitation marble counter top, beside her Avon products, other more costly colognes, perfumes, makeup brush, bracelets, rings, chains, tampons, cleansing pads.

"She lets others use her. Keeps silent about it and then wonders why she has so many upset stomachs. No spunk. She was *never* terribly wild. She was the obedient one in the house, but she still used to have some spunk. She didn't always sit around and mope. She didn't use to be such an all-fired little *saint* about every issue that came down the pike. She gets that from Mother. They're two of a kind. Just peas in a pod. They're both helpless. Lu Ann panicked when her first period came. I had to go out and buy the stupid Kotex."

Then on into the big bedroom—where she had had the new princess phone installed on her side of the bed, the dial glowing after dark, sitting primly among the ashtrays, glasses, books, papers. Glowing alone in its spot while they tossed and jerked. The cats sat in front of the window, washing themselves in the grainy winter dusk. He pulled the curtains, lit the lamp, still rubbing himself down—walking around enjoying his nakedness, looking for a cigarette. He had a great deal on his mind. He wasn't crazy about having a lot of people in at the moment: families, children, strange faces. Until he ended up feeling like an alien in his own house.

"She spends all her time running her children around, meeting their demands, taking care of this ridiculous schedule, and then that. She cooks every meal, and no two people in the house will eat the same thing. She waits on them like a hired hand. She spoils her husband and her children until they anticipate more and more. The family finally drives her crazy, but she *allows* it. She doesn't get out enough. She certainly doesn't have her own interests. I don't know why some women can't. *I* could raise three children and still have my own life. What about us, anyway? Do you want children?"

She took him by surprise. "I don't know, exactly. I'm not sure we're settled yet."

"*Settled*? We're as settled as we'll *ever* be, this side of dead."

"We're both pretty volatile."

"Oh, fighting's a part of *any* healthy marriage! Where did you ever hear otherwise? You don't have to run away from anger. You're still padding about half-naked, but sweet—looking so worried, so introspective, half put upon, as if you had to face your own doom at any minute. You have two ways of handling life. On the one hand, you anticipate the worst and on the other you won't face the simplest facts. You don't want to cope. I still say you have a cute bottom, though, particularly for a tall man. So nicely shaped. And boyish."

Kasey came, off and on. Like Fern, Sheila did not come, but, unlike Fern, she knew she was supposed to value the sexual life. So he saw in Sheila, in the continuing acceptance of her obligations, an unstated unselfishness.

"I'm going to have them for Christmas, anyway. I hate to lose all contact. Nieces, nephews. You don't know your family. Just because you reject it, I'm not rejecting mine. I'll show you what an old-fashioned Christmas is like!"

She threw herself into holidays and special events. She could concentrate on short-term projects, like holidays, before her interest ran out. She baked for days. She cleaned and she shopped—borrowing the Mercedes, dropping him off on Meridian, then driving away for an all-day jaunt. There behind the wheel in her crisp, waistless sheath, patent pumps, and pillbox hat.

She wrapped all the presents herself, turning them into elaborate works of art: huge bows and sprays, black and gold, red and silver, shiny stuff, standing couples and dancers like the miniature figures on wedding cakes. She bought a new cat box at the last minute and threw the old one out. She purchased the biggest tree she could find, sprayed the house with pine scent, put pine branches all over the place, and hung tiny silver bells on the two cats.

Then Lu Ann called. Arthur couldn't get away, and she claimed she wouldn't come without him.

Sheila was fit to be tied. "Well," she said, "I guess that suits you, anyway, doesn't it? Given the way you feel about family connections."

"No. I was curious about Lu Ann. I wanted to see what a cheerleader looks like when she grows up. *I* didn't know they grew up."

"Well, *you'd* be surprised. She's let herself go."

He could never tell when Sheila could adjust and when she couldn't. She wasn't going to have her holiday ruined. She still had energy to burn. They were fooling around with his shaving cream, called Rise, when she decided to get him ready for Christmas. She pushed him down and parted his legs. She lathered him, she shaved him, and she sent him through the roof.

She went back into the bathroom afterwards to spit and then sat down on the toilet seat. "There! *That* ought to hold you for awhile yet! Think of *that* when you start dwelling on Lu Ann! She doesn't have tricks like *that* up her sleeve, *you* can just bet!"

EIGHT Sheila stayed active during her first pregnancy. She refused to pamper herself and did not change her habits. Despite her doctor's orders, she continued to smoke and drink. She went everywhere. She refused to give up a shopping trip or an evening out. Aside from her swollen breasts and stomach, she did not change shape. She carried the child high until the last minute. Her skin glowed, as if the blood were closer to the surface; her pores grew visible and grainy; untouched, her hair looked dry and fiery, but she usually kept it frosted. Toward the end, oily, sweaty, constipated, she still kept her hairdresser's appointments because, she said, when she reached the hospital she still wanted to look vaguely human.

She gradually grew less strident. She had her resigned, reflective moments. She talked about getting a bigger house, considering the growing family, but when her hints fell on deaf ears, she dropped the subject. She turned Calvin's den into a nursery because she said he still had his downtown office, where he could rat around among his coleuses to his heart's content.

She cleaned her own den. She packed, sorted, and labeled. She put her art supplies away in the closet. She bathed often, which hadn't been a common practice. She pushed less about sex. She generally seemed less desperate. When they made love, she instantly dropped off afterwards, the crinkled gown still half-raised, furled around her big, hardening, blue-veined breasts.

He was out a lot, rambling around the countryside in all weathers checking into real estate investments. He did not like to let his land sit long, and when he bought, he bought just ahead of the developers. He would find what he wanted, or what he was pretty sure he wanted, and then sit there on a rock in the drizzle, staring into space.

Between his talk shows, his business investments, and his auction-going, he was often self-absorbed and cut off around the house. He would clump in after a long day, half-hidden behind his purchases. In this haze, he nodded while she talked, and then, when she finally quieted, he would pick up his own train of thought.

Talking about one project or another he had in mind. Talking, telling a long story, and trying to respond, or as best he could, because he didn't listen. "Or don't," she said, "when it doesn't suit your purposes. That's about the size of it." She said that he was going to drive her crazy. Send him out for more cat food, and he'll gradually get interested in the project, thinking about seafood, for instance. He showed up once with four bags of frozen shrimp instead, having forgotten the cats. When who else *eats* shrimp in the house anyway, but him? He lived in a closed thicket of his own making, a bramble patch of stubborn, thorny privacies. She had long since given up ever meeting Sarah Elizabeth. Except for the exchanged cards at Christmas, the two apparently did not communicate.

He was on the air when their first child arrived, a girl. He dashed over to the hospital where he managed to witness a feeding before a nurse threw him out. The infant's *thereness* was startling. Propped up against the pillows, the mother had the child against her breast, a wrapped, wrinkled, grayish-looking stranger, even its tiny, blue, boneless fingers bundled.

Having no pattern to follow, what kind of father would he make? How would he be? How could he know yet? Women invent the future; they take it for granted; they're ready before it arrives; the male just provides the raw material.

Sheila nursed the first six weeks. Sitting up in bed, propped against several pillows, she lowered the nursing gown's flap, removed the swollen, reddish, sore, milk-heavy, milk-soaked dug. While Shelley sucked blindly, losing the nipple every so often, grunting until she got it back, Sheila tried to get more comfortable, moving up higher against the pillows in her nest. He helped. She asked for a cigarette, and, involved, absorbed in the scene, he objected. "Oh, fiddle-faddle!" she said. "You're supposed to pamper me now, so let's see you get busy and do it!"

The sticky stuff, encrusting the gowns, turned up on the pillowcases and the sheets. He took everything down to the utility room and returned with changes, trying to move around the cats who followed him back and forth. He made the bed, picked up the bedroom, and carried down the dirty glasses.

When Sheila changed to a formula, she slept better, and Calvin often heard the child first. While Shelley was just stirring, while she was still waking, making the first rasping, grunting noises, he got up quickly, searching for his robe without turning on the light. He ran the tap until the water was hot, removed the lid from a sterilized bottle, and measured in the dry, flaking stuff.

When he reached the nursery, Shelley was already on her knees, her head and shoulders still down, trying to kick in the sopping nightdress, the padded bottom swaying from side to side. He picked her up from behind, the pacifier dangling from its string, and took her back to their bed, placing her between them, where Sheila could put the bottle in the infant's mouth. This close, everything smelled of infant formula, infant oil, faint, sweetish infant breath. At this silent five o'clock feeding, the bedroom was just beginning to appear, the windows framed in thinnish light. The house was both fragile shell and fortress, the center of the universe.

Shelley started to crawl. She crossed rooms undeterred, like a tank, going over everything in her path, heading toward some specified goal, like the kitchen garbage. He picked her up, strapped her down and fed her himself from time to time, involved in getting the hang of it. He first held the spoon, dabbing at the mouth with a wet cloth between bites, cutting down on the drip.

Sheila watched. "You're good at it, too," she said, marveling. "I never know what you can do and what you can't.

You can come up with some very surprising talents."

He was finally placing the bowl and the spoon in front of his daughter. She would sometimes deliberately drop the filled bowl over the side, then quietly lean down to look, to see where it had gone.

He dressed her when he found her still wandering around in diapers in the middle of the day. In the early stages she panicked while he was trying to get the cotton shirt over her head. While she struggled, screaming, turning red, the shirt stuck, caught around her ears. Her struggles made it worse. Suddenly, without his noticing the transition, she understood both the neck and the sleeve holes. Once he started the arms, they automatically poked themselves through the sleeves, the tiny fingers spreading around the cuffs.

When she was first trying to walk, she walked like an old-fashioned movie drunk, one step forward, two steps back. She grew into a dark, sturdy child with the Scudders' eyes, those sharp, intent, piercing blue points of light. She had their wills, too. She wanted her own way, and when she did not get it, she froze in place, her eyes blazing, her fists clenched.

She loved costumes. She was always walking around the house in some kind of strange getup. She once greeted him at the door in Sheila's panty girdle, the hose still attached, hanging loosely around her short legs, trailing behind. He picked her up and spun her around, the stockings waving like banners in the breeze. She howled with pleasure.

"Don't encourage her," Sheila said, banging the ice cube trays against the sink. "The child hardly needs that. If I were you, I'd cut back on her fantasy life just a bit."

He pulled heavy sweaters over her head and took her to see his investments. They walked around the frozen land together in the damp chill, their heads bent against the wind, their footing unsure. He took her to auctions. They came back together loaded down with junk, their piles separate in the backseat, their faces still reddish from the open air.

He went through the same ritual every night when he put her to bed. He chose a poem first, usually from *A Child's*

Garden of Verses. Why weren't parts of that as good as Burns?

> Garden darkened, daisy shut
> Child in bed, they slumber—
> Glowworm in the highway rut,
> Mice among the lumber.

Shelley would not settle until they went through what she called their "prayer."

She began it. "Who loves me?"

He touched her cheek and brushed back her hair. "God."

"Who else?"

"Mom and Dad."

"Who else?"

"Grandmother Foss."

"Who else?"

"Aunt Lu Ann and Uncle Arthur."

"Yes, but who else? What about the cows?"

"Oh, yes. The cows love you."

"Who else?"

"The horses, the rabbits, the chickens, and the ducks."

"Who else? What about the trees?"

"The trees, the flowers, the sky, the grass. Now go to sleep, sweetheart."

"What about the cars? You forgot about the cars."

"The cars, the tractors, the trucks . . ."

By then, Sheila was ensconced in the family room with a fresh drink. She would sit there absorbed, staring into space, eyes slightly squinted, rubbing her glass back and forth across the couch arm, which was now stained from the trick. "You don't ask her to face much, do you? She doesn't get disciplined unless I do it, and she isn't hearing much about how the real world works. She's going to be like you. A dreamer with a lot of potential. A bright child, but a dreamer all the same. Highly overprotected."

He did not know what she was talking about. He just didn't want Shelley neglected. "*I'm* doing all right."

"Oh, yes, your investments. But you're two people. She may just turn out to be one of them. She may not have your quirky business sense."

163

"She's an inward, lonely child."

"Oh, yes, granted. She needs some competition," she observed.

When the second child arrived, another girl, the parents decided that they were all going to church because the children needed some kind of religious base which they could later intelligently reject. While Sheila held the baby's chin, turning the fat, dimpled little face from side to side, peering at it critically, intent, she combed what fluff she could find up over the bald scalp, and when she was finally happy, or at least resigned, she would mop up the shapeless mouth, using an unclean dishrag. "Now stick her somewhere safe, will you, where she'll get the least mussed. See what you can do for your older one. I've got to get dressed myself." Calvin crawled around under Shelley's bed looking for something that matched and fit.

Once in church, Sheila had a snappish, dry, brittle tone that implied she could be tolerant of Christians if they did not threaten or push. She could go either way. She told the Anglican priest that she had always been interested in the dying and resurrected gods, but that, taken as a whole, the modern church was not mythy enough to suit her tastes.

Calvin was back in Sarah Elizabeth's faith, his childhood church, when he had lived with Sarah Elizabeth; and, despite this dim, half-comforting sense of homecoming, he still called it Sarah Elizabeth's faith, not his. While he went through the Collect and the Summary of the Law, he was still trying to settle in. His mind wandered through the readings and the Homily. He stood with the others for the Creed. Then they went through the Prayer of the Church, always a tedious business. However, he was gradually being caught up in the old rhythms. He finally welcomed the Confession of Sins, the Comfortable Words, the Absolution and the Peace, and when he reached the Communion rail, he briefly felt less anxious.

Coming home in the car, Sheila criticized the service. She said that although he could maintain it was high church, it

164

wasn't high enough for her. She claimed that if she was going, she wanted a good deal more fuss than that. "It's *supposed* to be a show," she claimed, a former Baptist, "and I want my money's worth. I want to hear some chanting. Why do we get all those tacky hymns instead?"

She cut down the average churchgoer. She gossiped. She said she knew she was being discussed behind her back. They were usually arguing before they reached the house, and when they finally pulled into the drive they weren't speaking. By now the children were ragged. Shelley nagged or threw fits. The baby, Gwen, was already yelling, strapped down in the car seat in back, her arms and legs flailing wildly. When Sheila got in she needed a drink. She was doing less and less around the house lately. While she fixed herself a stiff shot, Calvin checked the roast and peeled the potatoes. By now he was seething. He was boiling, just boiling.

Calvin met several transplanted eastern families through the church, staid, proper, older, upper-middle-class groups. In immaculate Tudor homes where Sheila was afraid she wasn't going to get a drink, and when she did she didn't always watch herself. She didn't actually drink more than when she was in familiar surroundings, but she seemed less able to handle it.

She usually protested going. "They're your fussy friends, not mine," she said, while he was wandering around trying to find the car keys, ready to pick up the baby-sitter.

"They aren't *my* friends anymore than they are yours. Come on. Get dressed. You'll like it. They'll have liquor there."

Unobservant, self-absorbed, telling stories about Sarah Elizabeth and the Cape, Calvin didn't always sense trouble coming. He told his hosts about the time someone had wanted to buy a small beach lot of his grandmother's. A retired music historian, the man had taught at Harvard, but she was soon calling him the singer. Nothing anyone could say ever disabused her of the notion, either. "'A singer,'" Calvin quoted, trying to catch her short, clipped speech. "'Well, most singers don't amount to much, do they? They don't amount to a hill of beans. They often get far too much attention, though, and that goes to their head. They don't lead very regular lives, either, do they? Singers!' she would repeat. 'I won't have a lot of wild people running all over my beach. Where's the sense in that?' She was still on the subject when the poor man had given up, gone somewhere else to look. 'Well,' she'd say, whenever she saw the local real estate agent, 'are those *singers* still pestering you? Are they still running around?' You couldn't argue with her, either. In fact, you couldn't *get* a word in. 'Singers!' she'd repeat, stamping into the local grocery, attacking the elderly clerk. 'George? If I didn't keep watch every minute, if I didn't keep my eyes peeled, we'd have these so-called singers swarming all over the bay. Living in tents, strumming their guitars at all hours. Oh, what's happened to the world, anyway? Why can't everybody stay home? Why can't they stay where they grew up? What makes everybody want to wander so? What's the sense in that? She turned up in town meetings, trying to get the zoning laws tightened, and when she couldn't, she stamped out, wearing her mother's old felt hat pulled down around her ears. Muttering about moving her ancestors out of the local plot, taking the bodies down to the next town where a little history was appreciated. She would have too, but she was usually fighting with that town as well."

Glancing up, he suddenly saw his wife across the room. He realized that something had thrown her off. Some person, some chance remark. She was in the middle stages of trying to deal with an insult, real or imagined. She was wearing that edgy, closed, half-surprised look. She was trying to walk straight. Her wrists were already loose, floating around her face. What had happened, anyway? He realized that he didn't want to know. Didn't want to have to deal. He faced any attempt to cope with dread. He felt too dense, too unequipped. Thinking about the problem, he felt swallowed up.

She wove around for awhile with her drink, but she was half-slumped over in her chair before ten o'clock. She was still holding onto her drink and talking to herself. "Why there

166

has to be all this ancestor worship is beyond me," she remarked, starting with that mild, quizzical tone which could soon turn strident. "What's so all-fired impressive about a senile, self-centered old woman like that? Why can't he just tell her to straighten up? Why can't he deal with his feelings? Why can't he get *mad* like everybody else, for instance? Why does he just store up his grievances like treasures in heaven? And *why* does he have to turn his life into an interesting story, as if he were just witnessing somebody else's?"

Calvin switched the subject. He was soon talking about Mercy Scudder, his great-grandmother, the ghost, who continued to have her differences with the local clam warden beyond the grave. He was going to have to try to get Sheila home just as soon as he finished this part, made his point.

She was growing louder. The guests started to avoid the chair where she was sitting, a disaster area. They did not comment or look in her direction. They just kept a wide berth. "Calvin has more money than King Midas," she was saying, "but do you know what he does with it? Nothing! Just nothing. He just collects it, like that junk he has in the barn back there. He just sits on his hoard, like the sleepy, fat old dragon he is. Breathing fire and flipping his tail. I'm never going to go anywhere. I'm never going to get out of Indiana. I'm lucky if I can get to leave the house. If I want company, I have the children."

Calvin tried to get her on her feet, but she would not budge at first. She complained about the rock music playing in the background. She said that she couldn't abide the Beatles. "Oh, *that* stuff!" She said several times. Although she had taken on all the other arts, she had skipped the musical ones. "Where's all the good music these days? Doesn't anybody have any taste anymore? Where are all the wonderful works of yesteryear?"

He eased the glass from her hand, stood her on her feet, and got her coat. She pushed his arm away when he tried to help. "I can put on my coat! What makes you think I can't put on my own coat? I've been putting coats on all my life!

167

I wasn't raised in a bed of lilies, like some around here, and I'm not about to be treated like an invalid now. I'm not dying. I'm not dead yet," she concluded, "my life as evidence to the contrary!"

She passed out in the car, but woke when he pulled into their drive. She wanted a drink. She wanted to go back to the party, and when he refused to take her back, she pushed him in the face. "Oh, he hates me!" she screamed in front of the baby-sitter while he was trying to help her into the house. "He's going to kill me! He's going to kill me! Call the police! Call the police! Oh, *how he hates me*, and the world doesn't know it!"

In mild shock, impressed with these clashing furies, she slowed down briefly after that. Humbled, having touched, then skirted, the irrational, she felt depleted, drained. She went around the house with a thoughtful, resigned look, and when he spoke, she didn't always hear. If she did, she said "Yes? What?" as if she were trying to come back down to earth. Once she said, "You're going to murder me one of these days, and I know it." She sounded removed, reflective. She walked off without waiting for an answer.

Sheila's mother stayed with the family off and on. Darlene Foss slept on the living room couch, and when he got down in the morning she was already up, dressed. She had the couch stripped, the sheets and blankets folded. She stayed in the living room, sitting up straight, tapping her fingers on the side of the chair until he had the morning coffee ready. She didn't feel comfortable around strangers in their kitchens. She didn't want to intrude, and unless Sheila was around, she stayed out of the way.

She was staying with them when his first poem appeared. Calvin hadn't mentioned its publication ahead of time, and when he put the small quarterly down in front of the women, the page turned back to his work, they both looked flummoxed. Mrs. Foss put her hand to her throat. "Why, Sheila!" she said, "just look! Isn't that nice?"

Sheila continued to register surprise. She read the poem

through twice. She was removed, amused. "It's a bit prosy, for my taste," she explained, as if she were trying to spare some child's feelings. "Bland, you know, but nice."

He went off to put the children down, and when he came back, the two women were sitting over Sheila's Ouija board with the evening's first drink. Sheila was good with the board. She could even work it alone, sober or drunk. She claimed that she could summon up the spirits with one hand tied behind her back. While she sat there in a torn T-shirt, his old work pants, a drink within reach, she got the plastic pointer moving at top speed, dizzily running from letter to letter. At that fast pace, it could not be deciphered. Mrs. Foss could not get it to move a lick. She was partly fascinated, partly disapproving.

"A poem published," Sheila said, playing with the board without looking up. "God help us, I could get a poem published if editors understood the genre these days, which they don't."

Every once in awhile she would hold out her glass toward him, her arm fully extended, and say, as she had been doing for years, years. "Would you freshen this? Would you freshen this, like the doll you are?" Although the glass was always empty, she always used the word "freshen," not "fill," which was what she meant. She often asked him why he couldn't say just what he meant, but in this case she certainly did not.

"Go freshen both our drinks, and then you can ask me something to ask the board. You can even ask me to ask it something about business trends if you like. We'll see how this thing handles the market. You might make a killing yet."

"It's late. I've got to get up early. I've got to run up to Chicago. Darlene may want to get some sleep herself."

"Oh, nonsense! Nonsense!" she said, getting up to fill both glasses. "Balderdash. The two of you indulge yourselves in entirely too much sleep."

Mrs. Foss was half-engrossed in the late-late show and half-engrossed in the board. She did not comment. She was tired. She yawned, half-covering her mouth with her hand, but she would not give up until they both did because she did not want to miss anything. She did not miss much.

"Oh, where has everybody's energy gone, anyway!" Sheila said, bringing the glasses back. "Mother! *Wake* up, *will* you? Get over here and see what you can do with the board. What's happened to the old days, anyway; where are they, when you used to come tearing down the pike? You're *both* just a couple of old hens! My goodness! I never saw the like!"

Mrs. Foss stiffened. "I don't know *what* you mean by that last remark! I never once came tearing down any pike! I was married young. I had *children* to raise, *if* you remember! Speak for yourself, if you have to, but leave *me* out of it. Heavens!"

"Oh, come *off* it, Mother!" Sheila had long since abandoned her first project, her central project in the beginning, their sex life, and because she had she wanted him around. Where she could still keep an eye on him. Where she could check up. Assuming she couldn't, she still needed company. "You're *supposed* to be on vacation, aren't you, Mother? Can't you look alive at least? Can't you *look* as if you're enjoying yourself?"

Mrs. Foss finally rose. She came over to where Sheila was sitting, absently brushing off her tight stretch pants. "Well, I ought to be in bed by rights. Because I know what I'll be like in the morning if I don't. I'll be half-dead."

"Well, you aren't dead yet. So get cracking."

Calvin picked up the children's litter and put it in the playpen. He shoved the playpen in through the utility room door, over the laundry on the floor. The cats looked up at him from inside the dryer.

Sheila and her mother were comparing actresses' breasts on the TV show. "What's *she* doing on TV," Mrs. Foss wanted to know, "when she's got no more that that? My word! How does she think she can get away with that dress? And don't tell me she can act. I've seen more talent on a goat."

She changed the subject slightly. Although she was not as endowed as her daughter, she considered herself to be in better shape. She turned sideways in her chair. "Look at you,

Sheila! You're getting so frumpy. You look like a *cow*! My word! Why would anybody let himself *get* like that?"

"Oh, what do you know! Maybe Calvin likes me like this."

"Nonsense. You don't exercise. You wouldn't *move* if you didn't have to. You're getting out of shape before your time."

"I can still *move*!"

The two women got down on the floor. They tried push-ups and then, on their bottoms, they pedaled their legs in the air.

Sheila spilled some of her mother's beer, and Mrs. Foss jumped up to find a rag. She dabbed at the soaked spot with a damp diaper. "You're just going to *ruin* this rug! You don't take care of anything! You don't *appreciate* everything you have!"

"Beer wipes," Sheila said, "so just don't go having a hissiefit, will you? Beer wipes! It comes right off!"

Calvin went to bed. He turned, listening to the women below over the board. Sheila got up every so often to freshen her drink. He could hear her getting into the refrigerator, then banging the ice cube tray against the sink. He finally dropped off.

She woke him when she came up. Blinking and wobbly, she reached for the light. "What are you doing up here, hiding out like a mole?" she asked, not untenderly. "Like the fuzzy little mole you are."

He did not try to deal with such a crazy question. He turned on his side.

She pulled off her short, gray T-shirt and the torn work pants. She still had shapely legs, but she had a soft roll around the middle now, there since the second child. She was nude except for her dangling cartwheel earrings and the big, battered, unclean bra. Her stomach curved down into her fiery, mussed, orange-red pubic hair. She sat down heavily on the bed. "Are you sulking, or what? Is there something bothering you? You don't want sex, do you?"

He turned over on his back again. "No, I don't want sex. I want a divorce."

171

Her mind stopped in its tracks. She was trying to focus, and then, for a minute, her mind cleared. "Fat chance of that and *you* know it," she said, just before she passed out.

Home. Home from town, he finally stood just inside the master bedroom door. Blinking in the big, brightly lighted area: a fanfare of children, cats, noise, TV going, tossed blankets, rumpled pillows, playpen, toys. When he returned from work these days, he usually found his family in this spot, unfed, half-dressed, in front of TV, watching anything that moved. While Sheila drank, still fairly sober, absorbed in soap operas, the children ate cold cereal directly from the boxes. They dug into the boxes, their cheeks full, then wiped their hands across the sheets, the pillows, the cats. The cats pawed the sheets, purring, or lay comfortably ensconced in the valley between his wife's legs. Wheat Chex and Corn Chex turned up in the sheets and in the shag rug.

Both children were still on bottles. A half-empty bottle, Gwen's, suddenly fell to the floor. A cat jumped after it, interested, but Gwen wanted it back. She started to cry. Sheila called their bed a boat, a barge. "There it goes, over the side! It's in the water! It's floating! It's still floating! Oh, Daddy will get it! Daddy will save the bottle, won't he?"

Shelley was bouncing up and down, overstimulated. Shirtless, in ragged underpants, she got it first. "We're having a party, Daddy! Look! Look at us! We're having a party!"

"I can see!"

She was wearing a collection of barettes, bobby-pins, and ribbons in her hair, just about everything she owned for her hair; she resembled the African gods on which natives stick anything they can get.

He squatted down in front of her. "Oh, pret-ty!"

Having recently passed the line of babyhood, she was learning to make her first distinctions between the gorgeously erratic and the somber mean. She knew she was a sight. She giggled and clapped her hands over her head.

Sheila, half-abstracted, got her heavy beer mug back down on the bedside chest with some precision, her attention still on "Dark Shadows." "Sweeties?" she asked, without looking up, "how did your day go?"

He did not answer, an answer.

She noticed. She just raised her brows. What came, came.

He could bear her, just, if he kept his mind on his girls.

The soap opera faded; Shelley turned the sound off for the commercial: a cheerful, upbeat pitch for toilet paper, a drain cleaner, and a diet drink. Then a preview, a slice of the news-to-come, an eye-catcher. The camera focused on rioting students— arms waving, mouths going without sound. Cops moved among them, trying to break them up. Several vans arrived. The soap opera returned. Shelley fixed the sound.

His girls were still bobbing up and down around his legs, demanding his attention.

He bent down again. "When I come in, you're all tucked up, like two raisins in a bun, but now what? You're jumping beans. Going off like firecrackers. What happened to my two girls?"

"Oh, Daddy!" Shelley screamed. "We're not! We're us!"

"Let me look closer. I don't think so. Let me see!"

The girls continued to jump around him, overstimulated.

Sheila's mood suddenly changed. Her mouth hardened. "Shelley? Tell your father what you did today." Everybody was supposed to straighten up, in that split second. "Go on. We said we'd tell him when he got home. Shelley?"

The child had that closed, cutoff look now.

He could not bear to watch her feeling pushed back, separated, suddenly abandoned.

He certainly didn't want to deal right now. He picked up her rabbit, a puppet. Kneeling in front of them, he drew it over his hand like a glove, holding it out, cocking its head. The children squealed, the tension increased. As he watched the group watching the rabbit, he realized that Sheila was worried about what the rabbit would say.

Shelley was jumping up and down. "Oh, Dad! Make it talk! DO IT! MAKE IT TALK!"

Everybody was still watching the rabbit. As in magic, needing the illusion, the time out from normal tensions, the

173

audience wants to believe. Amused, fascinated with the possibility, and if the ventriloquist gives the audience half a chance, it will keep its eyes glued on the dummy, having forgotten him.

Sheila broke first. "Shelley! I haven't forgotten! I was *talking* to you!" Shelley turned her back on her mother. "Calvin! I want her attention, now! If *you* won't cope, I can!"

A cat was going on the floor in the master bathroom. When it finished, it scratched at the bare tiles, automatically trying to cover its wet.

Calvin crossed the room and lunged for it, missing. "I'm *tired* of cat piss! I've had all the cat piss I can take!"

She sprang out of bed. She picked up both cats by the necks, one dangling from each hand. "KILL THE CATS THEN!" she screamed, no more than mildly beery. "KILL THE CATS, WHY DON'T YOU?" she continued, thrusting them toward his face. "GO AHEAD. HERE THEY ARE!"

Heart pumping, startled, frightened, he jumped back. The children, a blur, were screaming, running around both parents below the cats' squirming bottoms.

"So kill the cats! Just see what your children think!" She turned toward them, holding the cats out at arms' length while they jerked up and down in the air. "DADDY WANTS TO KILL THE CATS!"

He was suddenly yanking the scattered blankets off the bed. "Why am I sleeping in menstrual blood!" he screamed, deranged, finally feeling in control because wilder than she. Her pale, stricken face bobbed in front of him from time to time. "WHY AM I SLEEPING IN CAT PISS? WHY AM I SLEEPING IN CORN CHEX?"

Heart pumping wildly, breathless, his throat parched, his lips caked, his eyes dry, searing, his wrists numb, as if his body had used up its juices, oils, he dashed downstairs and back into the car. Fumbling with the keys, spilling his cigarettes on the floor, he felt calm with rage. As if directed, knowing what he was doing, he backed out into the street, going away, going away, going away, getting out!

174

He drove south, past Chester City, New Salem, and Boone's Bend. When he reached Boone's Bend, he turned west, toward Sylvan Grove. The last of the sun, setting in front of him, made driving difficult. It glinted on the windshield, casting a few reddish streaks. The narrow tar road wound through brown, unbroken fields on each side. A few spindly trees in the distance looked etched against the bleakness. He wandered past West Lemon and Cedar Corners. He went through the main street: two-story frame houses, a funeral home, a drugstore, a small, frozen park, and a concrete block Methodist church.

He was on the turning, narrow, shoulderless road again, some angles so sharp that he had to drop his speed, lightly touch the brake. He finally wandered into Rosemary Bend, past Auburnville, and then, at a sign with a familiar name, he turned toward Thebes. He missed Thebes, or could not recall passing through it, but he turned toward Morris City and Prophet's Fork. From Prophet's Fork, past New Lebanon and North Shelby, he blundered onto the highway which led back to the house.

Calvin suddenly heard from Fern's attorney. Fern wanted the child support increased, which puzzled him. Any request was unusual for her. He was willing. The boy was growing and had more needs, but wasn't it time to bargain? He ought to be able to see him now and then. He wanted visiting rights. "My son! After all, he's getting up there. He's twelve. He can travel now. He can be put on a plane."

Sheila was worried about her own family. Worried about what these divided loyalties could entail. What would the son take away from her two girls? Possessive, guarded, insecure, she didn't like loose ends. "He's not *yours*, and it's just sentimental to think otherwise. He's Fern's. She's made that abundantly clear. Why, you left her before he was born! You don't *know* him!"

What did he actually think he had to offer him in this wreckage, this battered house? A day did not pass now without arguments or long, bitter silences that tasted like salt on the tongue. "I know I don't *know* him. That's the point. I should. I've got to make contact. It won't be easy to do, but it's got to be done."

She realized that she couldn't refuse him. "Well, we'll see. We can talk about it again in the fall."

Sheila and Darlene were talking about going to Denver that summer to visit Lu Ann.

The country erupted that spring. The blacks rioted in DC in April. Three California cities went in May. Cleveland blew in June. Then Brooklyn, Baltimore, Perth Amboy, Providence, Minneapolis, Milwaukee, Detroit, Dayton, Atlanta, San Francisco, and Saint Louis. Saint Louis seemed too close to home. He wasn't terribly happy about getting on the road.

She told him that whenever she wanted to do something, he dragged his feet. He was just looking for an excuse not to go. She said that he would never leave his backyard if he wasn't pushed. She first told him that Denver was still peaceful because the black population was happy there, and then pointed out that Lu Ann did not exactly live in the ghetto in any case. "Cherry Hills," she said, "isn't your average slum."

He planned to fly, but, at the last minute, five major airlines struck, and, if they were still going, he was going to have to get on the road. She wanted to take the Dodge wagon, which had more room. He wanted to take his Mercedes because he wanted to do the driving; he didn't like to have others behind the wheel when he was in the car; and if he took his car, he knew she knew who was going to do the driving.

She finally gave up. "All right," she said, "we'll take that tank of yours, but you're going to have to stuff Mother in back with the children. I'm going to need all the room I can get up in front."

Calvin packed the car before dawn and put the children in back while they were still sleeping: Shelley on one side, curled up behind the driver's seat, Gwen in the portable car seat next, then Sheila's mother at the other window. Darlene had new shoes and a new hat. She wore a light summer dress, but carried a sweater because the car was air-conditioned. Sheila wore a new pair of gold pants and a dove-colored pullover with wide, elbow-length sleeves. She had had her hair recently done, and although she said she knew it wasn't going to stay that way, she was at least going to start out looking spiffy.

They dropped south to reach the interstate, and when they turned onto the highway heading west, the sun was already up. The day was going to be hot and humid. He put on the airconditioner. Darlene was dozing in back, resting her head against the seat, her mouth open, her hands still carefully folded across the black patent leather purse. Gwen was sleeping too, but Shelley was awake.

She was standing up directly behind Calvin's head. She was wearing a cowboy hat, her favorite, and a T-shirt with the Empire State Building stenciled across the chest. The hat was frayed and soiled, the brim down, pulled over her forehead and her ears, like a sharecropper's hat. She was already looking for the motel where they were going to spend the first night.

They crossed into Illinois around noon, where they stopped along the road for lunch. They ate in the car, keeping the doors open. Sheila hauled Gwen over the front seat and changed her before they left. They spent the afternoon finishing off Illinois and getting into Missouri without pushing it.

Sheila was quiet through the afternoon. She seemed content. She did not complain about their slow pace, and since she knew he would not let her touch his car, she did not ask to drive. She sat there chain-smoking and looking out. "This getting away means a lot to me," she said.

Gwen slept through most of the trip. Shelley was usually awake and restless. Darlene dozed from time to time, and when she was awake, she stared out with a glazed look.

"She's no help," Sheila said. "She's just going to sleep through the whole trip."

Darlene stirred in the back seat. "I HEARD that last remark."

"So? You may be awake at the moment, but you don't look

very perky to me. Why don't you sit up? Why don't you sit up, open your eyes, and enjoy your vacation?"

Darlene briefly pulled herself together. She pointed out the sights to Shelley. "There's cows. There's some pigs. They aren't as big as we have in Indiana, of course."

"There ARE, Mother. I thought you so love the language."

Darlene squared her shoulders and sat up straighter. She said that when she talked to children, she used their language.

"Well, *my* children don't happen to use children's language."

Shelley wanted to know if the motel was close. Nobody answered. Then she wanted to know why the car didn't have TV.

"Goodness," the grandmother said, "why do you need TV, child, when there is so much to see?"

"What?"

"Well, you missed that farm back there. You missed those tractors."

"I love Casper, the Friendly Ghost," Shelley said. "I love Casper because he's so cute. I don't love you, anyway."

Sheila turned, her arm across the front seat, holding a cigarette. "Just shut up and sit. I'm not going to tell you again to sit down."

Calvin was furious. "You can't stand your own children unless they're asleep, or at least not bothering you."

"Oh shut up," she replied, distantly. She had been looking forward to a pleasant trip and did not feel like arguing. "If you won't deal," she said, wearily, "then, obviously, somebody has to."

They spent the first night in Missouri and crossed into Kansas the next day. Darlene continued to doze off and on. Gwen slept, strapped into the portable car seat. She had her arms out, her fingers parted. She still had the pacifier in her mouth, and every once in a while she pulled on it in her sleep. Aside from these sucking noises, the car was quiet for long periods.

Shelley slept through that second morning, cramped be-

178

tween Gwen's car seat and the door, her hat still on, her head bent at an odd angle. In the afternoon, shortly after lunch, Sheila slipped off, too. She was still holding the diaper bag in her lap.

Shelley woke. Calvin could hear her moving back there, and then she was standing up directly behind his head. She was still for a long time. "Daddy," she finally asked, quietly, "why do robots don't have hair?"

"Because they're not people."

"Some people don't have hair."

He was trying to see against the glare. Dirt, wind, dust, corn. An isolated gas station or a wooden church, and then beyond these spots, the open fields again.

Gwen woke. She tried to stretch in the car seat, and when she couldn't she started to cry.

He woke Sheila. She lit a cigarette and fixed a bottle. The cigarette in the side of her mouth, she passed the bottle over the seat to her mother. When she saw she was still asleep, she poked her. "Here," she said. "Try to be useful, while you're still on board."

Darlene inserted the bottle, leaving the child strapped down. "She's *sopped*! She should be changed! My word!"

"She'll last," Sheila said wearily. "Just keep the bottle up there. Just do as you're instructed to do."

Shelley pushed her coloring book between her legs. She sat farther up in the seat and pulled the cowboy hat farther down over her forehead because she knew she annoyed her mother when she did.

Sheila grew restless and irritable. His slow, steady driving gradually wore on her nerves. She liked passing everything in sight. Every once in awhile she would say, "Take that truck, will you?" without expecting him to do it. She finally gave up trying. She tried to resign herself to his crawling behind everything that moved, if sometimes just.

Darlene announced that it was time for her pills. She needed some water. She asked if there was any water left.

Sheila did not turn around, "We'll be in the motel soon. You'll last."

179

Then Shelley wanted some water.

"Everybody keep this up," Sheila said, "and there'll be some heads knocked around back there."

While they were still in Kansas, they limped into the second motel just before dark. Shelley and Gwen were both asleep, back there among the torn coloring books, the scattered, broken crayons, the banana peels, the browning apple cores, and the balls of crushed wax paper.

He carried both children in. Gwen instantly woke and when he put the portable car seat down on the motel bed, she started to scream. Sheila picked her up and changed her. She wanted a drink, and she told Calvin to bring in the liquor supplies first. While he was out there, unloading the car, it started to rain lightly in the soft, dusk-colored air. He did not want to go back into the motel.

It rained off and on through the night and drizzled the next day. It cleared, briefly, when they crossed the Colorado border, but the sky soon closed in again. It was sticky and humid. The airconditioner wasn't working properly, and every once in awhile it blew the warmth into the car.

Calvin and Sheila argued in low tones. She snapped at him about his slow pace; he snapped back about her impatience. "Just keep calm," he said. "You'll soon be there and then you can paint the town red. You can hit every hot spot."

Shelley started jumping up and down in back. She was getting hysterical. She said one word over and over, just to hear it shrink into nonsense. "Potato!" she kept shouting, "potato, potato, potato!" When Calvin tried to quiet her, she got worse. "POTATO!" she screamed, collapsing into shrill giggles. The grandmother couldn't stop her.

Trying to deal with this, Sheila turned around and kneeled on the front seat among the maps, the diaper bag, and the insulated bottle bag. She leaned over toward Shelley, her hand in the air.

Calvin was trying to look into the rearview mirror. "Be careful! Be careful! Don't hit her!"

Sheila slapped toward her, but slapped at the air.

"You MISSED!" Shelley screamed. "YOU MISSED!"

"I won't miss again. So sit down and *clam* up!"

Calvin slowed the car, distracted. Behind him, a car braked and blew its horn.

Sheila turned around again. "You're going to KILL US one of these days. You're going to KILL US with your cautious driving! Oh, you're like an *old* hen!"

"Just shut up," Calvin said, quietly, five times in a row, like a litany. "Just shut up, will you? Before I lose my mind."

They had not fully pulled themselves together when they hit the Denver traffic on Colfax. Shelley kept wanting to see the mountains, and when she couldn't, she nagged. Sheila yelled at Shelley while she was trying to read the map in her lap. Gwen awoke. She started to cry. Darlene was trying to straighten up the backseat and did not know where to put the trash. She tried to smooth out her dress, but there was a stain in front, where a bottle had leaked. She kept saying that they were going to pull into Lu Ann's place looking like Okies.

He found Cherry Hills, but the sky opened up again. He pulled into the drive, leaned back and closed his eyes for a second. They had to make a dash for the house—everybody shoving in past Lu Ann, who was holding the front door open, and in the way, Calvin last, the in-law, the stranger, the TV personality carrying Gwen in the portable car seat.

Lu Ann studied the crowd as if she were not sure just where she was going to put everybody. She was a small, nervous, fat woman with a round face, a pretty complexion. Sheila instantly commented on the weight gain. Lu Ann could have returned the observation, but didn't. "It's the tranquilizers," she said. "I can't sleep without them, and they hold so much water."

Arthur was out, buying liquor, which was not a good sign. They evidently did not keep a stocked liquor cabinet.

Sheila was going to have to wait. "I hope he returns sufficiently armed," she said, doubting it, "because the caravan's run dry. We finished the gin in the motel last night."

Shelley was standing in front of the TV still wearing the battered cowboy hat. She would not take it off. She wouldn't speak to anyone, and when Lu Ann tried to kiss her, she just ducked her head. She said "Potato, potato," twice, in a dead voice, but stopped, without taking her eyes away from the TV.

"Now don't start that again, good grief," Sheila said. "Just don't go having a hissyfit in front of your aunt, who'll think you're demented. She pitched a hissyfit coming here," she explained, while she was trying to change Gwen on the coffee table. She was smoking, but she didn't have an ashtray. Lu Ann brought her a dish. Sheila held her cigarette out carefully, around the child's head, and flicked it into the dish. She did not take the dish. "Just keep it handy," she said, "until I can get done with these chores."

Lu Ann's children wandered up from the basement, where they had been trying to play pool. They came up arguing about it. There were three. The fourteen-year-old, their eldest, had Lu Ann's fair hair, her clear coloring. Other than that, she resembled Sheila. She already had a woman's figure.

When she was gone, Darlene wanted to know if she stuffed her bra.

"Mother!" Lu Ann said, instantly put out. "My word! She CERTAINLY does *not* stuff her bra!"

"Well, don't yell at me like your dog," her mother said. "I was just ASKING. My goodness!"

Arthur returned. The luggage executive was small, like his wife, but trim. He played golf, and, unlike Lu Ann, he was tan. He was in a conservative blue knit shirt with an alligator at the pocket, everything else matching. He was one of those people who dress carefully and stylishly even when off duty.

He had bought a fifth. He switched the bag to shake hands, then made drinks. He had the careful, limited morality of the literal-minded, and when he fixed the drinks, he measured a single shot into each glass.

Sheila fixed her second drink herself and carried the glass to the table. Lu Ann had prepared an Indiana supper, a lot

182

of cold dishes because, she said, she hadn't known just when to expect them. She had potato salad, macaroni salad, string bean salad, relishes, and pickled beets. The ham did not come from the country, but she had made her own sauce.

Calvin gradually realized that their coming had interrupted an argument. The couple never directly addressed one another, and the conversation, as a whole, seemed guarded and sparse. When the table was quiet, Darlene would try to get things going again. "Well," she would say, each time, "don't everybody talk at once!"

Lu Ann was trying. She asked Calvin about his work.

"Oh, he lives the life of Riley," Sheila said, keeping her drink close to her. She picked at the food between sips. "He loves talking, and what happens? Two talk shows fall in his lap. And on his second, held up by numerous grants, propped up with the tax payers' money, he goes on and on alone about this and that. He gets away with it, in part, because he stays so handsome, and, then, of course, he has that soap opera voice. I still keep waiting for the organ to fade out. He wrote a poem," she concluded, as if she still hadn't quite digested the fact. "*I* could write, *if* anybody could read these days, which they can't."

She slapped Shelley's hand when she tried to reach for the biscuits. "If you want something, I can pass it. I'm glad to see you tackling food for a change, but if you want something, ask for it. For pity sakes," she concluded, using one of her mother's expressions, "we aren't animals here yet." She looked up, as if she were eager to pass the information around the table.

She fixed herself a third drink while she was getting ready to put the children down. She was louder now, and in a few minutes she would be wound up. Arthur started to put the bottle away, and she put her hand on his arm. "We're here," she said, "all the way from nowhere, and we've got a lot to catch up on. I want to hear all the news from your wife. I want to hear about this sedentary life she's been leading. I want to see if I can't change her ways."

Lu Ann raised her brows at that last remark. She glanced at Darlene. The mother and daughter exchanged looks about the drinking.

Shelley did not want to go to bed. "I want to go home," she said. "I want to go home, where it's not raining. I want to sleep in my *own* bed."

Calvin did, too. He felt displaced, a half-familiar, unpleasant sensation. Both the strange, threatening house (because not his) and the unspoken tensions between the couple touched ancient nerves, primitive childhood feelings.

When Sheila returned from getting the children down, she said that she was just getting her second wind. She settled in to talk through the night, unworried about who had to rise early.

The men were both ready for bed. Arthur glanced at his wife, obviously wanting her to come along, but he couldn't catch her eye. Calvin said he was retiring. He anticipated an argument, but Sheila, fortified with the two women, did not need him now. She just nodded.

The men went up alone. "I guess they have a lot to talk about," Arthur said on the stairs, unsettled because his wife wasn't coming with him.

Calvin knew that Arthur wasn't comfortable with him, because of the poetry, or because of Sheila, or perhaps both. They parted at the landing.

Calvin walked into the guest room where their unpacked suitcases still sat on the bed. She had evidently put the children down in what they had been wearing all day. He unstrapped the suitcase which contained the parents' clothes and lifted the luggage up off the bed onto the floor. He showered, pulled back the covers, and instantly fell asleep, listening to the rain on the roof.

He had, in the dream, the child's sense of incompletion. The blunt, heavy passivity is ingrown, a habit, and if it is uncomfortable, he does not really know it, because he does not know any other state. He wears himself awkwardly, a long glove that does not quite fit. He feels dim, removed, numb. While he sinks further inside himself, the huge spaces

184

around increase in size and shape. Two adults are arguing, and while their shouting grows more strident, he feels as if he can help (or at least restore order) if he just keeps decreasing in size and shape. He has got to learn to take up less space.

She woke him. She came up blinking and weaving and furious. Talking to herself, she stumbled around the suitcases, turning on the light.

He turned on his side and glanced at the clock. She hadn't been down much more than an hour. "What happened to the party?" he asked. "What happened to the conference? Didn't Lu Ann want to get straightened out?"

"Oh, Lu Ann, Lu Ann," she said, fumbling around the dresser. "We drove two thousand miles, and *she* has to get up in the morning!" Feeling betrayed, humiliated, she was still trying to keep some grip on herself. "Her *children* and her *husband* come first. Her children and her husband! She's hiding behind them. She won't face herself. She's half-afraid of me. She's half-afraid of a moment's excitement, and she knows it."

He sat up and lit a cigarette. "I want a divorce, and I'm serious. I want a divorce, and if you won't give it to me, I'll get it. I'll get it in any way I can. I'll get it whatever it costs."

"Oh, BULL," she said, picking up the car keys. "BULL ROAR. I'm getting tired of that story. I'm getting tired of that same old song. You aren't going to give up your house, and you know it. You CERTAINLY aren't going to give up those two girls!"

She put the car keys in her pocket. She was stumbling around trying to find a fresh package of cigarettes. "You can *all* sleep your lives away if you want to, but *I'm* going out. I'm on my vacation, and I'm going out."

"Are you driving, in your shape?"

"Oh, God, you *never* quit, do you?" she said, just before she left. "You never give up! I could drive *circles* around you any day of the week, twice on Sunday. I could drive *rings* around you, I could do *figure eights*! You'll just dork along the rest of your natural, woolly, muddleheaded life, unable to tell the difference between a rose and a coleus. You'll just go on daydreaming your way down the pike!"

While the family lingered in Denver, camping out in that crazy place, Calvin drove back home to catch up on what needed doing. He reached town, picked up the cats from the vet's, and drove out to the house in a removed state. He felt half-glazed after the long drive and extremely tired. He unlocked the front door and pushed the cats through, but he did not go in yet.

He prowled around the backyard in the late summer exhaustion, staring at the sagging badminton net and the brownish, burned-looking grass. He was suddenly working on the net, all thumbs at first, trying to get the tiny, tight knots undone, the strings free from the poles. He took off his coat, loosened his tie, and rolled up his sleeves. The string was old and frayed, easily broken, but he unknotted every knot and then carefully folded the net up, as if he were working on a flag. He carried the net back out to the car and drove off to stay at a hotel in town.

He caught up on this and that. He stopped in to talk to his lawyer about a divorce.

"Who are you marrying this time? Listen. Don't tell me about it. I don't want to know," Ferris said, a golfing acquaintance. "Let me think about what judge we can get. This is your third divorce coming up. I don't want to go around throwing myself on the mercy of someone who's managed to keep the same little woman around for sixty years. I don't want to get down on my knees in front of some Baptist or Catholic. 'What?' he says, 'Blue Beard's back?' I'll check the court calendar and keep in touch."

"I have to have custody of the children, too."

He shook his head. "Oh, boy, that's rich. You don't want much, do you? The woman gets the children, and that's Holy Scripture in this state. You get your chance to fool around some more. In your case, you get a fourth crack at a new life. That's the package, that's the best I can do, and that's a lot.

186

Cut your losses, like everybody else, and maybe I can get you two or three weeks' visiting rights."

"She's a drunk. She neglects the children. They'll want to come with me when she finds out about this. She'll blow sky-high. You could put them on the stand. I'll take my chances there."

"What movies have you seen? One: most people drink these days, and the law can seldom make useful distinctions between drinkers and drunks. Don't you drink?" he asked, counting on his fingers. "Two: it's hard to prove neglect. It's usually *impossible* to prove neglect. What's neglect? It's too negative. Three: the children are still too young to testify. Most judges around here won't even *talk* to them when they're that young. Four—"

Calvin scoured the town looking for an attorney who would give it a shot. He finally ended up in the low-rent business districts across from used-car lots and plumbing suppliers.

Mrs. Fenstermaker was a big, well-preserved woman in her middle forties. She had a large, shapely chest and long black hair pulled back into a severe bun, emphasizing the face, the theatrical-looking bone structure. When he came in, she had her wastebasket up on her desk, and she was spreading the trash out across the blotter, looking for something she had misplaced. She was precise, crisp, and authoritative.

"You've had trouble because you've run into a lot of traditional people, but this profession is traditional. They have precedents for breakfast. However, there's more to the law than that. The law is like a fine musical instrument. You have to play on it, and you have to take chances. If you want to be interpretative, you have to be innovative."

"I want her served right away."

"Oh, no you don't. If she catches wind of what's going on while she's still out there, she could hold the children in Denver, where we don't have jurisdiction. You don't want her served until she's back in the state."

"She hasn't said when she's coming back."

"Well, we need time, right here. We'll have to pick our judge carefully," she said, putting the trash back without finding what she wanted. "I've already talked back to half the judges on the bench, and if I'm not going to blow this case, I've got to find a fresh face. I have a famous temper. I don't suffer these nitwits too gladly."

She was trying to prove neglect. She sent men out to the house to take pictures of the soiled rugs, the damaged drapes and woodwork. Calvin followed them around, pointing out the crucial features: the dirty laundry that Sheila had hidden from herself, stuffed under beds, piled up in the shower stall. He fixed drinks, and while the sun was going down, they took them out to the patio. He left when they did, keeping the cats locked up.

He missed his girls. Their voices on the phone seemed unclear and frayed, far away.

No hints about what was really going on, either.

"We've been on a farm, Daddy," Shelley said. "We saw a horse today."

"When are you coming back? Don't you miss me? Don't you miss your own bed?"

She didn't answer immediately. "I guess so. Daddy? Could we have a farm?"

What if she also dreaded walking back into the cat piss and the other solid comforts? What about a completely fresh start?

Mrs. Fenstermaker wasn't sympathetic. "Don't buy any real estate right now," she said. "It'll just come up in court. I've already got more assets than I can decently hide, and we're going to be lucky if we can get free with your skin intact."

He rented a place off the beaten track. The owners, recently divorced, wanted to sell, ready to sacrifice, but they hadn't been able to unload the property, sacrifice or not. The white elephant, a huge Colonial, sat on a treeless, weedy five-acre tract. The interior hummed and rocked with space: a game room and den down, besides the usual living room,

188

here like a ballroom, and a huge family room in cedar and brick. He counted six bedrooms, four baths. The ex-husband was also trying to sell his tools, his camping equipment, and his speedboat. He still had them stored in the heated, paneled, five-car garage.

Calvin was willing to let Sheila have his old house, but as soon as he got the kids, he was moving them out here where they could stretch. He looked around for a horse.

Sheila called from time to time, catching him at work. "Why aren't you ever home these days?" she asked, rattling her ice cubes against the sides of her glass. "Why don't you ever answer your phone? What're you up to now? What's going on? What do you think you're doing that I can't handle?"

She could lose that confidence in the next breath, a thin assurance these days that soon overextended itself and disappeared, revealing the wildly fluctuating fears and cross-purposes beneath. She changed her tone now. She was suddenly crying, and she wanted help. She said that Lu Ann had insulted her. However, she wasn't specific, and he couldn't make much sense of it. He heard some shouting in the background, and she hung up.

He was taking his books and his papers out of the old house when Lu Ann caught him several days later. "I've tried to be patient," she said over the phone, getting ready to go into a long pitch. "I've tried to be sympathetic. I've tried to help. But I have my own marriage and my own family, and if I've failed, I'm sorry. I'm letting myself off the hook."

What did all that mean? "What's going on now?"

"Well, you don't know what it's been like. She runs around town in a rented sports car—a tiny thing with red leather, and she's all over. She goes up into the mountains on weekends. She gets her hair done and then she disappears." Lu Ann talked about her continuous drinking, her underhandedness, and her feisty nature. "Why, she's propositioned Arthur! *Poor* Arthur, of all people. Can you imagine that?" she asked, pausing, because he would need time to imagine it.

"Where are my children? Are the girls all right?"

"I let it drop, of course. I didn't tell her I even knew. What's the point? Why, she's *sick*, of course, and she needs help. *I* can't help her. *I* can't tell her a thing. When I *try*, she gets completely out of hand."

"I want to talk to the girls, Lu Ann."

"She certainly got *completely* out of hand tonight! She started drinking earlier than usual. The house was a mess, just a mess: both TV's going, the kids all over, but I decided I was going to have to make a stab at it. I was going to be as tactful as I *could* be, but I was going to tell her she was going to have to do something about herself. I was going to tell her that if she didn't do *something*, she couldn't stay with us."

"Where are the girls right now?"

"Oh, they're all in bed *now*, mine and yours, both sets."

He finally sat down and lit a cigarette. He could hear the cats back in the utility room, running around, jumping up on the dryer. "I owe you something there."

"What am I supposed to do, just forget them? They're just *children!*"

"I'm coming out to pick up the children."

"Anyway, *listen*. I took her upstairs, back into the sewing room, where we could talk quietly, and I mentioned AA. I just *mentioned* it! Good grief! She *just blew*! She hit the roof. She screamed and screamed. She was all *over* the house. *I* couldn't handle her, and Arthur was working late. I decided that I was going to have to call him, but while I was still on the phone, she dashed out. She grabbed her car keys, and she was gone. In her state. I can't take much more of this."

"I'm getting a plane out in the morning. I'm picking up my children."

He called the airport about a morning schedule. When he put the phone down, he realized that he couldn't sleep. He had to keep busy. He continued packing books. He was still up in the den when Lu Ann called back. He took the phone there.

Sheila hadn't gotten any farther than Valley Highway. She had been trying to overtake a truck going down a long, curving ramp, and when she hit it, the small car rolled over the high, steep embankment several times before it finally stopped below, its fall broken against a utility pole.

Phones, phones, phones. He felt cut off from the world, certainly alone, back in this cold, silent house where the cats were prowling around upstairs now, eyeing him suspiciously, probably certain that something was up; but he still had a phone near him.

Organize, organize, organize, only organize!

He called his attorney at home, but he couldn't get her. He talked to a child for a minute, a TV going in the background.

He wanted a drink, but there was nothing in the house. Besides, he was going to have to keep a cool head. He had an early plane to catch. When he lit a cigarette, he realized that his hand was shaking. He felt cold, too, but other than the coldness, he wasn't sure just *how* he felt at the moment. How do you respond to a death? Any death?

He called Charley and got him out of bed. Charley had trouble following the news for a minute. "Sheila?" he kept saying, "Sheila?" as if he had trouble remembering just who she was, or perhaps which wife.

His voice finally came through clearer. "Oh, *Sheila*! Jesus Christ, buddy, what shape are you in right now? Where *are* you, anyway?"

He was sitting in the upstairs den watching the cats. He realized that he couldn't continue to leave them alone in the house. He was going to have to drop them off at the veterinarian's before he got his plane. Well, that was one chore figured out—one step taken. A step at a time, and then what?

He rubbed the side of his face. He needed a shave: another necessary action.

"Calvin? Cal? Are you still there? What's going on? Are you all right, or what?"

Calvin nodded. "Poor Sheila!"

"Oh, yes. She was *always* going ninety miles an hour, though, buddy."

"I know."

"She didn't make it easy on herself."

She didn't make it easy on anybody, and what could he have done about all that? Like everybody else, he couldn't handle her.

"Cal? What's going on now?"

He was still rubbing the side of his face. "I'm all right. I've got a busy day ahead. I've got to fly out to Denver. I've got to deal with a lot of wild people before I can get my kids back here. I've got to *shave* right now," he said.

"Listen, buddy, you sound numb. Can you deal? Take it easy, will you?"

"Oh, yes."

"What can we do? What if we take the kids for awhile until you figure out what you're going to do next?"

Charley was mellowing. He sounded authentically concerned. "No."

"You'll have enough on your hands in the next few months."

"No."

"We've got a large house, plenty of room, and Buffy won't mind a few more. Hell, she may as well spoil them while she's spoiling hers!"

"No, thanks. They've been away from home long enough as it is. Besides, I need them around. We'll all work it out."

"Do you want me down there?"

"No. There's nothing you can do."

"Well, I could be around, but I've got to be on the coast."

"I'll see you soon, Charley."

"Yeah. You know how that is. I've got to be on the coast. You know how those things work."

"I can manage. I'm fine. I just need a shave right now," he said, finally realizing that his shaving equipment was in the other house, of course.

He walked into a lunatic situation the next day: the mother and sister flying at each other, blaming each other, and then turning on him. Why couldn't he take care of his own wife?

A good question! A first class question!

He wasn't too balanced himself. "That's right. That's right! That's right! I don't know how to handle her troubles!" he shouted, still using the present tense. "I don't know anything about her!"

Arthur was mannish and helpful. He called his doctor, and he brought sedatives home, passing them around like candies.

Sedated, the two women got through the week looking glazed and remote, as if peacefully contemplating ancient griefs.

He finally calmed down himself. He took on one problem and then prepared himself for the next: the inquiry, the cops, the car rental agency, the trucking company, the insurance people, the newspapers, the distant relatives, and the funeral arrangements.

The women did not break down during the funeral service, but they did not speak to each other afterwards, either. The mother caught a plane out as soon as it was over.

Arthur wasn't particularly concerned. "They'll get over this," he said. "They need each other."

Calvin stayed close to his children whenever he could. He constantly worried about them, in part because they seemed so remote. If they needed him, they did not show it. They did not ask questions, and they seldom mentioned their mother.

Arthur put his finger on other matters. "You're going to need time to yourself, too," he said, just before they flew back.

However, he had to stay on top of things now because if he didn't, who would?

When the children first saw the Colonial, they wouldn't spread out. They looked pale, constrained, and uncertain. They dragged around, stayed close to each other, exchanging secret glances, holding whispered conversations, or just staring off into space.

Shelley spoke first. "Daddy? Is this a *farm*?" she asked.

Their cloth suitcases still smelled like cat piss, and the few scraps of clothing they carried would have to be replaced.

NINE Calvin was sleeping poorly. He lay there staring at the ceiling, reviewing his life: the jobs he had held, the people he had known, the investments he had made, the places he had lived in, the wives he had failed, the child he had already let go, having slipped through his hands in the courts.

When he slept, he could hear voices in his blurred, grayish dreams, a babble in the background, like a waterfall of changing sounds. When he woke, he could still hear the voices, his own, going on and on and on. He had things to get straight, and the talking always interfered. He avoided that center of muteness, his being. He needed to be at a loss for words.

He couldn't come first, either. He was constantly worried about his two girls, refugees from another life, little aliens, battered immigrants. Unlike him, they hadn't learned to pack up overnight, get out of where they were and move on.

While he was at the studio, he wrote little notes on what must be done at home. He would put down his pen and stare at the handwriting below the legend: from the desk of . . .

He was wearing his hair longer, and he had started a beard that fall—around his chin and kept trimmed fairly short, where he was just starting to gray. The face now looks less bland and round, the skin less perfect; the cheekbones have become accented, and the forehead has started to pick up some lines. He was a forty-two-year-old widower trying to raise two girls.

Still, given the curly dark hair, the beard, the chilly blue eyes, the tailored suits, the pale silk shirts, given his knowledge, his talking, his two shows, his constant going, he was a widower with some class, with interesting, preoccupied

194

airs, with mysteries. Nobody was supposed to assume that he needed a thing.

He was not a ladies' man, either, in the conventional sense of that term, and because he feared rejection, he could stay cool and distant over long periods of time.

He was sharper than his father, and educated, but if he wasn't careful, if he didn't watch himself, he could disappear into a ragtag series of personalities and roles. At the moment, though, his worries kept him focused.

Shelley picked up Gwen's baby talk, tried to climb into her sister's plastic training pants and wanted to live on her father's lap. They both fought each other for lap space. When they weren't in his lap, they followed him around the house, trying to hold onto his legs. He once found Gwen trying to lick the dustpan, just to get his attention, and while he was trying to distract her with the car keys, he caught Shelley carrying around the garden shears.

They wanted to wrestle every night before bed. While he lay on the floor on his back, they climbed up on top, across his chest and shoulders and sat on his face. He plucked them off carefully, one by one, but when he had one off, the other returned. The crazy mauling continued until bedtime.

The live-in cleaning woman did not approve of these antics. "You get them so worked up, they won't sleep a lick," Mrs. Pollett said, on her way upstairs.

He ignored her. He had specifically advertised for a live-in babysitter, a motherly type who would put his children's needs before the house's. However, she had missed the point from the beginning. She had taken one long look at the house and asked for cleaning supplies. "First things first," she had said, but, as far as he could see, she seldom got around to the second things.

She considered that she was finished after dinner. She went up to her room where she read paperback trash until she fell asleep. She had gone straight through *Fanny Hill*, and she was starting on *The Love Lives of Frank Norris*.

He couldn't fire her until he found someone else. He advertised a second time, taking a different post office box, stressing his particular needs, using phrases like "sustained affection, warm concern," but this show of desperation could have kept people away. So far, he had no takers.

Charley Klick turned up in early March. The children had both TV's going—one in the family room, which they had abandoned, and a second in the living room. They were still in front of the second, both wearing battered cowboy hats, having their lunch on fancy paper party plates, fancy paper party napkins decorated with cartoon characters. They did not like plain paper plates and napkins. They sat there chewing quietly, their eyes on the two men crossing through, trying to get around the toys and costumes.

The TV eye was focused on Central Park—a part of Calvin's innocent past, crossing it on Sunday mornings to reach the Paris, the private firm showings before the house opened its doors to the public at one; but these crowds could have come from the moon. On the twelve o'clock news, a love-in stretched across the grounds in every direction: silent, gangly, gentle children; silent, slouching, barely moving herds, the new, nonverbal wave.

"Stoned, stoned," Charley Klick was saying. "*Look* at them! Every last fucker! If you see it in one sense, it's a peaceful scene."

Talk, his generation's great drug, its chief vice. Talk, and his generation feels as if something's being explored, explained, accomplished.

"A medieval pageant, Calvin. Immigrating children in shapeless clothes. Secret powers, and the great con game: I know something that you don't. The incense helps. No wonder it's back. Incense and astrology."

"And you support the war."

"Hell, no, I don't. We're digging a pit for ourselves every minute."

Mrs. Pollett was sweeping in the den. He called her Mrs. Pullet in front of the children. He seldom remembered her real name. She resembled a huge, noisy, disapproving chicken.

196

They went on into the kitchen, where the floor had recently been scrubbed, the chairs sitting up on the table. He fixed gin and tonic and put the bottle in the ice bucket because he didn't want to come back into the house. They went out into the yard, where it was drizzling, and they ended up in the garage. When they couldn't find any other place to sit, they climbed into the speedboat, which was still up on its wheels. They sat in the boat drinking and talking, listening to the drizzle on the roof.

"I let the old place go, and I'm renting here," Calvin said. "I'm camping out for the time being."

Sheila's death limited their conversation at first, an unspoken subject that hung between them. "What are you going to do next?"

He wasn't making any plans. He wasn't putting in any work on the place. He wasn't planting this year. When he thought about the future, he could only envision vast, unsafe flashes of openness. "I'll have to think about that when I get around to doing it. Right now, we're lying low."

"You ought to come back East, buddy."

"I have to think about what I want to do with what I have," he said, jumping from problem to problem. "Last spring Fern's attorney wrote, asking for additional child support. I was going to hold back increased support until I could get the visiting rights squared away. I was going to go back to court in the fall. But then there was Denver, there was the accident, and I've had my hands full ever since."

"Floyd was in Saigon during the Tet offensive last January. He flew back recently with a helmet for the boy. Floyd's gotten pretty strange. Very grim. You can't talk to him anymore at all. Fern's lucky he didn't come back with a skull."

Calvin was only half listening. "I have to work through one problem at a time."

"Sheila was always going ninety miles an hour. She was very destructive, and you couldn't cope. Don't blame yourself."

She had taken no advice or assistance from anyone, and she had certainly asked for none. He had accepted her self-sufficiency at face value, needing to, and when he tried to pin down his uneasiness now, a recent feeling, he realized that he hadn't offered comfort because he didn't have it to give. He didn't want to be swallowed. So she was a stranger. They had tried to live together without getting in each other's way, at best. That was the most they could hope for. Sometimes, though, the house hadn't been large enough. *Mother of his children*, as the phrase goes, and she had been a foreign element—a series of noises and smells, densities and textures, a weighty, unspoken quantity beside him in the bed.

"We were both always going, and neither listened, but that doesn't put me in the free and clear. I didn't ask her what I could do for her."

"*What* could you do for her?"

The light was draining in the garage, and it was growing damper. The rain was coming down heavier. He had long since shut off the heat out there. Having to heat with electricity because the gas lines did not come out that far, he had shattering bills as it was. "I should have understood the trouble she was in."

Charley shook his head. "And then do what? Those are such murky waters. That's such a questionable, unsafe business, and it isn't your place. You couldn't handle it without taking advantage of it, or being taken advantage of, or both. You were a satisfactory husband in the world's eyes. You earned a good living, you loved your children, and you came home at night. What more could she want? So stop torturing yourself. Stop trying to hang yourself up on a hook."

Charley was not as open with him as he had once been. He criticized less. He could also detect concern in his tone, as if Charley now found him beyond help. But Calvin couldn't keep quiet. He had to talk. "I *needed* her drinking. I used her drinking against her so that I could keep my distance. And then, when I wanted a divorce, I had a first-class excuse."

"So what? A wife and mother shouldn't have *been* drinking like that in the first place."

An old-fashioned male, a classic Catholic, Charley produced children, made money, and kept a good roof over everybody's head. He did not go near the emotional life, and he apparently was not asked to. Buffy did not force such issues. But how did he get away with it? Why was he allowed to believe that he could handle women, when he wasn't close to them in the first place? Didn't he need intimacy? Didn't he suffer unknowingly? Who could tell? He played his cards close to his chest. Just because he avoided the emotional life, he had a certain advantage. All right, all right, Charley did not grow emotionally. He did not essentially change, but he was safe. He had roots. He knew where he was going to be in ten months' time, in ten years' time. He also had something to offer: pity. "I *know* she shouldn't have been drinking like that in the first place, but she *was*, and I wasn't helping a bit!"

Shelley was just learning to answer the phone, and when it went off, she would tear across the room to get at it first, dodging obstacles in her path and trying to beat out any adult in her way if she could. She answered it when Sarah Elizabeth's housekeeper called him the following month, a person-to-person exchange, and while Calvin was trying to get the phone, Shelley kept saying "WHAT? WHAT? WHAT?" getting nowhere with the operator. "DAD?" she finally screamed. "It's for you!"

Mrs. Fox was impatient and fairly unspecific. He could not get much information from her except that Sarah Elizabeth had been briefly hospitalized. "She's out now," she said, shouting, as if she had to cover all that space. "She's all right, she coddles herself, but she wants to know if you can come up for a visit."

The children wanted to help him pack. They dragged out more than he could take, or needed. They mixed the clean clothes up with the soiled, and they were generally louder than usual. When they lost interest in packing, they still dogged his heels.

He couldn't be sure how they were taking this latest turn of events. They partly wanted to go, partly didn't.

He couldn't take them, though, because he didn't know what he was getting into. If she had been sick, she might not be in any shape to entertain two small girls. When he thought about it, he could not imagine her ever being in such shape.

He was still on the Pennsylvania Turnpike when Martin Luther King was shot, but he didn't have the radio on, and he didn't hear the news until he reached the New York hotel. He kept the TV on while he showered and changed. He slept badly and woke early.

While he was shaving, he caught the morning headlines. Cities and towns were erupting all over the country, but he decided he was going to go on. He was going to keep a business appointment in Boston and then drive out to the Cape. He packed, ate breakfast, and checked out. He felt highly strung, and on the road he did not unwind. When he reached Boston, he checked into his hotel, moved into the bar and drank until he was tired. He slept poorly again, hearing his voices: the half-muted, cascading sounds that accompanied his hazy dreams like background music.

He woke with a light headache, but he felt purposeful. He showered, shaved, dressed, and took three aspirin. While he ate breakfast, he skimmed through the papers in the hotel coffee shop. He kept his business appointment, and then crossed the Boston Commons on his way back to his car.

He saw a group of students demonstrating ahead. They formed a loose semicircle, both sexes in ragged, castoff-looking clothing, and, from his distance, the tableau appeared to be allegorical in intent against the bleak sky. When he drew closer, when they no longer resembled aliens, holy fools, sacred clowns, he realized that they had probably come from solid, unimaginative middle-class backgrounds. The boys had long hair, but were clean shaven.

A big, fatty, pretty girl crossed his path in something soft and sweeping. She handed him her antiwar literature and pressed his hand. She was obviously from some curious religious sect because when she touched his hand, she told him she loved him. He felt self-conscious, imposed upon, but since he did not know what else to say, he told her he loved her, too. He quickened his pace, keeping his eyes on the ground.

He climbed into his Mercedes and sat there for a moment until he had his sense of privacy back. Then he drove around the Commons, off to see his grandmother on the Cape. The traffic was heavy around Boston, but it thinned out past Plymouth, and he turned on the car radio. He couldn't find much besides rock music. "Love's returning, love's returning, to the world."

He heard the same idea while he was crossing Sagamore Bridge. "Oh, Love, Oh Love, Give me love . . ."

He turned the car radio off.

He stopped at a combination gas station, grocery, and bait shop on Route Six just past Sandwich. The gas station was closed, but while he was inside the grocery picking up cigarettes, a transistor was going on the counter beside the cash register. *Oh, the world needs love!* everybody was still insisting, *love, pure love.*

It was a chilly day, the sky churning with leaden, fragmented cloud cover that promised rain or perhaps late snow. He picked up the carton of cigarettes without asking for a bag and put the carton on the seat beside him. He drove on, passing the turn for East Sandwich and West Barnstable.

He was just outside of Brewster when he saw the hitch-hiker. He paused on the narrow shoulder, and while the traffic whipped past, she took her time getting out of the obligatory backpack. She climbed in slowly, putting the pack between her feet on the floor. She finally leaned over and shut the door as if she had until tomorrow to do it. He thought she was stoned, but he couldn't be sure.

She looked sixteen or seventeen at the most. She was tall, lanky, and freckled, and she had short brownish hair pulled up behind the ears. She was wearing dungarees and one of those plain, thin blouses that does not quite meet the belt below. She sat hunched up, her knees against the dashboard, her hands folded between her legs against her crotch.

She was getting a cold. She blew her nose once, hard, and when he asked her where she was going, she studied the handkerchief for a moment before answering. "I'm going to P-Town, because where else? I'm tired, though, and I don't want to rap. I'll ball if you want to ball. I'll ball if you have a warm place, but if it's all the same to you, I don't want to rap right now."

He bought her a meal around Orleans, gave her motel money, and dropped her off just before his turn.

He passed Governor Prence Road, then took a left turn, down a dirt lane into the woods, passing the small places in among the trees. He found Sarah Elizabeth's without difficulty. The gray-shingled three-quarter Cape sat on a slight incline in a clearing, a single shuttered window on one side of the door, two on the other. A chimney rose above the bowed roof.

Mrs. Fox answered the door—first his great-grandmother's housekeeper and now his grandmother's. Mercy had kept no house help until the last six months of her life. Sarah Elizabeth had certainly never kept any around before. He realized that he had taken his time arriving because he was worried about what he would find. Mrs. Cox was a short, sturdy, broad-bottomed woman with a small mottled face and uncombed, wild-looking white hair. "I do for her now," she said, going ahead, leading him back, "because she's been pampering herself lately. You know how some will."

He remembered everything: the dark, low-ceilinged hall, the small, square parlor on the right, the small bedroom on the left. "Why was she in the hospital?"

"She's had a little breathing problem, but there's no general call to get alarmed. Well, here we are. She thinks she's queen for a day, but, I swear, I couldn't just sit like that."

He found his grandmother in the kitchen in a wicker chair she had brought up from Connecticut over twenty years back. She looked smaller and thinner. She was still smoking, and when she turned, she stayed encircled in that familiar, bluish gray tobacco haze.

Then the child, Calvin, intact, a solid mass, an animate weight, rose up through his chest and fitted across his shoulders and face, and when he moved his mouth to speak or smile, he felt his mouth returning to an old shape. There would be both something false and plucky about the expression, as if his whole being were on trial, anxious to please and placate.

She wasn't much on embracing, and when he leaned down she offered her hand. She looked terribly pale at close range, and the grip was less mannish than he remembered. She was still wearing the same kind of clothes, something shapeless and brown, belted around the middle, dropping unevenly at the calves. She had the easterner's sense of space, and when he told her that he had driven up from New York the day before, she looked at him with an air of considerable doubt. "You must be a very determined young man," she said, flicking her ash into a china saucer on her lap.

He had once tried to take her on, shortly after he had come home from the service, when he had thought of himself as an adult, but that bluff was now burned away like so much else. He couldn't adjust to her sitting down in the middle of the day. He wanted a lot of specific information about her health. What, exactly, was wrong with her breathing, for instance? Was it her chest or her heart, or both? However, he was worried about offending because she was such a private person.

He finally just asked her how she was—a conventional question which sounded shallow and hearty in his own ears, and he got what he deserved. She just shrugged, as if such faint pleasantness wasn't worth bothering with. Then something around the eyes seemed to crinkle for a minute, and she asked him how *he* was, as if she were paying him back. He felt innane. He heard himself saying that he was fine, just fine, and then, as her eyes grew duller, her brief look of amusement vanished.

Mrs. Fox brought in fresh kindling and dropped it by the stove. The kitchen was already uncomfortably warm, but she stoked the fire and stuck in more wood. She ran water in the sink and attacked the dishes, which had started to pile up. All her movements were abrupt, ungainly and impatient, and if you did not know the type, you could have assumed that she did not much care for the present company. She was worrying about what she was going to fix for supper, and while she worked, she talked to herself. "We could finish up that cold clam pie, of course, but do we *want* that cold clam pie?" she asked herself. "I am fairly certain that I do not. Because that clam pie wasn't like that clam pie we had before. I still say you can't freeze clam pie. You freeze a fresh clam pie, and something goes. You can not tell me it does not."

He was trying to get through to Sarah Elizabeth over that constant hum. He asked her if he could do anything for her. She said she could not imagine what. He asked her if she needed anything, and she said she did not. He asked her if she wanted any errands run, and she said that a delivery boy came to the door.

Mrs. Fox could talk to herself and still follow the conversation around her. "Well, we are not as squared away as she might indicate," she said. "That boy doesn't come until Wednesday, and we're low on cigarettes. We're also low on that dry sherry you like. Why, and then there are the prescriptions to fill, which are just lying about. Because if you see a doctor, and pay him those high prices he wants, you may as well take his drugs."

Calvin's spirits suddenly picked up. He was going to be useful after all. "I'm not going to drive back today. I'll find a motel and spend the night, and so, if you'll give me a list before I leave, I can drop in with everything tomorrow. Is tomorrow soon enough?"

"Tomorrow is fine," Mrs. Fox said. She assumed that he was just going to drop off the supplies then. She did not encourage his doing more than that. She assumed that he was on vacation, and she treated him like a tourist. "You will want to look around while you are here," she said. "You will probably want to see the old Jericho house in South Dennis."

Sarah Elizabeth put her cigarette out in the saucer. She made a small noise in the back of her throat and touched her chest. She was involved in her own thoughts. "There aren't too many of the old places left. There's the summers, when everything changes anyway, and that bay is gone. You wouldn't recognize it these days. All those strangers around with nothing on. They lie around back there, frying themselves up. Now where is the sense in that?"

"What happens in the winters, Grandma? Do you get a lot of snow? What happens when you're snowed in back here?"

"We generally don't get much, but when I am snowed in, I enjoy the privacy. I enjoy the silences."

"If you needed me, would you call? Would you ask for help?"

"What help could you be, where you are, out in Kansas?"

He didn't correct her. "I could get here quickly."

"Well, you know, I never think of you as a help because I never think of you as grown. You're still a boy, to me, with or without that beard. I suppose you're protesting the war."

"Some of those people can be pretty serious."

She raised her brows. She struck a kitchen match on the side of her chair and lit another cigarette. "Seriousness, at that age, is quite common, isn't it? But seriousness, at that age, doesn't amount to much. It doesn't amount to a hill of beans," she said.

He was worried about the various deaths and disruptions. "The Congress and the President have both been telling us a lot of lies lately."

"Well, *that's* hardly news, is it? What else have they ever done?"

"It's still incredible."

"Do you think so? Too many people, in all directions, getting themselves worked up, and then, when they do, why, they're surprised at how things turn out. They say, don't they, that it's a sinful state of affairs, but I've always taken sin for granted, and so I don't get too surprised over it myself. I'm more likely to be surprised when I see somebody behaving himself."

Mrs. Fox left the room to make out the shopping list, and as soon as the housekeeper left, Sarah Elizabeth changed the subject. She wanted to talk about her investments. While she kept her voice down, worried about the woman's return, she discussed the considerable holdings she still kept track of in Bridgeport, Connecticut. She also had things going on the Cape. She had something going in East Sandwich and West Barnstable, in Hyannis, and South Yarmouth, in Harwich and East Harwich. She had roamed as far as South Wellfleet, and now she was considering a piece of land just outside North Truro.

She took the creased real estate advertisement out of her pocket and handed it to him. She wanted to know what kind of investment he thought it would be, and she asked him to drive up there to look the situation over. "If nothing else, it could be a useful tax shelter," she said. "I've been giving entirely too much money to the government lately."

Her mind appeared to be as clear, and as set, as ever, and, as she talked about the property, he grew more hopeful about her health. Mrs. Fox returned, and she changed the subject abruptly. He took the shopping list and left.

He climbed past Eastham, past North Eastham and past Wellfleet looking for a motel that would be open so early in the season. He finally located one close to Truro. He checked in and went directly to the bar. The place was restful, empty, and dark. A huge cod hung over the cold fireplace. The dining room beyond was being painted, and while he sat at the bar, he could hear the painters calling back and forth to each other out there, moving the ladders and getting up and down. His stomach was empty, and after the second martini, his face felt stiff. He finally got something to eat in the coffee shop, but as tired as he was after the trip, he knew that he wasn't going to sleep yet. He took the clipping out of his pocket, and while he drank his coffee, he checked out the address.

He stopped for gas while he was still on Route Six, and while the attendant filled the tank, he opened the fresh car-

206

ton of cigarettes on the seat beside him. He started off just after dusk. He paused outside of North Truro and switched onto the alternate route, following the narrow, winding, single-lane road that curved along the bay in the softening dark. The few trees gradually disappeared, the grass thinned out, and the sandy stretches increased. The wind was brisk, and the tide was up. He passed rows of closed tourist cabins and a closed seafood place.

He was swinging in farther toward the water when he saw the house sitting by itself in an open field facing the bay. The vacant, sprawling, weathered, rambling, gray-shingled summer place had an unobstructed view of the bay, but it was in general disrepair. The roof and wraparound porch needed work, the shingles and screens needed replacing. There are always odd bits of lumber lying around old beach houses, and these stuck out from under the porch.

He pulled off the road and drove down the long, narrow, rutted lane that passed the house on its way to the bay. He stopped beside the for sale sign and got out with the clipping in his hand, pacing off the measurements. The land was pie-shaped, its apex toward the water. Once the house was down, you could get in a reasonably good-sized motel which would face the road, but you couldn't put in enough parking. So, why, then, was it zoned for business? Who was going to offer that kind of money just for a fairly pleasant piece of residential property? Who were they kidding? Why was everybody crazy these days?

He put the clipping back in his pocket, lit a cigarette, and strolled around. A thin moon threw an uneven sheen across the patches of grass in the rear, but the darkness predominated now. The dark stretched all the way from the rear of the house to the road. The road itself, going on into Provincetown, was empty, and in the darkness he couldn't even make it out. When a car finally passed, the road was lit for a moment, and then gone.

He went around to the front of the house again. He walked down through the rough clumps of poverty grass toward the open beach, where he could hear the tide coming in, fanning out along the breezy, open shore. The waves broke across the hard ridged sand just below him. Despite the sharp wind, he lingered there for a moment, breathing in the rank moistness, listening to the wash, the steady coming and going. The sea, the sea. It appeared to illuminate some basic meaning, some rudimentary idea of harmony which had eluded him through the years. If he felt this way, then, why wasn't he here all the time? Why wasn't he here, settling down?

He slept poorly, still hearing himself talking to himself in the back of his dreams, numerous background sounds, accents, imitations, disembodied voices explaining, arranging, defending. He finally fell into a deep sleep and did not wake before nine A.M. He shopped and reached her house just before noon.

As soon as he pulled up, he knew that something was wrong, and he jumped out of the car without shutting the door. He found Sarah Elizabeth still in bed in the front bedroom downstairs across from the parlor. She was conscious but she was having trouble breathing. She look dulled and spent.

"Have you seen the old Jericho house yet?" Mrs. Fox asked him. "I think you should see the old Jericho house in South Dennis and perhaps the Saconesset homestead in West Falmouth."

He paced, wanting a cigarette, staying close to the bed, refusing to leave her sight. He was terrified, and he was beginning to sweat. He touched her hand several times, but she appeared not to recognize him. Where was the damn ambulance? Oh, grandma, grandma, grandma!

"You will also want to visit the Atwood house in Chatham, of course. You will have to find out what day it is open to the general public. I do not go when they do, and I would not know. I also expect you will want to see the glass in Sandwich."

Sarah Elizabeth started to fumble with the sheets around her chest. Her mouth was moving, and she tried to raise her

208

head. She finally raised herself halfway, beckoning to him, anxious to communicate. He bent closer. While she tried to shape her words, she continued to pluck at the sheets with her long, thin, bluish-looking fingers. The loose flesh hid half the blunt, short, torn nails. "The Atwood place is *not* worth the admission price," she said, then, expended, she fell back on the pillows.

The ambulance pulled up, and the attendants jumped out with the stretcher. He stayed out of the way and followed it back to the small hospital in Hyannis, where she disappeared into the intensive care unit. Despite the hospital's size, it was half-empty because the tourist season had not started yet. It was on the bay. Small boats rode out there, and the water sparkled. He paced around the waiting room, smoking, drinking coffee from a machine. He knew she was dying, but he couldn't get into intensive care. She went abruptly that afternoon.

Sarah Elizabeth was buried in the old Cove Cemetery just off the Mid Cape Highway in the Scudder family plot, amid the Sparrows, the Hedges, the Snows, and the Doans. The plot kept memorials to three Mayflower passengers who had been buried there, the headstones themselves long since gone. The traffic, not heavy, whipped past on the highway, going at a good clip. The afternoon was bright and crisp, and, during the brief service, he could hear a high school band practicing in the distance somewhere.

He hadn't anticipated running into many relatives, but he was still surprised at the scarcity. He didn't recognize those present until they introduced themselves, and some did not. In most cases, he only knew the names. When, if ever, had he met the Westwoods' daughter from Birchley? Or Abner Scudder's boy, from around Buzzards Bay? Who were the Hallets, the Collinses, and the Sears? And who was Roland Crocker Joy?

He found himself leaving with Mrs. Fox. "I got along tolerably with your grandmother, myself," she said, "but a lot, of course, did not. She was a good woman, when you get right down to it, but, you know, just between you, me and the lamp post, she was not always truthful. She had her little ways. She liked to pretend that she was a native. She thought she was rooted in Nauset."

He spent a moment trying to digest this. "She was born and raised here! Those were all her people, back in that plot!"

"Well, some look at it different. She was not like her mother. She left when she got married, didn't she? She was away a long time. I don't know how they judge these things, where you come from, back in Kansas, but around these parts moving away wipes the slate. You'll be getting everything, of course," she added, changing the subject, "and that will come to a considerable amount, won't it?"

He stopped just outside the gate to light a cigarette. "Do you want a ride back?" He realized that, with luck, he could put up with her for another half hour.

"Well, I'm not so sure, now, just what 'back' even means. When I moved in with her, I gave up my own place. It was not much, but it was mine."

She caught him when he most wanted to escape her. "You can stay in her house until you find what you want. I haven't decided what I'm going to do with it. I don't want to sell it."

"Well, now," she said, and paused, as if she wanted to think about it first, "I suppose I could do that, yes. I could do that if it would accommodate you, of course."

When he dropped her off, he drove on to Truro, packed, and checked out of the motel. While he was putting his luggage in the backseat, he saw the groceries still sitting there, the sherry bottle leaning sideways, appearing over the top. He picked up the bag, walked across the motel parking lot and shoved the groceries into a garbage can.

He climbed back into the Mercedes and got behind the wheel before he finally collapsed. He could not cry, but he could not control the broken, tearing, ragged sounds which appeared to come from somewhere just below his chest. His chest was constricted, and he had difficulty drawing breath. When he finally quieted, he sat in the car for over a half hour—staring down the length of his long, unpurposeful life. He finally started the car and turned onto Route Six. He drove on past Wellfleet, Eastham, and Orleans, turning at the elbow for the stretch ahead. He passed East Harwich and North Harwich. He lit a cigarette, and when the smoke hit his lungs, he thought he was going to be sick. His nerves were on edge, and his hand shook. He realized that he had not eaten properly or slept well for days. He was in no shape to make the trip back. He was certainly in no shape to deal with the children yet. He left Six at the Hyannis exit, swung onto Route 132 and pulled into town looking for a place to stop. He ate in the motel coffee shop and then moved over into the bar before he checked into the place. He drank several brandies while he stared at the TV overhead without seeing it. He knew he still wasn't going to sleep, and he went for a walk.

He passed a big square stone church where cars were parked at the curb and in the lot in back. The lawn was lit with low floodlights and the basement was bright. A function of some kind was in progress below, and when he saw the hand-lettered cardboard signs, he realized that he had stumbled into another antiwar group.

He wasn't attending an official church function, as such, and when he went down there, he thought about the early catacomb culture, as if these church basements, where off-center groups met, could become an important if risky adjunct to a secret part of an otherwise normal life.

Sliding partitions had been pushed back, folded up, accordianlike; there were shelves against one wall, filled with Sunday school texts, various audio-visual aids; and the young priest was pushing an old blackboard on wheels toward the group. A kitchen, now dark, was at the other end.

Mixed ages sat around in a circle, if more young than old. (Why were these groups always in circles?) Most of the girls were curved and cute, in that fresh, serious, wide-eyed way, and unlike the group on the Commons, they were not in ragged, castoff-looking clothing. They wore denims, brief stretchy tops. He felt himself being possessed by that cloudy, buoyant, drifting feeling that gripped him from behind the eyes when he was both tired and around young girls.

A boy stood, speaking. "Well, we've been trying to do something pretty meaningful down here in the last few days. . . ." He cleared his throat and looked around, while his audience waited, politely encouraging, attentive. "Relevant, right? I think we have Father Anglin to thank for that." Everybody clapped. He sat down abruptly, as if interrupted.

The priest waited for the applause to stop. He thanked him. "Well? Does anybody else have anything he or she wants to share?"

A pale, plumpish girl rose next. She had a wide, wonderful mouth and large teeth. "I'm Cheryl Wiolis. I'm joining the group late, I'm afraid, but I'm still hoping to have a meaningful experience in awareness." She sat down.

The priest nodded. "Welcome, Cheryl, and thank you."

The priest spoke for about twenty minutes. He did not raise his voice or show any particular agitation; and the usual facts (figures on the bombing raids, statistics on the dead and wounded) did not seem commensurate with his understated delivery; the concern was calm, measured, and lucid. It appeared to pass from one medium to the next without a corresponding change in density. Calvin felt as if he were being spoken through, not to, and the effect was hypnotic, as if he were being asked to accept love without having to offer it.

A heavy short-haired woman finally interrupted him. "Father, Father! Please? Please! Let's get back to an earlier point. What about the phone tax? Does anybody here want to withhold his phone tax?"

Some did, some didn't. Others wanted more information about it first. Still others, living in student dorms, did not have phones. They sounded excluded. Father Anglin finally wrote "Phone Tax Committee" on the board in large letters.

The kitchen was suddenly lit at the other end of the basement. Middle-aged and elderly ladies started to tiptoe back and forth in their aprons. An altar group was preparing the

212

kitchen for a carry-in dessert smorgasbord, and while the group was still talking, the women cast worried glances toward the peaceniks. Would the anarchists be out on time? They started to set up tables and take down chairs. A sullen-looking, heavily bearded young veteran interrupted the woman. He discussed the atrocities from personal experience. While he talked, he looked around with unconcealed distaste, as if he were bored just being there. A big, fleshy man sat absurdly sideways in his chair, watching the veteran with slightly raised brows. The man had his legs crossed, his large, furry hands clasped across his knees. He was in slacks, expensive sports shirt. His hair, styled, fell in a curve across his ears, without being too long. A mod-looking businessman. He kept shaking his head while the veteran spoke. "I don't believe it," he kept saying, looking around at the others. "I just don't believe it, but, then again, I don't *want* to believe it, do I?"

A different type was suddenly on its feet, a thin, sharp-faced, frizzy-haired girl in overalls (not dungarees). "But why can't he be impeached?" she kept asking, without lowering her hand. "Why can't he be impeached?"

Father Anglin was still standing in front of the blackboard, holding the chalk, and when he got the group's attention, he talked about group responses, using key phrases like *dialogue, nonviolent,* and *creative tension.*

The frizzy-haired girl jumped up again. "I don't get it! *Shit!* Why can't we just throw him out!"

Father Anglin did not answer her directly. "What we need to do right now is to get our own heads clear. Starting with us, starting right here, in this room, before we part tonight. Do we know what we want? Do we know what we're about? Have we questioned ourselves? Do we understand our motives? We come from different parts. We come from different places. We appear together tonight with our own problems. Some of us may be lonely. Some of us may be lost. Some of us may feel as if we aren't receiving our own due share of affection and acceptance. Some of us may still be searching, still looking for the right path to take. So let's try asking ourselves some pretty heavy questions along these lines, concerning what's up ahead, and then let's carefully consider the possible alternatives. Yes, you had your hand up first. Peter?"

The boy ducked his head when he spoke, but when he glanced up, he did not look abashed. He wanted to blow up Harvard's business school.

The veteran jumped to his feet. "Well, I say shit on that! Shit on the colleges, anyway! Who notices the colleges? We need to take this to the people. We need to take this to the streets! What about street theater? Has anybody around here ever done any street theater? How about simulating an invasion? Does anybody here know where we can get a couple of good second-hand tanks?"

Father Anglin never lost that eerie patience. "Street theater has its drawbacks, Steve. What do you think, though? Do you see it as, perhaps, a form of disguised aggression?"

The frizzy-haired girl jumped up. "Well, but what's the *point* if we *don't* get into the street!"

The priest finally wrote "Street Theater Committee" on the board with some reluctance.

The talkative short-haired woman was up next. "Father, please . . . . Father? Please! What about coverage for these people? Don't we want all the coverage we can get? Don't we want to let the media in on this?"

The priest wrote "Coverage Committee" on the board.

However, behind his back, without his having noticed yet, the altar guild had started to file in with the desserts. Their turn, and noisy, making a point, they moved into the hippy camp without compunction. Still intent, Father Anglin had not noticed the invasion.

A stranger was suddenly on her feet. Short, crisp, butchered-looking, sandy-colored hair, and bifocals. A proabortionist, she was either confused about where she was or she was carrying her message into untouched territory. "The unborn have rights, too!" she insisted. "They have their own rights! Do we not owe them the right not to be born in the first place?"

The modish businessman got the priest's attention. He

214

pointed to the women who were now circling the group. "Time's winged chariot," he said. They were arranging on trestle tables the evening's main event: butterscotch pies, chocolate cakes, apple betty, baked custards, bread pudding, colored sherberts, and slowly defrosting fruitballs.

Father Anglin threw up his hands in gracious defeat. "Well, I guess this is it! If you're crossing the country tonight, if you aren't staying with the main group, have a safe trip!"

Scattered applause. People started pushing back chairs, standing and blinking. Talking to one another in smaller groups on the way out.

The businessman stood near the door with a separate clutch of youths waiting to go home. "Pittsburgh? Pittsburgh? Columbus? Columbus? Drivers going west? Any—? Driving? Going west? Come on, people. We're short drivers."

She was sitting near the door waiting for a ride, her face turned toward his while she was talking to someone beside her, her left arm out, over the back of the chair. She was in a man's white shirt, the sleeves rolled up. She had long, straight, bluish black hair which hung more than halfway down her back. A long, darkish, clean-looking girl in soft gray wool pants. "I could demonstrate, I think," she was saying as he passed, "if I just didn't have to do it in public."

Both her appearance and the remark (meant literally, or what?) completely charmed him.

"Pittsburgh? Pittsburgh, please? Columbus, Columbus? Come on, folks. We've got to get these good people home for Easter."

Calvin walked through the door. While the adult Christians arrived, coming toward him, heading for the smorgasbord, he lit a cigarette in the chill. He stood there for a moment, and then he took a deep breath. He went back in.

He was competing with another car heading west, and on the walk to the Mercedes (his little group spread out, following behind him), he could not tell if she was part of his haul or not. While he was opening the trunk, getting the luggage settled, he saw her there, all right, in the back, behind the driver's seat, her profile barely outlined in a street light. He came around.

A boy was standing beside the driver's door. "I'm Hank. I can spell you if you need spelling." A short, round figure with light, wispy-looking curls.

He had never let anyone touch the Mercedes, but he knew he wasn't going to be able to make it all the way back without help. "We'll see," he said, climbing in behind the wheel. He had two males in front, a third male and two women in the rear. Leaving the Cape, noboby talked much. Later, leaving the state, coming over the Connecticut line, he could hear part of the conversation in back. She was a sophomore, a biology major, a premed student in Columbus, Ohio. Which made her what? Around nineteen?

The other girl in the rear started to play a harmonica. Calvin felt slightly chilled and his throat was sore. He gave up just before Hartford. He climbed in back and turned the wheel over to the boy. He had a disorienting, fluttery sense of helplessness when the car started again. Well, what happened happened.

He was sitting beside Lisa, who had moved away from the window. She smelled like lemon face soap.

He tried to draw her out. She offered little besides her name, which he knew. He finally hit some sort of nerve when he mentioned the antiwar group.

"I feel sort of weird, as if I came under false pretenses."

"Why? Aren't you against the war? I thought everybody was against the war."

"Oh, I'm against it. That's it. I'm just a coward. Worried about doing nothing, and feeling false to boot."

Her beauty, her deepest appeal, he decided, lay in her reticence.

It was beginning to snow. He fell asleep smelling her face soap, listening to the windshield wipers.

When he woke, it was drizzling, just starting on the morning hours, and they had a rest stop in New York. When she climbed back into the car, her hair was damp. It smelled like clean, wet darkness. They unwrapped the dry sandwiches bought from a machine and passed hot coffee around. The steaming styrofoam cups were hard to hold. She did not smoke, and he tried to keep the cigarette away from her face.

His throat felt worse, and while he was trying to draw her out, he did not talk much himself. She was born, partly raised, in New Hope, New York, but she moved to Meriden, Connecticut. He told her that there were a lot of Giffords around Madison, Giffords around Guilford, Giffords around Old Saybrook, generally clustered along the coast.

"I'm not related. We came from upstate New York. When my mother died, I spent the summers in Meriden with an aunt."

"Did you like Meriden?"

"Oh, well, it was Meriden. Looking back, I realize that my aunt was pretty patient. I'll bet she breathed easier when my father married again."

"And did you breathe easier?"

"I like my stepmother, yes. She certainly makes more sense than my father does."

The other girl, now in front, was playing the harmonica again. She went through "Old Man River" twice, trying to get it right. She paused, tried again, and then put the harmonica away. She slid down in the seat, dozing behind an Eisenhower jacket she had pulled around her chin.

Hank looked into the rearview mirror. "Considering this drizzle, we're making good time."

Nobody answered.

Calvin fell asleep beside her for the second time.

He opened his eyes around eight o'clock, close to Pittsburgh. It was chilly and gray, but no longer drizzling.

She was awake, staring out.

"April's a cruel month, isn't it?"

She turned, her misty, sea-green eyes on his. "Good heavens! Do you usually quote poetry when you first wake up?"

"No. But then how often do I wake up like this?"

"Like what?"

"Like this."

The corners of her mouth deepened while her eyes were still on his. She said nothing.

They stopped on the Pennsylvania Turnpike. His throat

was still bothering him, and he bought some aspirin. He washed, shaved and changed his shirt. He got behind the wheel, both girls in front now. They drank coffee in the car. Lisa held his cup. The other girl, near the door, sat cleaning her glasses on a paper napkin. The boys fell asleep in back.

He asked her more about her roots.

"Roots? *What* roots?"

She had moved from Meriden to Wilkes-Barre, Pennsylvania. Then along the river in southern Ohio, around places like Wingis Corners, Kitts Creek, Huber-Knobbs, Big Bottom, Slocums Bend, and Sugar Fork—little stops with a gas station, a grocery, a feedstore before the farms began again. Then, the big time, Indianapolis and finally Louisville, where her father was an executive in a tractor company.

"I usually don't talk so much," she said, and then, as if the cliché bothered her, she glanced at him without saying anything else.

"It's this ride."

She was still watching him. "It's this ride, all right, I guess."

"I don't feel quite real."

"*You* don't talk much, do you?"

He did not disabuse her. "It's this ride."

The day was gradually growing less hazy. The sun finally broke through.

He told her about Connecticut and the Cape. He mentioned Sarah Elizabeth's funeral.

Two boys left at the Pittsburgh turnoff. Hank, the former driver, the last male left, spread out across the back seat. He dozed, his right hand against his crotch, his light ringlets matted across his forehead.

Lisa stirred. "It's clearing."

"Yes. It is, it is."

She was still watching him.

"I love those deep, green, gray-green, more than gray-green, misty-ocean eyes of yours."

She didn't drop her glance. "How's your throat?"

218

They ate in Columbus, where Hank left them.

They dropped south, toward Cincinnati, where they started to pick up country music and gospel singers on the car radio.

Meg was looking out. She put her harmonica back into her pocket. She said that she needed a rest room, and they stopped at a gas station just outside the city limits. He had his tank filled.

While he waited for Meg, he bought three Cokes. They sat there, drinking theirs alone.

He lit a cigarette. "This is crazy, Lisa."

"Why?"

"I'm ancient. I'm old enough to be your father."

"How old are you?"

"Forty-two."

"No, you're not. He's forty-three."

Meg returned. She climbed in beside them and took the Coke. "These always give me gas," she said, drinking it.

They continued on into the city. Meg played "Home Sweet Home" on the harmonica over the car radio.

Lisa raised her brows. "The trouble is, my home's not particularly humble."

Meg finished the song, wiped the harmonica, and put it back in her pocket. He stopped to let her off at the bus station in Cincinnati. She swung into her backpack and everybody left shook hands. "Well, see you folks around," she said, as if she would. Then she was gone.

The car, now so empty, seemed fuller, the silence more complex. "So? *Why* isn't your home 'particularly humble'?" he asked. His voice was growing hoarse. "Because you're so well-off?"

"Oh, yes, but I didn't mean that. I was talking about my father, who roars around like a bull."

"He usually gets his way."

"With my stepmother, yes. She keeps the peace. I just avoid most issues. I just stay away from home."

They crossed the river near Newport, through Covington,

219

and, as they dropped south along the river, the air grew muggy. They picked up the early lush, greenish tints and the flowering trees that would not reach Indianapolis for several weeks yet.

He stopped the car on a side road and kissed her. She was slightly reserved, but did not seem surprised.

"I'm not thinking. Okay?" she said, her arms still around his neck. "So if you want any thinking done, you do it. You're elected."

They entered Louisville shortly after seven P.M. He found a hotel on the river. The huge lobby had tall french windows, marble sills, tasseled velvet drapes. The sweeping stairs curved up to a second-story balcony.

Going up in the elevator, he set his suitcase and her backpack on the floor at their feet. "There it is," he said, looking down, "the difference in the generations."

She was irritated. "Are you planning to make a lot of that?"

Rebuked with such precision, he said nothing. Dead tired, disoriented, slightly feverish, he realized he could make a lot of orotund slips like that.

In the corridors, empty at that hour, she stayed behind him. When he turned, he saw her looking at the brass fixtures, the plush, red-textured wallpaper that matched the rug.

"Goodness! What splendor!"

He stopped at their door. "Why? Is all this grandeur offensive?"

"No. Of course not."

But he still felt vaguely mannered and stiff.

He dropped their luggage just inside the door.

She picked up her backpack, walked into the bathroom and closed the door. She started the shower.

He felt as if he were still in the car, and while he wandered around, waiting to take his own shower, the highway's moving images passed through his head.

She appeared in something short, pale and girlish. She

was still drying her hair. "*Try* it! You're next. It's wonderful. It's *hot*. I haven't felt so clean since I left home."

While he was taking his shower, he suddenly realized that he had first met her at just about this hour last night. What was next? Where were they going? Well, what happened happened.

She was sitting on the edge of the bed when he came out. She looked up. "You're thinking, aren't you?"

"Oh, yes."

"Don't."

"I thought I was elected to think."

"Well, I've changed my mind."

They lingered in the hotel close to a week. They stayed inside, eating and drinking in the small, half-hidden alcoves, the half-lit bar with a flagstone floor and fireplace. While the firelight shimmered on the pewter, the brass carriage lamps, they stared at each other without speaking for long periods of time. They played with each other's fingers. He was sleeping normally again, and his cold had disappeared. There were barges on the river below, and when he woke, he could hear the distant foghorns in the chill.

He was talking again. He told her about his marriages and his children. He told her about Sarah Elizabeth and Mercy Scudder, his great-grandmother. He told her about his father.

Dancing, carrying a cane, tipping his straw hat, his father could flop like a scarecrow, hop like a rabbit while looking over his left shoulder, checking for applause. A part-time, two-bit comic with walk-on roles. A sensation in costumes, a nun, a priest, a cop. A woman wearing a fur muff, an old man selling chestnuts, pulling his false beard like mad Lear.

Also a crazy, unemployed, morose-looking ventriloquist. With his long, spindly arms, wide hands. Tufts of blunt, black hair on top, shaggy brows, big, wet, loose, sad mouth. Talking to the dummy, the ugly, leering elf talking back. Turning to his family, widening his eyes, wondering what the dummy was going to say next. Keeping his audience's

221

attention on the elf, away from his own face, because his mouth was hardly still when the elf spoke.

He told her about his father's disappearance and then his abrupt return eight years later, when Calvin was fourteen. "My people on my mother's side were all talkers; Sarah Elizabeth was a talker. You couldn't get a word in edgeways when a Scudder got going. On top of that, my father was a talker. We waited for him to begin talking all the way back in the car from Mercy's funeral; we certainly waited for some explanation about his return, but none came."

He slept through the traffic; he slept through the muggy June day; he slept through the light and the growing shade while they dropped down through the small Connecticut towns.

Oh, a waiter, a vacuum cleaner salesman, a lingerie clerk, a service station attendant. Once, making ends meet, he had driven a bootlegger's truck. Once, later, during the war, just before Mercy's death, he had hung out with gamblers. Secretive, big-time stuff, but now he was in trouble, on the run. . . .

His father woke when they finally pulled up in front of the house. Back in Bridgeport, refreshed from his many little catnaps, he was ready to help with the luggage. Out, out, to make himself useful.

"'Is there any peace/In ever climbing up the chilly wave?'" he intoned, his rich voice back, some balance restored. "'All things have rest, and ripen toward the grave/In silence— ripen, fall and cease.'" While he quoted, while his in-laws fled into the house, he worked on the luggage rack, unknotting the ropes, removing the canvas. "'Give us long rest or death, dark death or dreadful ease.'"

And wasn't Calvin's calm, placid mother a wonder? With her soft, round face, her lovely dark eyes, plump, white arms, tiny feet. Her set Chopin pieces. Her high-neck dresses. Her hair in a bun in back, always pierced with a plain silver ornament. With her penchant for respectability. With her penchant for the earnest middle classes. An Emersonian, steeped in the Over Soul, in light, in cheerfulness, in hope,

222

in doctrinaire betterment, refusing to accept the worst, believing in heroism, in theory, she equated respectability with the pure in heart. Show her a man with property, with a nice suit, and she saw an honest man. Once taken in, now merely confused, in dread, filled with hatred and disappointment, out of character, she tried to hold her ground alone. What was she *supposed* to do? Was she *supposed* to take him back? "Dennis?" she said, close to tears. "Dennis! What do you *want*? Are you *really back*?"

Calvin lingered beside them in the growing dusk. He could smell the heat from the street, from the car, from the canvas luggage cover. He could smell the greenish freshness beginning to rise from the park across from his grandfather's big brick fortress. Fourteen, close to fifteen, both horribly innocent (even for the age) and pathetically bright (with figures, with languages, with literatures, with facts), he couldn't digest this stranger, this glamour, this actor from New York City, this talker from far places, this Tennyson-lover, this tall, mysterious, threatening being.

In his first gesture, his offering, his father made his first mistake. He leaned down. He pulled a dime out of the boy's ear and handed it to him, as if the boy were closer to five than fifteen. "'Surely, surely, slumber is more sweet than toil,'" he intoned, "'the shore/Than labor in the deep mid-ocean, wind and wave and car—'" He held out a silk handkerchief. He stuck it between curled fingers, then opened his empty palm. While Calvin flushed, disgusted, silent, his father waved his empty palm in front of his face. "'Oh, rest! Why wander more?'"

"Dennis! Be serious, for once," Calvin's mother said, sounding more like her mother. "What do you want?"

"I want to rest," he said. "I want to catch up with myself. I've changed, I've—"

"Well, you can't stay here."

He leaned down. He put his hand on the boy's shoulder, "All right, but we'll talk," he said, to Calvin now, taking another dime out of the boy's ear. "We'll all get to know each other again. I'll be at the Barnum Hotel in town, I'll be in touch. Grace," he said, straightening, putting the dime back in his own pocket this time, "I've got a lot to tell you."

"I don't know," she kept saying. "I don't know if I want to hear. Oh, I don't know why you had to come back."

"I've had problems. I had a breakdown. I was in a *Catholic* rest home. A pantheist, among the nuns. Our Lady of Peace took me in when I couldn't afford anything else. Oh, I was grateful! Our Lady of Infinite Pains," he began, swinging into an old routine. "Our Lady of Numerous Sorrows. Our Lady of a Thousand Troubles. Our Lady of Endless Qualms. Our Lady of—"

They heard the screen door open while they were still standing near the car. Sarah Elizabeth came out on the front porch in the hardening dimness. They could just see her cigarette spark, and they heard her cough. She was curiously silent for a minute. "Calvin!" she finally said, "I want you *up here*! I want you up here this minute!"

He sighed, releasing the air from his tight chest. He felt relieved, grateful.

His father misunderstood. "Go. Go on, son," he said. "We're all going to compromise. We're all going to try to get along with her this time."

His mother entered the house a few minutes later, and his grandmother followed her upstairs. "Sometimes I swear I don't know where your good sense is. Letting *that* boy—"

His mother sat down at her piano upstairs and started to play Chopin. She played through the rest of the evening. He could remember reading in his room across from hers—while she played until the last streetcar passed, and, in the summer air, while his window was open, he could hear his grandfather's sprinkler going. The soaking arc would hit the leaves overhead, making a soft, splashing sound, whispering, drenching parts of the foliage, and then the quiet, just the piano playing, until the arc returned, hitting the leaves again.

The atmosphere was now charged with half-finished sentences and abrupt silences. His mother's unspecified grievances increased. Her anxious cheerfulness picked up. "Everything is always for the best," she was fond of saying,

224

while she waited for everything to collapse at any minute. At the same time, without telling him anything, without sharing her fears, she exuded a helpless, disoriented air, asking for support and pity without actually putting the plea into so many words. Cold and numb, he felt that if he could just shrink in size, take up less space, he could at least diminish her problems.

He was alone in the house when his father returned in a friend's car. "Come on," he said, bouncing the car keys in his palm. "Don't look so frightened. Let's go. Let's see the countryside."

As soon as they reached Ox Hill, his father rolled his window down. A city person, he took deep breaths. He drove slowly, taking everything in. He left nothing unadmired: the low, rambling stone walls, the old-fashioned wells, the red barns, the cow pastures, the buttercups, and bees.

Calvin did not want to be doing this. He did not want to be there at all. It was also extremely warm for June, a midsummerlike warmth. Between his self-consciousness, his stiff embarrassment over his father's tastes, and that heat pouring into the car across his face, he had trouble staying awake. He yawned until his eyes teared, covering his mouth with his hand.

His father stopped the car as soon as he spotted the first church, as if he had been gravitating toward it all the time. The small white structure, with its narrow, short steeple, sat on a rise at a bend in the road, looking out on freshly planted fields. His father opened the gate. They climbed up the stone steps, then walked around the side to the small cemetery in back. The heavy air was filled with humming, buzzing, flying sounds and the smell of warm, freshly cut grass.

His father walked around the gravestones with those quick, abrupt, impatient movements of his, as if he had something on his mind that had to get done. "Listen! Look! Everything's busy. Breeding, feeding, dying."

Calvin felt drugged, heavy-lidded, and exposed. He looked across the fields every once in awhile, waiting for someone to order them out of there.

His father abruptly stopped. "*This* is God, you know. This

breeding, feeding, dying. This moment. This now. This air. Oh, the air! Go on! *Breathe* it, boy! Don't be frightened! *Breathe* it! Breathe in God! Look! Like this! Throw your shoulders back!"

Self-conscious, embarrassed, feeling exposed because his father was watching, because he was *noticed*, Calvin tried to breathe more deeply. He knew he wasn't going to be able to do it right. He sneezed.

His father laughed. He shook his head. He started back to the front of the church. "It's the pollen. You're rejecting the pollen. Why? What do you suppose could happen if you breathed it in? Does a *seed* threaten you that much?"

Calvin shook his head without knowing why. He pulled his handkerchief out of his back pocket.

"The New England soul," his father said, pausing, waiting for the boy to catch up. He shook his head again. "The New England soul refused and rejected the New World. It refused what was in front of it, the heart's desire and the body's joy. Old men in charge, all of them. What would have happened if a *different* breed had come?" he asked, finally entering the church.

The cool, formal silence greeted them without offense. "Why, this is maple," his father said, touching the creamy white pews, walking down the narrow center aisle. "Pure maple. Don't lower your voice in here. Don't cringe."

He mounted the pulpit while Calvin stood below, wanting to leave before somebody caught them there. "More maple," his father said, grasping the pulpit's edge. Then he held his hand out over the pulpit. He stared down at his palm, flexing the fingers. "This delicacy, this miracle, this marvel. Oh, this *hand*! I love my hand. I love my whole frame. I love my holy body."

Despite the building's contrasting coolness, Calvin could feel the sweat running down the back of his neck. He stood there without speaking, holding his handkerchief in his wet palm.

His father looked into his face. "What's wrong? Why does that make you blush? I love myself," he said, suddenly lowering his voice. Then he spoke up. "I love myself."

Calvin dropped his eyes. He could hear a lawnmower somewhere outside the church across the street.

"Now I want you to do something for me. I want *you* to speak the unspeakable truth. I want you to tell yourself— tell me, tell this place, aloud, now here, what you already know but think you can not face. Say: 'I love myself.'"

Pierced with shame, Calvin could not move a muscle.

His father was still waiting. "Well? *Say* it!"

"I— I—"

"Wait! *Don't* mumble! First, take a deep breath. And *pull* your shoulders back! That's it! Now stick your chest out. STAND UP STRAIGHT!"

By now, he was sweating and shaking. His breathing was shallow and quick. He wondered if he was going to be able to get through the words without passing out.

"Well? I'm waiting!"

He straightened, but he lowered his head at the same time. He finally mumbled the words while his chin was still resting on his chest. His breathing was growing more difficult.

"I CAN'T HEAR YOU!"

"I love myself," he said, louder, just above a whisper. His father left the pulpit. "All right," he said, not satisfied. "I guess that will have to do for the moment."

When they returned, the house looked less vacant. The screen door opened while his father was still pulling up to the curb, and his grandmother came down the steps.

Calvin was just opening his door when Sarah Elizabeth poked her head through, into his father's window. At the same time, she stamped out her cigarette on the walk. "I was just about to call the police. If you *ever* try this again, I'll call the police."

His father groaned and threw up his wide, pale hands. He finally put them down on the steering wheel and looked straight ahead. "He's my son, and I don't know what you think the cops can do about that."

"I don't imagine that you want the police around at all."

"I want to speak to Grace."

"All right, I'm going to speak my piece. I am going to have my say just *once*," she said. "I do not believe that divorce can ever solve anything. I do not believe that it can ever make anything better in the long run. I do not believe that it could even make anything better in *this* ghastly instance."

His father was still staring straight ahead. "I want to speak to Grace."

"However, my daughter's mental state at the moment isn't a whole lot sounder than yours, and I have stopped assuming I can get through. I have stopped assuming I have any influence on her at all."

"I want to speak to Grace," he repeated, in those same weary tones.

"She's gone. She's left. She's on her way to New Haven now, and I am not giving you her address. She does not want to see you again. She's finished. She's had her fill. Come to that, we have all had our fill," she pointed out.

He finally shrugged, as if all this probably did not make that much difference to him in the long run.

She pulled her head out of the car window. She stayed there on the walk beside her grandson, and she took his hand, a rare gesture. She did not go back into the house yet. She lingered there on the walk until his car was out of sight, as if she were going to stay rooted to the spot until it was.

Calvin stopped his story to locate his cigarettes. He wandered over to the bureau in the dim hotel room, lit a cigarette, and came back to the bed.

"My grandfather never said much about my father because he always kept his few feelings to himself, but I believe he despised him more than anyone else in the house. I think he had a special dislike for him because he was a man, and he could not understand how a male could be so weak."

He paused.

"Well? What happened?"

"He drove my mother back to New Haven. He was driving her back while that interview with my father was going on. He was still on the road when my father returned to his hotel in town." He paused, until his chest felt less tight. "My father evidently started to pack, then changed his mind. He jumped from the hotel window instead. Sarah Elizabeth and

I were still alone in the house when the reporters and the police arrived."

Grace stayed in the teachers' boardinghouse through the next few weeks, but her mind grew steadily more shadowy after her husband's suicide, and her parents finally placed her in a "rest home." She wasn't strong, anyway. She had several respiratory ailments while she was still in the home, and she finally caught pneumonia. She died in a New Haven hospital.

Lisa listened while she lay on her side, facing him in the big hotel bed, her eyes half closed, her hand in his, her hair half fallen across her chest, obscuring the small breasts.

"But what about *you*? You sound so removed in all this. So uninvolved."

"I wasn't involved," he said, changing the subject.

Calvin and Lisa! The names belonged together, already linked, familiar, but, at the same time, he felt as if an aura encircled their names, a faint, subtle emanation or exhalation, a charmed atmosphere. She reminded him of Kasey, before he had married her. She reminded him of that first affair, back in that golden period, when the world had seemed so outlined, touched with such breathless clarity.

At other times these days had a faint, dreamlike texture. They lived on shifting surfaces, moment-to-moment meanings. The new arrangement was still intangible because unknown, unexplored.

Sex was briefly enveloping. He loved watching her when she wasn't aware of his eyes on her. She would pull a minidress over her head and then pad around in flesh-colored briefs without a bra. The sparseness, the brevity of her clothing, always touched him—as if a part of youth's spare, indifferent essentiality, its exact uncoyness. He loved the disparity of their ages, as if it were some dispensation in nature itself, her eternality now his, altering his life.

"You have such wonderful little breasts."

She paused. She looked hesitant. Self-confident, self-assured, cocky—interested in the moment, in what's what, in the here and now, in the facts, the fact-as-itself, she could also change in a split second. As the self-confidence evaporated, she became uncertain, tentative, off-balance. "Why? Am I being too bold? Should I get dressed?"

What uncertainty explained such a leap in logic? Such a shadowy infringement!

She was *just* nineteen!

Easter was close, and they both had family responsibilities. They clung together on their last day, and they did not dress until the last minute. While they were sitting up in bed, he kissed her small breasts, like big buds, then dropped down between her legs. He clasped her knees.

She knew what was going on. She closed her eyes and threw her head back, until her long, straight hair, bluish black hair fanned out behind her. She had such thin shoulders, such long, straight, unfleshy arms and legs. She steadied herself on the bed with both hands. "Oh, I'm still not thinking. Should I be? Is that all right? I'm not going to start thinking until the last possible minute!"

He drove her over to the station to catch a local bus. The light was dazzling, unpleasant, the world larger and louder than they had remembered. When he pulled up to the curb, she jumped out quickly. She crossed into the station without looking back.

Dizzy with hope, he crossed the bridge alone, back in Indiana. While he picked up speed, driving faster than usual, he talked to himself in the car. She smelled like soap. She smelled like honeysuckle. She smelled like hyacinths. She was his love, his first love, and he was starting over. He soon picked up more speed, heading home for Easter, just getting in under the wire.

TEN Lisa's relatives spread across upper New York state. The Giffords, her father's people, lived around Batavia, Clifton, Shortsville, Montezuma, Lysander, and Dhurhamville, on top of the country where the sky rolls out and the woods drop back. The Breckenridges, a web of cousins, his first wife's people, Lisa's mother's people, clustered around the lake regions, close to Ontario, Oneida, and Seneca. The Talborts, his second wife's people, less prosperous, more easygoing, operated around the Catskills, around Climax, Freehold, Kingston, and Red Hook. They owned or more often managed general stores, service stations, and tackle shops.

A literal-minded, hard-working, God-driven, money-oriented lot, the Giffords and the Breckenridges ran their orchards and their vineyards like feudal estates, but escaping children gradually flowed over into the professions. At times, here and there, a boy or a girl turned up in physics, chemistry, medicine, or math. The outright failures seemed isolated in the herds, problems without specific faces.

A wealthy farmer's son, raised among five brothers and two sisters, Lisa's father first struck the clan as backward. Max was a stubborn center of inwardness. A visionary who worried about how things work, he was more often under the heavy equipment than on it. He took his first transmission apart when he was nine. When he returned from World War II, he designed a new spanner, as if he had gone off to Europe just to think the problem through. He left home, patented the spanner, and followed the restless flow into changing, seething, postwar Buffalo.

He studied engineering and went into design, but, at a quirky moment of his life, thrown off-balance after his first wife's death, he drifted into the junior executive branches, where he rose without noticing what was happening to him. He was constantly on the road after his second marriage, and the road changed him. He grew talky, melodramatic, and expansive. Finally a vice-president in a Louisville tractor company, he grew rich, settled, and unsure.

He was a big man, thick-necked, broad-shouldered, heavy-waisted. With bushy, winglike brows, piercing, grayish green eyes, a soft, ruined-looking face, filled with worry lines, sad, sensitive crinkles. He wore unmonogrammed, pocketless oxford cloth shirts, drank Chivas Regal, and turned his Lincoln Continental in once a year. His house, a cedar and stone structure, hung precariously over the Ohio River, looking luxuriously out of place. An intercom piped his voice through the rooms. He was always showing up with some new gadget, but he came home cursing about the highway robbery. "The fucking prices you pay for everything these days!" he would intone, with some pride, because with his money, he needed to be taken.

He wanted his daughter to make something of herself and then be independent. "Even from me," he shouted, always speaking as if he were trying to get through over high winds, roaring seas. He sent her off to college and then appeared in the dorm on weekends just to get the feel of her life away from him. (How was her independence coming along?) "I don't want to interrupt anything! Go! Go on! Go on with what you were doing," he commanded, dwarfing the room with his flair for taking over, filling space, commanding the good life. He fed the floor: giant take-out cardboard buckets filled with fried chicken, coleslaw, biscuits, mashed potatoes, and gravy. Coffee, Cokes, donuts. "Eat! Eat!" he instructed, not eating. He was too restless, too self-conscious to settle down himself. A stylish Jewish mother in French cuffs, the sleeves rolled back, showing the expensive computer watch, gold identification bracelet, and shaggy, blunt wrists. "Eat! It's honey-dipped!"

Lisa was also quick-tempered and abrasive. She was impatient and passionate, partly because she was young, partly

232

because she was his daughter. But she stayed closer to her feelings. She demanded a certain amount of honesty in herself and others. However, Max could abandon his dignity in the clenches. He could jump and duck, weave and dodge. He knew something was up now, if not what, and he increased the food supply.

"He doesn't visit. He invades," she wrote Calvin when she was back in school that spring. "It takes me hours after he's gone before I can believe I have my own space back again. By then, I'm too depleted to work, I'm so angry. I've told him not to barge in that way, but he never hears, or pretends he doesn't. He just *hears* what he wants to. He *uses*. He manipulates. He shouts. I know what he's up to, but he gets me *so* upset! I just shout back. Once I'm shouting, he has me where he wants me, and he knows it. He wins every time."

She put off telling him about Calvin until she was home that summer. She waited until he was getting ready to take the family to Maine, where he had a house (not a cabin) on a lake. She wasn't going, and she was ready to tell him why. She found him in his huge, two-toned kitchen, ensconced in an array of push buttons, built-in appliances, and copper pots. He was frying chicken—his oxford cloth sleeves rolled back, revealing the computer watch and the gold identification bracelet. When he was restless, when he couldn't cook up anything else, he fried chicken, baked biscuits, soaked beans.

He sometimes fancied himself self-controlled—measured, reasoned, philosophic. "You know, I knew something was up," he said calmly (falsely). "I knew there was trouble in the woodpile somewhere. What you know you know. I knew. You know? So," he began, in earnest, sadly looking down at the stove, his frying chicken, "since you've been sneaking around for months, behind my back, why do you bother to tell me now?"

His frying had raised the temperature in the kitchen. The airconditioner wasn't working properly, and the late afternoon heat had crept around to the back, where the sun was assaulting the two picture windows. "I *told* you! Because I'm inviting you to the wedding. *If* you want to behave yourself."

He was still feigning this, that, and the other. Now it was surprise."A wedding? *What* wedding? Why don't you two just go on sneaking around? Why bother with weddings? Why muck around with society's needs? Why get so formal?"

"Now *look*! I'm *not* going through a big scene with you! Do you want to come to my wedding or not?"

"Scene? Scene! Scene! *What* scene? Who's talking about scenes? What will you do when this broken down TV actor gets a little older than he already is? What happens when his plumbing gives out? What happens when you still want to see the town? Push him around some dance floor in his wheelchair? I want an answer! I *deserve* an answer!"

Her heart was thudding against its ropes, ready to soar. She hated her anger because it was his. She, too, wanted control. "I'm NOT going to answer you when you're intentionally being crazy! I don't have to listen to that!"

"*Crazy? Crazy?*" he shouted, using his normal tone now. He jumped back from the chicken and spun around. He raised both arms as if he was going to hit her. "Who's the crazy one around here! Who's the *crazy* one around here!" (Check the sleeves. Nothing up this one, nothing up that.) "TELL ME! WHO? WHO? WHICH ONE? POINT THEM OUT!"

She was dancing, too. "Listen! Stop it! I don't have to deal with this!"

He changed his tone. Lowered his arms. But his face was flushed, his breathing audible. "What about college? Are you going to let that go? What about your medical career? Are you going to give up *everything*?"

"I *told* you! I'm still going to college! I can transfer to Indianapolis, can't I?"

He shrugged. He smiled to himself. He turned the splattering chicken, lowered the heat and put on a lid. "They all say that until the children come. What do you know about life? You wait. You'll find out. You'll have *babies* crawling

234

over both shoulders. You wait, you'll see. You're finished, in fact, as of now. You'll *never* be an M.D. Nothing. Nothing!"

She started to walk away.

He followed. "Wait! I'm still *talking* to you! You do a stupid, senseless thing like this, and you're out of your mind! You're throwing everything away! You're dumping everything down the drain like it's so much garbage. Is *that* what everything means to you, a bright girl?"

"Oh, leave me alone! I love him! So leave me *alone*, will you?"

"LOVE? LOVE? YOU AND THAT OLD MAN? How many times has he been married before? How many other wives has he buried? You hand me something like that on the end of a shovel, and then you call it 'love.' Love! Jesus! Don't make me laugh! Why, I'll *shoot* the son of a bitch on sight!"

"Then stay *away* from my wedding! Stay out of my life!"

"Lisa? If you do this, then that's it! We're through. You don't have a home here!"

Myra Gifford turned up at the wedding alone. Later, Lisa's stepmother also visited from time to time "just to keep the lines open," as she put it. She came against Max's wishes, but she did not care. She called him "that old bear." She was three years younger than Calvin, but, because unfleshy, she looked older. The age showed across the tightly drawn facial skin, around the corners of the eyes. The eyes were pure blue—azure blue, perfectly clear. The recently frosted hair was severely pulled back across the shapely head.

Calvin loved the woman. He loved that combination: mildness and boldness. She kept her independence while she made things work. She kept a generous hold on the long view while she dealt with the moment on its own terms. He wanted her affection, too. However, despite her intelligence, she was an old-fashioned woman. She was a conventional woman used to conventional men, where borders were automatically maintained, and if he wanted her affection, she never even knew.

Was his own sense of balance lost on her? Did she appreciate his own long views? What was the point in the age difference between the couple if he didn't have them? "I can understand how Max must feel. I'm a father. It threw him, and that follows."

Myra never discussed relationships with men. She looked at Calvin for a moment, but when she spoke, she spoke to Lisa. "Oh, you know him," she said, sounding evasive, but she knew she was speaking bundles.

Lisa had just put the children down. She was trying to pick up after them in the big, shell-like family room. "Oh, yes. I know him. He said he was going to shoot my husband. He makes himself clear enough."

"Who, honey? Max? That old bear? You ought to know better."

Calvin felt excluded. "Well," he insisted, too self-righteously, "I can see his position."

Lisa wanted the subject dropped. "You aren't *supposed* to see his position. Whose side are you on, anyway?"

"Why do there have to *be* sides? How long can this feud last?"

"That's up to him, Calvin. So don't *butt* in."

Her directness finally silenced him. She had her own mind, a private person. Her own business was her business. His age and experience didn't cut any ice.

He watched her picking up, arranging the girls' things on a shelf. He bought them too much. She said so, and, as usual, she was right. The toys soon got scattered in that cavern, and they would not pick up after themselves. The smaller items soon got lost. She was constantly crawling around trying to find their Barbie dolls and Barbie doll parts. Barbie doll clothes appeared and disappeared in odd places: tiny slips, stockings, scarfs, plastic heels. Another complete, if miniature culture, a half-unearthed strata.

She was never comfortable until everything in the house was in its place. She couldn't take clutter. She was always worried about being inundated, ridden over, squeezed out—her space violated in some crucial way. Given this, she was frantic when she thought she wasn't in charge. She had to run things, be on top, and because she had her own methods, her own specific approach to every household problem, he gradually withdrew from most domestic chores. In deference, he stepped aside. For the first time in his life, he was not trying to paint; he was not fussing over the furniture, rearranging the pictures, or changing the drapes. He certainly stayed out of the kitchen. He let her clean and cook—a curious set of freedoms he was trying to adapt to, a slightly disorienting change.

Myra lit a cigarette and dropped the lighter back into her purse. "Honey, Max misses you, and he's drinking too much."

"He *always* drank too much. He hasn't grown up yet."

"Well, all right, but he's drinking more now."

"Fine. When he's ready, I am. He can say he's sorry."

When Lisa first saw the children, she realized that she was going to have to be a full-time mother for the first few years of their married life at least. She put off college because they *needed* so much. At the same time, she didn't want to impose. Their own rights, their potential dignity, overwhelmed her. She was constantly asking herself just how far she could go, and, in that role, she was removed and mechanically efficient, like a highly organized servant. She was willing to blend into the woodwork; and while she was trying to treat them as little adults, she created a gulf between her moral sensibilities and their ravaged, mother-starved appetites.

Myra raised her brows and picked up her brandy glass. "Now you know better than that yourself. He *can't* say he's sorry. It just isn't in the man."

"Well, he'll have to learn then."

"That's just the Gifford blood. They're all the same. You know that. *Stubborn* as the day is long. That's just the way they are. That's just the way they've always been, and we can't change them. I know I can't. I've learned to live with it."

"I know, Myra, and I'm sorry. But I *don't* have to live with it anymore."

"If you call him up now, if you invite him over, he'll come, too. Hot to trot. The whole subject dropped. That doesn't mean you actually have to say you're sorry, either."

"He'll think I am."

"Well? And what harm is there in that?"

"We'll be back where we started. He'll think he can get away with anything again."

"Oh, you two! Like peas in a pod. *Honestly!*"

Lisa finally couldn't be around the girls without taking chances, without presuming, and, as their strangeness wore off, she had them on her lap. They loved her long hair, and when she had them up there together, they wanted to comb it. They fought over the comb and stuck bobbypins in at odd angles. They parted the bluish dark, silky strands and stared through them at each other. They tried to get at each other through her hair, sticking their tongues out, poking their heads around it. She took them on shopping trips and then out to lunch, where they fought over who was going to sit beside her in the booth. Because they had grown attached to mirrors, she had less trouble getting them into clean clothes or into the nightly tub. They would soak until their fingers turned crinkly, and then, in new nightgowns, they would sprint down the hall, where they fought over the mirror.

They clung to her, needing constant attention and praise. They put on her old clothes and clumped around unsteadily on her heels, trying the stairs, her discarded patent leather purses dangling under their sharp little elbows, her hems dragging behind them. They would spend longer at this than most activities as long as she was in sight. When she needed time to herself, she would push them out into the backyard, where they could parade around the garage dressed to the gills. However, they would soon return, fighting over some real or imagined wrong, tripping over the dresses, slamming the doors.

She was worried about discipline. Like Sheila, they couldn't admit they were ever wrong, or even out of line. When she asked for a simple apology, they both stiffened as if they were being attacked, their spirits violated in some crucial way. When she tried to correct them, they both wore tight, defiant looks, as if they were merely playing for time, planning to wait her out. When she lost patience and shouted, they ducked their heads, covered their ears. But when a beating didn't come, they were both back five minutes later doing what they had been doing before.

He couldn't help her. "Do what *you* think," he would say, wanting the subject changed.

Myra wasn't much help on the subject, either. "Why, honey," she said now, getting ready to leave, "*I* certainly couldn't smack them around if I had them, either. A little love goes a long way."

"I'm not sure it goes far enough. They're great at taking advantage."

"Well, that's human, too."

"It may be human, but where does that get us all?"

Calvin liked to make his own martini. He wasn't one of those men who will climb behind a bar to show you how it was done, but he would fix his own as soon as he got in the house. There was something ultimately satisfying about watching him at it, too, as if you were watching a man doing what he does best. Home, getting out of his tie, rolling up his sleeves, he worked directly with the glass, a thick, good-sized tumbler. Home, talking, catching everybody up on the news, putting his car keys down on the counter, he poured himself four stiff shots, then just touched the Beefeaters with a very dry vermouth. Home, he was settling in. He stirred with his finger and added cracked ice. "I love Indiana," he said, adding a slice of fresh lime last. He claimed that he could not get really fresh limes in Indianapolis; he never used lemons; and when he flew in from an eastern business trip, he carried his own supply in a brown paper bag on his lap in the plane. "I love the TV bedroom suit advertisements—*suit*, not *suite*, and we all know what they're talking about."

Lisa was harried. She was trying to get a meal together before he had to go out again. "*Eastern* TV commercials often say *suit*, too."

He picked up his glass. He took his first tentative sip, then set it down again, a man who can afford to have just a sip because he's got a lot more where that came from. "Yes. I also love *drug* for *drag*. As in 'I drug it all the way up here.' I also love how the natives use *anymore* without a negative, a signal for the present progressive. As in 'I go shopping anymore out at the new mall.' I love the term *theaters* in the paper's *theater section*, when it means films—no, movies. When theater comes through, it's a show. I love the city's stylishness. Indianapolis spent *millions* dressing up the Circle, and then, of course, it put back its J. C. Penneys and its Sears. I love Indiana's huge, bulging educational systems. Every parent sends his child there because education is so *respected*, but they all get upset if the child changes, comes home with an idea. Which is, fortunately, seldom. I love Indiana's total *insularity*. I love its charming self-complacency. Oh, yes, and I love its sycamores," he said, pausing at the family room glass panel, staring out at the willows. (Lisa said, "You mean willows. Those are willows.") He picked up his drink. The gin was beginning to branch out. With one, he glowed. With two, he felt safe—enclosed in that necessary, helpful slammed-up-against-the-side-of-the-head feeling around five o'clock in the afternoon.

"Yes. They're cleverly after the central plumbing in this palace. Their roots are breaking through the pipes, which makes all four toilets back up. A crack has also started to flower across the garage floor, suggesting that, as a whole, the slab under us is beginning to go."

Mrs. Fox was still living in Sarah Elizabeth's house on the Cape, his, now, ensconced there rent free, based on his casual, offhand remark after the funeral—originally meant to be a temporary situation until she could relocate. She was keeping it up, and because he didn't *need* the rent money, he didn't push matters. Still, it was an embarrassment. She had been making plum jam when he last flew out, and when she finally came to the door, she did not open it more than halfway. He circled the house, looking at the roof, and she followed. "It's going to need a new roof very soon," she said, treating him like a landlord who must be handled firmly. "Also, the wind last winter blew off some shutters in back. I was up with a ladder, but I have no call to be up on ladders these days. My health is just tolerable. I have all I can do just to keep up on the inside."

Sarah Elizabeth had a chain of investments from Connecticut to the Cape. Problems constantly came up, matters that couldn't be handled over a long-distance phone. Why was he still in Indiana, anyway? Why couldn't he move to the Cape, where he could also get a little writing done? What was keeping him in Indiana, at the prairie's door?

The sea, the sea, the riddle endlessly rocking . . .

The children were sitting in front of the TV. At nine, Shelley had a hard, thin, strained-looking little face. She was already wearing glasses, and she had a sharp, worried, pinched, semiadult air. She was also shy, awkward, easily embarrassed. At six, Gwen was rounder and jauntier. She ran on a good deal of nervous, hectic energy. She seldom laughed, but she giggled constantly. She bounced around, giggling, gradually working herself up, and if she wasn't restrained before she went over the edge, she had abrupt, spasmodic, motiveless crying fits. She had his mother's weak chest, too. She had various breathing problems, complicated in this muggy midwest basin, and why, when you thought about it, wouldn't the whole family be better off breathing ocean air? Why couldn't everybody use a fresh start?

Shelley switched the TV channels, and Calvin suddenly appeared, in a two-year-old rerun. He was a guest this time on somebody else's talk show: talking, explaining, holding forth about high-risk, potentially high-return investments like venture capital pools. He also covered the mythic and ritualistic aspects of political assassinations, discussing and detailing the various archetypal deaths in the folktales of primitive tribes, in the Homeric epics, in the Icelandic sagas, in the Old Testament and in the Arthurian cycles. He talked about the reform movements within the Christian church, the Ecumenical Council, the important and unimportant changes in Protestant liturgical patterns and the doctrinal difficulties of people like Bishop Pike. He talked about quarks, genes, and primate sign language. Doing his old song and dance. Handsome and haggard, like a late afternoon soap opera star. . . . *Bullshit*, he thought. *Bullshit.* The kids were held, but they would watch anything that moved.

He still had his mind on the Cape. He was thinking about Nauset, one of his many enthusiasms. "'It is a wild, rank place, and there is no flattery in it.'"

Excited, he went off to find his Thoreau. He came back with the book open. "Listen to this, Lisa," he said, reading to her over the TV interview. "'Commonly, in calm weather, for half a mile from the shore, where the bottom tinges it, the sea is green, or greenish, as are some ponds; then blue for many miles, often with purple tinges, bounded in the distance by a light, almost silvery stripe; beyond which there is generally a dark blue rim, like a mountain ridge in the horizon, as if, like that, it owed its color to the intervening atmosphere. On another day, it will be marked with long streaks, alternately smooth and rippled, light-colored and dark, even like our inland meadows in a freshet, and showing which way the wind sets. Thus we sat on the foaming shore, looking on the wine-colored—'"

Lisa was running some water over a heavy pan. She turned suddenly. "I can't hear! I can't hear *both* of you at the same time!"

He turned off the TV and put down the book. While the self bloomed and burst with humiliation. He tried to relax before the anger hit. He walked back over to the kitchen counter and picked up the gin bottle.

Lisa opened the oven door. "Be careful, Calvin, please? You told me you had to go out again."

He didn't answer her. With the TV off, the kids stood, stretched, bored. They began to bicker.

"Can't you do something with them for a few minutes?"

He felt restless, irritable. He carried his freshened glass outside—skirting the willows and the patio, on into the ga-

242

rage, where he stored the possessions brought back from weekend auction trips: several Eastlake love seats, a walnut cradle, an oak drop leaf table, a cherry wardrobe in bad shape but still solid, a sleigh, a meal chest, a dough box with drawers, wagon wheels, old tools, old locks and chains, an early milking machine, a butter churn, a cigar-store Indian, several steamer trunks filled with nineteenth-century photographs, postcards, costumes, several boxes filled with carnival items. When was he going to dump all this stuff? When was he going to start simplifying his life? When was he going to cut back?

Calvin returned in a gorilla suit. The monkey had a wonderfully gentle, wise old face, as if it had a store of ancient wisdom to impart, but when it bent over the two girls, it merely cracked them up. Gwen rolled around on the floor, unable to contain herself. "DAD!" she cried, giggling, half-hysterical, trying to get her breath, "DAD! STOP IT!" Shelley was not much better. "DAD!" she screamed, "*come out* of there, will you! We know who you are! Why don't you grow up!"

The land and sky dipped and ran through the early spring. The slush lingered in the culverts, the low places around the trees. Calvin's gutters were jammed with twigs, leaves, seeds. He climbed a ladder, and wearing a dirty pair of cotton work gloves, he pulled out the clotted, dripping compost, dropping it onto the concretelike ground below. He scratched out the new growth sprouting up there, in among the heavy, sopped, dead foliage.

The stock market was down, and nothing was moving much. Unemployment, at 6 percent, was reaching recession level. Nixon stopped the gold flow that summer. He also froze prices, wages, and rents. With luck, Calvin just got out from under a motel franchise. He was steadily liquidating his Indiana interests. When the depression swept in, the tide was going to hit the Middle West hard.

While Nixon was trying to demolish Hanoi, busily bombing it around the clock, the young were raiding the Army-

Navy stores. The older, softer styles were going. He saw pea jackets, petty officer shirts, bell-bottom trousers, square toes, low, clunky shoes, shiny plastic. A lot of hard, metallic fabrics, and then those tailored pants suits. At twenty-three, her hair pulled back, showing the square forehead (a harried stepmother), Lisa wore tailored pants suits when she dressed up at all. Oh, where had all the miniskirts gone? Why was the world suddenly so mannish?

If he was several people, she was several people, too. First, that quiet nineteen-year-old who had crossed the country with him four years ago—that self-assured, mysterious young being telling him not to think. Telling him to take time out. Well, she didn't take time out now. He had caught further glimpses of that second girl: tentative, uncertain, unexpectedly off-balance, a charming human in her way. But the third person (a woman) was steadily predominating. *She* thought, all right! She thought and thought. She brooded. She often seemed strained and driven. She was often trying to redress some inner idea of order, balance. After wild sex, she cleaned the house from top to bottom.

Charley called to talk about Nixon's price and wage freeze. They talked about inflation and the war.

"Floyd was killed in Laos," Charley suddenly said. "They flew the coffin back to the west coast. It landed in San Francisco, waiting to be shipped east, but it disappeared. The morons finally tracked it down in Dallas, but by then it was on its way to New Orleans. There was some unpleasantness next, but it finally ended up out here. So. Good Deeds is gone. It's official. The poor son of a bitch is dead."

They briefly talked about the past: the trips to the Metropolitan, the Russian food, the blowy New York winter, and the rainy spring. Calvin could only dimly remember Fern's apartment with the river view—the Sunday *Times* scattered across the furniture, books everywhere, the rain blurring the windows.

"She's had a lot of trouble with her son. He's been in and out of therapy lately. She says she's never known anyone so filled with hatred."

"That's Fern, too."

"No, not exactly, not like that."

"Well, then, like what?"

"Well, you know, the usual things, really. The world. Life. How things work."

"Another voice being heard from the counterculture."

"Good Lord, no! He's the opposite. He listened to his crazy uncle a lot through the years."

"Exactly why is he in therapy?"

"I don't know the details. You'd have to ask Fern."

Calvin wrote his ex-wife a long, sympathetic letter, mentioning Floyd's death. He also suggested that he ought to get to know his son. He enclosed a large check to help cover the therapy expenses.

Fern cashed the check—which could have been a measure of her desperation, considering her usual independence, but she didn't answer the letter.

He stuck the canceled check back in with the others.

"That's just pure vengeance, coming from her. The *uncle's* influence meant more."

Lisa was concerned. "How old is he now? Fifteen? Sixteen? You ought to write him yourself."

"How would I get through the enemy lines?"

"Well, you've got to try."

He tried. He enclosed another, smaller check, made out to his son, but he was right. He didn't even get a canceled check back this time.

He told her while he was fixing a martini before dinner. "I haven't voided the check yet, and, as a result, my account's always off at the end of each month. That's bothersome, because so unneat. I need to tie up ends."

Lisa was pregnant. She was always hungry, and she craved junk food. She often resisted buying it, but when she was home, she went through the refrigerator with a dreamy, abstracted air—moving bowls around, looking for something that wasn't there, as if it might materialize at any minute. She opened the refrigerator while he was talking now, but she could hardly hear him over the children's TV, blasting

245

in the game room in the middle of the afternoon. "Why aren't they out *doing* something? They watch too much TV, anyhow. They watch it until they glaze over, and when they finally turn it off, they're not here."

"Well, then, cut the TV-watching back."

She shut the refrigerator door and opened the cupboard. "*You* tell them, for once. Why do I always have to be the heavy around here?"

He moved into the game room and turned off the TV. "This Special, Limited Time Offer: Life! Absolutely will not be repeated! Act now! Out!" he said, while the girls scattered, wide-eyed, off-balance. "Get some air! Take a bike ride!"

He came back with divided feelings: guilty because he had moved in on his children, pleased because he had taken a stand for her. He waited to be rewarded. "Well, that does it."

She was leaning against the kitchen counter eating a Ding Dong. "Does what? Did you have to make a production out of it?"

But he could not deal with such issues head on—seriously stripped down, the basics stressed."I *did* the best I could! You wanted it off, didn't you? Well, it's off."

"I didn't hear you say anything about a TV schedule."

"That can come. We can play it by ear."

"That means you're not going to deal. Doesn't it?"

He sighed. "No, Lisa, it doesn't."

Being younger than he, she lived closer to the surfaces, could hide less, was often impatient, abrasive, quick-tempered. "Oh, yes it does! NOTHING'S EVER GOING TO CHANGE AROUND HERE!"

"All right, all right. Fine! Then you handle it."

She turned her back on him. "Myra's on her way over, and if I want anything done, *I've* got to get it done. On top of everything else, I've got to clean up the *trash* around here!"

Both Giffords arrived. They rang the bell, but then opened the door before Calvin could get to it. Myra held the door because Max was loaded down with packages. "Is anyone here? Is anyone home?"

Max wasn't comfortable in other people's houses until he

246

could first establish his own base. He moved in now with the baby presents, just barely able to see around them while his wife held the door. So loaded, he was soon setting up a command post. He made his way down the stairs, past the sunken living room, down the central hall, into the kitchen. Lisa was just coming out of the utility room.

"So. What can I do for you, baby?" he said, his booming voice taking up the last of the space.

ELEVEN The huge, sprawling, weathered gray-shingled beach house was being repaired and remodeled, partly torn down, partly enlarged, generally modernized. The family lived in the clutter while the work was going on. They lived around the lumber, the tools, the heavy equipment, the sawdust, the curled shavings, breathing the plastering mist and the fine drywall silt. They ran into open spaces where there had once been a wall; they stepped across loose flooring, or no flooring at all, and opened doors that had not been there before. The porch was now gone; a redwood sundeck was going up in front, facing the bay; the yard was strewn with loose, rotting wood, rusty nails, shattered glass, bits of ancient screening. Plumbers crawled in and out under the foundation. Carpenters leaned up against the house on ladders, calling back and forth to each other. On the roof, they hammered with their heads down in the wet, misty mornings and the high noon shimmer.

The children created more clutter: Calvin's two from his third marriage, Shelley and Gwen (twelve and ten), his two from his fourth marriage, David, now four, and Karen, their baby. In the girls' rooms at the back of the house, among the shell collections, the weathered bits of driftwood, the horseshoe crab shells, Calvin ran into old wiring, abandoned electrical sockets, rusty pipes. (Why, for instance, save five old doorknobs?) David hoarded extra pieces of carpenters' wood, which he used for bridges, highways, garages, ramps. The wood turned up in the hall, on the stairs, or in the middle of the living room floor.

Since one room or another was always being remodeled, or torn up completely, one room or the other was shut off, and the adults' bathroom was now closed. When Calvin used the children's bathroom, down the hall at the back of the house, he usually found the sink half stopped up, emptying sluggishly, a bent toothpaste tube and slippery pieces of soap lying at the bottom of the bowl, under grayish, scummy water. There were never any clean towels back there; damp ones lay strewn around, some still gritty from the beach. Sand turned up in the sink, on the floor, and in the tub. When drained, the gritty tub was still filled with the younger children's plastic boats, empty detergent bottles, the kitchen's measuring spoons. The wastebasket overflowed, Pampers curled beside it, a tampon sitting in a Dixie cup on the floor. When the chore hour arrived, Lisa would herd the two older girls in ahead of her with mops, pails, Lysol. The girls would work feverishly for several hours, down on their knees, getting everything shipshape. They would sometimes throw themselves into the task without complaint when the room looked its worst, just because challenged; but, after a beach day, after the evening baths, the room was freshly wrecked, struck down again, returned to the shambles it was apparently meant to assume.

When first waking on Saturday mornings, crossing the hall to the children's bathroom, then coming down the stairs, when he could hear his children's strident voices clearly etched against the unaccustomed stillness, the novel silence that permeated every level of the place—including the strewn yard, where the heavy equipment sat idle over the weekend, he would deliberately pause on the landing to announce his great discovery. "It's Saturday morning, everybody! No workers! No noise! Notice? Let us praise the peace!" He stood there for a moment longer before he descended in the eighteenth-century judge's robes, his costume for the Bicentennial pageant. The father-priest at fifty, he looked more blemished, less padded than he had at twenty-one, but he was still handsome, slightly grayish, neatly bearded.

Shelley and Gwen looked up, raising their brows, a gesture older than their years. In many ways, they *were* older than their years because muddled with bits of street wisdom. Like Sheila, they seldom showed much life before noon and did not bother to comment now. Still in their rumpled gowns, no robes, they sprawled on the couch looking sullen and ill-used. Once in a while, their eyes narrowed; partly coming alive, they hissed at each other, but, at that hour, their hearts weren't in it. "He doesn't even know you exist," Gwen said to Shelley, half stirring. Shelley was staring into space, knowing what she knew. "Oh, yes, he does," she insisted, not yet really baited.

Shelley, already built, was into boys. Clumping around the vacant beach lots in wooden platform shoes, skimpy tops, loaded down with terrible mixtures of junk, all the costume jewelry she could get, she walked with a chip on her shoulder, keeping her eyes peeled. She combed her hair on the beach, waiting to be noticed, and when boys passed, she rushed upstairs to catch a final glimpse from the window. Like Sheila, she was never wrong. When confronted, cornered, found up there, she was instantly furious. "I was just *looking* for something!" she hissed, spitting, outraged, injured, her face blood-darkened, her sharp little jaw set. (Sheila's jaw.) Gwen was more realistic, more direct; and because still ten, she loved the truth. "*I* know what you were *looking* for!" she would say, using it.

They had inherited their mother's artistic talents. When they sketched, they were completely absorbed, evidently at peace for long stretches, sprawled across the living room floor, self-contained, a separate unit. However, when they were finished, they couldn't rest with their accomplishments. They carefully put the prices on the bottom of each picture: $.25, $.50, sometimes one dollar. "Dad? Dad? Is that too much? Do you think it's *too much*?" (What am I worth? What, precisely, am I worth?)

When nothing else was doing, they swung on the refrigerator door, looking for the Twinkies, the apples, and the milk they had already polished off between breakfast and lunch. They sometimes briefly worried about their weight. They exercised; they kept their statistics on the refrigerator door. Although they ate less at the table during that period, they got into snacks between times, as if snacks didn't count. "Will a banana hurt me?" they asked, every five minutes. "Will just *one* banana hurt?" When Lisa wouldn't lie, they gave her injured, outraged, close-mouthed, bruised looks, as if they had both been vitally ill-used once more. They put more pressure on her than on him—because she was the woman, the mother-figure.

His son, David, the darkest in that clan, dark from both sides of the family, was playing with his toy cement mixer in the doorway between the living room and the kitchen. At four, he had a shut, intent look. When so concentrated, he appeared to be independent, self-contained, as if a bomb could go off without disturbing him. His miniature cars and Fisher-Price people (round, wooden, neckless figures with big faces) lived all over the house, another strata, like the girls' earlier Barbie doll period. Having concerns of their own, they rolled under furniture, lived under rugs, turned up in Lisa's big, battered leather purse. Calvin touched his son, his prize, when he stepped over him, around his toys, and, surprisingly, the boy looked up, if still self-contained, self-absorbed.

Calvin was after his morning coffee, his first cigarette. Their last child, Karen, not quite two, was silently leaning across a kitchen chair watching a bug on the screen. The screens were still webbed with moisture; the early morning was foggy. The curling haze blurred outlines, muffled ridges. But the fog, as the natives said, would burn off by noon. He parted the judge's robes, picked Karen up, sat down at the table, and put her on his lap. She spotted a piece of cold, leftover toast. She was no eater. She seldom touched anything beyond her bottle, but she wanted the toast. He broke off a bit.

Lisa was cleaning the refrigerator. She was in shirttails, shorts, her bottom concealed, her straight black hair loose around her shoulders. Her small breasts just pressed the shirt, then disappeared in the folds. Her thighs, now less wide after children, not more so, were only slightly fuller than the long, uncurved calfs. Always thin, she lost weight after pregnancies instead of gaining it. "That robe," she said, without turning around, "is going to be in *sad* shape by the time you really need it."

He was watching his youngest devouring all the cold bits of toast that she could get. "I just put it on to cheer the family up."

She was constantly forced to distinguish between the serious, potentially chaotic possibility and the merely erratic, a choice she often had to make on the spur of the moment; and since she was by nature literal, serious, analytic, thinking best when given time, he often put her under an unnatural strain. She was learning, though. She said now, just to gain time: "You could drive me crazy. Do you know that?" She turned back to the refrigerator.

Tupperware bowls partly filled with leftovers dotted the domestic landscape, sitting on the table around his coffee cup, perched on the chairs and the counter: bits of this and that the girls stuck back in the refrigerator after meals, under orders not to throw anything out, which they took literally. In one bowl, she found a quarter cup of soggy peas, still in the pan, in another a few string beans, in a third some congealed macaroni, in a fourth part of a baked potato still in its skin.

He lit a cigarette. He had a full day ahead of him because he was on several Bicentennial committees, and, of course, he was doing the legwork. In their infinite wisdom, the Town Fathers had put prominent natives' names up on their letterheads: Fox, Hallet, Doan. But when they needed anything done, then they called on him. "I've got to run several errands, and I've got to pick Charley up at the airport." Charley was flying in from Boston for a visit. "He comes at a bad time. I wanted to put him off but I couldn't. You know how he is."

Lisa removed two milk cartons, three sticks of butter, all partly used, on three separate dishes. Then three ketchup bottles, each opened, someone's medicine, unfinished, now abandoned; the bottle, with its reddish stuff, was sticky, the cap broken. "There's been *milk* spilled in here."

252

She was righting, correcting, ordering, trying to restore her balance. Her private need for order stood between them, as if she were struggling alone against everyone else. She held up two battered, browning grapefruit, which had been pushed back behind a giant mustard jar, outside the vegetable drawer. "Did you notice what Shelley was wearing last night?" He hadn't. "She got it yesterday, didn't she, when she was in town with you?"

The girls loved Provincetown's *good* parts, where they could mill about in the crowds, the Coney Island section: the blocks that smelled like boiling fudge, dope, hotdogs, fried clams. Shelley headed for the cut-rate bargain basements, where she could pick through the barrels filled with luridly colored, elasticized rags that apparently turned out to be halters. He shifted Karen on his lap. "She bought a halter. *I* wouldn't have bought it, but I couldn't stop her. She had her own money. I can't say what she can do with her own allowance."

"Well, then, *I'll* have to tell her she can't parade around in that. *I'll* have to be the heavy. I'll have to be the one she resents. Again. Don't you suppose it *gets* to me?"

He couldn't deal with anger. His wrists, particularly, felt cold. He did not want to touch his own flesh. "All right, all right! I'll tell her!"

"Will you? When? Could you take the children on your errands this morning? I could use the break."

He did not answer her. He now had his undivided attention on the child on his lap. He was still feeding her bits of cold toast. Deep in some sort of game, Karen accepted the pieces of toast from his hand one at a time. She wouldn't be rushed, and she chewed thoughtfully. She nodded before she took each bite, as if she wanted to get it right, then show how eating was done. "She's so *meditative* now," he said, withdrawing from his wife, as if engrossed elsewhere, completely held.

His shirt undone, still getting himself together, looking for his pants, he wandered from the front bedroom through the hall into the den, around the packing crates. The books, papers, and folders sat partly unpacked, in stacks on the floor, his books mixed-in now with his wives' collections. He unpacked a few boxes at a time, going through, sorting, just to see what was what; and while he was absorbed, picking up pieces of the past, he would turn a corner and unearth earlier marriages, strata after strata: old letters, cryptic notes, grocery lists, furnace bills, household budgets, canceled checks, bank statements, unfilled prescriptions, abandoned diet plans, postcards, photographs, children's drawings, report cards, baby shoes, baby bonnets, baby spoons, birth certificates, faded newspaper clippings, colored ribbons, scraps of Christmas wrapping paper, champagne corks, theater stubs, restaurant menus, tourist guides, pressed, faded flowers, old eyeglass frames (one lens missing), broken watches, perfumed handkerchiefs, pajama bottoms, somebody's original poems (not his), somebody's silk panties, torn, but preserved, obviously carefully saved from the flux. Whose? Why? And why was everything now so affecting?

Ref. Pastor's Refusal

1. What do we do now about religious night?
2. You haven't written that letter yet, have you?
3. Does it strike you that neither of us is exactly in shape to go through with this?
4. Back to the basic point: We can hardly push through the home Communion as planned when the pastor isn't speaking.
5. Could we talk all this over with Don?
6. What will we do about Charley?

What was he supposed to make of all this? *What* religious night? *What* letter? *What* sort of shape had they been in? *Why* wasn't the pastor speaking, and if "Charley" was Charley Klick, *who* was Don? He couldn't remember any "Don" in his life.

He worked on his poetry off and on among the packing crates up there. He hadn't glanced at "The Divorce Sonnets" for months, a manuscript lying about in several folders, chiefly notes. He kept his accounts and he wrote letters to the local papers. He was by now into politics. He had helped to push through an ordinance against loitering. In town meetings he had campaigned against nude bathing beaches because the tourists, who drove out to see the nudes, created such parking problems. He belonged to a historical organization that was trying to save old walls, windmills. He was on the Bicentennial committee, a loose collection of unorganized people who spent the bulk of their time arguing with each other. They broke appointments, missed meetings, and generally did not know what they were up to. He kept the books, of course, but, beyond that, he ran every errand.

First, Mrs. Fox, where he had to pick up some folk singer's motel reservations, then over to the clam warden's for other valuable documents before he swung into town: the printer's place, and then over to pick up the singer at the bus stop that evening.

He was stepping into his pants when Lisa passed the door. "First, Mrs. Fox, that harridan, then over to Halibut's place."

She paused in the door. "Halibut? That's a fish. Do you mean old Mr. Hubert, the clam warden?"

"Nobody, of course, tells Mrs. *Fox* when you can clam and when you can't. They're thick as thieves, those two. But him and her," he added, enjoying the local grammar, "always has been. They're tolerably close. They prowl around the dunes together, seeking who they may devour. Charley and I are taking you out tonight. Once I get this day over with."

"Calvin? Why don't you two just go?"

"I'm not sure why you don't like him."

"I don't like the way he treats women. I don't like the way he treats his wife."

"He isn't always *divorcing* women."

"Why should he? They don't *mean* that much to him."

"He's a family man."

"Then where's his wife? Why doesn't he ever take her with him? Why isn't Buffy coming?"

"He's in Boston on business. He's passing through."

"Well, I've never even *met* her."

"Why, they're Catholics," he explained, working on his hyperbole slowly, "and so, you see, she *wants* to stay home."

Lisa's practical nature, her one-dimensional view, left him free to float, and he was able, without entanglements, to stay half out; but now, as if harried, because down, as if tired of his elaborations, she refused to take him unseriously, "Oh, *bull!*"

"I'm teasing."

"I *know* you're teasing! I'm not *that* dumb!"

"I love you."

"I love you. Now I've got to get the girls on their rooms if they're going out with you."

The phone rang while he was back in the bedroom trying to find his shoes.

"Calvin? Look, buddy, I've got some news."

"Where are you? I'm supposed to pick you up around noon."

"Boston. I'll be there. But I flew up with your son. He wanted to come along."

"*Who?* Fern's boy? My God! It's short notice. How did that happen?"

"Wait a minute," Charley said, putting down the phone.

While he waited, Calvin could hear Lisa calling the girls upstairs to get on their rooms. They came, grumbling.

"It's a long story," Charley said. "I'll tell you when I can."

He hung up, lit a cigarette, and sat down on the bed to put on his shoes.

He was on his way downstairs when the phone rang again. "*Calvin?*" the voice boomed, "this is Max! We're in Maine."

"Hold it a minute, will you, Max? I'll get Lisa."

He found her back in the girls' room, giving cleaning instructions. "Oh, God, him! That's all I *need* now! Tell him I'll call him back. You handle it. Tell him *anything!*"

"I can't get her right now, Max."

"When're you coming up here? When are you bringing the kids?"

"Up? Where?"

"Maine! What's wrong with you down there? We wrote. We've been waiting to hear! What's going on down there? What're the plans?"

Because why would anybody want to be on the Cape when he could be in Maine? Because Calvin disliked him so, he stayed pleasant, reasonable, and calm. "I don't know, Max. We've got a lot of family here. I've got a friend coming—"

"Hell, bring everybody! Bring your friend! We've got room! Does he like fishing? The fishing's great! It's been a long time since we've seen the children."

"I don't know, really," he said trying to stall. "Why don't you come down here?"

Now. Where were his car keys? How long before he could get the children organized?

Lisa came out of the girls' room. "Take mine, then. They're in my purse—back in the kitchen, I think."

He finally located the worn leather mother-bag sitting on the washer in the utility room. He brought it out to the kitchen and sat down at the table beside his son. David was drawing in the moist, gray light.

If women's purses usually broke him up, hers demolished him—all the vulnerability, all that duty in the clutter, layer after layer: Handi-Wipes, tangled Kleenex, Roll-Aids, Life Savers, mints (there to keep the smaller children quiet in church). He ran into several Fisher-Price people from "Sesame Street." He found her checkbook, credit cards, credit card slips, trading stamps (long since invalid), supermarket tapes, sunglasses (loose), and sunglass case (in another pocket). Then tampons. (When just Karen's age, Shelley had once brought him a tampon, holding it at the end of its string. "Mousie," she had said. He had kidded around. "No, that's a firecracker.") He ran into two Flair pens, two miniature Hallmark calendars, and several church bulletins, which she would never leave in the pews because someone else had to pick them up. A damp washcloth in a plastic bag. Pampers, training pants, Barbie doll slippers. The children were constantly coming back from the beach loaded down with junk, which they carried up to her. ("Here. Hold this, will you? I need it.") So he found broken bits of seaglass, seed pods, and cracked clam shells down toward the bottom of the gritty leather saddlebag. He finally ran into three empty bottles used for urine, which she had taken to the doctor's office when pregnant. She picked up a new bottle each time because she could never locate the previous one. All in order, all accounted for; but no keys.

David wanted attention. "When're we going to the airport, Dad?"

"Soon. Soon. Later. Just as soon as—"

"Dad? Look at me. I'm making a *D*. Do you want to see my *D*?"

Calvin picked up the piece of paper just as Karen appeared. She tried to climb up onto his lap. David pushed her, but Calvin moved her over, onto his other knee. She sat there with her head against his chest, getting as much of his chest as she could. "That's a *fine D*. That's a first-rate *D*!"

Lisa appeared with the car keys. "I'm sorry. I left them upstairs."

While he had his arm around the two squirming children, trying to talk above the chatter, their claims for his attention, he told her about Charley Klick's phone call. "I don't know what's going on, though. I hope Jeff's coming is okay with you."

"Is it all right with *you*?" She was worried, gentle, concerned, wondering how she could help. "Will you be able to handle it?"

"Oh, yes. It's sudden, it's unexpected, but I've been *trying* to meet him for years." Then he told her about Max's coming down, and her face instantly changed.

"*When?*"

"I don't know. He didn't say. We left it open. Lisa! I handled it the best I could! Don't blame me! I *need* you! I worship you! I worship your purse!"

"I could use a little *less* worship around here and a little *more* common sense."

The battered bag, strap hanging down, still there beside him, just out of the children's reach, now looked raw, harsh, inert. He couldn't have touched it. "Jesus Christ! I'm *tired* of hearing about common sense! You're just tied up in knots!"

"Oh, go, if you're going, will you? Go play your *games*!"

He put Karen in the infant car seat beside him, David on the other side of her, strapped in. The two girls climbed in back, where they liked to sprawl.

He decided that he was going to make a long, leisurely morning of it. He drove around the Wellfleet bay, curving along the shore roads above the little beaches. The fog was starting to lift in separate patches.

He was enjoying everything: the inlets, the sudden open stretches, the small low houses scattered in among the dwarfish pine.

Karen fell asleep, her chin on her chest. David was wiggling around in his seat belt, trying to see the girls in back. They sat slumped down, grumbling because they weren't out on the beach.

He turned back onto the highway, heading for Eastham.

Bored, the girls started to sing a TV commercial.

> Plop plop
> Fizz fizz
> Oh! What a relief it is!

Then, as if they shared some inside joke, they both broke up back there, going into fits, into gales of laughter. Giggling, torn apart, howling, their eyes wet, they glanced at each other. They slapped their thighs and doubled over into knots of helplessness.

When Shelley spotted the adolescent hitchhiker, she abruptly straightened, looked behind her. She punched Gwen. "Did you see *that*?"

At ten, still groggy on the subject, punchy, mystified, Gwen was trying to keep up. "Yes, I *did*!"

"Wasn't *he* a fox!"

"I *say*!"

259

"Oh, Gwen, he *looked* at me!"

Gwen put her hands on her hips, a solid lump of truth, honesty. "He did *not!*"

"Oh, yes, he *did*, Gwen!"

Because less desperate, she could be realistic. "Don't *lie!*"

Shelley's whole being changed. She grew crimson. She stiffened against any possibility of self-recognition, as if she could ward it off through blunt, physical force. All of this was Sheila. "You take that back! I'LL KILL YOU IF YOU DON'T TAKE THAT BACK! I MEAN IT! I WILL! Dad? *Make her take that back!*"

Calvin pulled over, trying to quiet them both. While he kept his temper, feeling ill-used, he could recognize the self-pity in his tone.

"Well, she is," Gwen said, refusing to back down when the truth was in plain sight: concrete, whole. "She lies." (What's more obvious?)

"Let's enjoy the ride! Let's enjoy the day! It's starting to clear."

Gwen slumped down again. "Then why can't we go swimming? It's so *boring* in the car."

He picked up some speed, but the highway was crowded. The cabins turned over on Saturdays—new people streaming onto the Cape toward him, the old leaving in his line, everybody trailing boats, loaded down with luggage, bikes.

He finally turned toward Sarah Elizabeth's three-quarter Cape—his now, though Mrs. Fox was still living there, rent free. Just how small was her pension, anyway? She was constantly trying to save every cent. She would not use the electricity a toaster needed. She put the bread directly on the rack in the wood oven. She had no phone.

As soon as the children saw the place, they wanted to get out. He wasn't going into a long argument. "I'll just be a minute," he said, climbing out without looking behind him. He was going to have to learn to lay the law down more.

She wasn't home, and her car wasn't around. She seldom went far. The clam warden would know where she was. He backed up and took a side lane, bumping over ruts, scraping against the sides of bushes. He passed sunken little salt ponds, still misting in the dampish woods.

Humbert-Humbert lived back there alone in a trailer. Calvin knocked, but he had to cool his heels for several minutes before he could hear the old bachelor stirring back there. He came to the screen carrying a coffee mug.

"Good morning! Do you know where Mrs. Fox is? She has some motel reservations, and I'm supposed to pick them up."

"Bastun," Humbert-Humbert said, holding his thumb over the top of the mug. He stayed inside the screen door. "She's in Bastun 'till Tuesday, mebee Wednesday."

"I've got to pick up the singer today. Do you know where she's supposed to be staying?"

"Nope. I don't."

"Well, I'm also supposed to pick up some receipts from you. Do you know anything about some receipts?"

"Sure. Mrs. Fox has 'em," he said. "I give 'em to her, the last time I seen her."

"That helps. Since she's in Boston."

"Yep. Do you drive that car out there?" he asked, looking toward the Mercedes. Calvin suddenly realized that the clam warden did not know him, or pretended not to. "That's a big car."

"I have a lot of children."

"I got to go."

Calvin hit the highway in record time. The traffic was picking up, and on his way back, heading into Provincetown, the driving was wilder. Cars ducked in and out of the passing zone and veered across the break-down lanes. They darted out of side streets.

In back, the girls were discussing boys again. Shelley started it. "Hal's the best swimmer in the *whole* world."

Gwen looked at her for a minute in silence, her mouth set. "You *can't* say *that*!"

"Oh? And just *why* can't I say that?"

"Because it's unfair to all the other swimmers in the *whole* world!"

David was studying Karen, who was still sleeping in the infant car seat. "Dad?"

Calvin waited, wondering why the boy was studying his

sister. He preferred his age to the girls'. He preferred children before puberty, before sex struck. The boy was still thinking, trying to form his question.

"What? What can I tell you, sweetheart?"

David switched questions, probably, because he changed expressions. In any case, he didn't ask about his sister. "What would happen if you put your hand on a bee?"

"He'd fly away."

"Yes, but what if he *didn't* fly away?"

"Then, I suppose, he'd sting you," he admitted, with some reluctance.

"Would he poison you. Would you die?"

"No!"

"You *could* die," Gwen said from the backseat. "*People* die from bees!"

David was still involved in his own thoughts. "What if you put your hand on a butterfly?"

Space suddenly opened up. Blueness: the strip of gray from the sand, then the dark blue band, the sky another band of light blue above. The tide was in, but the bay was calm. The sea came in long, steady, even, slightly rolling swells.

"Dad? Dad!" Gwen said. "When're we going swimming?"

"I have some errands to run. This is a busy day. We dip into town first, then over to the airport, and then we swing on back."

"But the tide will be out by then!" they both observed in chorus, in the rear. Trapped in the car, they gave up all hope. Their day was ruined.

He didn't answer.

"Dad?" David asked, "When we get to town, can we have some ice cream?"

"Mother will have lunch ready when we get back. You don't want to spoil your appetite."

"We won't. I promise."

He didn't answer.

He parked up on Bradford, pulled Karen out of the car seat and grabbed his son's hand with his free one. The girls

262

scrambled out of the back. They wanted to have lunch in town; they wanted to go shopping, but they didn't have time. While everybody crossed Bradford, then cut down into town through an alley with roses just starting on white picket fences, tall sunflowers growing in clumps in tiny side yards, their huge, shaggy heads drooping over with their weight, he tried to deal with each demand. At the same time, he tried to scoot them around the cars climbing Bradford, kept them together in the alley. He finally got them pointed toward the next stop, the hardware store.

The street wasn't crowded at that time of day; the tourists stayed on the beaches until the sun went down; but if the going wasn't difficult, Karen's weight dragged against his arm, and he had to keep shifting her, changing hands with David. The girls left his side in the hardware store, and when he found what he wanted, he had to herd them together again. The printer's was closed, giving them some extra time. The girls wanted to poke around. They drifted on past their turn, toward lower Commercial, where their fun started, where the tasteless cut-rate stores and the fast foods began.

Shelley wanted shrimp. She was just starting to try sea-food, largely for him. She would pick at the shrimp for awhile and then push the plate back.

"We have to get home soon. We have to get to the airport, and then Lisa's planning to fix lunch."

"Shrimp's *dis*-gusting," Gwen said.

Shelley assumed an innocent stance, prepared to defend shrimp all the way down the line. "Why?"

"Because it is."

"Just because *you* don't like shrimp!"

"Don't you feel *sorry* for them? The poor little things!"

"Well? You eat *hamburg*, don't you?"

"Yes, but, at least, that's not *alive*!"

"Oh, Dad! She's crazy! A hamburg's *a cow*!"

"Well? *So*?

"So? So you're eating *a cow*!"

Because he wasn't feeding them, and wanted to, he let them drift in and out of the cheap shops. Shelley wanted to buy an orange glass ring. "Dad? What do you think? Don't you *like* it?"

Karen woke. She squirmed in his arms, increasing the awkward hold he had on her, and he stopped to shift her, still gripping the hardware store purchase behind her back. Shelley was still waiting. He didn't like the ring, of course. Why did she need *more* rings, anyway? "Well—"

She was already opening her ragged, cheap cloth purse, not a woman's yet because too small, too uncluttered. "Oh, Dad, please? I have my own allowance, and this is on *sale*! Oh, I love it! What do you think, Gwen? Won't Hal love it? Oh, Dad, please?"

He was still trying to deal with Karen. He didn't argue.

She paid the clerk herself, then came back. "Dad? I need four cents."

He fished through his change and held out a nickel.

She lingered behind, still poking through the sales counter. She finally appeared in daylight with her penny. She held it up.

He braced himself first, then took it.

Gwen was usually a lot tighter with her money, but she wanted to spend some now because her sister had. They continued on down Commercial and stopped inside a shell store.

Shelley and David were now both bored. He wanted to know when they were going to the airport. He didn't yet care about shells. When he was on the beach, he gathered up discarded beer cans, bits of broken styrofoam.

Engrossed, Gwen walked around among the bins and shelves. Completely taken, she finally picked up a tiny bottled octopus floating in formaldehyde. "Oh, *look*, Dad! *That's* gross!"

"Isn't it?"

She looked at him uncertainly. "Dad? Can I have it?"

"It's your money."

Shelley was waiting to go. "I thought you said it was gross."

"It is! I want it!"

"It isn't cheap," he explained, worried about her allowance.

She didn't part with money without great deliberation. She looked unsure now, but as she continued to stare at the bottle, she seemed to cross some line. "He's cute."

"Oh, *Gwen*! Now you *know* you're just saying that to be contrary."

She ignored her sister. She was enclosed now. She went through her purse until she found her unbroken allowance, saved over a two-month stretch. She held up the five dollar bill. "How much does it cost? Is this enough?"

"Two dollars."

"Is that much?"

"It isn't much if you really want it. How much do you want it?"

Shelley was impatient. Annoyed because left out. "Well? Yes or no?"

"Yes. Dad? I want it."

He liked the baby octopus better than the lurid ring.

He had to resist paying again. He took the five dollar bill and went off to find a clerk.

When they reached Race Point, the small plane from Boston was already circling overhead. The day was now blowy, bright, and clear. He picked Karen up again, and the other three piled out.

So Jeff was coming! *Ghosts and more ghosts*, he thought, inaccurately—the four literal deaths in his life all undealt with, too, all improperly mourned because not faced, merely registered as more vacancies. Now his son's appearance threatened to touch the edges of his unanalyzed life.

"Come on, everybody. Let's watch it land! Let's watch Charley and Jeff come in!"

Gwen was dragging behind. "Who's Jeff?"

"Why, he's your half brother."

Shelley had her hand raised, admiring the new ring. "*Who's* Jeff?"

"He's your half brother."

265

"How *old* is he?"

"Oh, twenty-one? About twenty-two."

"Is he handsome? Is he a fox?"

Gwen had been taking a good deal of this in. "He's your *half* brother, *stupid!*" she said, still looking at her father. "How could she be in love with him? Are you glad he's coming, Dad?"

"Now I'll have *all* my children together, won't I?"

"Is he going to live with us?"

"We'll have to wait and see. Come on, everybody!"

David was trudging along close to his legs. "Dad, what's air?"

When the children fought, they seldom crossed lines. Shelley fought with Gwen, David fought with Karen. Shelley was particularly solicitous with the younger ones. She bent down now, and, with a bogus, overbright manner, she took David's hand. "Why, air is just up, like heaven, where our own mother is now, sweetie. Right, Dad?"

He was trying to herd everybody through the waiting room, then out the backdoor toward the small enclosed area. The plane was coming down.

Gwen stopped in her tracks. "That's different! THAT'S NOT THE SAME THING AT ALL!"

Shelley dug in, just because corrected. "Yes, it *is!*"

Gwen was having trouble breathing now. "NO, IT ISN'T! DAD? DAD? TELL HER IT ISN'T!"

He was still trying to settle them down while he watched the few people who left the plane, ducking their heads as they came through the door, looking glazed: three women, a child around ten, two dapper-looking elderly men who came off engaged in conversation. They both looked up together at the same time, blinking in the raw light.

Shelley turned around. "Well? Where's Uncle Charley? Where's your son?"

He pulled several children from that ragged pack against him. "I don't know. I don't understand. Come on, everybody! Let's go! Let's get some ice cream!"

266

TWELVE Doors slamming. Children running around, fanning out. "We're back! We're home! Look at us! Look at what *we* have! Look at what we brought!" They came through a galaxy of light exploding over the bay, fragmenting across the empty space where the sundeck would be, streaming through the glass panel, spinning upon each barrier and object, from the freshly painted stark white walls to the sprawling tropical coleus, pieces of African sculpture. The space, recently cleaned, ordered, seemed wider, ecstatically expanded. Lisa coming through, drying her hair after her shower. As she bent down over the children, the shifting pack, the white terrycloth robe parted, showing brown skin, part of the small, crinkly, flesh-colored bra that completely covered the little breasts. She knelt to see the children's treasures. She listened to the stories, the complaints, and appeals, trying to get them to speak one at a time. She had to deal with the children first before she could get to his adventures.

While he was waiting his turn, he went off to get the ice out, the gin and vermouth down. Why not draw back, get a fresh start? Why not put their differences behind them, again? Why couldn't they spend some time together this afternoon. He wanted sex, but when they tried to go to bed together in the middle of the day, they seldom got away with it. The younger ones sensed the unusual quiet. Up from naps early, they huddled outside the locked bedroom door, breathing heavily, trying the knob, pushing their drawings and notes under the crack.

She finally appeared while he was slicing his lime. She looked withdrawn, anxious. She needed the clean house. She needed the shower. She needed the spotless order, a reflec-

267

tion of some necessary internal structure. However, she was still on edge when she had the place the way she wanted it because she felt let down, sensing that the parallel didn't hold.

"Mrs. Fox fled town, probably carrying the committee's funds. I struck out next with Old Humbug, the clam warden. He gave *her* whatever I was supposed to pick up. Why do you suppose he hides back there in the woods in that trailer? In any case, I have to pick up the folk singer at the bus station tonight, but I don't have her motel reservations, and nobody knows where she's staying. What do they *want* with a folk singer anyway?" he asked, his drink built, now done. He tasted the edges first, a sip, then put the glass down to admire his work.

She sat down at the kitchen table. "Cal? Could you be careful with your drinking today? It's *only* noon now."

"I'm just having this one."

"Yes, and that glass *holds* at least three martinis. You've got it to the brim. You didn't talk to Shelley about the halter, did you?"

"We reached the airport on time. We got to watch the plane come in, a successful operation, complete in itself from David's point of view. He wanted to watch a *plane* come in. He wasn't interested in who was or wasn't on it, but, as you see, Charley wasn't on it. Not hide or hair."

The girls appeared, wanting lunch, wanting to go swimming, and Karen was crying in the other room. Lisa put the girls to work on the meal. She fixed a bottle and took Karen upstairs.

Shelley making a salad. Sheila again. She cut the lettuce up into tiny, dead chunks with swift, blunt strokes, then swept the mess up into a glass bowl. (Get the lettuce before it gets you.)

"Dad? What happened to those people we were having?"

"I don't know. It beats me."

He couldn't observe the painful operation without trying to explain how it should be done, but if he explained, the child felt criticized.

Carrying his drink, he crossed the room to the back door,

watching a cat, which had come down from one of the private cottages along Route Six-A. The animal was walking across his stoop rail, across the freshly beaten rugs hanging up out there, its tail up stiffly.

"And I haven't met him, have I?"

She was still wondering about Jeff. Trying to put him together. "No."

"And what was *his* mother like?"

He was still watching the cat. It stepped very precisely, very carefully, as if it were trying the job out to see if it could get it done, and done just right. "I'm not sure I ever knew."

Lisa returned. "When, exactly, did you say my father was coming?"

"I didn't set a date. I stayed vague."

He was still standing at the screen with his drink. He was trying to make it last. Small white butterflies, like scraps of paper, hovered over the bayberry, the beach plum, and the wild roses crowded out with woodbine.

"So we don't even know *when* they're coming?"

"Lisa? It's beautiful beach weather out there. Why don't we *all* go to the beach? Why don't we try to salvage this day?"

She didn't answer. "Max throws me off balance. He gets to my guilts, and when that happens, I have to keep from offering him the moon."

"Well, that's your trip, then. Just don't try to lay it on me. Just don't go around offering him the house, like the grand host you are, and then expect me to entertain on top of taking care of everybody else."

The children were still high. While they were having lunch, David leaned forward, across the table, toward his father, and, without warning, without saying a word, he put his fingers under his eyes, pulled the skin down until the strained flesh showed the veined, reddish parts beneath—an offering, a love gift. Calvin put his fingers under his eyes and pulled his pouches down. Shelley and Gwen squealed. "Monsters!" They both screamed, collapsed in laughter. "Two monsters loose!" Lisa was still trying to restore order when the phone rang.

Calvin took it upstairs because of the noise in the kitchen.

"Listen, buddy. All this is a long story. Jeff wanted to come along."

"Yes. I know that. You told me. Where are you now?"

"We flew up yesterday because I had to see some people in Boston. He said that he was gathering information, and on the plane, all the way up, he kept asking me questions about you, your wife, your children. He wanted to know what kind of house you had, what kind of car you drove, things like that. All natural curiosity, I guess, after this length of time, but he's like a damn computer. No expression. No signs of approval or disapproval. Nothing. He would just nod every once in a while and file away the facts. He could have been trying to unearth an ancient burial ground."

"So what happened? Why weren't you on the plane?"

"Well, while I was on the phone with you this morning, he slipped out—to get a paper, he said, and he didn't return for several hours. He showed up just before we were supposed to get the plane out to the Cape, and he said he changed his mind about coming. He said he was going back home."

"*Why?*"

"For somebody who wants a lot of information, he doesn't offer much. He just kept saying he was going back. My guess is he lost his nerve. Anyway, while all that was going on, while he was packing, I missed the Cape plane."

"Shouldn't I try to reach him? He was welcome, Charley."

"I don't know how you can. He isn't living with his mother right now. He's staying with some friends in the city."

"Do you know their names?"

"How would I know their names? Listen, buddy, I'm sorry, but I don't think it would have worked out anyway. I'm staying over here tonight and catching the same plane out tomorrow. Do you still want to see me tomorrow?"

"It doesn't matter. Every day here is like every other day here."

"That's the same everywhere," Charley said, hanging up.

Calvin organized the crowds while Lisa was getting into her

bathing suit. He got Karen up, dressed her, and found David's trunks. He hunted down the beach equipment: towels, lotions, toys, playpen, rubber float. While he assembled the stuff, while the children ran around, hunting down other needs, the place gradually lost its pristine shape. Several balloons showed up, lying around in corners, leaking air, growing smaller. Shells, stones appeared. Some shells, not empty, would soon be smelling.

He put the girls on these last minute chores: pointing out this, pointing out that because if he didn't *point*, they didn't see it. Get this; get that. Then he went up to see if his wife was ready.

She was in her bathing suit, going through her bureau drawers looking for something to hold her hair back. She kept talking about having it cut short these days because she believed that, at twenty-seven, she was already too old to wear it long. He stopped her—trying to hold onto the nineteen-year-old as long as he could. She finally gathered her hair together, out of the way, then drove a clip through. She was frowning at herself in the mirror.

He couldn't hurry her and now did not try. He sat down on the edge of the bed to show her he wasn't pushing; he had time. "It's a wonderful day."

"Is it?" she said, still looking in the mirror. "Oh, the Cape's so wonderful, too, isn't it? The house is so wonderful, the family's so wonderful—this poor, demented, falling-apart, ramshackle bunch! You don't help a bit! Oh, that *meal*! You *contribute* to the general hysteria! I have *five* children, counting you, now six, probably, if your *first* son comes!"

His lids quivered, went dry, and when his anger hit the rest of his body, he could feel himself generally losing vital fluids; his cells leaked sap. He would be hoarse if he spoke, but he did not care to speak. He was too furious to care. There was a roaring in his ears, and his wrists went numb. He felt through his pockets but he had left his cigarettes downstairs. His new drink, too. How was he going to get successfully enclosed if he stayed up here, in this cell? "Lisa, Lisa," he said in a low voice—sounding crushed, infinitely wise, infinitely tired, "I'm not responsible for *all* the inundation you feel. I'm not responsible for *everything* that makes you feel overwhelmed."

She turned around so abruptly he thought she was coming after him. She had her back to the bureau, and her hairbrush hit the floor. Her color was high, her cheeks roaring. "*I didn't say you were! Just carry your share!*"

Children called, eager to get to the beach. Some started to climb the stairs, and Lisa turned. She shut the door. "Let's have it out now, once and for all. You can say whatever you have to say, and I'll say what I have to say. I'll be as calm as possible."

He got up. "All right, but later. We promised to take them to the beach."

"No! *Now!*"

He had his drink downstairs on his mind. "We can't do that now! I *promised* to take them to the beach!"

"Oh, great! You only worry about the children when you think you have to confront me! Otherwise, who talks to them? Who talks to them *seriously* about their problems? Who *listens*? Who has to sort out what's *really* going on? Who *bothers*? You? They'll survive—for an hour alone now. All of them! But I don't know about me. *I don't know about us*! Or don't you *care* about the marriage anymore?"

He could hear David breathing heavily just outside the door. "All right, but I've got to get them settled down first. I've got to get them organized and I'll be back."

He went down to check, picking up David on the way. He confronted the full tide in the living room. The girls were jumping around, red-faced, arguing between themselves. When he showed up, they turned on him, shrieking, wanting to know when they were going swimming. All followed, swirling out into the kitchen with him. "We're going, we're going!" he kept saying, while he freshened his drink. "We're just delayed. So take it easy! Take it easy! We're just arguing. We aren't fighting. Everything will be all right. We'll be out in the sun before you know it!"

He put Shelley in charge. He talked her into getting down

some games while he picked up his drink and a fresh pack of cigarettes.

He found Lisa sitting on the bed looking down at her shower clogs. She glanced up, looking comparatively calm. "You can start," she said.

"You have a lot on your mind. You start."

"No, you start," she insisted, starting. "I know you also have a lot on your mind. I know you have your side. I know you think you married a different person. You think I've changed. I have. But I was never easy to live with. I know I'm quick-tempered and impatient."

He went over to the window and put his glass down on the sill while he lit a cigarette. As long as she talked, he could stay withdrawn, waiting for her anger to pass. He wasn't particularly interested in discussing his "side" because if he stated his case, if he tripped himself up by discussing his own resentments, he would merely prolong the unpleasantness. He wanted all this over with. He wanted to hold her. He wanted his children around him. He wanted to get out on the beach.

"I *know* I've been too tightly wound. But don't tell me again that my father set this off. Yes, he did. But so what? Do you want to go on telling me about that or do you want to deal with us? Do you want to have it out, for once?"

The little breeze was gone. Kites were out, but high up, hardly moving above the beach grass. A dory lay pulled up, over on its side.

She stirred, as if she were going to stand. "Well? *Are you ever going to face yourself?*"

"When you feel overwhelmed, you end up overwhelming everybody else around. You're so afraid everything's going to fall apart, you end up insisting on complete control. Yes, I married a different person. I thought you were so intrepid. You can't *stand* a slightly different environment, and you've been worse ever since we came here!" He was on his way, but where was all this going to lead? Beating heart, pumping organs, gathering hatreds. Where was the *sense* in this? *"Oh, what's the point?"*

273

"NO! GO ON!"

"You've completely taken over the house! I like to cook, too, I like to clean, too, and for your reasons—because they give me a sense of order, but when *you're* into the house, you don't even want anybody else around! I don't *mind* taking the children off your hands, if it's my idea, but you *run* everything. You dole out duties! You assign! Goddamn it, if you aren't wearing the fucking *captain's* hat, you think you're going under! There's no sharing, Lisa," he said, suddenly lowering his voice. "So I feel displaced. Abandoned." He was through. Through, through. Drained. He wanted to hold her. He wanted to finish his drink in the sun.

"Are you through?"

He didn't answer.

"All right! I can let you cook more! I can let you clean! You do most of the decorating now. Every *color* in the house you've chosen. I *know* you think your tastes are better than mine! It's just that you'd rather do *any* of this than deal! Than be a father, than *face* what's going on! You'll entertain your children, but you won't raise them. *I* have to raise them!" She was standing now, and too close to him. He backed up. "I'm only asking for help! Oh, God, how can I get *through*! You *haven't* talked to Shelley about that halter, and you don't *intend* to."

"I don't see why that's such an issue."

"That's right! You *don't*, do you? It's a rag in the first place, but have you ever *looked* at her in it, with her *size*? Have you ever watched her strut around in it? Do you ever *really know* what's going on? Because if *I* don't watch her every minute, she's hanging around a thirty-two-year-old lifeguard!"

"What thirty-two-year-old lifeguard? Is that Hal?"

"Yes, that's Hal! I'm suprised you even know the name! I'm surprised you got it *straight*, for once!"

"All right, all right! I'll *talk* to her! Oh, Lord, why *waste* the day like this? I just want to hold you!"

She grabbed her terrycloth robe and slipped into it as if she couldn't bear to be lightly dressed around him another minute. "Oh, you're charming! You're engaging! You're better looking than when I first met you. I'll be *wrinkled* before you are at this rate. I'm starting to wrinkle now! You're a perfect delight, you are," she said, while he was pacing, carrying his drink around, trying to get back to his burning cigarette on the sill. "*All* your wives got hooked the same way, didn't they? You have such a boyish air of erotic availability, but, after awhile, they must have all realized what you *really* want! You want to *be* held. But while you're *being* held, you aren't happy either. Because you're *afraid* you might have to *hold*, too! You're worrying about having to take your turn!"

Karen was crying below. Usually able to distinguish between kinds of crying, a serious fall, say, from mere discomfort, or boredom, Lisa wasn't sure about the sound this time. She was too distraught. She listened for a second longer. "Check on that, will you?"

When he got down, Karen was bouncing in her playpen, her bottle out of reach on the floor. He picked it up and handed it to her.

David was running his cars around a tangled pile of Pick-Up Stix.

The girls were playing cards. They held them close to their chests, a grip that turned their knuckles white, as if they were worried about having them torn from their hands at any minute. They slapped them down hard, resenting each move, ready to take the card back. They watched each other closely, their faces tense, as if it were a duel to the death. Gwen would usually throw her cards across the floor first. Then Shelley would say, in that clipped, breathy voice, "*Typical* of you!"

"She *cheats*, Dad!" Gwen was saying now, while he was heading toward the kitchen to freshen his drink. "She cheats! Oh, yes, you *do*! YOU CHEAT!"

"LIAR! LIAR!"

He couldn't deal with his children until he had his wife back. "Goddamn it, Shelley, I *asked* you to take care of things for an hour! Can't you do that *for five minutes*?"

Lisa was standing at the bureau combing her hair again— perhaps ready to drop the quarrel, forget, move on.

"Let's get out of here. Let's go swimming."

She shrugged. Landlocked, brought up in small pockets, hummocks, rolling stances that broke the view, she was often uncomfortable around openness. The bay side was better than the unbroken ocean, but when the tide was going out she felt particularly unencumbered, unsubstantial. "We'll have to walk a mile before it reaches our waists."

He noted the *we'll*, not *I'll*. The pronoun connected them again. "That isn't the point, Lisa. I just want to be with you." She didn't answer. "At least, then, take off that robe."

"I don't want to."

The sense of deprivation, displacement struck him directly behind the eyes, and his joints felt weak.

She put the brush down. "I'm *tired* of trying to work all this out. Alone."

"You once said you were going to leave all the thinking to me."

"Oh, don't remind me! I was *nineteen*! I was such a silly, stupid, vacant little girl. I didn't know which end was up. I didn't know what I was doing. When I woke, I had a family!"

He backed against the wall. "You *weren't* silly! I loved you then!"

"You still love me 'then.' But I'm not 'then.' I'm now. *Look* at me!" She opened her robe, revealing the fragile ribcage, the tiny, unfleshy bosom, the prominent shoulder bones. "But here we are! I'm ready to accept my family! I haven't ducked my share, have I? I'm just asking for another adult in the house!"

"Goddamn it, being a father's difficult too. I didn't have one. To see how it's done," he said, realizing he had not made the connection before. The truth had been torn out of him in one large, unwieldy chunk. He felt weaker, hollowed out.

"*I* didn't even know you *knew* that! So, if you do, *handle* it!"

"HOW?"

"Stop *drinking*, for one thing!"

276

The phone rang. He took it in the den. A hangup, and he came back.

"Somebody's got to be with the children, Calvin. Could you check? We can't leave them all day, and I want a nap."

Karen was sleeping in the playpen, the empty bottle between her knees, her arms stretched above her head, the palms up, open. David was also gone. He was out on the floor on his stomach, his grubby T-shirt up around his shoulder blades—human wreckage, Calvin thought, and his already overworked heart skipped a beat.

The girls were on the stoop in the hot late afternoon brilliance. Shelley was perched up on the rail combing her hair. Gwen was sorting through her rock collection. Absorbed, they didn't notice him in the screen door.

He carried his liquor supplies over to the sink, making several trips. The gins and vermouths first, down the drain, then the dark rums from Jamaica and Haiti. There was a little scotch left, less whiskey, and they went next. He started on the red wines and then on the whites, domestic and foreign. He rinsed out the sink with great care and then dropped the empty bottles into a carton under it. He closed the cabinet door and lit a cigarette.

He had no need to talk about this yet, and he felt pleasantly alone in the house, where most of his family was sleeping and the rest occupied. He did not feel self-righteous yet. The experience was still too new, but because it was so novel, he felt uncertain: a man trying to step into another way of life without knowing just how it was done. Like every change, it would involve practice and substituted habits.

He walked back into the living room with a new sense of purpose—feeling cleaner, lighter, and slightly disoriented, as if his nervous system were already disturbed. There was, in fact, a drink left—his last martini, watery and half-finished, still sitting on the windowsill upstairs. He couldn't have retrieved it without waking Lisa, and he wondered if he really wanted it, anyway.

He stopped to kick the Pick-Up Stix into a neat pile with the edge of his foot. Then he lit a cigarette. In the span of a few minutes, he had changed—opened himself to unexplored stretches of time. Oh, where was he going? What was he going to do when the standard four o'clock drinking hour rolled around every day for the rest of his life? What was he going to do during the gin hour, that mauve period, that moment when the rest of the world settles down, when everyone else is high on this spinning planet? Oh, and what do you do at parties? What do you say to your hostess? I'll have what the children are having? I'll have what the heart cases drink? And what do you do when you're out on a business lunch? Do you lose all your contacts when people realize they're dealing with a Seventh-Day Adventist? Finally, how was he going to go back to a world without color, depth, or softness?

The phone went off, waking the two children on the floor. The back screen door banged. The two girls appeared.

He had his second hangup that afternoon. He was beginning to wonder about it. He wanted a drink, and he went back into the kitchen to put the coffee on.

The girls followed him out there. They wanted to know if they could make some Kool-Aid. They always spilled the sugar, and he decided to mix up a batch for all four of them.

He was fixing the Kool-Aid when Lisa appeared. She was still in the terrycloth robe, her hair loosened again, lying across her chest and shoulders in stiff points. She looked groggy and unfocused, and while she was moving things around in the refrigerator, she talked to herself. "I thought I had some beer in here. I was sure I had some beer in here. Didn't I have some beer?"

She found the beer.

He had forgotten about the beer. He opened the can and found a glass for her. "I love you."

She was still preoccupied. "I love you, too."

He finished making the Kool-Aid and sent Gwen off to find Karen's bottle. He poured the Kool-Aid and put the paper cups on a tray. Shelley carried them off into the living room while Gwen was coming back with the bottle.

"I love it when everybody's organized. I love it when everybody's a team, working smoothly."

She sat down at the kitchen table with her beer. She didn't answer him.

"We were going out to eat with Charley. Now we can eat alone tonight. Get dressed, and we'll pick up the folk singer on the way. We'll get her into a motel somewhere, and then we'll have some scallops. We haven't eaten out in a long time."

She looked up at him without speaking for several seconds. "Everything isn't settled between us, Cal."

"*I* know that!"

"Do you?" He wanted a drink, and he was not himself. Her persistence made him edgy. "Do you know some of the reasons why?"

"We can talk about it tonight."

"Oh, sure! Or tomorrow, or the next day, or never. Do you remember what I wanted to do when I first met you?"

Her direct question, her direct, brazen gaze, and then her silence—pinning him down, asking him to consider what he had allowed himself to forget: her, as distinct from him. What is the great cry? What is the final, ravaging cry? *What about me!*

He put the lid back on the sugar canister. He pushed the dry washcloth across the counter, and turned it over, looking for sugar grains. And half listening to the children. Shelley was arguing with Gwen. He wanted a drink. Standing there—when the late afternoon sun reached the kitchen, while he was considering the dishcloth, the children, his thirst. He sensed his general blankness, his woolly retreat. His eyes smarted, and his breathing was shallow. "Lisa? Listen—"

"All right, all right! I just wondered if you remembered. You obviously don't!"

"Do you *still* want to go to medical school?"

"I don't know. I'm not sure. I know I want to go back to college."

"How could you commute from here?"

"*You* fly back and forth from Boston when you want to!"

The sun was in his eyes, and the kitchen was boiling. "Well, but that's different."

"*Why*?"

"I have to keep the family together."

She was up. Moving into the living room, past the children, and he followed, feeling helpless. "*You* keep the family together! *You* keep the family together! Oh, that's wonderful! That's *got* to be one of your gems! Oh, why don't you go away? Why don't you get out of here! Why don't you just *go*? Why don't you start looking for your fifth wife!"

The father and the four children grew mute. When she withdrew, when she climbed the stairs, she took their space with her. Alone, separated, baffled, they stayed silent. They felt smothered, cramped, crowded in on.

He stormed out.

He stopped first up on Bradford, a place with a lot of glass and chrome. He hoisted himself up to the bar and pulled out a fresh pack of cigarettes. "Where's Governor Bradford these days? What's happened to the Governor?" he asked the young bartender, who was reading Nietzsche. "Where are all the sundry, weighty, and solid troops? Where are the Lord's free people?"

The boy raised his brows and looked up when he was ready, still keeping his finger in the book. "Pardon me?" he said, as if he had already seen everything in his time.

Calvin decided to disabuse him. "Could you wait on me? Could you wait on me, sir? Could I point you toward your homely and necessary offices? I want a drink. I want a very dry, very businesslike martini, if you think you can get that done with some dispatch."

"I don't have to take this," the boy said, without raising his voice.

"No, you don't, do you?" Calvin got down from the stool. "That is precisely why we are all here. In this age."

280

He left just as the preholiday crowds were beginning to fill the streets, and the bar's parking lot was busy. A dusty, green pickup had him blocked off. He walked around it, past its headlights, and on over to the Mercedes. The pickup backed and waited, then followed him out onto Bradford.

His second stop was more cheerful: a lot of imitation pine paneling, garishly painted shells, and several mounted cod. "How would you rate the ambience here on a scale from one to ten?" he asked the second bartender when he had his martini in front of him. "How would you rate the atmosphere, that special air, that deep down, old-fashioned Cape Cod *charm?*"

The second bartender was wearing a single gold earring and a black net shirt. He had a huge chest and huge, solid-looking arms. The place was packed, and he was busy. He picked up Calvin's money without actually listening. "I just work here," he said, moving off.

Calvin watched the pre-Fourth of July crowds until he finished his first drink. What precisely characterized this age? This hurrying and going—the dusky, jaded youths in cut-off jeans, bracelets, dirty feet, in among the solid burgers, the touring middle-class couples in seersucker suits and backless dresses? The screeching music and the powdered lonely grandmothers with rinsed hair, bare midriffs, open-toe sandals? Why was this theater so joyless?

He wanted another drink, but he couldn't get the bartender's attention, and he left without leaving a tip. He turned at the top of Bradford without noticing the dusty, green pickup behind him, moving slowly, keeping him in sight. He drove back down Bradford and swung around the fork onto Commercial, where the serious action was. Crowds jammed the walks and milled around the bumper-to-bumper traffic in the middle of the narrow, one-way street. A few annoyed drivers, unaccustomed to the town's ways, honked at the walkers, but they did not bother to look up.

A short, fatty woman passed in front of him, dragging a screaming child behind her. "Look at you!" she kept saying, without looking around at the child. "Just look at you! You're the only little boy crying in the whole street! You're the *only* little boy crying in the *whole* street!"

The cars waited, gradually inched forward, looking for parking places. He moved on, past the antique shops, the art galleries, and the weathered, shingled boardinghouses with improvised side sundecks, earlier gingerbread trim, ships' bells beside several doors, the small yards enclosed behind white picket fences.

He stopped at a crowded restaurant on the bay side, where a Pachelbel record was playing in the background and the waiters wore red jackets. The tide was in, the place breezy, filled with fresh brackish smells. The candle flames were flickering inside their glass bowls, and several waiters were busy lowering the windows behind the diners.

He sat down at the bar. The bartender was talking to the customer beside him while he set his watch. He wound the watch and put it back on his wrist. He was going to Boston University. He was a business major, although not young, and he was branching out into computers. "Do you know what's going to be big?" he said, stopping by Calvin, still talking to the man beside him. "They're going to be big. They're already big." He took Calvin's order.

"I'm waiting for the *meaningful* computers to come along," Calvin said, when his drink appeared. "I'll be interested when they can write long, rambling, incoherent letters that they never mail. I'll be interested when they pick fights, spill their drinks, and wander around their backyards in their underwear. I'll be interested when they have complicated, menacing dreams that leave them feeling disturbed and wiped out the next day. I wouldn't *trust* any information that did not come from a battered soul, but—right now, at the moment, as things are—they aren't *tragic*, are they?"

The bartender was still having trouble with his watch, and if he was interested in the monologue, he did not bother to challenge it. He took his watch off again and shook it. Then he looked at the ship's clock over the bar. The customer beside Calvin was gone.

282

Calvin tried his drink. "The tragic hero has a fatal flaw that never lets him off the hook. Bound to be determined, he is less clever than the rest of us because, being obsessed, he has less edge. He is also a person with no low profile, and so don't we all enjoy a good shudder when he makes a spectacle of himself?"

The bartender shook his head. He was probably in his late twenties, but he was already beginning to thin in front. He had a clear, polished, sensitive-looking skull, and, unlike most on the Cape, he was not tanned. "Don't ask me about these things," he said, "I just wear the red jacket." He tugged at it.

"However, the Greek audience wasn't civilized enough to see what Sophocles was *really* saying, and although they made a stab at it, they missed the crucial point. What would have happened if Laius and Jocasta had done the sensible thing in the first place? What if the parents had decided to *keep* the child, just to keep an eye on him? What would have happened if they *hadn't* stuck him out on a limb? *Nothing! Nothing!* Don't you see? The primal curse *isn't* incest. It's child abandonment."

Calvin was sitting sideways on the barstool without paying a great deal of attention to what he was saying. He was staring at a table below him where three middle-aged men were eating clams. They wore tourist sport shirts, but they looked authentically weathered. He heard a Cape accent. Generally, though, like natives, they ate without talking. They were throwing themselves into it. They ordered more beer.

He felt a depression coming on, and he glanced at his watch. He was going to have to go. He was going to have to pick up the folk singer at the bus station. He still lingered for a moment, wondering if he was going to bait them or not. "Those are natives," he told the bartender, feeling light-headed. "They're very rare around these parts. They clam a lot."

The bartender was counting some change in his hand. He put the change back in his pocket and straightened. He sensed that Calvin's mood had shifted, and he followed his gaze.

"So how are the clams biting, or whatever clams do?" Calvin said, shouting across the room at the table below him. He felt more light-headed. He was determined to get a rise out of them. "Catch any good clams lately, Captain?"

The men, deep in their disapproval, did not bother to look up.

The bartender put his hands on the bar in front of him. His skull was flushed, and a muscle in his neck was showing. "Hey! Listen!"

"The natives are all deaf. That's another way you can spot them. They're all deaf, and they're all a bit slow witted. High winds, howling seas. It comes from so many years in the rigging, keeping a sharp eye out for clams."

Two waiters started to move in.

Calvin swung off the stool with his tab. "Well, I've got to go. I've got to pick up a girl."

While he drove down to the huge public parking lot on the wharves, where he was lucky to get in, considering the crowds, he wondered if he was going to be able to shake the coming depression—those clouds that rolled in, covering everything, trying to obscure what was half determined to break through. What unpleasantness was?

He had to park in the last lane, close to the bay—where the tide was high, still coming in, frothing lightly, quietly, moving in steady, curling edges around the piles, arriving farther up against the narrow, hard, gradually disappearing rim of sand, darkened in places, faintly glimmering in others. The mauve-colored air was brilliant across the water—varying from that brilliance to a bruised, bluish red across the town's peaks and steeples.

He cut through the cars toward the public rest rooms, the fast-food shacks and the bus station—past the vans and trailers, the bulky campers, and family pickups that still smelled like boiling engine parts, cooling motors, various fuel vapors, steadily diminishing, disappearing energies.

All right, what fixes the times? How do we live now? While he was attending Sarah Elizabeth's funeral, while he was staring out the open window at the clumps of blowing poverty grass, the tourists' high-priced, weathered shanties, balconies, and porches, all real estate for expensive sunning, he suddenly saw a figure appear on one of the raised sundecks: a blond fairy in a blue bathrobe. He was obviously listening to the Anglican liturgy. He finally yawned, stretched, crossed himself, and went back inside.

A parody? The gesture was too mechanical, too understated; but, if serious, how do you define that kind of seriousness? Seriousness and parody now crossed each other's borders at will—the time's obsession with a finely tuned imprecision, an elegant ritual that was supposed to keep the furies at bay. However, the age expanded all its vital energies on this without coming up with very happy results; and when he considered his wife's impatient straightforwardness, her intense, earnest, sometimes strident insistence on calling a spade a spade, he felt graceless and impoverished in comparison. What is art? What is truth? He was by now a masterpiece of disguises, like a medieval knight who wears so much junk he can't mount his own horse unassisted.

There is an unacknowledged conspiracy against at least half our needs, and the half-crippled spirit wearily plays along, as if it has partly convinced itself that it, too, wants what the flesh wants. And poor sex, which was left to carry all the burdens, which was left to bear more than it could properly sustain: ecstasy, wonder, adoration; in short, holy awe!

He was on the walk, at first, but, because of the weaving packs, he was soon in the street. He fought through the standard tourist crowds, the grandmothers in tight knit slacks, bare stomachs, bare backs, these conventional people in the majority; but he also passed two young men, in denims, holding hands, two middle-aged women in capes, their arms around each others' hips, and then a bearded elderly man with gold loops in his ears, his shorts so sparse they outlined the huge, bulging groin. He was talking to a young traffic cop on duty.

The big, grubby bus had trouble getting through even with the cop's help. It lumbered across its sharp turn without saving much other space, but people did not scatter until the last minute. It finally stopped without shutting off its engine, and the small group descended through cloudy carbon smells, whirling bits of dust.

When the girl separated herself from the others, when, really, the others rapidly disappeared around her, he could recognize his catch without difficulty because she was wearing such a disoriented, ungathered expression. At the mercy of strangers, of someone's kindness, she put the guitar back around her shoulder and picked up her pack.

He waved while she was still standing in the middle of the street, and waved back. Her face almost instantly relaxed. She had a large, round, cheerful, homely face, like a Dutch painting, but she was also lush, like those distant burghers: full breasts, a rolling swell that the small, cinched-in waist, wide jeans belt, merely accented. Oh, she was grand, and how could you look at her without thinking about a bed?

He picked up her pack without trying to talk in the crowds, without trying to tell her his troubles yet, but as they threaded their way through the people, heading back into the public parking lot, she spoke in breathless little fragments. She had almost missed her bus. Then she had almost gotten off in Hyannis by mistake. She was starved. She was really starved. She stopped in the middle of the parking lot and put her hand on his arm, lightly, just below the elbow. "I have a confession to make. I've *got* to have a large Coke before I drop."

He was up because he was so tired, between depression and elation. He felt shaky and out of breath because he was balancing himself up on the high, isolated edge of another adventure. He was going to put her up at Mrs. Fox's in the empty three-quarter Cape. He grew precise, almost prim. "Then," he said, "we'll have to find the large Coke."

286

While he drove down Commercial, up Winthrop across Bradford to Shank Painter, he realized that he now recognized many different people; many different voices were familiar; but when he was first on the edge like this, he *was* prim, stiff, as if he were waiting for the woman to break down his reservations. If she didn't, then he lost nothing. He pulled up and parked in the Dairy Land lot, thinking how everything fit: the neon lights' buzzing shimmer, casting a guava color that made the building pulsate; her soft, pale, blond, moonlike face; and then her name, her wonderfully indolent, useless name, Melaine Tuss.

Stiff across the shoulders, more tired than he had first realized, he got out to get the orders. He felt highlighted in the neon glow, a lurid contrast, given the darker stretches of Shank Painter, where the traffic was thinning. A green pickup passed slowly, as if it were going to turn in, but it crossed into the Cumberland Farms lot instead.

When he returned with the orders, he found the car radio going, just enough self-assurance there to alert his own. He was reasonably certain that he could seduce this girl without much difficulty. He was also reasonably certain that he had weathered an old compulsion. He could sleep with her without asking her to marry him, keeping his own family intact for once. He could satisfy a robust sexual appetite without committing himself, and, in that case, he would just be like everybody else. He also realized that he did not like what he was up to, and, because this was true, he could not do much more than manufacture enthusiasm over the night ahead. Then he knew that he wanted to go home instead. Oh, Lord, yes! He wanted to get back home as soon as he could. He wanted to go on fighting if fighting was necessary. He wanted to come to terms with her, if he could, and before they went to bed, but, in any case, he wanted to get back to the fort.

The pickup was still parked in the shadows across the street. Someone was still sitting in it behind the wheel, its lights off. He could see a cigarette glowing in the dark. He had noticed the truck before, but where, when? Then he realized that he had seen it several times during that long evening.

He was overtired, alerted, highly strung. His eyes smarted, and the back of his throat felt dry. While he drank his coffee, tapping his fingers against the wheel—trying to explain the motel reservation mixup, he had his mind on the truck across the street.

He could hear her ice rattling in the paper cup. She poked around it with her straw. She didn't appear to care about the motel problem or anything else. She put her head back on the seat. "Oh, I'll go most anywhere," she said. "Why, I could pass out right here."

"You won't have to, though. I can find you a house."

While she still had her head back on the seat, she turned her face toward his. "Oh?" she said.

"Oh, yes. I can drop you off, before I have to get back."

He started the Mercedes and turned on his lights. The pickup's lights came on—the blinding, steady, accusing brights. He swung onto Shank Painter, heading toward the highway, which wasn't going to be crowded at night, up there at the tip.

The girl did not stir. "I love driving at night."

The pickup followed him onto Route Six, its brights in his rearview mirror, and he adjusted the mirror. He increased his speed—passing the dark scrub, the pale dunes, the shadowy open places, and the truck increased its speed. It did not exactly tailgate, but it stayed close behind. He passed few cars.

Melaine still had her head against the back of the seat, her face toward him, but he could not clearly see her face in the dark. She was quiet, and he supposed that she was asleep. If she was awake, he had nothing to say, no interest in talk. Her hands lay open on her lap, the paper cup on the floor at her feet.

He couldn't shake the truck. Because he was so tired, he was not thinking clearly, and when he finally reached the North Eastham turn, he pulled into a breakdown lane to let it pass. It didn't, of course. It slowed and pulled up behind him and the driver got out. Calvin rolled his window down. The tall nervous youth was under a streetlight for a moment. Fern's wavy auburn hair, Fern's wide forehead, Calvin's jawline; but the face as a whole resembled Floyd's. He was what? Twenty? Twenty-one? He was unshaven, but because he was covered with acne, he looked younger. He was in army fatigues and combat boots. The boots, like the stolen truck, looked muddy and serious. If he was in costume, he probably did not realize it.

He stopped to light a cigarette before he reached the open car window. He was in the dark again, and at that moment the skin on Calvin's arms prickled. "I've come because I am gathering information about you, Calvin. I want to understand. I want to forgive you," he explained, without any inflection in his voice whatsoever. He could have been commenting on Pompeii. "I have only heard my Uncle Floyd's side. Then he died in the service of his country. But perhaps you don't look at that war that way?"

The girl finally stirred. She lifted her head and looked around, but Calvin ignored her. "We've got to find a place to talk, Jeff. I *still* want you to come out to the house."

The boy nodded, perhaps to himself. "I have since found other . . . people. I have learned to pray a lot. Do you pray?" he asked, leaning forward, but he still did not appear to be addressing him directly. "I do, and when I do, I always feel better. Then I am at peace. I can experience total peace . . . I see that you have a girl here."

"I've got to drop her off. I'll drop her off and then we can talk about all this. We can have a drink."

He nodded again. "I'll follow you," he said.

Calvin's mouth was dry; his jaw hurt, and when he reached for a cigarette, he had trouble getting it lit. He eased back onto the highway and the pickup followed.

Melaine was now sitting up straight. "My *God! Who* was *that!*"

"My son."

"Who?"

"I'll drop you off quickly, and then I'll take care of it."

289

The pickup followed closer than before. When Calvin turned, the truck was tailgating on the deserted back road, trying to decide if it wanted to bump the Mercedes or not. There was now no moon, and, given the trees, he was driving through the pitch black dark.

Melaine looked back. "*Listen* here! I don't know where *we're* going, but *you* ought to be calling the police!"

"I can't."

"*Why?*"

"Because I can't. He's my son."

"He's dangerous!"

"Is he? How do I know? I'm not positive."

He pulled into Mrs. Fox's drive. They both jumped out without looking around. He was getting the front door open when the first shot hit the side of the house. The girl screamed, exactly like a movie scream. He was in the middle of a melodrama now, and, because it was a melodrama, he was completely out of his depth. He opened the door and pushed her through into the dark hall.

"I don't *believe* it! I don't *believe* we're being shot at! *Now* will you call the police?"

"Mrs. Fox doesn't have a telephone. She lives too close to the bone."

"Oh, *great!* Then what are we supposed to do? Let him shoot us?"

"He just may have blanks."

"*That hit the side of the house!*"

He turned around in the hall and partly opened the door. "Jeff?" he called, unable to see him. "Jeff? You said you were gathering information. You said you wanted to talk. Wouldn't you like to put that gun away and then *ask* me what you want, face to face?"

Silence. A bush cracked. Then nothing. He could hear the girl's harsh breathing just behind him.

"There's a girl here. Couldn't we let her go?"

"*I* know there's a girl there."

"Well, then . . ."

The bullet went wild, low, hitting the millstone doorstep;

290

stone chips, stone dust. Then the silence again. He shut the door.

Melaine pressed herself against the wall. "Oh, God," she said, "oh God, oh God!"

He was shaking when he pushed her into the small side bedroom where the shade was lowered. "We'll be okay here. Stay away from the window."

"What if he decides to shoot off the locks?"

"He won't shoot off any locks!"

"HOW DO YOU *KNOW* THAT!"

He could hear a car door slam. "Calvin? Calvin! I'm going! I'm leaving you alone!" The laughter was harsh and wild, and then abruptly stopped. "I'm leaving you alone with your girlfriend there!"

"He isn't. Is he? Oh God, I know he *isn't*! It's a trick! Are you going to tell me *now* he isn't crazy?"

He was having trouble breathing. His left eyelid twitched, and his face felt stiff. The back of his neck itched. However, if he stayed frozen, if he didn't scratch it, the boy wouldn't shoot again. He knew he was being irrational; he knew he wasn't making any sense, but he still didn't scratch it for a second or two more. He finally moved, and nothing happened. He was finally breathing better.

"Well? Now? What're we going to *do*?"

"He's going to expect us to try to get to the car. He has to keep his eye on that, which means he has to stay around in the front somewhere. What if we go through the back? We could try to make it through the woods. There's a trailer back there."

"Are you kidding? I'm *petrified*! *I'm* not going anywhere!"

"He could also be counting on that."

"Well, he can count on it!"

"I could try to make a run for it."

"Oh, *no* you *don't*! You aren't leaving *me* here!"

"He wants me."

"Don't be *too* sure! What kind of crazy person is out there, anyway?"

"He's my son."

291

"Well, you've *said* that!"

"He wants to talk to me."

"So he *said*! Try again, will you? See if he'll let *me* go, then."

He wanted to get away from her, and he mounted the side stairs. "I'll see if I can talk to him from an upstairs window. It'll take him a few minutes before he can locate it."

"Oh, no you don't! You aren't leaving *me* down here alone!"

He crossed into the tiny upstairs bedroom and struggled with the side window in the thick, unfresh air. He leaned out, where it was slightly lighter. "Jeff? I'm here. Over at the side." He could hear some groundcover crack.

The girl was right behind him. Breathing heavily against his neck. If he moved back abruptly, he would step on her. "Oh God, get your *head* in, will you? What happens to me if he gets you?"

Was all this like a dream? Was that the word? It struck him as too formal, too ordered, too definite. "Jeff? It doesn't make any sense to keep the girl, does it? Can't she go? I'm going to give her the car keys."

There was low laughter. Nothing more.

Calvin waited.

The boy laughed. "Oh! Sure!"

He shut the window.

Melaine moved closer. "*Now* what's he up to?"

He was trying to get around the girl, away from both her and the window. She was shaking so she couldn't speak. When he moved, she moved, still in his way. He put his hands under her arms to keep her in one place while he got around her. She was soaking under the arms, and the back of her shirt was wet. She clung for a moment. He was enveloped in all those mixtures: the damp, sweet sweat, the meaty, oily odors. "Nobody's thinking! He *can't* let you go! You'd call the police!"

"I *won't* call the police! I *promise*!"

Oh, that was beautiful! Beautiful! Perfect! Just listen to her! Wasn't she speaking for everybody? Wasn't Dostoevsky

292

right? *One drop, one drop of your own fat must be dearer to you than a hundred thousand of your fellow creatures. . . . There's* the fall! There's man! Just refute it!

She was very, very bitter. *"Well? You* said you wanted to talk to him!"

He wanted to keep moving. He went back down—this time into the rear of the house, into the long, narrow kitchen, the girl following, breathing heavily, talking, talking now, wanting to know what he was going to *do.* He pulled the curtains over the sink.

The doorbell rang.

Melaine jumped. "Oh, God, we're saved! Somebody's at the door! Somebody's come! Oh, go *answer* it! Go answer it *quick,* before they *leave!"* She paused. "Oh, *he's* ringing it, isn't he?"

The bell would stop. Then start. Then, when he had it jammed, it did not stop at all.

"Oh, I can't *take* this all night! I'll go as crazy as he is. *Do* something, will you? When are you going to *do* something?"

All right, all right! Why wasn't he just breaking in? Wasn't he just playing a game? He was trying to make his point. Well, he had a right. Who said he hadn't?

There was an explosion; the girl screamed, and the town's fireworks lit up the dim kitchen behind the closed curtains, a trial run; they couldn't wait for the Fourth. Because everybody was trigger-happy. Violence was in the air! Her face leaped up in the sudden blaze, masklike, hollow-eyed, the open mouth huge. He tried to explain, but she was hysterical. She slumped to the floor against a wall, her head down, her hands over her ears. Then, in the comparative silence that followed, he could hear her crying just below the constantly ringing doorbell.

The warped kitchen door stuck. He could turn the knob freely, but the door itself wouldn't budge at first. He pulled on it several times before it opened. He stepped across the back sill, facing the dark, ferny woods—off to deal, to talk to his son, his firstborn. He couldn't hear because of the pounding in his ears. He couldn't see much in this altered, fresher darkness. He felt lightheaded, airy—from fear, from renewed confidence, from having reached a decision. He was already choosing his words of greeting, the right words this time because they were both going to get a fresh start.

When he came around the side of the house, the fireworks exploded again; a rocket suddenly flowered, filling the sky with lurid stars and stripes. He saw the figure in the army jacket at the same time. Calvin was ready to cope. He waved, too, but Fern's boy shot him, and he went over—too surprised to feel wronged or mistaken. The boy cut and ran. Calvin passed out.

When he came to, he could hear the car motors, car horns, and the voices—faint at one moment, louder the next, as if someone were adjusting a volume button. ("Here. *Here*! OVER HERE! Here.") Then the underbrush. Movements, lights, more stamping. Exhaust smells. Being lifted up—carried, swaying, and then put down, an enclosed space. Canvas, linen, steel. A car door slams. His mind is clearer for a moment; consciousness lingers, like a light briefly holding before it burns out. He did not feel any pain. He felt cold, but aside from that he felt strangely peaceful. He was dying, but at the same time he was curiously unconcerned. He passed out again behind a webby, bulging, dullish red screen.

He was in costume on stage, strutting his stuff: talking, explaining, lecturing, digressing. Tipping his straw hat, waving his cane. He had the small attentive audience to himself. Heads lifted, faces rapt. At the same time, while he was still facing the audience, wondering about his last, best shot, he was trying to work his way toward the right wing. He started to exit, but, just as he reached the dark wing, he caught a glimpse of his father back there in the shadows. His shirt sleeves rolled past his knobby elbows, his long, spindly arms exposed, he was holding up his wide hands. He kept shouting over the din. "No, no—not yet! Get back! Get back! Get back! You're still on. You still have to keep going!"

He woke just before surgery. He woke again in the recovery room. He finally woke on a sunporch in Hyannis over-

294

looking an inlet—the hospital where his grandmother had died, and he remembered that inlet. He watched the rain dabbing the windows, then coming down harder, obscuring the small boats. He shifted positions. The pain was trying to work its way through the drugs. The weak light shifted, and the room grew darker. He dozed, but some movement woke him.

She was standing beside him in a red raincoat, trying to take his hand. How awake was he? How real was she?

"I never saw that raincoat before."

"I just bought it."

"You look, well, different."

"Oh, Cal! I'm not *'different.'* I just bought a raincoat. I didn't have one."

"All right, Lisa, I'll get used to it. A red raincoat. It will gradually assimilate itself among the familiar, become one less awesome object. I'll accept it. Trust me. It's practically unalluring already."

"Oh, God! You don't know how *frightened* I was! I didn't know what shape I was going to find you in! But even your *color's* better than I thought it was going to be, and you're in great shape, aren't you? You're still the same!"

"I love you."

"I love you, but we haven't *solved* anything yet!"

"What do you want me to do?"

"Cope?" she said. "Please? Try. I'll try. I'll try to be less impatient."

"When do you want me to get going? When do I talk to Shelley about that lifeguard? Who's the child molester? Who's the pervert? What's his name?"

"Don't *ask* me. *You* work things out! That's the *point*!"

The room was steadily growing darker, and he could hardly see her face. The rain was coming down harder. He wasn't leaving her; he was through running, but what if she left him? What if she found out she didn't need him? Could he prevent that, though, if he kept her hopping? "His name's Hal. She calls him Hal."

"Oh, *Calvin, I* know you know his name!"

He felt exposed. He felt exposure's unpleasantness—that

ancient bite and sting; but, at the same time, he didn't instantly try to move away from the feeling. He was wary, but still attentive. At any rate, he didn't try to bury it underneath boiling anger. "You know a lot," he said, in all honesty and innocence.

She was still on her guard. "Yes? So? *And*—? Is that irony?"

He briefly shut his eyes, wondering when he was going to get his next drug; the pain was beginning to spread, to branch out. "No. I'm cutting back on irony, Lisa. That's just the truth."

"Well, don't over*estimate* what I know, either. *That* won't help."

He was looking over her shoulder at the rain falling against the window in the last of the room's light. He was still too young for her, but she wasn't eighty-seven, either. She was right. She didn't know everything, and she was vulnerable too. She broke him up now. She was in pain now—insecure, uncertain, like a child; but, if he treated her like a child, if he tried to reassure her, he would be seen as moving in, trying to take over, and she would be off and running. He knew her. Once feeling patronized, she would try to kill him. She wanted comforting, but she also wanted her freedom.

There was no health in them, no help in sight, short of a few creature comforts. He took a wild chance, and he pushed her head down against his bandaged chest. She gave up. She wept against the padding. She sobbed as if she were going to come apart. Her chest heaved, her shoulders trembled. What kind of stress had *she* gone through in the last several hours! There she was—dependent, leaning on him, all over him, in fact, and he wasn't breaking under it! Could he always count on coming through now? He doubted that, but he didn't think about it. He just held her instead. He stroked her neck, the back of her head; her hair lay across his chest, across the hospital's heavy bandage—tape, cloth, gauze. "That's all right, that's all right!" he kept saying, trying to reassure them both. "That's all right! We'll make it, won't we? We'll make it!"